TANK HILL

TANK HILL

A Tale of Suspense and Horror

Don Otey

iUniverse, Inc.
New York Lincoln Shanghai

TANK HILL
A Tale of Suspense and Horror

Copyright © 2004 by Donald Vaughn Otey

All rights reserved. No part of this book may be used or reproduced by any means, graphic, electronic, or mechanical, including photocopying, recording, taping or by any information storage retrieval system without the written permission of the publisher except in the case of brief quotations embodied in critical articles and reviews.

iUniverse books may be ordered through booksellers or by contacting:

iUniverse
2021 Pine Lake Road, Suite 100
Lincoln, NE 68512
www.iuniverse.com
1-800-Authors (1-800-288-4677)

ISBN: 0-595-33688-4 (pbk)

ISBN: 0-595-66992-1 (cloth)

Printed in the United States of America

This story is dedicated to my big brother Ken.

ACKNOWLEDGEMENTS

Writing a novel is never a solitary achievement, even though it does involve long hours of isolation and creative labor. The experience is made so much richer by those who offer inspiration, encouragement and honest criticism of the work in progress. I offer to these special people my heartfelt gratitude for sharing with me the experience of writing Tank Hill.

First, I thank my brother who has had more of an influence on who I have become than he could ever know.

My special collaborator on all of my novels to date has been a unique person who I am privileged to call friend. His name is BLUE, and he is a multi-talented individual who has kept me focused and served as my foremost critic.

The helpful members of three writers' groups, the Hudson Writers, Tarpon Wordsmiths, and West Pasco Writers, have patiently listened and immeasurably improved my ability to express ideas in my various works.

The most understanding and patient woman in the world has shared my life for forty seven years. Jo Ellen knows my passion for writing and tolerates my dedication to the craft through long and sporadic hours. She is the inspiration for everything I do and the model for a key character in each one of my novels.

Chapter 1

▼

"Maybe this isn't such a good idea after all," Kyle Owens mumbles as he steps out of Jenny's van. A brisk February wind buffets him, and his first gulp of the frosty air chills his lungs. He exhales. A cloud of vapor rises in the night air. Why does he feel so vulnerable, so exposed to some danger he can neither see nor define?

Kyle raises the collar of his blue winter parka and pulls his knit cap a little lower over his head to cover his ears. Owens has recently passed his fortieth birthday. He has always had the look of someone years younger than his actual age, slender and fit, tanned from his two passions, golf and home gardening. Now time is catching up with him, etching worry lines at the corners of his eyes, coloring his hair with flecks of gray.

He removes the van's gas cap and reaches for the fuel pump hose. His eyes sweep across the service station. The outline of a lone attendant shimmers in the subdued glow of the lights inside the Lakeside Exxon. Springlake's East Main Street is nearly empty at this late hour. Nobody afoot, and only an occasional car passes by trailing vapor into the winter air.

Owens waves and calls out, "Hi, Sam." The attendant, Sanjay Samderiya, can't hear him from inside the warm building, but he returns his greeting. Kyle glances at his watch. The time is well past eleven PM and only the two of them are stirring. At least Sam has the good sense to be indoors while Kyle stands outside shivering. Another gust of wind races across the open pump area and Kyle feels its force through his coat. He senses an involuntary chill rippling the length of his spine. Looks around and wonders again why he feels so uneasy, so threatened when there is nothing around him but cold and solitude. No sound. In fact, the stillness is eerie.

Kyle thinks about the events that have unnerved and disoriented him for the past week. His nights have been disastrous. He's been sleeping no more than two or three hours each night since that terrifying event six days ago. The rest of every evening he spends tossing and twisting, fretting and worrying until the stark fear once again seeps down into his bones. Until fright takes hold and sets him to staring blankly through the darkness. While he agonizes, Jenny sleeps beside him, unaware of the torment he is enduring. The dawn always finds him physically and emotionally drained, facing another day of confusion, of dread for what nightfall will bring.

Kyle has taken to sitting later and later every night in his den, absorbed, or so it would seem, in an endless procession of television documentaries, the replays of old sports events, travelogues about the reptiles of the South Pacific, accounts of the blitzkrieg of London. But the truth is that he's trying to fill his mind with bits and pieces of trivia, anything to avoid the inevitable flashbacks to another agonizing memory from long ago he thought he had put behind him. That memory and the recent loss of his lifelong friend Jimmy Moore, has jarred him to the core.

Then the gruesome package arrived and, since that shocking moment, his world has been in a maddening downward spiral.

As the gas tank slowly fills, the deathly silence of night is broken only by the chime announcing each gallon dispensed. Kyle's mind drifts back to earlier this evening.

His wife Jenny came to the den and interrupted his hypnotic television escape.

"Can you do me a favor, Kyle? The van is low on gas, and I have some early errands to run in the morning."

He had acknowledged with a wave and a head nod, scarcely taking his eyes from the TV.

"Sure, Jen, I'll take care of it" he had answered. Then he'd returned to the documentary and riveted his attention on the account of the Johnstown Flood.

For another two hours he had sat mesmerized by the images on the television screen, suspended somewhere between reality and the return of the cold fear. Only minutes ago he had finally emerged from his numbing travels through the Discovery and History Channels and remembered his promise to Jenny. One more excuse, too, for delaying his climb up the stairs where Jenny already lay in bed and where he faced another sleepless night. He had peeled himself from the den chair and plodded toward the hall closet. The weather report predicted temperatures in the mid twenties and windy conditions in the valley overnight, so he found his parka and knit cap and bundled up before heading to the Lakeside gas station.

Kyle forces himself to shake off the mental pictures and return to the task at hand. Stares at the whirling numbers on the gas pump. Four gallons…five. Stands with his hands jammed into his coat pockets. He's parked at the island farthest away from the building and nearest the exit to Main Street. An intermittent light flickers overhead.

Have to stop in and see Sam, he mulls. *Remind him to have the bulb in that annoying light replaced.*

He peers into the moonless dark toward the mountains. A black mid-winter night in Southwest Virginia. A barely visible line separates the peaks of the Blue Ridge from the sullen sky. Kyle's eyes feel heavy, and they ache from the strain of too many sleepless hours and too much television in the dimly lit den. He wants so desperately to blank his mind, shut out the unwelcome memories, find some peace from his mental agony.

The quiet wraps around him. The silence is overwhelming.

A noise suddenly sounds behind him, a rustling in the wind, a footstep on the pavement. Kyle starts to turn toward the sound but is met with a jarring blow to the back of his skull. The faltering light overhead gives way to an explosion of red and yellow flashes. His knees crumple, sending him reeling toward the pavement. He grasps for support and yanks at the fuel nozzle. It comes free from the car, its trigger locked in place. Gasoline sprays crazily across the asphalt. Kyle slumps heavily against the pump. He goes down, his shoulder slamming into the pump's metal frame.

Pain races through his head and shoulder. He closes his eyes tightly and grits his teeth. Then he rolls onto his left side and looks up. Kyle blinks at the blurred vision of a dark figure crouching over him, someone in a heavy coat who is dropping astride him to grind a knee painfully into his groin. He raises both hands to ward off his attacker but without success. Hands pound him with blow after blow; something rips at the flesh of his cheek. Kyle's eyes clouded over and watering from the cold and the pain, can not get a clear picture of the attacker. Everything about the man gives Kyle the impression of deepest black: the coat, the cap, the piercing eyes. Kyle thinks he can see a coal black beard as the darkness crowds in on him. His eyes dim until only pinpoints of light remain.

He feels the hot breath of his attacker near his cheek. A voice whispers, "Got you, Owens."

Searing pain wracks his right ear as if some ferocious beast is ripping it from his head. He hangs precariously on the edge of a deep vortex that threatens to suck him down into weightless nothingness. He concentrates on fighting the urge to give in, fearing loss of consciousness from which he may not awaken.

It really is true, Kyle's muddled brain tells him. *Just before you die, your life passes before you. It comes in vivid color frames. Special memories surface from the secret places where they've been locked away. Treasured memories come to calm and take away the unbearable hurting.*

He has a vision of Jenny bending near, pleading. "*Fight hard, Kyle, stay with us.*" His two sons whisper encouragement, take his arms, lift him up. A bright light hangs like a beacon above him. Dave, his little brother, tugs at his arm. Calls out, "*Don't leave, Kyle. I need your help.*"

Through the pain, Kyle tries hard to focus on the figure looming over him, the mugger who is savagely tearing at his face, screaming in a high-pitched voice, "I didn't forget, I didn't forget."

From somewhere in the dizzying haze he hears another voice, a shrill shout with an edge of urgency and urgency drawing nearer. "Stop it! Get off him."

An object gleams in a hand raised high above Kyle. A knife?

Sam charges across the pavement, hurdles the first island, and bears down on the assailant who sits astride Kyle Owens. He is brandishing a menacing club and shouting at the top of his lungs.

"Get off him. I will brain you!" The club makes a swishing sound as it cuts through the air.

The figure in the long black coat and stocking cap stops his assault and peers toward the station attendant. For an instant, his arm remains frozen in midair. Sam swings the club again and knocks the object from the dark man's hand. The attacker leaps to his feet. Before Sam can deliver another blow, the mugger turns away and springs off into the night.

"Oh my, it *is* you, Mister Owens!" Sam shuts off the pump, kneels over Kyle, and feels for a pulse.

"Made a mess of you. Almost ripped off your ear. He had a knife, too."

Sam picks up the shiny blade and stares at it oddly, as if it were an alien object. Shakes his head in disgust.

The battered and bleeding Kyle Owens can only manage to mumble something in garbled words and touch Sam's arm.

"Hang in, my friend. I will call for help," Sam reaches for his cell phone. Punches in 9-1-1.

Kyle blinks at the fluttering fluorescent light. He slowly slides down and gives in to the black void folding its arms around him.

Chapter 2

Someone once said you can never go home again. The way things are going for me lately, I think home is the only place for me to turn. Springlake gave Helen and me some happy times. Just wish I wasn't going back now for *this* reason. Dave Owens, prodigal son, rushing back to my brother's side.

Can't seem to press the gas pedal down far enough. I'm hurtling through pre-dawn Carolina near Statesville. My mind is racing. How can I be drenched in a cold sweat? The heater's on high and the car is almost stifling inside. But the beads streaming down my cheeks and soaking my collar feel like ice water.

Zipping along the Interstate. Don't see any flashing lights in the rear view mirror. Lucky, damn lucky. Doing a reckless, headlong sprint toward the valley. Just ahead is the climb up the mountain. Then I'll turn east and make the final dash for home. Back to Springlake.

There's a wild-eyed face staring back from the rear-view mirror. The look on that pale face leaves little doubt about the stark fear that has taken hold of me. I could lose the best friend I've ever had, my brother Kyle. I've rubbed and tossed my brown hair till it's standing on end. Those drooping lids belong to someone who's barely awake. Have to fight to focus on the road. My eyes, more bloodshot now than gray, peer back at me with a strange, hollow quality.

Should have known from the outset that Jenny's frightening call last night would be a turning point in my life. The ups and downs of the past few months have been a blur for me. Dave Owens, small town boy with a golden touch. I'll never be a threat to Bill Gates, but I've carved out my own neat little niche, very profitable sliver of the software world. And what have I lost in the process?

Success can't dull the pain of being separated from Helen and Melody, the two most important people in my life. The mistakes and bad judgment that brought it all about are entirely my own fault. If only I could go back and change some of my stupid moves. But I can't. Now there is a terrible emptiness, a void where the love of my wife and daughter should fill every day.

For all my success in chasing the almighty dollar, my rapid climb in the business world now seems much less satisfying than it should. Now I have a new crisis to face. Makes all my victories seem hollow. My one remaining link to stability lies in a hospital fighting for his life. Dave Owens has been reduced to an insecure, shivering wreck of a man. My big brother, the person I've admired all my life, has been viciously attacked, and I'm scared witless.

Time to try Jenny's number again. Must have dialed that number twenty times without success during the long night of driving frantically through the deathly quiet from Atlanta. I know my sister-in-law sat by Kyle's side through the night, but sooner or later she has to go home. I need to know how Kyle is, how he's meeting this crisis with me powerless to be at his side.

I pull into the mountainside rest area, heave a long, exhausted sigh and debate giving in to the urge for a short nap. But I can't take the time for even a brief refresher with Kyle in serious condition. The best I can do under the circumstances is to stretch my legs and hope the frosty air will jostle me awake. Unfold from under the wheel and swing unsteady, jean clad legs toward the cold outdoors. Grab my winter jacket draped over the seat and wrestle into it, zipping it over my sweater. I drink in the air and try to clear the cobwebs from my brain.

Mom used to delight in standing us side by side, Kyle with his short underpinning and me with my compact trunk and long legs. She'd laugh and say she'd built us from different patterns. I'm the taller, heavier one at six feet and 180 pounds. He's four years older, at least three inches shorter, and his waist squares up at mid-thigh level on me. But inside I'm much more like Kyle than one would suspect. He's been my role model for as long as I can remember.

Squinting through the dark, I gaze back down the valley I've just crossed and see the winter gray sky that hovers, not wanting to yield to the first burst of dawn over the horizon. A fine mist is falling. The brisk gusts blowing against the mountainside buffet me. The night air is invigorating, though, not as frigid as I expected. I lower my head and walk toward the brick structure for shelter from the gusting wind. Wander off the pavement and nearly tumble. Both feet skid in the slurry mud the drizzle has left. I thrust out my arms to regain my balance. Stamp my soiled ankle-high boots on the concrete walk, take a deep breath of the damp mountain air, and try to stay awake.

Under the rest stop's roof I stab at my cell phone with cold, wet fingers and wait impatiently for an answer. Finally, after several rings that seem to take minutes, my stubborn persistence pays off. An exhausted, barely audible voice drifts back to me.

"Thank God I finally reached you. How is he, Jenny?"

"It was a long night, Dave—a very long night. Doctor Gray says there are no guarantees yet. We just have to pray he has the will to pull through. His fate is in the hands of the good Lord." Her voice is thick with hopeful uncertainty. "Someone beat him terribly, left him battered, Dave." She begins to sob.

"Jenny, you know he's always drawn on your strength when the going is tough. You'll make it through this together."

"He asked for you, Dave. There were moments when he knew I was with him. Twice he asked about you, and I told him you were on your way."

"I'm driving flat out on I-77, Sis. Climbing up the mountain toward Wytheville. Just stopped for a breather. Should be there in another hour and a half. Have you had any rest since this happened?"

I look at my watch and realize I've reached her well before seven AM. She must be sleepwalking by now.

"I dozed in his room. The doctor left orders I was to take a break, and the nurse ran me out 30 minutes ago. Soon as I can freshen up, I'll be back at the hospital."

Her voice sounds ragged, hoarse. There's no need trying to convince Jenny she needs to slow down and rest. She won't leave Kyle any longer than is absolutely necessary.

Walk back to the car, cupping the phone close to my cheek and protecting it from the drizzle with my coat collar.

"Can I swing by and drive you to the hospital? Let you catch a nap til I get there? That may be safer for you at this point."

"No, I'll meet you there, Dave. Valley Hospital, Intensive Care. I'll take you in to see him."

"Okay, we can talk later. You need to unwind for awhile."

"Don't hang up," she says. "There's no way I can relax now. I need to talk."

Sounds like she's found her second wind and wants to fight letting go just yet. This gal is going to crash and burn once she stops moving. Back in the car, I swing out and speed up the mountain slope Wrestle around in my seat and it chafes my back, sticks to my clothes in the blast of the heater.

"Tell me exactly what happened, Jen, if you're up to it. Still can't believe this is real."

"Dave, I'm so confused and puzzled. Somebody came up behind him, beat him viciously and ran away."

"You said earlier he was pumping gas when he was blindsided."

"Yes, my van needed a fill up. He promised to take care of it, but he waited until really late to go out. Guess he forgot. Hasn't been himself lately, sitting up late with his mind somewhere else whenever I try to talk to him. It scares me." By now she's close to tears again.

"Hang in, sis. We'll get to the bottom of this. First we have to help him mend."

"Oh, Dave, if Sam hadn't run that terrible man off, he might have…He had a knife!"

I feel an involuntary shiver.

"Do the police have any leads, Jenny? A possible motive?"

"That's what makes the whole thing so frustrating. We don't have a clue why somebody would want to do this. He wasn't robbed, and you know Kyle doesn't have an enemy in the world. Why would they pick him to hurt?"

"Well, there's one thing for sure, Jenny. I won't rest until someone pays dearly for what they did to him. When they hurt Kyle, they're messing with me. I intend to stay as long as it takes to put his attacker away."

The anger wells up in me, and I realize how concerned I am that Kyle may not recover.

"But first we have to help him heal and get over this terrible shock, Jenny."

A long silence follows.

"Jenny?"

"I'm here. It tears me apart, Dave. He's a good man. Why him of all people?"

"No accounting for random acts of violence, Sis. Maybe he was just in the wrong place when someone was looking for a victim—any victim. Has he told you anything about who mugged him? Did he get a good look at the bastard? Sorry, sis. I'm hopping mad."

"I understand. The fear of Kyle lying in the hospital fighting to recover hurts something awful, but I'm angry, too, over the senseless act that put him there."

"Well, I'll be there as soon as I can. Just took a break to wake up."

"You asked whether he saw the mugger. Maybe you can make some sense of this. He blurted out between his lapses into some sort of deep sleep. His words don't mean anything to me. Said something about a beard and dark eyes and mumbled a word two or three times that sounded like 'damp' or 'sank'. I told the policeman who came in to check on him, and he wrote it all down."

I reach for a scrap of paper in my pocket. Scrawl a note with a stubby pencil.

"The most important fact is that he knows you've been there with him, Jenny. That's the greatest comfort he could have right now. Let the police work on it. I'll jump in with both feet. You just coax him back to us."

"He did seem to be resting more comfortably when I left him. The last time he spoke, I told him his little brother was on his way, and he managed a smile."

I chuckle. Old Dave hasn't been the *little* brother for years now. I'm a head taller and twenty pounds heavier than Kyle. But in my eyes he will always be someone to look up to.

We talk on and I sense some of her tension lifting. They both need me there as soon as possible to share their uncertainty and to encourage them. And unless I can find a way to make this car sprout wings and fly, I'm getting to them as fast as humanly possible.

"Just keep believing, Jenny. He's more than earned a break. He can also be a pretty determined guy. We'll both pray and he'll be fine.

That rings a bit tinny in my own ears, but it's what she needs to hear at the moment. Both of them are pillars of their church; a model couple who live their beliefs and have raised two sons to be fine, Christian young men. I, on the other hand, consider myself a moral man but do little to practice my religion formally. All the lessons of so long ago grow dimmer as I find less time for anything outside striving for success in business. But if prayer can help Kyle pull through, I'll reach down and remember.

I hurry on through the mist and the awakening day, blinking through wet eyes, a plea forming on my lips.

Chapter 3

▼

My frantic trip to my brother's side is almost behind me now.

I find the Interstate exit and turn in at the entrance to the Valley Hospital. My heart races, pulse threatens to burst my veins. When I realize Kyle lies inside, the rush of excited anticipation gives way to cold fear. A clammy fright washes over me. What will I find when I get to Kyle's room?

I maneuver into a parking slot and set the brake, lean back in sheer exhaustion from the stress of the scramble to get here. Grip the steering wheel and try to calm my nerves. For a long moment I consider settling back and letting my fatigue take over. Maybe I can sleep away this bad dream and awake in a saner world. No, there's no avoiding it. I have to face whatever lies ahead of me.

Operating on pure adrenalin and beyond the point of reasoned thought, I somehow extract myself from the car. Force rubbery legs to carry me forward. Must be a sorry sight after my harrying drive. People hurrying through the parking lot seem to be giving me a wide berth—or is it only my imagination?

Purely on instinct I manage to stumble through the lobby and ask the receptionist, "Intensive Care?"

Everything around me seems to be moving in slow motion. I wait impatiently for an answer then realize the pounding in my ears is drowning out her reply. "Excuse me?" I say.

She looks slightly annoyed and repeats. "Down the hall—elevators on the left. Down to Level One and follow the signs." Then she casts a look of puzzled concern as I struggle to process her instructions. She shakes her head, points and repeats once again, "Elevators—down to One (holding up a single finger) and follow the signs."

I nod when her words finally come through to me. Hurry ahead toward the hallway; take the ride down, my mind racing. When the doors open I see the sign on the opposite wall pointing toward Intensive Care to the right. As I reach a waiting area and peer around, I suddenly feel very alone in the stark surroundings outside the large double doors to the IC unit. Several people are there, but Jenny is not among them. In my confused state, all sorts of disconnected thoughts speed through my clouded brain. *Am I in the right hospital? Did I hear her correctly on the phone? Why is that guy over there looking at me like I'm a spectacle of some sort? What do I do now?*

"Dave! You're here."

I turn to see Jenny rounding the corner into the waiting room. She heads toward me with arms outstretched. Her crisp appearance, auburn hair placed just so, freshly pressed white blouse and dark wool skirt and a coat draped over her shoulders, her normal light step make her seem alive and ready to tackle anything. But the weariness in her brown eyes betrays the hours of tension she's endured. She smiles bravely, but there's little doubt Jenny's been stretched to her limit. I hug her and she trembles.

"Tell me, Jenny, how's he doing?"

She looks up at me through her tears and manages, "He seems to be slowly improving, but you should be ready for a shock. The attacker beat him badly, Dave. The bruises and swelling will upset you. But he desperately needs to see that you're here."

A helpless feeling of inevitability hits me hard, washes over me like a gray funk. Am I up to this? Kyle's always been the strong one, but now it's squarely on my shoulders to keep it together for his sake. I reassure her somewhat weakly. "I'm ready."

She takes my hand and walks to the wall phone. I only dimly hear her speak, but the word 'brother' comes through loud and clear. In a matter of moments one large door opens, and a nurse motions for us to enter the unit. The nurse smiles sweetly at Jenny and gives a nod toward me as she turns to lead us to Kyle's side.

For an instant I'm certain I will be ill. But somehow I hold it in. Tell myself I have to get past the feeling of nausea for myself and for Jenny. She's staring into my eyes, reading the pain they show at Kyle's appearance. The person lying in that bed is a twisted, bloated version of my brother. Both of his lips are mangled, both eyes are blackened and one cheek is a swollen, bruised lump. His right ear is heavily bandaged and his eyelids flutter as if he were trying to see without success. Kyle's forehead is red and beneath the cover of a white cream, I see signs that a clump of his dark hair has been snatched from his scalp. If I didn't know better, I would swear a wild animal had mauled him.

He reacts to the sound of our approach and turns slightly, painfully to fully face me. Jenny holds back and urges me forward. Kyle manages a half smile; mutters something through swollen lips. I do a double take and realize he's greeting me by an old nickname I haven't heard him use in years. A special uncle once dubbed us with his own names. Kyle was Mugwump and I was Flywheel because I talked incessantly. Being called Flywheel by my brother at this tense moment has broken the pall that hangs over us. I laugh out loud.

"Hi, Mugwump," I manage. "Looks like you jumped into trouble face first."

He nearly produces a chuckle, but it seems to take more effort than he can muster. All he can produce is a weak cough, and it's obvious even that is painful.

"They're taking good care of you, Kyle, and I know Jenny's working you through this. I'm here for as long as it takes to get you up and out on the golf course with me. Just take orders and let 'em work their magic on you."

He raises one hand with great effort, and I take it in mine. Kyle squeezes my fingers weakly. Appears he's agitated and restless. His lips move but no clear words form. I look over at the nurse. She's signaling for us to cut the visit short, pointing to her watch and nodding toward the door. Kyle is still trying to tell me something but without success.

I look down at him. The expression of helpless frustration on his face cuts me deeply. But there will be time later. I'm not going anywhere for as long as it takes to sort this all out.

"You and Jenny visit. I'll be back later. We'll talk then. You need rest right now." I turn and leave the two of them. A tall doctor in a long white coat passes me as I leave the room.

Later, outside the IC unit, I stand and dry my eyes as Jenny reappears. She takes my hand.

"What do you think, Dave? How does he look to you?"

"What you see are mostly tears of anger, Jenny. I want at his attacker so badly I can taste the revenge. I want five minutes alone with that sucker—five minutes he'll never forget."

"But what was your impression of Kyle?" she presses.

"He's gonna be okay, Sis. It would take more than this to set him down. Must have been rocky for him, but I think he's turned the corner. Just give it some time."

She smiles weakly, reassured but not convinced.

"You must have seen Doctor Gray on your way out, Dave. He says Kyle has weathered the worst and is coming around. Had the doctor worried for awhile, but Kyle seemed to fight really hard. Now it's a slow process of getting his strength back."

"We'll have him up and at 'em before you can say Jack Spratt, as Mom would have told us. You can bet she's watching over him, too." Jenny smiles at the mention of the departed mother Kyle and I adored.

"Let's go home now," she says. "You must be worn out."

"I'm not the one who sat up all night and kept watch. Where are the boys?"

"They're both at school. I told them it was better they stay busy and that I'd let them know if Dad needed them."

"Then you go get some rest and see to the boys when they get home. I need to make a couple of stops then I'll be along."

She looks at my bloodshot eyes. "You must be dragging by now, Dave. Don't push yourself too hard. Don and Tom are going to want to see you. Better find a spot to curl up before you crash."

I know she's right, but there is more to be done. I have to know the details now. I'm consumed by the need to get to the bottom of this attack and avenge my brother. My mind won't rest until I find some logical answers to this puzzling and illogical act.

"Tell me exactly where the attack happened, Jenny."

She bites her lip and holds back the tears. "As I told you, Kyle was up reading and, for some odd reason, waited until very late to go to the Exxon at Lakeside to fill up my van. The police think his attacker caught him totally off guard, maybe hit him from behind. Pounced on him and beat him until Sam, the station attendant, chased him away. Sam said the man was holding a knife like he was about to stab Kyle. The police have it now."

"Then the report will be at the Springlake police station?"

"Yes. I guess."

"So that's my next stop. Is Len Darden still the sheriff?"

"Yes, he is."

That could make my task somewhat easier, I think to myself. I grew up here and know some of the local policemen. The current sheriff, Len Darden, is a friend and former high school classmate of Kyle and Jenny. And I may as well jump in now and get involved. I give her my cell phone number in case she needs me for anything. Then I head for Main Street and the county jailhouse.

Chapter 4

▼

I drive up to the county courthouse in Springlake and marvel at the sparkling new building. Almost seems too modern for this small town. See a side entrance marked 'Sheriff' and hurry inside.

"Nice facility. Never been in here," I say to the bored looking officer sitting behind the desk.

"What can I do for you?" is his curt response.

"My name is Dave Owens. I'd like to see the sheriff."

The sergeant looks me over carefully and asks, "Can I tell Sheriff Darden why you're here?" By now, with my disheveled appearance and bleary eyes, I must look like some vagrant who crawled in off the street. Guess if I were the man at the desk, I'd be a bit leery, too.

"Just tell him it's Dave Owens. I think he'll see me. Only need a few minutes of his time." The name seems to have a ring of familiarity, but he gives me another scan from my unruly hair to my boots still soiled from the mountain rest area. Then he slowly responds.

The officer rises and walks to a closed door where he raps sharply. I hear a voice from inside, and the sergeant opens the door a crack to speak to someone. Shuffling sounds follow. A big man with sandy hair appears in the doorway. He's as bulky and ruddy as I remember him, but he's showing a definite middle age paunch. Sheriff Len Darden walks toward me with a wide smile and his hand outstretched.

"Hot damn, it's been a long time, Dave. Kyle keeps me updated on you whenever I see him." With a note of concern he asks, "Have you seen him? How's he doing?"

"As well as we could expect, Len. Kyle took some hard lumps, but I think he's working his way through it."

"Good to hear, damn good," he offers. There is genuine relief in his voice. "Come on back, Dave."

We walk to his office. He offers a chair so I sit down facing him. The sheriff bellows, "Really pisses me off that somebody would do that to your brother. Having enemies goes with the job for me. Doesn't make sense in Kyle's case. You know we go way back, and he's one of the nicest people I know." Darden shakes his head. His cheeks glow with anger. He picks up the butt of a cigar from his ashtray and chews on it.

"Why Kyle, Len? Did they take anything or was it just a senseless attack? I've been thinking about this all night, and I'm ready to kill something."

The sheriff looks me over and chomps even harder on the stogie. In spite of the tension in my voice, I smile at him. But it has nothing to do with our discussion. I'm remembering when all of Kyle's buddies used to call Len by his nickname, Broadus, a slurred reference to his most prominent feature. Wonder how many people realize they've elected as their chief lawman someone known by his childhood friends as Broad Ass Darden? He looks a bit puzzled by my sudden grin but answers.

"We're on it, Davey. Give it some time. I guess you want to find out exactly what happened?"

"Yes, I want to know as much as possible about what took place at that gas station last night, Sheriff. It just doesn't make sense to me."

"Got that right. Must have been totally random. The perp won't get away, though. We're gonna be on him like stink on shit!" His big fist pounds the desktop.

"Save some of his hide for me, Len. I owe him."

"Whoa, there, Davey boy. Don't let your mouth overload your ass. Hate to have to bust your balls for interferin'. Let us find the asshole that did this." He's staring intently at me and the warning is clear. He just gave me my butt-out orders.

Well, he's certainly the same old Len. I wonder how he's been able to curtail his foul mouth in public long enough to be elected to his post three times. To me, Darden will always be a rowdy, garbage-mouthed kid. Now he's the county's chief law enforcer.

"I know you'll track him down, sheriff, but I have to help somehow. Can't just sit idly by."

"You got no choice, friend. This is police business, and you'd better leave it that way. Don't make things hard on yourself. Last thing we need is a well-meaning amateur messing things up."

His reaction has also told me I'd better be very careful about signaling my real plans. *Well,* I think to myself, *I have no intention of leaving this situation to the police force, no matter how capable they may be. It's up to me to exact a payback from the scum who hurt my brother.* But I accept for now that I must bite my tongue and soft-pedal with the sheriff.

"Understand, Len. But can I read the full report of the incident?"

"Sure. Bet your ass you can." He takes me back out front and turns to one of his uniformed staff.

"Hey, Charlie. This is Dave Owens. He's a good ol' boy grew up right here in Springlake. Known him since we were kids. Get him the report on the beatin' down at Lakeside last night."

The deputy reaches into his out-basket and retrieves the report. He looks at the papers then at me and asks, "Owens? You related to the victim?"

"He's my brother," I say. "Thanks, officer."

He strides to an empty desk, turns on the reading lamp, and motions for me to have a seat.

I begin to carefully absorb every detail in the report. The crime took place at the gasoline station at the corner of East Main Street and Ellery Road at approximately 11:30 PM. Since I've used that service station a number of times, I can picture exactly where Kyle was standing on the east side of the building when he was set upon. He's told me how he goes to that station to pick up his favorite snack of slaw dogs at their food counter. Seems odd he would wander there so late at night, though. I add that question to my list of things to discuss with Kyle when he's up to it.

The perpetrator approached him without his noticing and struck a blow to the back of Kyle's head. He suffered a large lump at the rear of his skull, which the officer deemed to be the result of a blow from a heavy object. Open wounds near both eyes made it appear the attacker had punched him, possibly with heavy rings on his fists. Kyle's right ear was lacerated and had wounds that looked suspiciously like tooth marks, a matter for a physician to confirm. When the officer arrived, he noted that the victim was barely conscious and his right cheek had already begun to swell. The paramedics arrived minutes later. One of them reported that two teeth were loose on the right side of Kyle's mouth. He had also bruised his shoulder when he fell to the pavement beside the gas pump. The other injuries were apparently the result of blows delivered by the attacker and not due to the fall.

"Damn coward," I mumble. The anger returns full force. I want to crush something, but there is nothing near at hand to absorb my vitriol. "He'll pay for this...I swear it!"

The officer hears my comment. He turns toward me with a frown.

An amendment to the initial report states that the victim later gave a partial identification of his attacker when he said something about dark eyes and a black beard. During periods of consciousness he had also been heard to say the word 'damp' or sank' at least twice. The victim's wife reported his mumbled outbursts.

I jot down notes and reread the entire report to be sure I haven't missed anything. Nothing in the account gives me the slightest clue as to the reason for the attack. That's something I'll have to dig out for myself, and I'm more than ready for the task.

* * * *

Have a couple of important chores to finish before I can rest. I pull in at Huggins' Diner on West Main Street. Need a shot of caffeine to keep me conscious, and there are two phone calls to make. The first number I know, the second will require a look up.

Pace the parking lot as fatigue and nervous energy battle for what's left of my consciousness. Jab at my cell phone and connect to the number in Raleigh. The voice that answers is the one I've longed to hear.

"Helen, it's Dave. I'm in Springlake." My words are met with a long silence.

"Yes. So?" This is not an encouraging start, but at least we're talking to each other.

"Kyle's been hurt. I drove all night from Atlanta."

"Oh, no! What happened?"

"Somebody beat him up last night. Really worked him over. He's in the hospital."

"I'm sorry, Dave. You know I'd come if I could." She pauses. "It's just not possible right now."

"More than anything in the world, I want to see you and Melody. But I understand."

"Maybe I ought to call Jenny," she offers. "Give her a word of encouragement."

"She's out on her feet right now, Helen. Soon as she wakes up she'll be back at the hospital most of the day."

"You'll keep me up on Kyle's progress then? And give Jenny my love. I'll call her tonight."

"I will. And Helen…"

"Thanks, Dave." *Click*.

She's gone. Helen has postponed my attempt to break through our impasse by avoiding any further conversation. I'm foreclosed before I can even get the words out. The instant pain of another missed opportunity speeds through my system, forms a tight little ball in my stomach and rockets up to slug me in the chest. I lean on the car until the nausea of failure passes.

Walk into the diner. Find the entryway pay phone, look up the number of the Barnwell House Bed and Breakfast and jot it down. Then I plop into a booth. The waitress glides over with a coffee pot, looks me over, and offers tentatively, "Breakfast?"

"For starters, I need some of that."

She manages a half-hearted smile and pours my cup full. I eat only because I know my last meal was too many hours ago. What I need most is the hot, strong coffee I slug down as fast as the young lady can re-supply it. When she brings my eggs and bacon I feel obligated to explain why I have the appearance of a fleeing fugitive.

"Sorry I look so grungy. Been on the road too long. Drove all night. Any motels close by?"

The question is my way of making conversation. I already know where I want to stay. My words take the edge off her apprehension, though.

She answers, "A couple here on West Main. You look like you could use some rest." She grins and hurries away.

That's the understatement of the year. I'm avoiding mirrors for fear of what may squint back at me. Tired, sweaty, dirty, mud-spattered. Probably look more like I need an *extended* rest, just short of interment. That's all the more reason for booking at the Barnwell House by phone rather than in person. Show up like this to register and they'll run away screaming. Punch my cell phone. The cordial voice on the line informs me they have a room available. Book a seven night stay; tell her I'll check in later this afternoon.

I polish off my food and a fourth cup of coffee. Leave a ten on the table and head for the bathroom. The cold tap water helps to make me feel human, and I comb my hair and straighten my clothes. Even manage to get some of the mountain mud off my boots. Hope a quick once over with my cordless shaver will make me look like a credible risk as a boarder.

Now I have to force my eyes to stay open to check on Jenny and the boys.

Chapter 5

Don, my oldest nephew, answers the phone.

"Hi, big guy. You okay?" I ask.

Don is twenty, a junior at the local business college. He's a near carbon copy of Kyle in looks and mannerisms.

"Hi, Dave." I've never been Uncle Dave to these boys, just Dave. "Is dad really all right?"

"He's tough, Don, and he's on the mend. Your Mom must have told you by now."

"Just wanted to hear it from you, too. Mom had to crash soon as she got home. She's totally exhausted. I convinced her she shouldn't try to make it back to the hospital for awhile in her condition."

"Glad you talked some sense into her, Don. She's out of it with worry. The best thing for her right now is to sleep. How's your brother taking all this?"

"Tom's pretty shook, Dave. But he'll be better as soon as he sees Dad. We're all three going there when he gets home from school."

There is an awkward pause in our conversation then Don asks, "Are you going back to the hospital this afternoon? Mom insisted I go on to classes this morning then wait here for Tom to get home. How does Dad look, Dave? Really?"

"Look, I wouldn't mislead you. Your dad is bruised and swollen but he's tough. Your Mom and I are being straight with you. The worst part is behind him now. I'll see all of you at the hospital later."

"Okay, Dave. I believe you. We're all glad you're here."

"Listen, Don, I'm out on my feet. Need to sleep and catch up. Expect me at the hospital between five and six. And tell Tom not to worry about his dad because he's gonna be fine. Got something you can write on?"

"I have this." He reaches into his notebook and fishes out a notepad. "Go ahead."

"Write down this phone number. It's at the Barnwell House Bed and Breakfast on Main Street. Tell your Mom I'm staying here so the three of you can have the privacy you need while Kyle gets squared away. But you know I'll come any time you call me."

Well, I hope that reassures Don. Wish I was as confident as I sound that Kyle will make a full recovery. Refuse to accept that this can turn out any other way.

It's time I call it a morning and head for the Bed and Breakfast.

* * * *

The Barnwell House looks pretty much as I remembered it. An impressive three-story mansion sitting high on a hill. Overlooks West Main Street near the center of town. A steep driveway leads to a guest parking lot in the rear. I turn in and drive up past the old house.

A slender elderly lady with a broad smile emerges from the rear when I enter the big open foyer. She takes off her apron as she approaches me and brushes back a wisp of gray hair at her brow. Calls out,

"Busy in the kitchen getting dinner started." She offers her hand. "I'm Mrs. Starkey. How can I help you?"

"I called earlier and booked a room for seven nights. I'm Dave…"

The bubbly lady chimes in before I can finish; her eyes twinkle and she says, "Oh, yes. You're going to be in Room 203. Just need a little information." She hands me a card to fill out and does a double take, almost as if she recognizes me. I certainly remember her, but there will be time for us to visit later. Right now I have an appointment with a pillow.

"Good to be off the road, Mrs. Starkey. I've been driving all night." She nods and seems to be searching my face for something. I stand there thinking what a pleasant lady Mrs. Starkey is, energy belying her years and a smile that lights the room. Must be late fifties, early sixties. About the age Mom would be if she were still here.

"Your room is up those stairs. Second door on the left. Welcome."

I take the key, and she points me toward the staircase. The gleaming hardwood floor of the entryway and the ornate Oriental runner down its center give the appearance of subdued elegance from times past. The chest high armoire she uses as a registration desk has a starched, dazzlingly white doily and an antique lamp. All around me is the feel of a stately home meticulously cared for and proudly presented to her guests. I acknowledge her greeting and turn toward the winding staircase with its massive polished banister and carpet covered stairs.

The inviting room feels large and comfortable. Sweeping beige curtains with a subtle rose pattern. Windows with shades up to let the light of the mid-day sun fill the room. A big, quilt-covered poster bed beckoning to me. I set down my bags and go to the windows. Pull the shades down to darken the room. Kicking off my boots, I plunge headlong onto the soft bed without undressing.

So much confusing information is pounding away in my skull. I'm too confused to ponder what it all means at this point. Surely the world can stop whirling long enough for me to have a little quiet time. I close my eyes and drift away.

But this won't be the peaceful sleep I'm seeking. The restlessness begins from the moment I spin off into a deep sleep. I float somewhere above the quiet streets of Springlake, detached from my body, a silent observer soaring over the landscape. Childhood memories flood in. As I let myself go, my last conscious picture is one of Kyle in his early teens.

Then the dream begins.

Everything around me seems so clear and real. I'm a youngster tagging along behind the object of my admiration. He's my source of learning and an authority on the real world. I believe Kyle has experienced so much more, understands the people and events around us far better than I do. Everything I do flows from watching my brother and imitating his actions. I try my best to be just like him.

We're sitting in the local movie house. The logical side of my brain tells me this can't be real because that theater was torn down at least fifteen years ago. But a feeling of comfort and well being sweeps over me. I want desperately to be safe in the Colonial Theater with Kyle seated beside me. He's bought my ticket with part of the earnings from his newspaper route. I'm watching in awe as the Saturday morning characters parade before me on the giant screen, secure in the fact that my big brother is at my side. All is well in my ten-year-old world.

Kyle is, in my eyes, almost grown up now that he's a high school freshman, all of fourteen years behind him. He has discovered Jenny and spends a lot of time with her. She and his pals must be so much more interesting than the string bean, towheaded kid sitting next to him in the dark movie house. But he makes me feel important, like I'm the one person who he would spend his Saturdays with, chewing on popcorn and fending off the jibes of his more mature pals who make fun of him for always having me hanging around.

He merely shakes off their comments and confides, "They're just being wise guys, Davey. Most of them wish they had a brother like you" My chest swells with pride.

Then we're on our way home after a double feature, a cowboy flick and a horror film. My friends and I enjoy the shoot 'em ups and rooting for the good guys, but I never could understand why anyone would want to muddle our minds with Frankenstein, Dracula and the like. Kyle and I are hurrying home as the sun starts to sink. One of those days when we've gone to a late matinee and evening is about to close in on us.

Kyle stops dead in his tracks and says, "Listen to that, Davey. Was that the wail of a wolf?" Then he jumps back and looks startled. "Oh, no. It's the Wolfman!"

What would normally have been a fifteen-minute walk from the movie to our house suddenly becomes a rapid sprint. I take off like a homing projectile for the safety of our back porch. All the way back, Kyle is somewhere back there shouting for me to slow down. But he's energized me, and I'm not about to lose ground to the creature looming behind me. I'm certain that half-man half-wolf is about to reach out for me. I can imagine him panting hot against my neck, opening his jaws, baring his dripping teeth and preparing to finish me off.

When we reach the shelter of Mom's kitchen it finally dawns on Kyle what he's done. He comes over to me and says, "Davey, I'm sorry for scaring you like that. It was mean. I'll never do it again." Then he can't help laughing, and I join him in sheer relief. "Somebody asked me the other day what does a guided missile look like," he says. By now tears are streaming down his cheeks. "Well, now I know, little brother. Looks like Dave Owens leaving a cloud of dust between himself and the Wolfman."

Kyle laughs about that to this day. He delights in telling the story about how little Davey set a new speed record and a pace he couldn't match. Said he knew how to make me a track star, but he wasn't sure my nerves would survive the repeated shock.

I feel myself stirring, trying to return to conscious reality. My mind tells me to break away from the dream, but I can't seem to get back from where I've wandered. I drift and seem to float somewhere outside my body. Toss around and search for a way back, but my fatigue won't turn loose. The old house fades slowly away.

A new scene slowly takes shape. We're back inside the movie house, and through my dreamy haze I'm watching one of my favorite cowboys on the screen. Kyle is dis-

cussing something in whispers with his pal Jimmy Moore, who is seated behind us. From looking at Kyle and Jimmy, I surmise I must be watching through the eyes of a skinny, tow-headed youngster of nine or ten. Then a very disturbing thing happens. I look up to see a thin man with a short, coal black beard reach across me and tug at Kyle.

"You'll have to shut up or leave," he says in a threatening tone.

Kyle says, "Sorry," still snickering at something Jimmy said to him. The bearded man bristles at his laughing.

"You smart aleck," he says, and puts one hand roughly on Kyle's shoulders, shakes him hard.

My brother has never been one to go looking for trouble, but I've never known him to back down when pushed. That includes bullies and bigger kids. But this is a grown man. Kyle starts to get up from his seat, and the tall man steps in front of me, leaning toward Kyle with a raised open hand. "All you smart-mouth kids are just alike. Always looking for trouble. You need a lesson."

I'm nailed to my seat in panic until Kyle moves his eyes from the usher to me, and I see his helpless look. He's ready to do battle but knows he's out-muscled. At that sight, I lose all sense of reason. Hurl myself at the bearded man. He screams in pain when my teeth clamp down hard on his forearm, and he drags me into the aisle, my teeth sunk firmly into the flesh of that hairy arm. He tries to tear me away then grabs me with his free hand and yanks me roughly off my feet.

I hold on tight, lock my jaws and bear down that much harder. The taste of blood fills my mouth. With my legs pedaling in the air, I dangle from the usher's arm. Kick my legs as hard as I can at his middle. He moans and cries out, "Little shit!" Lets go of me, doubles over and rolls on the floor, both hands pressed below his stomach. Round two goes to the skinny kid with the strong teeth and pumping feet.

This is our opening. I grab Kyle's hand and tug. We hurry up the aisle through the cheers and laughter from the young movie crowd. As the movie stops and the theater lights go on, a beaming young Len Darden thrusts out his hand and says, "Good on you, kid, busted him one in the jewels. You're all right." He reaches out and slaps my hand.

*   *   *   *

I awake, sweating profusely, my head pounding with images I can't explain. Find myself tangled around the bed covers, trying to kick them away so I can stand. My mind replays the dreams frame by frame like a slow motion reprise. I grope for the meaning of the unsettling visions. The frenzied run home I remember as vividly as if it had happened yesterday. That's a shock to my nerves I'll never forget.

But why that scene in the Colonial Theater? Memory tells me there was a particular usher at that movie house all of us kids disliked. Fragments of the scene I've just witnessed come back dimly, but it must not have been all that important to me when it happened. Can't say I've ever thought of it until now.

What possible explanation could there be for my memory banks dredging up that incident in such detail now? Could it have some obscure connection with my current dilemma that isn't yet obvious to me? May be just my exhaustion working tricks on me. My mind fighting for some tie with the past and better times for Kyle and me to help calm me down.

I can't deal with it until my thoughts are more organized. Gulp down aspirin and strip my clothes away, leave them in a pile. Then I slip down between the sheets and let sleep carry me away.

Chapter 6

▼

Sometime later I stir and slowly focus on my surroundings. Where am I? Then it hits me like a splash of cold water that I'm back in Springlake. I'm sleeping when there's work to be done. Look at my watch and see it's nearly five o'clock. I've slept through the afternoon. Have to get cracking. Once the nightmare from the movie house passed, I had actually enjoyed a deep sleep that began to rejuvenate me.

With a new burst of energy, I hurry to the shower and shiver under a cold stream until I'm fully awake. The water isn't the only thing that causes me to tremble. I flash back to the mystery man in the movie house threatening to hurt my brother. The mix of fear and anger sends goose bumps up my arms. I have to shake that picture and get moving. Kyle and Jenny will be expecting me at the hospital soon. But the image of that obnoxious movie usher won't go away. On instinct, I pick up the phone directory to look up the number for the sheriff's office.

"Sheriff Darden, please."

"He's busy. Can somebody else help you?"

"No. Please tell him it's Dave Owens. I'll stop off to see him later. It's important."

"Oh, then, let me try to get his attention," the deputy says. Maybe he recognizes the name.

Hope I'm not becoming a pest. And maybe this is nothing, but my dream worries me, and there is a question that I need to settle now.

"Yeah, Dave," Darden answers. "Can you run this by me quick like? It's pretty busy around here today." Sheriff sounds testy.

"Len, do you remember the usher at the old Colonial Theater?"

"Yeah. Why?"

"Did he have a beard?"

"Yeah, and a sharp honker of a nose. Looked like a damn turkey buzzard. What about him?"

I smile. This could be important or it could be a total fabrication on my part; but it has me thinking about possibilities. I have to be a part of the search for Kyle's attacker.

"Did he ever throw Kyle and me out of the movies while you were there?"

"Well, if I recall it right, you sort of threw yourselves out, but not till you'd done something we all wanted to see. You damn near crippled him with a well-placed boot. Bet he was walking spraddle-legged for a week. And you took a healthy chomp out of his arm, too. Somebody told me later you thought he was gonna smack Kyle so you took after him big time. Hell, if that had been a few years later, some lawyer would have hauled the Colonial into court and the Owens family would have owned that place. But that was before the days of everybody suing each other."

"And he wore a beard?"

"Had a black beard and eyes to match. He was mid-twenties or so. A real odd duck. Always had it in for us kids so we deviled him every chance we had. Why would you think of him now?"

"It was just bothering me for some reason. Thanks, Len. By the way, do you remember his name—the usher, I mean?"

"Beats hell out of me. I'm not your world's best for remembering names."

Darden isn't quite through with me yet, though. Seems he's made the connection, and an alarm has sounded in that big old noggin.

"Hold on there, Davey. You're reaching. I read the report, too, you know. That scuffle at the movie house was damn near thirty years ago. Gotta be a lot of guys running around with black beards. Hell, that usher's probably long gone from here by now."

"It was just playing on my mind for some reason, Len."

"Don't forget what I told you. This is a police matter. I don't need you running around making up bad guts in your mind. Already have one unsolved death on my hands, and I don't wanta come fishing you out of the river."

"What unsolved death?" I ask.

There is a sudden silence. Did I only imagine he muttered 'Damnation' under his breath? Has he opened a touchy subject by accident? Finally, he replies.

"Jimmy Moore, friend of your brother's and mine. We found him butchered out in the woods a few days ago. Terrible scene. I don't need any more complications, so you just back off."

"Jimmy?" I repeat in shock. "Oh, no, not him. He and Kyle were like Siamese twins."

"I know, Dave. His death must have gone down pretty hard with your brother."

"But you said he was 'butchered', Len."

"Forget about it, Owens. Told you more already that I should have. It's not your affair. Just do as I told you and stay out of things better handled by my police force."

"I hear you," I reply. "Don't want to get in the way. But you can imagine how this whole mugging matter has me looking for connections."

He must know by now, too, that I'm not through searching for clues to find Kyle's assailant and have my own revenge. This new input about Moore is chilling. What's going on in this peaceful little valley? Jimmy butchered?

*　　*　　*　　*

The nurse meets us at the door and leads us into Intensive Care. My first impression is that Kyle is improving. His bruises are still obvious and the lumpy cheek is ugly. But his manner is somehow more encouraging than when I went to see him a few hours ago. He manages a weak smile when he sees me approaching with Jenny.

"*Is* you," he says through swollen lips. "Not a dream."

"Let me talk and you just listen," I reply.

Jenny bends and kisses him on his good cheek. He gives a head nod toward the nightstand. She picks up the ice bucket, gets an approving nod from the nurse, and gives him a spoonful of ice shavings. He works to moisten his mouth and turns toward me to speak.

"Must tell…" His voice falters, and all that comes out is a squeak.

"Lots of time for that, Kyle. It's so good to see you snapping back. I like the fact that you're showing some color besides black and blue." *Pretty dumb statement*, I think, but his upper lip curls in what I hope is a smile, not a sneer.

"I saw Len Darden today. You know, old Broadus? He asked about you. Also mentioned something to me about Jimmy Moore."

That strikes a cord. Kyle turns his face toward the wall.

"Sorry, Kyle. Forget I said that." *Clumsy*. I chastise myself silently.

He rolls his head back in my direction and mutters. Wets his swollen lips and slowly croaks out the words, "Beard…Mugger…Jimmy…Tank." His eyes are weak but the fright registers in them. Then he coughs and his eyes water over. The nurse steps in to silence him.

"Save your voice, Mister Owens," she admonishes.

But with those words he has established a connection for me between two violent events, his beating and the death of his good friend Jimmy Moore. I have no idea how they may be linked, but the events are somehow related in his mind. The sheriff also doesn't realize what he's accomplished with his slip of the tongue. Far from discouraging me from snooping, his comments about Jimmy Moore and Kyle's reaction to hearing me say Jimmy's name compel me to continue.

The race is on, sheriff. You and your deputies better beat me to the guilty party or you'll be handcuffing me for pounding him to a bloody stump.

* * * *

I go to the waiting room and wait for Jenny. She finally comes out of the IC unit, eyes me with concern and opens with a question.

"You're getting yourself too involved in this thing, aren't you?"

"How could I *not* be involved, Jenny. He's all that's left of the family I grew up loving. You know how much he means to me."

"That's not what I meant. You're about to do something dangerous. I can feel it coming. Let the sheriff take care of this, Dave. I have enough to worry about with Kyle lying in there."

I ignore her warning and prompt, "Tell me about Jimmy Moore."

"Oh, well, I suppose you'll find out one way or another. He was found dead in the woods off Wildflower Road about a week ago. There isn't much that's been released on what happened. The police have kept all the details quiet. It really worked on Kyle's mind when he heard the news. He and Jimmy had been close friends for a lot of years. Kyle sort of went into a shell, and he hasn't gotten back to normal yet."

"They were practically each others' shadows for as long as I can remember," I tell her. "Always off plotting some minor mischief. Not bad kids, just two guys with vivid imaginations. Occasionally got them into trouble, and Mom would have to tighten the reins on Kyle for awhile. Jimmy was my favorite of all of Kyle's buddies."

Jenny smiles. "They stayed close. Kyle knew he could use Jimmy as a sounding board. They often confided in each other. It was a terrible loss for Kyle."

"Darden used the word butchered when he told me about Jimmy. What else do you know about his death?"

"Nothing more, Dave. I think Kyle does, though. Maybe when he comes around he can deal with it better. But please don't press him yet. You saw how even hearing Jimmy's name upsets him."

I squeeze Jenny's hand and drop the subject. But it's still high on my list of things I need to know. And I now understand that the word Jenny misheard was actually 'tank.' Somehow *beard, mugger, Jimmy* and *tank* are bound together. Kyle can't tell me how just yet. It's a puzzling combination, but I'm determined to learn why he's tied them together.

We're about to leave when a slightly pudgy, balding man hurries into the waiting room and goes directly to Jenny. He puts his arms around her and says, "I just heard about Kyle. How is he, Jenny?"

"He's holding his own, but he's badly bruised and beaten. It's awful."

She steers the man toward me. I think I recognize him, but can't quite come up with his name. He's barrel-chested and has big, sinewy arms, but his face is beginning to show a fortyish sort of puffiness, and his eyes make him look like he's carrying the weight of the world.

"You remember Billy Logan, Dave," Sis says, and it comes together in a rush. Of course. Billy. Kyle's pal since childhood, a big, lovable guy with a heart as big as all outdoors. I reach out and he pumps my hand vigorously.

"Hi, Dave. Man, it's been ages. I know Kyle's glad you're here to help him through this…rotten thing."

"Well, he's strong-willed, Billy. You ought to know that. Give it time and he'll be good as new. Great to see you again."

"Don't guess they'd let me in there, would they?" His question is addressed in general to both Jenny and me. She shakes her head.

"Family only for the time being, Billy. But I'll tell him you were here. Thanks for coming by. I'll let you know when he's able to see visitors."

She touches Logan's hand and turns to me. "I have to go check on my boys now. You coming back here this evening, Dave?"

"Have a couple errands to take care of, Jenny. Want to talk to Billy for a minute, too. Then I badly need some rest. Feel like I've been sleepwalking for the past few hours. I'll be in touch in the morning unless you need something before then. Here's my number at the Barnwell House. You have my cell phone number."

I hand her the business card where I've penciled in the Barnwell's phone number on the reverse side. She looks at the card, nods and turns to leave.

"What do you think, Dave," Billy asks. "Is he really okay? I mean, is Kyle out of danger?"

"Kyle will pull through fine, Billy. He has his faith, a good woman, and a will of steel. By the way, when's the last time you saw him?"

"Let's see. Must have been about three days ago. Yeah, it was around the middle of the afternoon on Wednesday. Went by his house."

"How was he, Billy?"

"What do you mean?"

"Did he seem normal to you?"

"He was mighty fidgety, Dave, and he acted distracted. Kept wandering from one subject to another. I asked him if he was having a bad day. He said he'd had more bad days than good recently. Then he stared out the window like I wasn't even there."

"Did he mention Jimmy Moore?"

Billy visibly sags and begins to stammer. "I...I...that's the main reason I went to see him. Jimmy's death really shook me so I knew it had to get to Kyle. I mean, we'd always been good friends, but those two were about as close as you can get without being blood kin."

"And?"

"He said he couldn't talk about Jimmy, wasn't up to it yet...maybe later. He was torn up real bad about it."

"Thanks, Billy. Can I get back to you? I'm trying to fit together what happened to Kyle and why."

"Just give me a holler, Dave. Anything I can do to put this guy away for what he did to my buddy." He turns to walk away then hesitates for an instant. Looks as if he wants to say something else then reconsiders and waves as he leaves the room.

* * * *

Too many unanswered questions. Can't keep pushing the sheriff, though. He's going to sit hard on me if I make any further show of playing amateur sleuth. So I'll have to find other sources of information. Maybe it's time for a visit to the offices of the Springlake Times.

Haven't seen the inside of this place in years, but it hasn't changed in all that time. Still smells of must and newsprint, filled with badly worn furniture and framed samples of old headlines. Recent editions of the Times sit on the counter and more papers on the coffee table in the sitting area. I casually thumb through the counter stack and check the headlines. Last week's paper features a story on the death of lifelong Springlake resident James Moore. Has a class photo of the blonde-haired kid I remember so well.

"Like to catch up on the hometown news, miss. Been away. Can I get copies of the past four weekly issues?"

The young lady behind the counter leafs through wall shelves and produces the copies I've requested.

"Missed the icy spell, I take it."

I think, *Sure did, and a lot of other happenings since I strayed from the valley.*

"Yeah, been gone for a while," I tell her.

She takes my money, and I retreat to an armchair in the corner to scan the local news. Spot what I want almost immediately, but I can't make a big deal out of asking questions about Jimmy Moore. First I have to find another story with the same reporter's name and ask about that.

Thumb through the papers looking at the bylines. This week's edition has an article about the new bridge that has just been finished on the west end of town. That will do for an opener. I look up and catch the young woman's eye.

"Excuse me, miss," I say, returning to the front with my finger on the story. "Is Randall Bean in? I'd like to ask him about one of his articles."

She picks up her phone and hits a button. "Randy, can you come up front to see somebody?"

A red-faced man comes in from the back. He introduces himself simply as Bean. We shake hands. He looks to be slightly older than I am, and fits my picture of a reporter with too many years of hustling small town news. The boredom is clearly stated in the eyes behind those thick glasses.

"Want to ask you about this article on the new bridge over the river above town," I say, pointing to the photo in the paper. "When I was a kid in Springlake, there was a flour mill out past the leather tannery. The mill sat across the river on Rohr's Mill Road. Your article says there's now a warehouse complex out there. Can you tell me what happened to the mill?"

"Burned down some time back. Hadn't been in operation for more than a dozen or so years. Some big outfit bought up the property and built storage buildings. The deal was the town would put in a new bridge that could carry wide, heavy loads to those warehouses. Turned out to be a good deal in terms of bringing new money and jobs to Springlake."

"Thanks. Do you have any idea where the Rohrs are now? The family that ran the mill?"

"Last I heard of them, they had moved somewhere out west."

"Thank you, Mr. Bean. That clears up a couple of things for me."

Actually I'm not the least bit interested in the bridge, the mill or the Rohrs, but it gives me the lead-in I want for my real topic.

As he stands to return to work, I mention, in an off-hand way, the headline in last week's paper. "Great piece of reporting, your story on the Jimmy Moore death." That resonates with him. Probably the most important news he's covered in months. He won't need a lot of prompting on that one.

Bean returns to his chair and begins. "Said you grew up here. Did you know Moore?"

"Knew of him, yes. He was a couple years older, but I remember him.

"Strange case, and really tragic. Biggest crime around here in years. I heard the emergency call on the police band. Arrived almost as soon as the rescue team. Of course, there was no hurry. Poor Jimmy was already dead." Bean shakes his head.

"The story doesn't say how he died."

"All I saw was that he had been stabbed in the throat," Bean replies." The police hurried me away and told me to check at the station after they had all their facts together. Wouldn't let me take any pictures, either."

Stabbed and 'butchered', as the sheriff had termed Jimmy's condition, don't seem to be consistent. And why did the police want the newsman away from the scene immediately? Something doesn't quite compute. I have the uneasy feeling that Kyle understands something about his friend's death the police don't yet know. Whatever it is has him scared witless, and that's not like Kyle. But he can't—or won't—tell me yet.

Chapter 7

The peace and quiet of the Barnwell House is a welcome relief. It's been a frantic day.

I take a while after dinner to relax in the parlor and think about what I've learned so far. The attack on Kyle and the mysterious death of his close friend both have me rattled. And the fact that they came so close together in time is disturbing. Could be there's no connection, but my imagination is running wild.

Sit in the toasty warm parlor, the fire in the hearth casting shadows across the room, and sip at the coffee Mrs. Starkey has thoughtfully provided. I'm alone in the parlor except for the myriad of thoughts that crowd in on me. A flood of questions and doubts about what my role will be in the events unfolding here in Springlake.

My return to the old home town has also raised new questions about where my personal life is headed. I think about how tranquil Kyle's life has been, at least up until the past twenty-four hours. Wonder where I got off track. He's always been the steady, stable one. Never showed the slightest desire to leave Springlake or change a life he considered to be fulfilling. When we were growing up, he couldn't wait to get his first car, an old Plymouth he spent long hours tinkering with whether it needed his tinkering or not. Loved to get his hands on anything mechanical—bicycle, motorbike, auto, didn't matter as long as it involved wheels or gasoline engines. This is a love he has passed along to Don. His son has taken it another notch, becoming something of a collector and restorer of classic autos. Kyle and Jenny are hometown products and perfectly content to stay here. Their success and beautiful family seem to confirm that was a good decision. He's had opportunities to leave with promotions, but he valued the home town and old friends more than advancement.

Meanwhile, I was out there thrashing around, always chasing something—even I didn't know exactly what—getting more dissatisfied with each passing year. It all started innocently enough. Seems, as far back as I can remember, I was the one destined to reach beyond the valley for my future. I had a natural ability to breeze through school without exerting myself. Learning just seemed to come easily for me, so easy it always made me less than energetic about my study habits. Bone lazy probably more nearly describes it. I had a reputation as an insider, a leader, and enjoyed much success in high school. With great sacrifice, my parents found the money to send me on to college, and I continued to excel academically. Then I struck out for the high-pressure arena of the electronics revolution carrying all the tools I needed to take on the world.

There was a time after we were married and I had my first full time job when Helen and I were happy here in Springlake. Melody thrived and we were perfectly willing to stay right in my old home town forever. After my parents were taken away in that car wreck, Kyle, Jenny and the boys and Aunt Ethel became my small and treasured remaining family. Helen's folks were a short drive away in West Virginia. Our jobs paid enough to provide us with all the necessities including a cozy little apartment. We even began our search for a first home. Helen thoroughly enjoyed her work in an accounting office, and I was part of a small engineering firm.

One summer afternoon Helen, Melody and I were down by the river. The three of us finished the fried chicken picnic basket Helen had prepared. I was dozing off in the June sun, my head in Helen's lap. I stirred and looked up at her. "Honey, are you really content in this small town?"

"That's a strange question, Dave."

"There's a big, exciting world beyond those mountains."

She gave me a knowing smile. "Itching for bright lights?"

"Just want to make my two girls as happy as I can."

Helen pointed to our rosy-cheeked little girl romping nearby and said, "What more could I possibly want? Melody is thriving here and we both enjoy our jobs. Your family is close by. I'm contented wherever you and Melody are."

But I was already caught up in my greed for something more. I wanted to be a part of the fast moving, big money world of the young engineers who were advancing electronics technology at a blurring pace. I had ideas and the industry was ripe for thinkers with the ability to visualize and follow through.

"Helen, my engineering degree should be worth more to us than this mediocre job I have. The computer world is red hot. There are exciting jobs to be had. I already have a lead on a great position in North Carolina at a good deal more money than I'm making now."

She let me set the pace. I was too blinded by the possibilities to see that she was less than enthusiastic about relocating away from our friends and family.

"I love Springlake, Dave, but we'll be happy anywhere you are. You have to be satisfied with what you're doing for a living. Whatever you decide, I'm okay with it."

"You've said you'd like to be a stay at home mom. This is our chance with me bringing home more pay. You can always go back to work later, if that's what you want."

Her financial skills would be in demand anywhere we went. What I wasn't considering was that she derived a large measure of self-fulfillment from putting her talents to work, and she would miss that satisfaction if she stayed at home. At my insistence, we moved to Raleigh, and at first she enjoyed the extra time with our beautiful daughter. Helen thrived on nurturing Melody, but there was a spark missing that only her own sense of professional achievement could have provided.

I ignored the obvious. My own fresh ideas drew rave reviews. My corporate climb began, and I was intoxicated by success. Spent more and more of my spare time on schemes for advancement and currying favor with my employers. It all worked wonderfully well. Even won a patent on one of my brainstorms. The company financed the patenting process, and we shared the royalties on sales. Sadly, I disregarded the fact that Helen and Melody were taking a back seat to my desire to personally get ahead.

All the time my spiral toward becoming a workaholic was capturing me in its siren clutches, Kyle labored along, earning his way up the supervisory ladder, building a solid home life. Now that I reflect back objectively on those days, I realize that he hinted to me on several occasions that I may be too wrapped up in my career. But even though I had always heeded his advice in the past, I turned a deaf ear to his counsel.

"Ever long for some quiet time, Dave? A chance to unwind? Clear your head? Must be a real pressure cooker down there in the Triangle area."

"Never happier, Kyle. The sky's the limit now. I have lots of ideas to put to work that should be real money makers. There's a rumble I could be in line for a nice promotion, maybe a Director's position."

"Sounds great. What does Helen think of the faster pace? Is she making friends and finding ways to fill her time?" He made the question seem almost routine as he reached for the TV remote and switched between Sunday football games.

"Melody is plenty to keep her busy. We're fine, really great, Kyle."

That sounded good, but there was a warning light flickering somewhere deep in my brain. I just wasn't paying attention to it.

* * * *

Mrs. Starkey interrupts my drowsy musings with freshly brewed coffee and warm cookies just out of the oven.

"Ever been in our little town?"

"Grew up here, Ma'am."

That gets her attention. "Springlake boy, are you, back for a visit?"

"Been away too long, I'm afraid. Didn't remember how comfortable the folks around here make me feel. These cookies hit the spot. They remind me of the ones Mom used to bake. I love them still warm."

She says, "You know, I just now realized I didn't even look at that registration card to check your last name. All I really heard was Dave. Guess I assumed you said Davis. My hearing isn't so good at times any more. Just didn't give it another thought."

"No. It's Owens."

Her face lights up. "Wait! Owens? You wouldn't be Ruby Owens' son?"

"Sure am. Number two son. My brother Kyle still lives here."

Her voice goes up an octave. "Ruby and I were girlfriends back in grade school. You must have thought I was a little odd when I kept looking at you. I was trying to place your face. Last time I remember seeing you was when Ruby and your Dad..." She catches herself and stops short.

"I know. You were at the funeral. I was a college freshman at the time. Lived here for awhile after finishing school then left for Carolina and Georgia. Always wanted to see the inside of this place, and I must say I'm impressed, Mrs. Starkey."

"What brings you back now? Sorry, it's none of my business." She turns away and busies herself with straightening the doily on the lamp table.

"That's all right. My brother Kyle is in the hospital, and I came home to see him." The word home has a warm feeling about it. "He's been my only family since the car crash that took our folks."

"Oh, yes. I read the story about Kyle in the paper this morning." She looks concerned. "How is he?"

"He's some better now, thanks. I plan to stick around until he's fully recovered. Hope the room is available for awhile longer."

She touches my hand and says softly, "You stay as long as you want. And just let me know if you need anything at all. Ruby was a dear friend, so you're a special guest."

I plod up the stairs and wearily undress after a long day of worry and wondering. Pile up clothes to take to the cleaners in the morning. Choose a shirt, pants and a sweater to wear tomorrow. Then I turn out the lights and put my head on the pillow.

Tomorrow I'll make a fresh start.

*   *   *   *

Sanjay Samderiya has been nervously watching as each customer enters the store. After his experience last night, he's not sure he should even be working this evening. Maybe he won't ever have a normal workday again after seeing that brutal, senseless attack. Made him wonder if his adopted country was, after all, any safer than the remote province in India he'd left ten years ago.

"Here, you boys! If you want to play, please do it somewhere else. This is a place of business."

The two youths in their mid teens interrupt their horseplay and look at him with contempt. One of them throws out a comeback Sam doesn't even understand. The other jabs a middle finger in the air. Sam sees that both of them are carrying open bags of snacks they haven't paid for. Sam is slight of stature, but he is on his turf. No one is going to cut up like this inside his station and steal from him.

He charges past the counter and chases the boys out the front door. They snatch up their bikes and pedal away. Sam catches his breath and says, "Get a job, punk boys."

Sam looks at the pumps standing idle outside. It has been a slow night so far. After running off that man with the knife trying to hurt Mister Owens, he had welcomed a shift without incident until now. Rude kids weren't the worst thing he could be contending with.

Then he looks up and sees the last face he ever wanted to see again.

"Boo," says the dark man with the black beard. His eyes flash and he grinds his teeth together. Sam is immobilized, rooted to a spot just inside the front door; he can't speak, can't run, stands frozen.

Sam throws both hands up to cover his face. He tries to concentrate, to remember what he's been told by his manager about situations such as this.

"You may have anything you want. Just take it and leave, please. I am opening the cash register for you." Sam slowly inches toward the counter.

"Damn meddler," the man roars. "Don't want your money. I'm after payback. You whacked me on the arm. Ruined my plans. Now you have to pay the price."

The dark man produces a long, ugly looking knife from under his coat and steps forward.

Chapter 8

▼

I sleep soundly and awake ready to tackle the puzzle of Kyle's mugging and Jimmy's death. The face of that bearded theater usher returns as I shower, and it makes me wonder why Kyle blurted out the word 'beard' at the hospital. That's still on my mind as I walk downstairs and take a seat in the dining room.

Mrs. Starkey greets me with a big smile and a steaming cup of coffee. She says, "Hope you slept well, Dave."

"Closed my eyes and the next thing I remember was sunlight streaming in the window."

She beams. "Juice?"

"Orange would be great," I answer, and she whisks away to the kitchen.

The lavish country breakfast Mrs. Starkey serves me is delicious. Can't resist overdoing to the point of stuffing myself. Must be somewhere I can stroll and work off the excess calories. I return to my room briefly then retrieve my coat and leave by the front door. Head down the long driveway to Main Street then turn right to walk westward.

Another of the four words Kyle uttered on my last visit also has me totally stumped. Have to walk and think about it. What could he have possibly meant when he said 'tank'? I hurry along in the crisp February morning thoroughly enjoying the feel of the invigorating air on my face and the clear winter blue sky. Rising on my left and right are the rounded peaks of the Blue Ridge that guard the valley on two sides. Mountain ridges that provide the water to replenish its many natural springs. As I walk down the hill I remember the fresh water pond that gave the town its name. Three blocks later I see it. The fountain at Lake Spring sends its spray in a halting stream this morning, no doubt the result of near freezing temperatures. A thin layer of ice has begun to form at the pond's edges. No one else is afoot near the spring. The townspeople are probably still huddled warmly in their homes. I feel strangely alone.

Then I notice a solitary old man sitting on a bench by the lake and approach him. He appears lost in thought. As I draw nearer he takes a long draw on an unfiltered cigarette and coughs, his chest noticeably rattling.

"Morning, sir. Bit nippy out, huh?"

His reaction is delayed so I assume he has a hearing problem. As he slowly turns toward me, I speak louder, "Real chilly day."

"Heard you first time, son." Again that wheezing cough. "Just thinkin' about when me and Molly used to sit here for hours on end and watch the younguns dip their lines in that lake. You know, they was plenty of fish in here back when the town stocked the pond."

"Yes, I remember. I've fished in that spring many times. Can't say it was productive, but I sure enjoyed it."

"Home boy, are you?"

"Born and raised right here in Springlake, sir. Been away awhile, but it's great to be back."

That seems to pique his interest. He looks me up and down, and his tone hardens with concern.

"Used to be a quiet town. Don't seem like the same place any more. Too many people movin' in and too much mischief goin' on. Folks devilin' each other, tryin' to steal 'em blind. Even had a killin' here last week."

"You mean Jimmy Moore?" I inquire.

"Yeah. Terrible thing. That and all the rest of the shenanigans nowadays." He shakes his head to show his disdain for the way things have changed in his hometown. Takes a last pull on his cigarette and grinds it out under his heel.

The cold wind is cutting. The old man must surely feel its effects as much as I do. He rubs his hands together and blows into them.

"Sure could use a hot cup of coffee," I say. "Want to walk over to the Burger Chef? My treat."

He nods and peels himself off the bench. Takes a wobbly first step then falls in line to cross the side street.

Over hot coffee we work off the chill. I'm curious about what he said and ask, "Not the peaceful place I remember, huh?"

He glares up at me. Moves his head slowly side to side.

"Nosiree. Seems we got a new scandal or somethin' every time I turn around. Folks used to leave one another alone and go about their own business. Now all they got to do is try and run everybody but their own selves."

"What did you hear about the Moore killing?"

"I understand somebody cut him up pretty good. Feller told me he heard from one of the deputies that he'd been mangled."

"Mangled? How?"

"Didn't say. Cop just told him it was so downright ugly it made him sick. Then he clammed up."

That makes me feel suddenly icy all over again. The sheriff slipped and said Moore was butchered. Now I find a deputy used the word mangled. Sounds like it must have been an ugly scene, indeed. Both of them had apparently blurted out without thinking. That bit of information, the fact Moore was butchered or mangled, could be the key to their whole investigation.

The town water plant across the street catches my attention. That moves the wheels in my slowly awakening brain, and I roll over the words then blurt out, "Tank...water tank...of course!"

My companion casts a puzzled look at me as I excuse myself and step out onto Main Street.

Crossing the street in mid-block against almost non-existent traffic, I look for what I remember as a gravel road around the corner. See an overgrown grassy path and the remnants of an old fence where the back road once wound to the leather tannery's back gate. Maybe Kyle has put me onto something. I can't wait to check it out. During my college days I spent every school break, the holidays, and all summer long working at the old tannery lab. The chemist who supervised all of the mixing of tanning solutions and testing of finished products took a liking to me. He mentored me and confided that I would make a great replacement for him when he retired soon. All I had to do was change my major to chemical engineering and continue to train under him until graduation. As tempting as the offer sounded, I found it difficult to put behind me the desire to ride the new technology wave in electronics.

My decision turned out to be another lucky stroke of good fortune. Within five years the tannery shut down as the demand for leather was replaced, in large measure, by synthetic materials for industrial uses and shoe soles. Now the old plant is gone, leaving hardly a trace in the overgrown fields behind a strip shopping mall. There is a low fence with a padlocked gate, which I easily scale. I stand where the old wash house had been. Think about the days when the hard-working men, their clothes covered with the stains from putting animal hides through the tanning process, trooped to the tin shack and washed away the day's grime.

Straight ahead had stood the tanning vats filled with their steaming, pungent tanning liquors into which the workmen dipped the hides and cooked the color into them. I picture myself hurrying between those vats and the laboratory carrying samples of the liquids to test their tannin content. For the first few days on the job, I had been nauseous every day from the overpowering odors of raw cattle hides being scalded to remove their hair and the sweet smell of the tanning vats. Then I think I my sense of smell finally gave in to the inevitable.

The bellies and backs were immersed into the deep vats with carefully mixed tanning liquors and the desired colors were cooked in for days. I had always marveled at how the end product, after drying and rolling to a lustrous finish, could become such beautiful and pleasant smelling pieces of finished leather.

But today there is no sign that any of that activity ever took place on these grounds. The vats have long since been filled in and weeds have taken over. I stoop and grasp a handful of tall reeds that grow up out of a marshy spot and look ahead for the one landmark I've come to see. The old water tank still stands, though it is battered and weathered. Twisted vines climb its rusted metal legs. The concrete base is cracked. Rusted bolts hold the feet in place. Curled, bleached out warning signs warn trespassers to stay away. I find myself wondering if the tank tower is a serious safety hazard. Probably too costly to tear down. It wouldn't have much salvage value.

I stand and stare up at the ancient tank, my eyes watering in the bright February morning glare. What connection could this crumbling old artifact have with Kyle's beating? Its significance totally escapes me as I recall the sheer fright in his mumbled words…'Beard…Mugger…Jimmy…Tank!'

I stand and ponder this question for several long minutes, then turn away. I hop over the low fence and start to retrace my steps back to the Barnwell House. Walk along carrying on a one-sided conversation.

"You've stumped me, brother. But it will come to me. Somehow, some way, I'll break this thing down, run it through my stubborn engineer's brain, and come up with the connection. I know you have the answers I need, but I've made a promise to Jenny. You don't need me pushing until you're ready and able to help me fit the puzzle together." I self-consciously look around in all directions, relieved that no one is in sight who could have watched me going on to myself.

I take a quick check on the time. Visiting hours at the hospital begin before long, and I want to stop by to pick up Jenny on the way. Maybe Kyle will be

more alert today so we can pursue whatever it is he seems so anxious to tell me—
on his schedule.

Chapter 9

Billy Logan gathers up the six-pack he's bought at the corner quick stop and strolls out into the evening chill.

He's absorbed in thought. *This layoff sure hit me right in the chops. Couldn't be a worse time to be out of work. If Doris didn't have a good job, we'd be in a world of hurts. The plant may never gear up to full tilt again, so I've gotta find something soon. 'Bout to go stir crazy sitting around the house.*

A brisk gust of cold air sweeps around the corner of the Ridge Mart and tugs at his cap. Billy grabs for the burgundy and gold Washington Redskins cap with one hand and clutches his package tightly with the other. He steps off into the darkness beyond the store front and hurries toward his pickup truck.

He hears a sound off to his left. Sounds like footsteps on the asphalt. There is a rush of air past him. He turns to face the noise. A blur of motion looms into view and crosses in front of him. Billy instinctively draws his head back and away. An indistinct object—an arm?—rises and then sweeps downward in a wide arc toward his face. Billy ducks to his right. He automatically mounts a defense, swings the beer carton as hard as he can. With a dull thud, his blunt bludgeon strikes something solid at the same instant a sharp stinging sensation punishes his left cheek. He hears a moan, and tries to make out what or who he's hit.

A dark figure slumps and goes down in front of him then rises again in a headlong charge. Billy drops his impromptu weapon as suds spew from a ruptured can. He whirls right and narrowly avoids a second blow from the attacker. Billy brings one of his big arms down hard across the attacker's black-clad, outstretched arm. This blow brings a whimper of pain from the assailant, and Billy hears an object clatter across the pavement.

Now Logan is enraged, a bull of a man bent on doing damage. He's determined to dismantle whoever has been foolish enough to set upon him. But by the time he prepares to put his weight behind the next punch, his adversary spins and sets off across the parking lot in full flight. Billy swipes at his burning cheek with the back of his hand, and the hand comes away bloody. His vision is dim, but he can make out the figure, a swath of deepest black, retreating down the hill toward an open field. Billy's always had a reputation for brute strength, but he's never been known for his speed. This would be a no-contest foot race, he decides. So he leans against a parked car and reaches for his handkerchief to stem the flow of blood from his lacerated cheek. Watches the dark man bound across the fence line and disappear into the murky night.

The counter man is at Billy's side, excitedly asking questions in rapid fire fragments. "What in the hell…who was…are you okay?"

"Yeah, just took a blow to the cheek. I'll be all right."

"Looks like he cut you with something sharp. Left a nasty gash that needs stitching up, mister. You need a doctor."

"It'll be okay. He just nicked me."

"Come inside and let me call the police," the clerk insists.

"What good's that gonna do. The son of a bitch is gone. I managed to whack him a good one, though. Should have a sizable lump somewhere on his sorry hide, but he got away."

"Still, the police need to know, and they'll bring an ambulance. Help you file a report. You need to sit down, anyway."

As an afterthought, Billy's eyes sweep the pavement all around him. He locates the object that fell and bounced several feet away. Walks over and stoops, a bit unsteady, to pick it up. It has a four-sided wooden handle and a nasty looking metal rod narrowing to its end. Billy runs his hand down the metal and notes that it's been sharpened to a fine point.

Oh God, Billy thinks, *it's an ice pick!* In a wink he is a boy of fourteen standing on a snow-covered hill as a bitter wind whips about him. The fear from that night sends a deep shiver through his body. The clerk looks at him with concern and says, "Come with me."

A long-suppressed memory has returned with sudden force. It is like a fist shoved hard into his gut. He tries to straighten up, doubles over and stumbles back two steps. The counterman reaches out to keep him from falling.

"Go inside with me and sit down, please."

Chapter 10

When Don answers the door, I shake his hand and give him a hug. He seems a little taken aback by my move now that he's so grown up. But he and his brother Tom will always be youngsters to me, very special youngsters.

"Almost had a flashback, Don. You look so much like your Dad at the same age."

"I saw him for awhile last night, Dave. I really feel for the twisted mind that did this to him."

"Rest assured, he'll get his," I answer. "I'm not as forgiving as you are."

"Mom and Tom have already left for the hospital, Dave. Tom wanted to see for himself how Dad is recovering. Said he couldn't keep his mind on schoolwork until he saw first hand how he looked. They left about thirty minutes ago."

"Then I'd better hurry and catch up to them. Keep good thoughts."

I hurry along to the hospital and wait in the room outside ICU until Tom and Jenny finish their visit. They both come out smiling.

I grab Tom's hand and pull the slender, blondish lad toward me. He's a strikingly handsome kid with long hair, big blue eyes, and a look of innocence that must drive the girls wild.

"Has to be good news the way you two are beaming."

"The doctor says Dad can go upstairs for a couple days and then come home," Tom tells me.

Relief is clear in his voice, and Jenny is positively radiant.

"They're going to move him to a private room," Jenny confirms. "Said he should be settled in enough for us to see him by noon."

"You look ninety-nine percent better today, Sis. Now maybe you should take a few hours off to get back into your routine. Why don't I come back here and spend some time with Kyle after he moves upstairs, and I'll give you and the guys a full report."

She thinks about that and finally answers, somewhat reluctantly, "Okay. Better get this guy to school for the rest of his classes. Call me, Dave." Jenny wheels to leave, her step definitely bouncier than before.

My questions for Kyle will have to wait a bit longer. My watch shows it's almost ten AM. Since I can't see Kyle until noon, there should be time to pay a visit to the one other person I always look forward to seeing on my infrequent trips to Springlake. I put the morning sun at my back and drive toward Aunt Ethel's house like a homing pigeon.

* * * *

For as long as I can remember, Kyle and I and all our cousins have congregated at our Aunt Ethel's place. We can look forward to hugs, food and a large helping of love in that house. My mother's older sister is a four-foot-ten reservoir of motherly affection. She's always had enough love to go around for every kid that crossed her threshold. And once you're one of her 'kids' she's forever your other mom.

She meets me at the door with her ever-present smile.

"Well, lookee who's here! Come in, Davey and give me a big hug. Now I know why I made that big old banana puddin' last night."

The tiny lady puts her arms around me and snuggles her head to my chest. Her words bring a rush of warm memories; mental pictures of hot biscuits and gravy, corn bread with home made preserves at her kitchen table; fascinating stories from the one remaining family member who can trace our ancestors back several generations.

We walk to her kitchen, and I sit at the table where I took so many meals as a child.

Cautiously I ask, "You know about Kyle, Aunt Ethel?"

"I heard. Durn ol' troublemakers got nothin' better to do than hurt one o' my boys. Like to get after 'em with a pitchfork."

"Kyle's doing much better. I'm going back to the hospital in a little while. Just couldn't wait to see you again."

She is already at the stove pouring coffee. No need for her to ask. I'm in her kitchen—that automatically means she has to feed me.

"What possesses people to do things like that, Davey? Why can't they just mind their own business?"

"Don't know, but I intend to find out. I'm here to stay until we get to the bottom of this. How have you been, Ethel?"

"Can't complain. Waste of time to complain, anyway. Got plenty to do, and my kids come by real often. How do you like the way I painted in here?"

I notice for the first time that the small kitchen has a sparkling new coat of paint. Imagine Ethel on her step stool, brush in hand, in her element. She and Uncle Thurlow bought this place fifty years ago when it was a couple rooms and a bath. Over the years they had added on, rearranged, and remodeled until they had three bedrooms, a covered back porch and a screened in porch for summer sitting.

Aunt Ethel had been right there every step with hammer and paint brush. Now that she was alone in the house, it just wasn't in her makeup to slow down. Had to have some project going all the time.

"Great job. Looks like your usual handiwork."

She beams and serves me my coffee and banana pudding.

"Took me awhile, but I whupped it." When she took a notion, this little bundle of energy could work circles around any man I ever met. She cut her teeth on walking behind a mule and plow when she was the oldest child on the family farm.

"You're amazing."

I think to myself, *Hope I have that much energy when I reach seventy-five.*

"How are your girls, Davey?" The question hits me suddenly. I pause before answering.

"Haven't seen them in a while. Talked to Helen briefly after I got here to let her know about Kyle."

"Just breaks my heart to see you two kids at odds. I love Helen, and that Melody is the most darling little girl."

"Not so little any more. She's going on fifteen. I really miss both of them."

Ethel pats my hand and says, "Don't quit trying, honey."

We move into the front room, and she goes to shelves filled with what she refers to as her 'what-nots'. Every one of those figurines, pitchers, mementos and photographs has an often told tale behind it. As many times as I've heard her stories, though, I never tire of her telling how she came by each item and how it reminds her of some significant time for her or a member of her family. On this particular day it's time for me to be refreshed on the family history. She retrieves a small faded photo of five bearded men in their Sunday finest sitting in front of an old wooden building I take to be a barn. I sit attentively as if I'm about to hear the story of the men in that portrait for the very first time.

"Did I ever tell you about my granddaddy and his brothers?"

I shake my head, all the time fully aware that I've seen that picture and heard her story of Granddaddy James Edward Palmer more times than I can count. One of the beauties of her family episodes, though, is that there is always something a little different each time, a new fact I never heard before. She never contradicts herself, just adds to the richness of the story.

"Which one is he, Aunt Ethel?"

She points to the man in the middle of the photo.

"He was the oldest of five brothers. Let's see, there was James Edward, Virgil Kent, Herbert Lyle, Raymond Kyle and Iry David. Your brother was given this one's middle name and you got Iry's middle name. Our family always took great stock in honoring our ancestors by reusing their names for our children."

With the size of families in those days to man the plows and hoe the rows, I wondered if it also had to do with simply running out of names for new offspring.

"You have an amazing memory, Ethel. You're a walking catalog of family facts. Wish you'd write them down for future generations. It's so easy to lose track of our heritage."

She smiles, but I know that will never happen.

"The youngest brother, Aunt Ethel. How was his first name spelled?"

"I-r-a. You know, Iry. Got *his* name from my great great granddaddy Iry who fought in the War Between the States."

I could stay all day and listen to her. But there is much to be done. After awhile I rise and say, "I'll be around for at least a week, Aunt Ethel."

"Then you come on back. And remember what I said about those sweet girls. Family is everything, Davey."

She is so right.

Chapter 11
▼

Kyle is sitting up in his hospital bed watching television.

"Looking better, Kyle. But no football, huh?"

My brother is a rabid NFL fan. I've known him to have four games going on separate sets in his basement on Sunday afternoon. One of his hobbies is TV repair and he always has multiple TV's sitting around.

"Goo seeya," he manages to get out through still swollen lips.

"Well, I understand you've really snapped back. Doc wants to let you out of here real soon."

There is so much I want to ask him, but I'll honor Jenny's wishes. Have to work up to my hard questions slowly.

"The boys seem to be doing well. Just keep growing. I swear Don looks more like you every time I see him. He's changed even in the time since I saw him last."

"Monfs."

"Yes, it has been months. I'm a little embarrassed over that. Got myself too tied up in my work, and the time slipped completely away from me."

"Slow dow." He struggles to speak.

"In my business, every time you slow down, somebody gets a step ahead of you. But this trip is an exception. Told my partner I'd be up here at least through mid-month. He can handle things, and I can get back into the down home mode for a change."

Finally he's able to organize a smile on his swollen face.

"This is my wakeup call to stop spinning so fast and grab some reality, Kyle. Helen and Melody are too important to me to let them drift away from me. I think you tried to tell me that a long time ago, but I was too pigheaded to listen."

Kyle opens his mouth to speak, but his throat refuses to respond. I raise a hand in caution.

"I have lots of questions, but let's get you healed first."

He shakes his head. Points toward the table where a pencil and pad lie.

"Okay. I ask and you write?"

Kyle nods. I hand him the note pad, and he works hard to hold the pencil. Finally manages to arrange his stiff fingers so the pencil stays put.

"First of all, why were you at Lakeside so late at night? I know it wasn't for a midnight slaw dog."

His hand moves haltingly across the pad. He writes *Can't sleep*.

"Jenny says something's been bothering you the past few days. Want to tell me about it?"

Kyle's expression changes, and his hand trembles so violently that he loses the grip on the pencil once again. Looks frustrated.

"I know this isn't easy, but I want to help. You have to trust me, Kyle."

He fumbles for the pencil, and slowly begins to write *Jimmy*. Now we're getting somewhere.

"You know something you're not telling about the way he died." I realize this is pushing him dangerously fast, but he has to get it out into the open. Some secret about Jimmy's death is eating at his insides.

His eyes water.

"I'm sorry. I have to know, and you need to get it off your chest."

He grips the writing instrument so hard his knuckles turn white. Bears down hard, and the letters on the pad are bold and dark. The lead breaks under the pressure. Kyle knocks the pad away with a backhand. I feel guilty that I'm putting him through this agony.

I retrieve the pad and read the words he's written. *BIT OFF HIS T O N.*

The scrawl at the end shows he has stopped short of finishing. For a long moment I rack my brain then a frigid cold fills my mouth.

"Ohmygod!" I say and touch the tip of my tongue with my forefinger.

He nods yes. The gurgle in his throat tells me the mere thought makes him gag. It also gives me the answer I really would have preferred not to confirm. Whoever killed Jimmy Moore mutilated him by removing his tongue!

But why would he say BIT? I point to my mouth and clank my teeth together. Then I stare at him in disbelief and mouth the words, "*Bit* it off?"

Again he nods agreement then he turns away to face the wall.

I start to speak again, but Kyle is through. He holds up his hand to stop me. I know he's given me all the information I'll get for now. The searing question of how he could possibly know about the butchery of Jimmy gnaws at me, but this is no time to press for an answer.

"Okay. Let's talk about things we can deal with. It always impresses me when I see your beautiful family and their obvious devotion to you. If only I..."

I stop abruptly, but his look tells me no more words are necessary. Kyle already knows the pain I'm feeling and how badly I want to reconcile with my own family. He knows, as Aunt Ethel put it, that 'family is everything.'

He waggles his fingers at me as if to say 'keep going'.

Why should I be surprised? Here he is lying in that bed beaten and bruised, only hours past hanging on for dear life, and he's urging me to unload to him. I could always expect a sympathetic, if at times critical, listener in my brother. For the next hour or more I bare my soul to him. Say things I have never entrusted to anyone before.

I tell Kyle of my neglect and inattention that progressed to an addiction to work; about my inability, in the face of certain estrangement from Helen, to set my priorities in order and work out our difficulties. He hears how my bitterness at the loss of intimacy with Helen drove me to seek solace in alcohol. Finally, I break down and share the one secret only my wife and one other person know—the single act of infidelity that brought our marriage crashing down into a bitter separation.

As he has always done, Kyle listens patiently and quietly. Then he reaches for my hand and smiles. He must know that I feel cleansed of the secrets that have tormented me. Closely-held secrets that caused me to turn inward when I needed encouragement most.

Our bond is as strong as ever. I'm happy to be home.

Chapter 12

▼

The dark man with the intense eyes walks from his rumpled bed to a tiny bathroom.

"Damn that Billy Logan! I caught him flatfooted. Had him off guard and on my terms. Another second or two and he would have been bleeding out of two sightless holes. Maybe I'd just finish him off right then and there. Put that ice pick through his heart to see how he bleeds; leave him in that parking lot to die alone."

He looks into the mirror to inspect his throbbing shoulder.

Don't know what he hit me with, but it hurt like blazes. That's a big, ugly bruise. Gives me another reason to settle a score with Mr. Logan. Every time I look at it, I'll think about driving that pick into his sockets and scooping out his eyeballs. Wonder how blue eyes taste?"

The figure hunches over in front of a bathroom mirror lit from above by a single bare bulb. His dark eyes pierce the glass with raw anger, his nostrils flare with the thought and the scent of revenge. He sets his jaw and resolves there will be no more failures, no frustrating near misses.

He makes a stabbing motion with a pair of scissors.

"Logan, you're gonna be sorry you didn't die in that parking lot. Now I have to make it especially painful for you. Should have accepted your fate like that little greaser at the Exxon. Gave him a lesson about getting in my way. Damn, it felt good watching him die."

He straightens up and runs his fingers through his coal black beard. Wonders if he should shave it off to change his looks, further frustrate anyone that comes looking for him.

"Hell," he mutters, "I doubt anybody even remembers me. After all, I was never noticed in this one-horse town. Not a soul wanted to give me the time of day or a cordial 'how do you do'. As far as they were concerned, I didn't exist. I was just an accessory, a piece of furniture."

No. He wouldn't get rid of the beard. Just give it a neat trim. After all, if either of those two piss ants caught sight of him before he did them in, his beard would help make sure they knew who was about to kill them. That was the most exciting thought of all, his being able to watch the fright in their eyes while he was exacting his long-awaited revenge.

"No looking back now. Nobody ever cared about me but my sweet Margaret. The rest of them can go to hell and see if I care!"

He steps away from the mirror, puts down his trimming scissors, and stares back at his stern image. Put his fingertips to one corner of his mouth and wipes away the spittle. He smiles, knowing now that nothing he has ever done could be as satisfying as stubbing out the threat those two pose. The idea of totally extinguishing the chances of their ruining things for him has become a tangible thing to be savored, to be chewed on and digested again and again, to be tasted until he salivates.

Chapter 13

▼

My visit to Kyle has lifted my spirits. There was a time when I wouldn't have hesitated to share my most private thoughts, my deepest secrets with my brother. He'd always been the one person who would listen to me without judging. But with everything else brought into question in my life lately, I'd even come to doubt that our strong brotherly bond had survived the years.

We hadn't talked, really talked, on a personal level for so long.

Now I have finally shared my darkest thoughts and misgivings with Kyle. It's cleansed me and uncluttered my confused mind, made me feel like a new man. I return to the Barnwell House and sit alone in the cozy parlor, my heart much lighter. The fireplace glows its warm greeting, bids me to drift away into its fluttering flames. Mrs. Starkey's gentle background music floats through the room and the relief courses through me.

I snuggle down in the big chair and let the soft music surround me and take me away. Time slows. The hurried pace of the past few days becomes a dim and fading memory. I recognize a composition that made a strong impression on me during my youth. Grapple with a memory that returns in fragments and try to bring it into focus. Close my eyes and drift.

I'm drifting back to when I was first aware of that music. Kyle and I are tucked into our bunk beds. He's dialed in the local classical radio station.

"Why do we have to listen to that long hair stuff, Kyle? Let's turn on some rock and roll." I must be all of eight or nine. Really don't know what people mean when they say long hair music—just know it isn't supposed to be cool like Elvis or The Fifth Dimension.

"You should learn to appreciate all kinds of music, Davey," he tells me. "Every song or melody tells a story. Listen and I'll tell you what's happening."

He turns the radio up slightly and says, almost in a whisper, "The White Knight is kneeling by the side of a babbling brook, resting from his ride in the noon heat. He dips his water skin into the creek. Fills it with pure, clean water. Then he raises the vessel to his mouth and drinks long and deep. It cools and soothes his dry throat."

The music does, in fact, describe to my young ears a fast flowing stream in a forest. How does Kyle know the music is telling this story? I can almost feel the cool water in my own mouth quenching my thirst. Then the pace quickens, the music rises and Kyle says softly, "Listen. The knight must hurry away. He is on a mission. He mounts his snowy white horse and rides off. Up over the hill he gallops and down from the crest into a green meadow. The evil Scarlet Knight sits astride his coal black mount in the middle of the roadway. The White Knight knows a battle is near at hand."

My pulse pounds in my ears. My mouth goes dry with anticipation and excitement.

"They draw their swords. Back and forth across the meadow the two knights battle. The Scarlet Knight is strong and he presses the fight. The White Knight is wounded; he stumbles and falls. Scarlet sends his blade in a sweeping thrust. White narrowly manages to escape the blow. White swings his sword as the evil Scarlet Knight hovers over him."

The music draws a picture of the battle. I'm captured by the scene.

"Finally, White strikes the decisive blow, and he watches his enemy fall. White knows the castle of his lady love is ahead of him, but he is wounded and bleeding. The White Knight manages to sit atop his horse and move forward. His heart is filled with love, but the pain is deep. Ignoring his pain, he spurs his horse and gallops ahead."

"I see it, Kyle! I see it. I'm there with them in that meadow. The visions are so clear. But who told you the story?"

"The music is whatever you want it to be, Davey. Just close your eyes and listen. It will tell you what to see. When everything is all a jumble around you, relax and let the music sweep you away and send you to a better place."

Years later I learned that the music I had grown to love was written by Franz Liszt. He had subtitled it "What May Be Heard on a Mountain." It had nothing at all to do with knights or battles. What a shame that my big brother had never pursued his love of great melodies by developing his musical talents, whatever they may be.

I later worked very hard for several years to play the piano, first taking lessons paid for by an aunt then spending the few dollars I earned at odd jobs to continue my weekly lessons. The innate talent was never there, but I never lost my love for all music. Those nights in our dark bedroom had instilled in me a new passion as Kyle entertained me with his stories.

* * * *

Slowly I become aware that someone is in the parlor with me. My eyes blink open and shut as Mrs. Starkey bends near to see if I am sleeping. I look up at her and smile.

"Sorry, Dave. I didn't mean to wake you. You looked so peaceful."

"Seeing you standing over me took me back, Mrs. S. We lived a few streets over when I was little. I can remember coming to your door on Halloween nights. You knew all of us kids. You used to say when you saw me, "There's my little tow-head all gusseyed up.""

"But you're grown up now, and I didn't even know you at first. Such a fine young man."

"In some ways I'm just beginning to grow up, Mrs. Starkey. Springlake has brought back some sobering thoughts."

She looks at me as if trying to read past my eyes to find the meaning of my statement. I sense that she already suspects in some unexplained way the heavy weight that threatens to crush me. Her soft smile and her reassuring hand on mine tell me everything will be all right. If only I could believe that.

"Well, what I really came to tell you is that dinner is ready any time you are. Some of the guests are already enjoying my country ham and apple pie."

"You don't have to invite me but once, Mrs. S. Remember I was there for that fabulous breakfast spread."

I stand up, and she instinctively takes my hand as if I were still that little tow-head. I ask, "How long has it been since you converted your home to this lovely bed and breakfast? I seem to remember you and Mr. Starkey starting the business. You've done a masterful job."

"We've been open to travelers for almost twenty years now. The mister learned he was in the early stages of a muscle disease that would force him to leave his job as head of the bank before long. The children were grown and out on their own. There is still so much of him in this old house. We bought it when Jack was picked to run the Farmers Bank."

She guides me toward the dark oak mantle. Proudly shows off framed pictures of her son and daughter and of four grandchildren.

"We decided to put the house to use to see others enjoy it," she tells me. "I enjoy my guests even more now that Mr. Starkey isn't here to keep me company. Looking for another helper, though, to clean rooms and help me in the kitchen."

"This old house must have quite a history behind it," I remark.

"That it does. Why, we even have our very own spirits that roam the halls. It's part of the charm of the Barnwell House that two ghosts turn up every now and again and appear to our guests. I've had people return and tell me they came back hoping this time they'd see our resident spirits."

"Tell me about them. Do you know who they are? Anything about their past lives?"

"One is, by all reports, a young lad with blonde hair. A Confederate soldier. I've only caught a fleeting glimpse of him a few times, but others claim to have seen him clearly when he wandered from room to room upstairs."

"Why do you think he's a Confederate soldier?"

"He appears to be wearing a cotton uniform of some sort. There's a small patch on his arm. Those who have seen him plainly agree the patch seems to be the Stars and Bars of the Confederacy. I'm told a lot of boys from around here volunteered for the army or the local guard, and they went off to battles up the Shenandoah Valley. They even fought in some skirmishes closer to home. In fact, there's a small cemetery up the hill in back that's been there since some time in the nineteenth century. Several Confederate soldiers were laid to rest among the graves of other town folk."

"You said there are *two* ghosts."

"Yes. The other vision is a young woman. She appears to be a teenager. She's from much more recent times by the look of her clothes. Wears a skirt and saddle shoes. Seems to be searching for somebody she thinks is here in the house."

"And the guests are okay with these specters roaming around?'

"Oh, they never bother anyone. Just drift about quietly. I've been told they've tried to speak to boarders on more than one occasion. But though their lips move, either the words don't form or at least none of the guests have ever heard what they're trying to say. Some of the boarders have seen the girl try to talk to the lad. He looks annoyed and turns away from her."

"That's fascinating, Mrs. Starkey."

"Now that you've had your local history lesson and ghost story, it's time for dinner." She smiles and leads me away toward the dining room.

* * * *

After dinner I steel myself for another try at engaging Helen in conversation. I want to update her on Kyle's condition and ask about coming to see her and Melody over the weekend. But most of all I want to open a dialogue about how much I need her back in my life for good. When she answers I savor the sound of her voice; want so desperately to be there with her.

"Kyle's much better, Helen. I was scared to death he wouldn't be the same, but I see the old spark. How are you and Melody?"

"We're fine, Dave. I'm happy Kyle is recovering." She falls silent. It's a nervous silence.

"It was touch and go for him for awhile, but he's slowly getting back to normal. I intend to stay here until I know he's fully recovered and see someone pay for hurting him. Jenny sends her love to both of you."

"We'll keep them in our thoughts. That's good news," she says.

Here goes, I tell myself. *Time to test the water.*

"Helen, I'd like to come down this weekend to see both of you."

I realize I'm actually holding my breath waiting for her reply.

"Your daughter would enjoy that. She hasn't seen you for nearly three months. You know you're always welcome to visit her."

I ignore her jab. This is no time to start an argument.

"So can I come down for a visit on Saturday and stay till Sunday morning?"

"We'll be here all weekend, Dave."

"Good. And that'll give us some time to…"

She cuts me short. "I'll have the guest room ready. We'll be home from Saturday noon on."

"And, Helen, can we talk about us?"

Her silence tears at me. I wonder if she's heard my question.

"Helen?"

"Let's just take one step at a time, Dave. I'm not sure I'm quite ready for anything more."

"I am, sweetheart."

"Just come for Melody and we'll see what develops."

"Helen, baby, I love you with all my heart. There's so much I have to say to you. Please don't shut me out now."

No reply—only dead air then the receiver falling. I feel heartsick. But maybe the door between us did open just a crack. I can't wait for the weekend.

The staircase seems longer tonight. My footsteps fall heavy but muffled on the carpeted treads as I climb to my room.

CHAPTER 14

▼

I awake from a great night's sleep in a comfortable bed. It's done wonders for me. Feel rested and ready to tackle the baffling puzzle of Kyle's beating. So much to dig out, so many bits of information that need to be collected and studied. Kyle is definitely holding back, though, numb with fear, and it's connected somehow to Jimmy's death. My guess is he has information so dangerous to Moore's killer or killers that they tried to do *him* in, too. Up to me to coax him to tell me what it is that has a strangle hold on him. Kyle has to open up and tell someone, or whatever it is will simply tear him up inside.

Have to move fast today. The weekend is coming, and my trip to Raleigh won't wait. Have to know first hand how I stand with Helen, and need to do all I can to draw her nearer to me. But I can't slight my obligation here in Springlake, either. Kyle could still be in mortal danger. Important questions need answers before he has to face another attempt to silence him.

Sit down to a hearty breakfast in the Barnwell dining room. Rub my hand against the cold window pane. The chill outside air and the warmth of the dining room have fogged over the windows. I clear a circle and peer out into the frosty morning. Winter has taken a firm hold on the valley. Yesterday's glaring early winter sunlight has yielded to a gloom that hangs low and shrouds the entire landscape. I've soon seen all I want of that dreary scene, so I return my attention to my last bit of coffee. Mrs. Starkey is standing by my table ready to refill my cup.

"Hope you had enough to eat, Dave. If you're thinking about going out soon, I should tell you the temperature is down near freezing. It's overcast and foggy, a real nasty day."

"So I see. But I have no choice. Places to go and people to see, Mrs. S." She smiles. I take that as approval of my new nickname for her.

"Well, watch your step in case there's ice." She pours my coffee and turns to leave.

"Wait, please. You mentioned a cemetery nearby that has some Confederate graves. Where is it from the house?"

"If you go down the hall past the kitchen and out the back door, it's only a short walk. Bear off to your left and you'll see it. There's a low iron fence, and you can see the headstones."

"Thanks. I need a walk. The cold air may help me think through some things this morning."

I retrieve my coat and galoshes from the room and strike out, crossing the back porch, walking across the driveway toward the hill and the trees beyond. A heavy fog hugs the ground and blocks the morning sun from view. I pull my head down into my heavy coat. Feel my leg muscles flex as I begin the climb.

Straining to penetrate the fog and crunching along over the hard ground, I am struck by the sameness of the whole landscape; the ash gray pall that dominates and conceals its features. I look to my left and realize I've almost passed by the cemetery plot. No more than twenty feet away I see the low black iron fence protecting what appears to be the burial area. An engraved metal marker, obviously added many years after the ancient resting place was created, reads West Ridge Cemetery. I find myself approaching this somber spot with an odd feeling of reverence. Somehow I know this is a special place.

The area inside the fence is surprisingly well kept. In all my time growing up in Springlake I never knew the cemetery was here. Someone has kept it carefully maintained. If Mrs. Starkey's information is correct, West Ridge has held the remains of some of the town's citizens for well over a hundred years.

I walk around the inside perimeter to read the markers and headstones. Some are almost lost in time, letters worn by the seasons. I count thirty two grave sites in that place of repose. Carefully stepping between the rows, I take a closer look. Determine that eight of the graves are those of men who served the Confederate Army during the War Between the States. Their brass markers have clearly been set as replacements for the original headstones. Each one is etched with bold letters and a small Confederate flag. I imagine a dedication ceremony honoring the town's heroes on some glorious spring day in the distant past, the speeches and placement of the shiny new plates.

Just as I turn to go, something registers. I work my way through the soldiers' markers once again. There it is! The inscription reads "John Palmer, Private,

CSA. July, 1847-May, 1864. Died at Battle of Cloyd's Mountain." Palmer is my mother's maiden name. Aunt Ethel had mentioned no John Palmer, only that her great great grandfather Iry, as she calls him, had been in the war.

I have an eerie feeling about this grave. The other soldiers' resting places are sunken and sparsely covered with grass. But this one grave seems as level and fully covered as the others that bear dates from more recent years. Why would that be?

A tingling sensation works its way along my spine. I am sure it's more than the cold morning fog. This calls for a return visit to Aunt Ethel. If anyone knows of a connection between John Palmer and our family, it will be her.

Chapter 15

▼

Kyle is sleeping comfortably when I go to his hospital room. Can't bear to disturb him. But he's due to be released by the time I return from Raleigh, and I need to talk to him today. I glance at my watch and quietly leave his room. Go to the hospital cafeteria to have coffee and wait for him to wake up.

The coffee is fresh and strong. I might even call it good. One thing about these dedicated people who rush about the hospital at all hours of the day and night—too often they're running on caffeine and will power after too many hours on duty. Poor coffee in the cafeteria would surely be sufficient grounds for a full riot by these caffeine zombies.

An attractive young blonde approaches my table. I look at her closely cropped golden hair and bright eyes with long lashes. She registers as familiar. Then I realize why. I had caught a quick glimpse of her somewhere up on Kyle's floor only a few minutes ago. She flashes a radiant smile and speaks to me.

"Pretty crowded in here. Mind if I join you?" A quick scan around the room confirms that there are no empty tables, but there are certainly other places for her to sit. Maybe she wants company as well.

"Please," I answer. Take a longer look and note that she's wearing a sweater that does little to conceal the fact she's generously endowed. Pretty face and a disarmingly pleasant smile. My hasty estimate is that she is probably several years younger than I am, maybe in her early thirties.

"Visiting or do you work here?" I ask.

She sets down her tray, takes a seat and begins to slowly peel the wrapper from around a muffin. When she looks up at me, it seems her beautiful eyes are peeling my exterior right down to my soul and peering into me. It's a strange sensation to have someone I never saw before affect me this way almost immediately. But it's a warm feeling.

"Actually, I'm interviewing for a hospital position," she answers. "Work is scarce right now. I really need a job."

"Oh, I thought maybe you came to see somebody. Saw you up on the third floor earlier."

She fidgets with the muffin, pulling away bits to munch on. "Did go up there to check on a friend since I was already here. But I really need employment."

Why does her answer seem made up on the spur of the moment? Guess I'm beginning to cast a suspicious eye on everyone these days.

"So what do you do?" I ask her.

"Just want cleaning work or whatever I can get. I have a son to look after. I'm a good cook, but they tell me they don't need that kind of help at this time."

I take a long look at her. She's a genuinely attractive woman. Slender and pretty with golden hair and deep, liquid brown eyes—an unusual combination. Seems personable and alert. It's a shame someone who wants honest work can't find it. These days there are so many lazy people out there who sit back and expect a handout.

"I'm Dave Owens. Visiting from out of town. You a Springlaker?"

"Name's Meg Kane. Yes, I've spent most of my life right here. Do you have friends here, Dave?"

"Grew up in Springlake, I have a soft spot for the valley. Been away out in the big, cold world for a long time, though."

"You make it sound like you've escaped back to Springlake. Surely it can't be that bad wherever you come from."

"Oh, no, it's been good to me. Just realized how great it is to see all the old familiar places. Came home this time to see my brother. He's upstairs."

Something, surprise, a spark of indecision, registers in those liquid brown eyes. She hesitates then asks, "Owens? He the one that was beaten up the other night?"

"Where did you hear about that, Meg?"

"You of all people should know this is a small town. Everything is news around here. Just remembered the name Owens and wondered."

"Kyle had a bad time of it, but he's coming through it now."

"I'm glad." She's looking down at my ring finger. Self-consciously I twist the ring around and explain.

"Kind of unattached right now. Came home alone."

Find myself wondering why I would feel a need to volunteer that bit of information.

"Will you be here long, Dave? It's not very lively this time of year. And the night life is almost zero." She gestures with a downward thumb.

"Oh, I remember Springlake as a tame place most of the year—every year. But someone like you shouldn't have any trouble finding interesting pastimes."

"What does that mean?" she asks, more playful than defensive.

"Just meant you have everything going for you: looks, grace and the gift of gab. There should be lots of guys around here smart enough to look you up."

She laughs, her tone light and lyrical, and I find myself liking her more than I should. We seem to be quite comfortable talking to each other, not like we just met. And she isn't wearing a ring, so she must also be 'unattached'.

"Don't mean to put it down, Meg—after all, it is my old hometown. But watching the planes land out at Woodford Field with a six-pack in hand is about as exciting as dating used to get around Springlake."

Again that lilting laugh of hers. She tosses her head and places both palms on the table, leaning in toward me. "Or counting the ducks at the spring lake and feeding them greasy french fries. Doesn't get much better than that, does it?"

"Must be more to do than when I lived here, though, Meg. Maybe even somewhere I can find a meal a cut above average. Any suggestions?"

"Well, there is a new night club over off Grandview Road. I understand it's classy—but pricey. Their food is supposed to be outstanding. French name. Auberge."

"Sounds like my kind of place. Thanks." We fall silent, and I search for a way to prolong my visit with this delightful person. I offer to fetch a coffee refill for her. She nods so I set out for the coffee urn with an idea forming. When I return to the table, she speaks up and rescues me from the awkward pause.

"So what do you do for a living, Dave?" She places one hand under her chin and leans forward to hear my answer. I get lost in those eyes.

"Engineer. Developed some software that's enjoyed a bit of success," I reply. "Have a small company down in Atlanta."

"And that's the big, cold world, huh? Sounds like you did all right for yourself. I'll bet there's a lot more to know about you." When she flutters her lashes I feel myself melting.

I try to dodge her implied question. Didn't set out to talk about *me*. It's Meg I want to know more about.

"Your family here, Meg?"

"Just the most beautiful little boy you ever saw. That's why it's so important that I get this job. I'm all he has, and right now I'm out of work."

"Don't know how they could possibly let you get away, Meg. Landing a job here should be a snap for you." She beams.

We talk on and I learn that she's a single parent with a five-year-old. She likes music and dancing, although looking after her son leaves little time to dance. Reads everything in sight, and she has a sweet tooth for ice cream and chocolates. Neither of those treats has hurt her figure. We have fun comparing notes on the differences between Springlake and big cities like Atlanta. Meg Kane is beginning to get inside my head, and I like what I'm feeling. She stops now and then to look at her watch.

"My interview is a few minutes from now. Wish we had more time to talk. This has been a bright spot in my day, Dave Owens."

She pronounces my name slowly as if she's savoring how it feels. Closes those big brown eyes to accentuate the feeling, and I squirm in my seat. Suddenly the cafeteria has grown much warmer and my vision has narrowed. All I can see at the moment is this lovely creature who has presented me with a very large opening to pursue. I've come to a decision, and it's time to float my question. Our conversation has made me wonder if Meg might not be a pleasant diversion from the meat grinder I've been going through. I know I'm not behaving rationally with all my other problems, particularly my need to get things straightened out with Helen. But this woman has my attention and I can't seem to set myself right.

"Glad I stopped off down here, Meg. Talking with you has been a real lift. Our visit has been entirely too brief."

"Well, I certainly feel better, Dave. Came in here awfully nervous about the interview and a little down. Searching for work is downright frustrating. Thanks for the company." She starts to rise from her seat. Time to make a decision, even id it may be the wrong one.

"Wait. Understand I wouldn't normally ask this of someone I just met, but we probably won't see each other again unless I ask you now. And we seem so natural together it would be a shame to just say so long. How would you like to join me for dinner? We can see if that restaurant lives up to its billing."

She lowers her head slightly and looks up at me through her long lashes. "And I wouldn't consider an offer from a virtual stranger under most circumstances. But I like you, Dave. You seem like a very nice person. I'd say we have a date."

"Wow, this is starting out as a great day," I tell her and lift my paper cup in a toast of sorts.

"By the way, it's coat and tie, and I hear they insist on reservations," Meg says.

"Not to worry. I'll give them a call. The Auberge, huh? Can I get your phone number and address?"

I produce a slip of paper and a ballpoint. She writes down the information and hands it to me.

"One seventy two Juniper Street," I read. "Let's see, that's out near the lake spring, isn't it?

"See, you're more of a home boy than you thought. Now I have to run to my interview."

"Pick you up at, what, seven o'clock?" She nods and hurries away.

I take a last gulp of my coffee and toss our cups away. Kyle should be awake by now. I certainly am, awake and looking forward to this evening. The elevator takes me to the third floor.

*   *   *   *

On my way from the elevator to Kyle's room I run into Billy Logan. He's looking for the elevator. We stop in the hall to chat. He's sporting a large bandage on his bruised and bulging left cheek.

"What happened, Billy?" I ask.

He pulls me aside. Speaks very softly. "Had a scary experience night before last. Some dirtbag tried to waylay me, and he damn near succeeded."

"Oh, no." I'm already racing ahead of him. *Jimmy, Kyle, the station attendant, now Billy. Who has it in for Kyle and his circle of friends? Feel as if I've stepped off into some kind of weird shadow world, and it's closing in on me.*

"Scum snuck up on me in the dark and swung an ice pick at me. Ducked just in time, but I took a deep cut on my cheek. Got several stitches for a souvenir."

"Did you catch sight of your attacker?"

"Dark figure, black as coal tar."

"A black man?" I feel great relief that Kyle and Billy's attackers may be different people.

"No, Far as I could tell, he was a white guy. But he was wearing dark clothes and probably had a black beard. I wasn't seeing too well after he cut me and my eyes teared up on me."

The twinge of relief turns to a cold lump of fright in my throat.

"Do the police have him?"

"You kiddin'? I knocked the ice pick out of his hand and was ready to level his butt when he turned tail and ran like a rabbit. Cleared a rail fence in one jump and was gone."

"Is there something I'm missing here, Billy? Beginning to believe these aren't just random attacks. What do you think?"

He hesitates, almost continues. Then he stops and says, "Not my place to tell you. Ask Kyle. This goes back a long way. Has to do with him, me and Jimmy. I tried to talk to him about it just now, but he shut down on me. Maybe you can get something out of him."

I tell Billy I'll try and will call him later. Then I walk to Kyle's room.

* * * *

Kyle is sitting up. He appears more alert today.

"Morning, sport. You're looking better every day. When do they spring you?"

Kyle beams at that prospect. "If everything checks out, I'll be out of here by early tomorrow morning. Won't be ready to whip any wildcats, but I will be back home."

"Sounds like progress to me. Just do what Jenny tells you."

"Haven't I always?"

"Yeah. Guess that's why you've aged so gracefully." I hesitate and consider my next question deliberately. "Are you ready to talk about Jimmy Moore?"

"Won't give up, will you?" He momentarily averts his eyes then looks at me like he's trying to beg off continuing this line of conversation.

"Kyle, I know this isn't easy for you. But I have to know what's going on in your head. Talked to Billy just now. I want to know what's happening here. I did a total dump on you. You know things about my past I wouldn't dare tell anyone else. Now it's time for you to open up. Whatever is deviling you, I want to help."

"Dave, don't ask me to deal with this yet. Let me get home and think it through first. I want to tell you everything, but you can't imagine how..."

He stops short and waves one hand in front of him. Clearly I am not going to have any success this day. Maybe he does deserve a reprieve over the weekend while I work on patching up things in Raleigh. Then we can both turn our full attention to untying the knots in this mystery about why he's terrified. Maybe then I'll learn what, if anything, it has to do with his having been so badly beaten.

All right, I think, *you win for now, big brother.*

With Kyle on the mend but unwilling to let me share his heavy load, I'll have to play a waiting game. The next step on that subject is his call. We'll just try some light banter today, see how he really feels. But before I can begin, I hear Jenny.

"What a pair! The Owens brothers in person. And look who I brought. My own Owens boys."

Jenny comes in with Don and Tom trailing behind. She's noticeably rejuvenated. Her man is on the mend, and she's all smiles.

When the three of them have hugged Kyle, she turns to me and says, "What's on your agenda today? Going to come by the house to see us?"

"Sorry, Jen. I have a visit and an appointment. And tomorrow morning I'm driving down to Raleigh to see Helen and Melody. I'll be back Sunday evening."

Thankfully she doesn't ask me to elaborate on my 'appointment', so I don't have to make up some off the ceiling story. Feel kind of dumb about the way I talked myself into the date with Meg Kane. Not my coolest move.

Jenny's reaction to my mention of the girls is spontaneous, pure joy.

"Oh, I'm so glad, Dave. Give them my love, and tell them we look forward to seeing them soon." She puts her arms around me.

"Just a visit, Jenny. I'll hope for more, but…"

"I understand. Come by for supper when you get back Sunday."

"Have some things to do now, so the four of you have a grand visit," I answer.

"Don't forget, Dave," she tells me, "Sunday night at our place. I'll have Kyle eating normal food by then. Please be there."

"I will, Sis. Take care of everybody. I'll see all of you on Sunday."

Kyle stares intently at me. I wonder what's going through his mind. Will he really open up to me once he's home, or is this just a delaying tactic. How do I convince him that telling me what's going on will be for his own good? Sunday night has to be the showdown on that matter.

Chapter 16

I spend the afternoon driving around town, reorienting myself and seeing some of the prominent landmarks. No particular reason except maybe recapturing the feel of being home again. Then I steer my car toward an old familiar place and home in on that warm hearth.

"Hi, Aunt Ethel. It's me again. Hope you're not too busy to sit and talk."

"You know I'm never too busy for one of my boys. Get on in here, Davey." Her face lights up in that way that only she has of hinting there's some delicious little secret she wants to tell you in her own good time.

"Well, I never know when I'll show up and you'll be doing some little job like moving walls or pounding new shingles on the roof."

"You give my old bones more credit than they deserve." She laughs. "Today I just want to sit and enjoy. Doesn't feel like a working day."

"Good, 'cause that way you won't be looking for me to do hard labor. You'd probably put me to shame, anyway." She gets a chuckle out of that. Then a look of concern crosses her face.

"What's troubling you, son?"

"Can't fool you, can I? All you Palmer women are alike. You and Mom could always read me like a bold print newspaper."

"Something's got you worried, Dave. It doesn't take a wizard to see that."

"First I need to ask you about family history, Ethel. What do you know about a John Palmer from back in the eighteen sixties?"

"Been to the old cemetery, haven't you?" Her answer catches me totally off guard.

"Uh-uh, yes. Mrs. Starkey told me about the place on the hill behind the Barnwell House. I found a Confederate grave marked Private John Palmer. Is he a distant ancestor?"

"Matter of fact, he was the youngest brother of my great great granddaddy, Ira." Her mouth turns up in a smiled gotcha when she pronounces his name the way it's spelled. "John went off to join the home guard and be with his brother. Took his horse along and served as a messenger. He was still short of his seventeenth birthday when he was shot and killed in a battle up near Dublin."

"Dublin? Never knew there was a battle there."

"Seems like my granddaddy called the place by some name of a mountain when he told us about poor John. Lot of boys lost their lives in that battle. John was just a boy when he was taken away. Ira was heart broken over the loss. According to my granddaddy, John had nearly been snatched away when he was just a little tyke—seven or eight. Horse threw him and stepped on him. Left a nasty hoof print on John's cheek that he carried the rest of his days. Ira calmed the horse down before he could do more damage and took John to the house for his ma to attend to him."

"The marker on his grave said John died at Cloyd's Mountain in 1864."

"That's it. Cloyd's Mountain. Not far from Dublin. Mostly in those days the dead were buried near where they fell. But Ira put his brother across his horse and rode back here to bury him so the family could grieve proper like."

"Brought him back to West Ridge Cemetery?"

"Yes. They put him in the ground in that little burying place up on Tank Hill."

A light goes on. "Say that again, Aunt Ethel."

"You mean about the cemetery on Tank Hill?"

"That's it! Why didn't I think of it sooner? When Kyle blurted out 'tank' he meant the old *town* water tank. Had me totally stumped."

"Whatever are you talking about?" she asks.

I lean over and kiss her cheek. "I love you, Aunt Ethel! You just opened my eyes about something that had me buffaloed."

"If you say so. Now, how's your brother."

"He's going home tomorrow and everything's going to be all right. I'm heading down to Raleigh in the morning to see Helen and Melody. Be back here Sunday evening."

"*Now* I know what's bothering you. You're worried about how Helen will act when you see her. Just be yourself, Dave. Show her you love her as I know you do. It'll be okay."

"I hope so. I want them home with me. I'll go wherever she wants if she'll just say we can get back together."

Aunt Ethel talks on and gives me the benefit of her years of wisdom. I begin to feel encouraged, can hardly wait to be on the road to Raleigh. She cautions that I must, however, take it at Helen's pace and let her call the shots. Even though I've never told her what actually caused our breakup, somehow my aunt has figured out that it was mostly my fault we split. I take her words to heart. Promise myself that I won't hurry Helen.

She sees me to the door. I leave feeling much better than when I arrived.

* * * *

Don't know why I'm keeping this date with Meg. It certainly can't lead to anything. I'm committed to patching things up with Helen, and I don't need any complications. Oh, what the hell. It's just an innocent dinner with a delightful young woman I'll never see again. Go and enjoy the moment. Besides, my hormones have been raging for too long. Something keeps telling me it couldn't hurt if I should get lucky with this dynamite woman. Keep telling myself I deserve a break. It's been too long since I felt the softness of a woman next to me. I'll deal with the guilt later.

When Meg Kane gave me her address, she told me it was only a couple blocks west of the lake spring on West Main Street. That wasn't necessary. I already know exactly where Juniper Street is. In fact, it is within easy walking distance of the Barnwell House. That strengthens an idea that occurred to me after my conversation with Meg, one I want to explore further if this evening goes well.

Shortly after sunset I drive the short distance to her small house in the modest neighborhood and go to the door.

She answers my knock, appearing in a stunning midnight blue dress, her hair combed back and glistening like spun gold. She smiles and invites me in.

"I have to tell you I'm impressed, Meg. You're beautiful tonight. I feel almost informal in this blazer with you looking so classy."

"You look fine, Dave. Handsome and fine." Her eyes sparkle.

She offers me her coat to put around her shoulders, and picks up a small purse from a table by the door.

"Seriously, I feel like I should be showing up in a coach. You are dazzling."

We walk to my car, and she beams her approval of my compliments.

"So. This restaurant is on Grandview Road? I forgot to ask for directions when I made our reservation. You know the way, I hope."

"Can't go wrong if you follow my lead. I'll steer you right."

She looks at me with a twinkle in her eyes. I totally lose her words. She stifles a tiny giggle and points at the road. "Just drive."

The Auberge turns out to be all that she advertised. It's at least three stars above anything I remember in the valley. But then most of my time around here in my youth was spent at burger and barbeque joints or wrestling dates around the Coffee Pot Café's dance floor. The maitre d', true to his word, has found us a quiet corner in the back overlooking the lights of the city. I acknowledge his attentiveness with a generous token of my appreciation.

"Lovely place, don't you think, Meg?"

She's so busy taking in the elegant surroundings that her answer is slow in coming.

"Do you like it?" I ask.

"It's like nothing I've ever seen before, Dave. Almost feel like I'm in another country—and in over my head."

"Oh, no. You're the most beautiful woman in the room. Relax and enjoy it. All the other women are chartreuse with envy."

Meg settles in and her nervousness subsides. She seems to be more at ease now.

"What would you like to drink?"

"Surprise me." She produces a smoke. I motion for her lighter. Touch the flame to her cigarette. She draws deeply then stares at me across the dimly lit table.

The waiter appears. "Two very dry martinis, Absolut with an olive."

We linger over our drinks and a second round before ordering dinner. Meg is slightly flushed by now, so I surmise she isn't accustomed to drinking like this. Better get some food in her empty stomach or I'll be carrying her out.

As we dine she begins to probe for information.

"I'm fully aware, of course, that you're wearing a wedding band," she says. "You said you came to Springlake alone on this trip. Made a reference to being unattached."

"That's a long story. For now, let's just say I'm on my own. I'm here alone to see my brother.

We're enjoying dinner together. What else matters?"

Once again I silently sound a note of caution. I'm not acting normally. Right now I'm more like a giddy kid on the make than a man trying to set a marriage straight. But I push that thought back and go with the moment.

"Just curious, Dave." She seems taken aback by my rather curt reply.

"How about you, Meg? Told me you have a son, but I see no ring. Divorced?"

"Something like that. For now I'm out with a charming man for an elegant meal and sharing delightful company. As you say, what else matters?"

"Your son. What's his name? How old is he?"

"His name is Trevor. He's the joy of my life. Turns six in a few weeks. Do you have any children, Dave?"

"One. Melody. She's fourteen. My little darling."

"And her mother? You're not together?"

It suddenly occurs to me that I've prolonged a line of conversation I'd rather not pursue. Pangs of guilt are stealing back in, threatening to spoil the evening. She's found a way to pump me for more information than I want to give her.

"We don't live together right now. I'd rather talk about something else."

"You brought up the subject." She flashes a coy little smile and sips at her martini.

We fall silent. It's an uneasy silence. Some mental pictures flash through my head that are better left alone for the moment, visions of the two of us in a much more intimate setting. She opens the top two buttons at her neckline and dabs at the hollow of her throat with a lace handkerchief. Then she uses the hanky as a fan and I note that her cheeks are more than a bit rosy. The room isn't overly warm, so I conclude it's not the temperature. Must be either the alcohol or our nearness that's affecting both of us. Something magic could be working here, and I find myself no longer harboring guilt. I just want to feel her close to me. Want to enjoy the female essence that has been absent from my life for months.

Our waiter comes by and breaks my too-real daydream. Finally I venture, "How was your interview at the hospital this morning?"

"Not so good. They don't have an opening right now—or so the lady said. I need a paying job as quick as I can find one."

"I have an idea, Meg. Do you know the Barnwell House on Main Street?"

"Sure. It's not far from where I live."

"I'm staying there. Mrs. Starkey told me she needs someone to help with the cleaning and cooking. Do you think you'd be interested?"

"Of course. When can I see her?"

"Why don't you come by mid-morning before I leave for…a short trip I'm taking. I'll introduce you."

With the serious matter behind us, and her disposition much brightened, we move into an easy banter about all manner of things. I find, much to my amazement, that we share a love of classical music. She also loves to dance. Before our meal arrives, she proceeds to show me her skill on the Auberge's dance floor. As we whirl around the floor, I can see the ladies' eyes on her, at once admiring and despising her youthful grace and poise, her confidence. She feels oh, so firm and warm in my arms.

We have an elegant meal with a bottle of good champagne. I'm completely into what's going on right here; all my problems are pushed into the background, not forgotten, just put on hold. I watch Meg's movements, her natural grace, and marvel at how she's captured my attention so quickly. She catches me staring and asks, "What?"

"Just reflecting on my good fortune, Meg. A chance encounter that turned into a lovely evening."

"And I can't remember when I've enjoyed myself more, Dave. But the drinks and the champagne were a little too much for me. I feel a bit woozy. Need some fresh air."

"Shall we go then?"

"I think so."

* * * *

I drive her home with her window rolled halfway down and the cold night air pouring in.

"How are you feeling now?" I ask.

"Much better. Not used to martinis and wine at the same meal. Set my head spinning. Of course, you had already turned my head long before that." A mischievous little grin turns up the corners of her mouth.

I let that go without comment. We've had a great evening, but I don't expect the interlude to last beyond this evening. I still can't let go of the notion of one night of forbidden pleasure with the beautiful Meg, but then I'll have to find some way to bring it to an end. It's no time to get involved with Meg or anybody else other than my own wife. Still…it's so tempting.

When I reach her house she takes my hand and urges me out her side of the car toward the front door. I rationalize that I can at least see her to the door like any gentleman would do. Then, despite my indecision about my next step, perhaps we should say our thank yous and goodbyes. That is, unless she has other ideas. *Sure. Blame it on the lady, Dave.*

But she soon makes it clear this night won't end at the front stoop. She turns the key and draws me inside with her. The room is dark except for the dull glow of a night light somewhere. Scarcely giving me time to react, she closes the door behind us and turns to press against me. Takes my mouth with hers.

I've been kissed many times but never like this. Without warning, the demure little beauty has turned into an inferno that threatens to engulf me. I put my arms around her, and she moves so close to me that I feel like I'm wearing her. She takes my hand and places it on the soft skin at her open neckline. I feel her heart beating fast.

The hall light comes on. "Mommy, is that you?"

A child is standing in the living room rubbing the sleep from his eyes. He's a handsome little lad with his mother's eyes but raven black hair.

Meg releases me and goes to the boy. "What are you doing up? Where's Marcy?"

He points, and for the first time I see a figure huddled up under an afghan on the sofa. The teenage girl stirs and manages to sit upright.

"Sorry, Meg. I didn't feel so good after dinner so I brought Trevor back home. Figured if I had to call you, at least he would already be here in his own bed."

"Thank you, Marcy. That was very thoughtful. And how are you now?"

"Some better, and relieved now that you're home."

"Dave, this is my cousin, Marcy." The girl stands and tests her legs, then bends down to kiss Trevor good night. Meg sees her to the door.

The boy looks up at me. I step forward carefully to make friends with him, crouch to his level and extend my open hand.

"Hi, Trevor. I'm Dave. I hear you're the man of the house." When he smiles it seems to light up the room. He's a beautiful child.

He lowers his head and offers his tiny hand. I give him a hearty handshake and say, very formally, "Happy to meet you, Mr. Trevor Kane."

When Meg returns to his side, he flashes those coal black eyes and long lashes at her and tells her, "I met Mister Dave." Then he crooks a finger for her to lean closer. Cupping one hand over his mouth he speaks. His child's whisper is loud enough to reach my ears. "I like him," he says.

Meg pats his head then looks up and casts a disappointed look at me. "So much for the rest of our evening. I'm sorry, Dave."

"I enjoyed it. Even got to meet a special young man. Best we call it a night now. Trevor needs your attention."

I'm still excited, and my state has to be obvious to her, but this is no time to press.

I make a show of repeating the boy's gesture, placing my open palm beside my mouth and telling her so he can hear, "He's quite a guy." He smiles and clings to her leg.

"I guess I'll see you in the morning at the Barnwell House," she says as we walk toward the front door with the boy in tow. "I'll keep my fingers crossed that Mrs. Starkey needs my help."

After that one moment of passion she's back to normal. But just before I leave, a flash of heat returns. She grasps the edge of the open door and leans closer to me, her dark eyes flashing hidden signals.

"You and I have unfinished business, Dave Owens. Another time…soon."

I look down at the tyke beside her and back to the now slightly disheveled but intriguing young woman. All I can manage in response is, "Great evening, Meg. See you tomorrow."

My light kiss on her moist lips is definitely anticlimactic after the way she explored my mouth only minutes ago. I return to my car and sit for awhile as I try to unravel just how I feel about our date tonight. All the while, alarms are going off telling me to drop this as a pleasant but fleeting experience. But something inside me can't let go of the most tantalizing woman I've met in a long while. Against all logic I want to know more about her. I have to admit I have a strong physical attraction to her. What I want to know about her certainly isn't all on the intellectual level. That brief encounter in her entryway holds promise of who knows what to follow.

Keep it together, Davey boy. Don't stoke up the coals any higher. You already have enough irons glowing on the hearth. Just think about the trip to Raleigh tomorrow and the important task facing you with Helen. Cool down and keep your focus.

Chapter 17

▼

At breakfast on Saturday morning I manage to corral Mrs. Starkey long enough to ask for a few moments of her time. Once the busy work of serving the meal is past, she comes from the kitchen in a bright yellow apron, drying her hands on a kitchen towel. She sits downs at my table with a long sigh.

"You wanted to talk, Dave. Think I have everyone taken care of now. What's on your mind?"

"From what I saw in here this morning with you on a dead run, I think my first question may already be answered. You said you're looking for someone to help with cleaning rooms and cooking."

"Lord knows I could use an extra pair of hands today. Felt like I was swatting flies trying to keep up this morning. Why do you ask?"

"I may have the right person for the job. She's a delightful young lady, very personable, mother of a small son, and she lives nearby."

"Is she available now?"

"Wants a steady job in the worst way. I could have her come by and talk to you."

"Ask her to stop in today if she can. The sooner the better. I'm tired and the day just began. Guess there really is such a thing as business being too good."

"Can you see her before noon, Mrs. S? I'd like to introduce you two, and I want to leave for Raleigh by mid day."

"That's fine. Bring her around." One of the boarders hails her, and she hurries away.

I set about preparing for my trip and pause to call Meg on my cell phone. She answers in a very sleepy voice.

- 80 -

"See you slept in this morning," I chide.

"Not accustomed to such late nights, Dave. Trevor and I are still huddled under the covers. What time is it, anyway?"

"Almost nine, Meg. Trevor must be missing his Saturday TV cartoons."

She pauses and I hear whispering. "Trevor says hi. You made quite an impression."

"So did he."

"Dave, did I make a fool of myself last night? Things got pretty hazy for awhile, but I seem to remember losing my cool about the time we reached my house. Did I do anything that embarrassed you?"

I had to pause to think about that. Embarrassed, no. Surprised, sure. Even shocked and more than a bit delighted. But was it calculated on her part or was it the alcohol working?

"Hard question, huh?" My hesitation must have confirmed what she suspected. "Sorry if I went over the edge. It was the most enjoyable evening I've shared with a man for as long as I can remember. Hope I didn't spoil it by being crass or impulsive."

"You were totally charming. But you need to get moving now. Mrs. Starkey will see you at eleven AM to talk about the job at the Barnwell."

Rustling sounds and muffled whispers over the phone line. I picture her leaping out of bed on those terrific legs that danced me around the floor last night—a pleasant vision.

"I'm up now! I'll call Marcy and get moving." She calls out, "Trevor, put on your cartoon show and Mommy will fix your breakfast."

"Slow down, Meg. There's plenty of time. We're only a couple blocks away."

"Eleven o'clock," she says breathlessly. "I'll be there. Thank you, Dave." Then she hangs up.

* * * *

I make a quick run to the nearest shopping mall to pick up a gift for Melody. She's never outgrown her delight over gifts from me. The fact that I show up bearing some token will at least get our visit off to a decent beginning, something I desperately need about now. Then she can tell me, as she undoubtedly will sooner or later, that some boy has taken over my spot as the number one man in her life.

My gift to Helen on this occasion is my heart delivered in person, ready to be made her lifetime possession. If only she will let me explain that I want her back on whatever terms she decides. I'll do anything to have my family back together. Thanks to Trevor, I avoided a bad mistake at Meg's house last night. It's time I got my act together and forgot about dallying, no matter how inviting she may look.

I hurry back to the Barnwell in time to meet Meg at the front door. She looks perky and confident in her robin's egg blue sweater and charcoal skirt, her blonde hair glistening in the morning sunlight. I carefully remind myself that this is merely a matter of helping out someone in need. It has nothing to do with any feelings I may briefly have for her. And if I keep saying that I may even believe it soon.

"Do I look all right, Dave? Am I overdressed, underdressed?"

"You're perfect, Meg. Mrs. S will love you. Just be yourself."

As I finish my quick pep talk, Mrs. Starkey emerges from the kitchen and joins us in the parlor. She pushes back a stray gray curl and exhales noticeably as if she's already weary at this early hour.

"And this pretty lady is the friend you told me about. I'm Mrs. Starkey, honey. What's your name?"

"Meg Kane, ma'am. I'm pleased to meet you." She extends her hand and smiles warmly.

I retreat from the parlor to let the two women talk. Still have to put my dress clothes in a hangup bag and get everything to the car. I'm as nervous as a young suitor going to meet his sweetheart. Everything must be perfect. Don't want to forget anything that may enhance my chances of success. Do I have the aftershave Helen always liked? Does my hair need trimming? Have I packed the right clothes? I'm a veritable bundle of raw nerve endings, and I will be until this weekend has passed. Today could be a watershed in my life.

Half an hour passes. I return to the parlor with my travel items and set them down. Minutes later the two women come down the hall from the kitchen laughing and talking like old friends.

"Dave, I'm grateful you put me in touch with Meg. She's just the person I want to help me keep this place in order. Knows all the ways to make our rooms just right, and she shows real promise as a cook, too. I've asked her to start work tomorrow morning."

Meg is beaming her unspoken thank you to me. I answer, "I'm happy you two hit it off so well."

"See you at seven AM, sweetie," Mrs. Starkey says. "And if your cousin can't watch your son on short notice, bring him along the first day. We'll find something to occupy him." She takes Meg's hand in one of hers and pats it with the other. Then she disappears to continue her work.

"I owe you," Meg tells me. She steps forward and kisses me full on the lips. I work to regain my lost composure and manage a reply.

"Only gave you the opportunity. You clearly won this job on your own. Congratulations."

"You're packed and leaving. For how long?" Meg seems disappointed.

"Taking a weekend trip down to Carolina. I'll be back tomorrow night."

"Good. Guess I'll be seeing you more often now that I'm part of the Barnwell staff."

Don't know if I like what I've gotten myself into, but it's too late now.

Chapter 18

▼

"So, Dave Owens has family in Raleigh. How interesting. Saw him drive away with luggage, so he must be on his way down there. Could be a good time to check in on his brother, maybe even attend to that dummy Logan that got away from me."

The dark man sits shirtless in a straight chair picking at a plate of canned beef stew. He raises his tumbler and gulps down the shot of Old Bluegrass he's poured. Puts his head against the chair back and touches the sore shoulder. Bruise is almost gone, but the mental wound Billy Logan has inflicted still enrages him.

"You're going to suffer for this," he mumbles, and stares out the trailer window at the snow falling on Shaws Corner. "Yeah, you'll pay big time, you toad. Nobody gets the best of me and walks away. Not for long, anyway. Two people tried and one ended up floating in the river. The other one didn't leave that bar room alive."

He picks up the Times and rereads Wednesday's article about a customer being attacked outside the Ridge Mart on Peters Branch Road. The victim suffered a deep wound requiring multiple stitches to close. Police recovered the weapon, an ice pick, but found no fingerprints. Chuckles and looks at his black knit gloves lying on the counter top.

"Those scruffy youngsters from the night on the hill. One of them dared break the code of silence I imposed twenty five years ago. He tried to stir up that dumb sheriff. Good thing Darden is too thick to follow up. I made the blabber mouth that talked to him pay for his mistake, too. Lying cold in his grave. Can't speak out ever again." He touches his tongue.

He smiles as if he's sharing a delicious inside joke. And he is. The joke's on everybody who tries to defy him. They won't even know he's coming until it's too late.

"Never going to catch me with a bunch of halfwits like Darden and his gang. Broad Ass, that's what they called him. Now he's got a butt like an elephant and a head like a watermelon. You were young and stupid thirty years ago, sheriff, and you're fat and stupid now. No match for me, that's for sure." He snatches up the newspaper. Throws it across the room.

He's been slouching around his mobile home for the past several hours, slugging away at the contents of a now half-empty bottle of booze. It doesn't help, though; can't take the edge off his need to strike back. He shakes with the excitement of settling some old scores so he can leave this rotten town forever. Springlake has never done anything for him but tear his family apart and chase him away, off to years behind bars. Then his bitchy little wife betrayed him, but he took care of her. Drove her over the edge with his taunts and sending prison mates to threaten her when they got out. She finally did herself in. And that punk Johnny tried to take away his sweet child, but he paid dearly, too.

He pours half a tumbler of whiskey, and drains it in a single long pull. Belches and holds the glass high above his head.

"Here's to you, all of you, the ones that are long gone and those about to die."

The bearded man stumbles toward the living room area; collapses in a drunken stupor. He lies half on and half off the sofa, one arm dangling to the floor, the empty glass in his hand. In less than a minute he is snoring away.

Chapter 19

The drive from Springlake to Raleigh is a relatively short one, but in my current jittery state it seems to take forever. I fret and worry, wondering what kind of reception I'll meet and how the weekend will develop between Helen and me. The events of the past week weigh heavily on my mind. Even though Kyle is progressing well in his recovery, I'm not nearly through with doing my part to exact revenge for his pain.

Now there is a new concern to cloud my thoughts. What of the evening with the perky little Meg that I enjoyed far too much for a married man? Where might that lead unless I make it clear to her that my wife and daughter are my priorities? Here I go again. Trying to walk too many diverging paths, and I can't negotiate all of them at the same time. Making my life a tangle of mixed emotions. My own fault for being so damned indecisive. The last time this happened to me, I slipped into addictive work, alcohol, even another woman on a single night. Can't let myself backslide now.

Well into the journey to Raleigh, I realize almost too late that I'm daydreaming. Not paying attention to my driving. Pull out into the passing lane on an interstate somewhere in North Carolina and nearly buy it. Snap out of my haze just in time to avoid being sandwiched between an eighteen wheeler bearing down on me from the rear and an oncoming tractor trailer hurtling toward me.

I nearly lose the breakfast I wolfed down hours ago. Brake hard to shoot over into the right lane; tuck in behind the brake hard to give the trucker I was trying to pass. That tears it. Time for me to find an exit, get over the shakes, try to ease down a bite of lunch.

*   *   *   *

The big two-story colonial stands waiting for me when I turn into the driveway. If only I had stayed here in this home rather than running off to Atlanta seeking my fortune. That's a decision I have regretted many times, even though it brought me a fortune. No amount of money can replace the love of a devoted wife and daughter.

Melody comes running to me before I even open the car door. I'm taken aback by how much she seems to have changed in the weeks since I last saw her in October. Still kicking myself over missing Christmas here in Raleigh with the two of them. But I was convinced that business trip overseas was more important at the time.

"Hi, princess. How's my little girl?"

That brings a grimace from the budding teenager. Maybe she doesn't want to be thought of as a "little girl" any more.

"Okay, then, how's my beautiful young lady? You are, you know."

That suits her much better. She hugs me with more enthusiasm. "I'm fine, Daddy. It's so good to see you. I have lots to tell you."

"I want to hear it all, sweetie. Where's your mom?"

"Says entertain you and she'll be back soon. Went to the store for something."

Melody takes my hand. I follow, leaving my bag in the car.

"Come in out of the cold. I made hot chocolate." She puts her arm around my waist and steers me inside.

We chat and joke with each other. She brings me up to date on school, her gymnastics and ballet, the neighbors, boys, everything but her mom. Seems she's carefully avoiding that subject. I know she understands most of what's been causing the rift between Helen and me by inference, even though I'm sure Helen has told her as little as possible. There's certainly nothing vindictive or petty about my wife. I'm confident she'd never purposely try to turn Melody against me. Still, it must be terribly painful for our daughter to see us at odds like this with no sign of reconciling.

Time passes swiftly, as it always does when I'm in the company of my daughter. I listen intently to her stories, and marvel at how she is maturing so fast in so many ways. She shows me photos of some of her recent activities. Says proudly that she is still a straight A student. I'm aglow with a father's pride.

I can't help glancing at my watch periodically. Find myself wondering why Helen could be gone so long. An hour and a half has passed since I arrived with no sign of her yet. Am I being snubbed from the outset of my visit?

"Tell me about Uncle Kyle again, Daddy. Is he really going to be all right?" Melody asks almost as if she is afraid to hear the answer.

"Yes, honey. The worst is over. He's going home today to finish mending. I'll be in Springlake for awhile to see that he recovers fully."

"Good. I'm so glad. Now if you'd just come home to us." She snuggles up closer to me.

"Your mom and I need to talk about that."

"I know you do. I'm going to disappear after dinner and give you the chance." She looks up into my eyes, her expression pleading with me to bring this upset in our lives to a conclusion. Heaven knows I want to.

There are sounds from the kitchen. Helen walks into the living room. I take one look and almost melt. She is still the most beautiful woman in the world to me. Brown haired, brown-eyed, in the prime of her life, looking even younger than her thirty five years. I rise and start toward her. My instinct is to sweep her up in my arms, but that would be premature at this stage.

"Hi there, gorgeous. Need help in the kitchen?" I quip.

"No. It's under control. How are you, Dave?"

She manages a quick peck on my lips, probably more for appearance than anything else. The air in the room is so charged it's a wonder my hair isn't standing on end. My nerves are shot, and she's only been here for seconds.

"I thought we'd have something light tonight. Hope you're not real hungry."

"No, whatever you fix will be fine, honey. Sure I can't take the two of you out to dinner?"

"Rather stay in if it's all the same to you."

I nod. God, she's beautiful! How could I have ever let her drift away? Or was I the one that did the drifting? No matter, it's time to change all that.

We share a pleasant dinner at the table where we've sat so many times in happier days. The chatter is light and cheerful, if a bit forced at times. Melody's glances back and forth between the two of us tell me she senses the undertow just below the surface of our conversation. I have always credited Helen with being unusually perceptive. Our daughter seems to have inherited the trait. Melody reinforces that conclusion when she accompanies her last bite of dinner with an announcement.

"Judy and I are studying at her house tonight. We have a history test tomorrow. I'll be over there for awhile—couple of hours, anyway. Don't turn in before I get back, Daddy."

"I won't, darling."

She's cleared the way for me. Now it's my ball to carry. I sneak a glance at Helen. She's fidgeting nervously, twisting about in her seat. Probably trying to plan how she will handle time alone with me on a moment's notice.

Melody gives me a kiss then crosses to Helen and kisses her. It's like she's building a connection between us with her own love, entreating us to act.

As soon as our child leaves the room, an awkward silence hangs heavily around us. Eventually Helen gestures toward my cup and rises from the table, saying, "Let me get you a refill."

When she returns with the pot and stands nearby, I inhale the familiar fragrance of her. How many times have I remembered her essence on cold, lonely nights when I cursed my stupidity? Now she seems an unattainable dream, so near to me and yet on the other side of that invisible wall we've built.

Our small talk continues. I grow more impatient to cut to the real reason I'm here. I grasp for the instant when she will give me some opportunity, the slightest opening, to turn our meaningless banter aside and move on to the real issue—us and our future. But she holds back. There is no invitation in her words. The conversation drags and falters, and she stands up to clear the table.

"Better do the dishes. Here, let me get that." She reaches for my plate. I touch her hand lightly with my fingertips.

"That will wait. Don't you think it's time we cleared the air, baby?"

She answers my question with a look of resignation. Turns toward the living room, placing herself stiffly in a chair near the sofa. I follow and take my place on the couch facing her. She breathes deeply, appearing to prepare herself for what she must have long anticipated. I don't know how to interpret her movement, but it doesn't seem to bode well. She sits with arms crossed over her chest, legs tightly entwined. I fear I'm conducting an uphill advance.

"Let me begin by saying that we both know my mistakes are what got us into this pickle. I know how badly I acted, how the job got to be too important and the pressure and the alcohol sent me into a bad downward spin. Have only myself to blame for that. But you know I never loved you any less. Just lost my perspective. Please believe that you'll always be the most precious and important part of my life."

She drops her palms to the chair arms, and relaxes the death grip her knees are holding on each other. Still her face remains expressionless.

"When I went to Atlanta to start up the new company, it was a temporary arrangement," I remind her. "I believed we'd be together there in a new home as soon as Melody finished the school year. My weekend trips back to Raleigh were what I lived for. Then the work took over, and I found too many lame excuses to miss those trips and work straight through the weekends. One day ran into the next. I lost track of time and priority."

Helen reaches for her purse and finds a cigarette. I had noticed there were ash trays sitting about. Wondered about that since she hasn't smoked for several years. As she lights up I take it as a signal that she, too, is under more stress than she wants to admit. I found my hiding place in a bottle when she began to withdraw from me. Now it seems she's returned to tobacco as her emotional crutch.

"For the rest of my life, Helen, I'll punish myself for that one night of indiscretion when the frustration and the alcohol took over and I let down my guard. That night meant nothing to me. I don't think it was even an act of defiance, just a way to cope with all those conflicting stresses exploding inside me. You have to believe it had absolutely nothing to do with my devotion to you. But you had become unreachable."

She breaks her silence. "What was I supposed to do? When you did choose to grace us with your presence, you made a beeline to the liquor cabinet. Then it was upstairs for wham, bam, thank you ma'am, and you were off to Atlanta again. I was losing you and I didn't know how to cope. My reaction, right or wrong, was to close up to you and hope you'd eventually wake up."

"I can see that now. But then the word somehow got back to you about my one big slip on that business trip and you confronted me, Helen. Everything closed in on me at once, and I lashed out. I know it's a lot to ask, but I need for you to forgive me for that."

"Yes, you compounded your error, Dave, by trying to blame me for your actions. When you accused me of having found someone new here in Raleigh, it hurt me like I've never been hurt before."

"If I could take back those words and choke on them, I would, darling. It was a poor defense. I knew you'd never be unfaithful. But that's all part of the past. Can't we work on putting it behind us? I could quit work tomorrow and we'd be set for life. We need each other, and Melody needs us both, together in the same house. Give it a try, Helen."

I can feel her mellowing, but she isn't ready to buy my plea just yet. Helen would never be one to string me along for payback just to watch me suffer. Isn't in her makeup. She obviously still has genuine doubts about the sincerity of my words.

"I do believe you're sorry for the things you did—and didn't do, Dave. It's too important a decision to make quickly. Let's make this weekend as near to normal as possible and a time for Melody to remember. Give me time to think about what you've said. You have all you can handle up in Springlake right now. We'll talk seriously when that's over."

Reluctantly I have to agree. She's the cautious, conservative one. Time does heal, but there are some gaping wounds in our relationship that need major binding up. I trust her to come to the right conclusion, and no amount of coaxing from me will speed her decision.

"Fair enough, Helen. I'm only a phone call away. When you're ready, I'll be here in a flash."

For all the uncertainty our conversation leaves gathered about us, I immediately notice a loosening of the tension, a bit of lighthearted fun finding its way back into the way we act around each other, even casual touching from time to time. Melody sees it, too, and she brightens in the improved atmosphere. We spend our time on Sunday morning on an impromptu trip to a nearby park shelter with a brunch suggested by Melody and prepared by my two women. For this time of year the day is surprisingly bright and mild and so are the three of us. At least for a time, it's like nothing has ever come between Helen and me. But, except for my hastily captured glances at her and the feel of Helen's eyes studying me obliquely from time to time, there is no hint of last night's discussion.

Now that I'm here I don't ever want to be out of their sight. But there's the matter of settling what happened to my brother. And Helen needs time and room to decide on her own about my plea for a truce and a return to normal, if that's still possible.

We stand in the driveway at 1820 Autumn Drive, and I hope the next time I'm here it will be as more than a visitor.

Melody hugs me and asks, "When are you coming back, Daddy? It's been wonderful having you here. Please hurry back."

I peer at Helen. Her smile is encouraging but inconclusive. "Soon, sweetie. Mom and I will be in touch. You have my cell number and the number at the Barnwell. Call me whenever you can."

"Give our best to Kyle, Jenny and the boys," Helen says. She comes over to kiss me. Her lips linger on mine for a breathless instant that buoys my hopes.

Chapter 20

▼

The drive back from Raleigh is filled with a jumble of emotions raging through my skull. I want to be encouraged by the way the weekend played out. Helen and I ended our heart-to-heart talk on Saturday night on a hopeful note. Our Sunday picnic was much more than I expected. It was like old times; like nothing had ever happened to interrupt our happiness. The possibilities feel good. There is a warm glow that tells me better days could be ahead. It's up to Helen now.

The afternoon is almost gone when I pull into Kyle's driveway. Today is Groundhog Day, but the creature couldn't have seen his shadow in this valley. February has loudly announced its arrival with a snowfall of several inches. Threatening gray clouds skim overhead in the strong winds that toss and swirl the fallen snow.

Tom meets me at the door and sees me in. The kitchen fragrances tell me dinner preparations are well along. Kyle is sitting in the living room with Don. Looks fit if still a bit pale from his ordeal.

"Back from tarheel country, huh, Flywheel?" Kyle tosses out. Tom looks a bit bewildered by that name, but his older brother grins knowingly.

"Guess you never heard about his nickname, Tom," Kyle says. "Thought I'd told both of you boys. Uncle Hap called him Flywheel because he never shut up. Dave had a real run-on mouth as a kid. You see he's a lot more reserved now." Both of the boys snicker.

"Bet you never told them his name for you," I counter.

"Yeah. Never did understand what that one meant," Kyle replies.

"Well, I looked it up a long time ago. Uncle Hap called you Mugwump. Whether he meant it this way or not, a mugwump is a fence straddler. Never knew you to be indecisive about anything, though."

"And I don't want that repeated by either of you guys," Kyle says, waving a finger at them.

Jenny comes in from the kitchen. "Well, it's about time! How's the weary traveler?"

"You said it. Mostly weary about covers it. This was a fast weekend but a great visit. The girls are fine and Helen sends her love."

"Well, I hope you're not too tired to eat. This is Kyle's first real meal back at home, so there's plenty of everything. I'll have it on the table in a few minutes." She disappears back into the kitchen. We men get down to the important stuff like sports and cars.

Jenny has outdone herself with her culinary welcome home for Kyle. We sit and she asks Don to say grace. He thanks the good Lord for having Dad home safe and well again, and for having their uncle at their table. He blesses the abundance of the meal his Mom has lovingly prepared. Gives thanks for the joy of a caring family. I can certainly say amen to that. I eat like it's my last chance for calories.

After dinner both boys hurry off to see friends. Jenny busies herself in the kitchen, and Kyle and I walk back to the den. He's walking at a slightly slower gait but, considering the shape he was in little more than a week ago, that's not bad. Once we've talked for awhile, I'll be able to conclude whether the trauma has noticeably affected his mental processes. I feel a tad guilty about probing just so I can study his reactions, but it's purely a matter of being concerned for his welfare and his immediate future.

At last it's only the two of us and I have my opening. "Kyle, I had an interesting experience this past week. Went up the hill back of the Barnwell House and found an old cemetery Mrs. Starkey told me about. It's called West Ridge. There are several Confederate soldiers buried in that cemetery."

"I know the place." There is a halting tone to his words, as if he's reluctant to continue.

"One grave caught my interest. There's a Private John Palmer interred up there."

That seems to be a new input for Kyle. He apparently didn't know about that particular grave. He stiffens and sits up in his leather easy chair to catch my words.

"I asked Aunt Ethel about John. She tells me he was the younger brother of her and Mom's great great grandfather, Ira Palmer. Lost his life at the battle of Cloyd's Mountain near Dublin in May of 1864."

"That's a curious discovery. Never knew about him."

I find his reaction equally curious, as if his mind is elsewhere. He averts his eyes and picks at the arm of his chair like he's trying to catch some fleeting object.

"But she threw in a surprise about the burial plot."

"What?" Kyle asks nervously. I've struck a chord somehow.

"She called it the cemetery on Tank Hill."

Kyle pales. He looks away from me out the window into the dark. I wait for a reply. When he removes his hand from the chair arm there is dampness where his palm and fingertips have clung to the leather. I hate doing this to him, but he has to spill out whatever is tearing him up inside.

All he can say when he looks back at me is, "So?" Even that comes out weakly.

"You know, Kyle. You've repeated the word tank, and it totally stumped me. I even went to the tannery and looked at the old tank trying to figure out what it may have to do with the torment you're obviously going through. But now I'm convinced your reference has something to do with Tank Hill where the town water tank stood for so many years. Where we had our winter sledding run that scared the willies out of me. The one you stopped taking me to without an explanation."

"Don't do this, Dave. I can't…it's too much."

"Don't put me off. I saw Billy at the hospital, and he told me about being attacked with an ice pick. Says it had to do with you, him and Jimmy."

Kyle's whole face drops. It's like I've let all the air out of him.

"I know you're going through some private hell you won't share with me, Kyle. Get it out. Release it. You have to do this now."

Kyle kicks his recliner to upright position, stands and walks toward the door. Looks like I've pushed too hard. Now he's going to shut me out completely. But he closes the door and sits down on the couch with me. His hands tremble. Beads of sweat cover his forehead as he forces his words.

"I don't want anyone else in this family to know what I'm about to tell you. Don't think Jenny could handle it, and the boys don't need the shock."

"You have my word. Just let me help carry the load, whatever it is."

He wipes his brow and begins slowly.

"Something happened to me up on Tank Hill a long time ago that changed me forever. It was just before Thanksgiving the year I was in the tenth grade. I've tried to forget that night, but it keeps coming back. Now I'm going out of my skull with fright. This time the incident isn't just a distant memory but a real threat to me and my whole family."

"Then it's also a threat to me, and I want to stand with you and fight it."

The words begin coming in a rush. "One day I was on Tank Hill with Jimmy Moore and Billy Logan. We'd had a good snow and really cold air that gave us an icy crust for our sled run down the hill. We worked on that run most of the day. Had it fast and slick by the time the sun was about to set. We wanted to take a couple more trips down the slope before we went home."

"You know how I feared that hill, Kyle, after Len Darden broke his collar bone crashing into the gate at the bottom," I interject. "I still get sweaty palms every time I hear the name Tank Hill. For all your encouragement, I was sure one day I'd meet an untimely death on that hill, miss a turn and cave my head in on a gatepost."

He manages a half smile remembering my unreasoned fear of his favorite sledding spot. Then he continues.

"Jimmy heard noises over beyond the water tank and went to check. He was gone for awhile, but we just figured he stopped to pee in the snow or something. Then he came running back sputtering something about a man with a shovel. I couldn't understand what he was saying but there was no doubt he was scared crazy."

Kyle coughs and tries to wet his lips.

"Let me get you a glass of water. Don't go anywhere. We're on a roll now."

I go to the kitchen and find two glasses. Jenny casts a quizzical eye at me. She says, "Must be something serious going on in there. He never closes that door. Is he okay, Dave?"

"He's doing fine, Sis. Just reliving old times and didn't want to bother anybody. You know us when we start telling tall tales about our exploits as kids. We're a bit loud and raucous sometimes."

Grinning, she fires back, "Yeah. Gets pretty deep at times. Just go easy on him, Dave."

"I will," I say as I hurry back to the den and close the door again.

Kyle drinks and clears his throat. Now he's ready to go on.

"Jimmy had good reason to be frightened. There was a tall, bearded man running behind him with a spade in one hand and a flashlight in the other. Now all three of us stood rooted to the ground, scared out of a year's growth, as Mom would have said."

"A bearded man?" That jolts me, and I have to know.

"Did you recognize him?"

"Coal black beard and black eyes that could burn a hole right through you. It was the usher from the old Colonial Theater. The one you kicked and almost put out of commission the time he tried to smack me."

Okay, Len Darden. Now who's imagining things? I won't stop Kyle now to tell him, but the irony of my having that dream my first day backing Springlake about the incident in the theater has to make it more than an eerie coincidence.

"He had us. If we tried to get away, at least one of us was going to feel that shovel in some tender place. We could only stand and listen to his ranting.

He nudged Jimmy with the shovel and said, '*Forget what you saw, you little piss ant. If you tell anybody, including these other two pests, I'll rip out your tongue.*'

I recognized him and shouted out his name before I stopped to think. '*Lester. It's Lester Kanicki*'. Lester wheeled around toward me and his eyes narrowed as he looked directly at me. '*And you, Owens, I'll get you and that smartass little brother of yours. How would you like for me to bite off one of your ears for listening to your friend's story?*' He put the flashlight under his chin and clanked his big teeth at me. I covered my ears and held on tight. I don't scare easy, Dave, but the pure evil of what he'd said made me shiver in my boots.

Then he laughed and said, '*I already owe your brother for kicking me. Maybe I'll just get my knife and neuter him*'."

Those words are like a blow to my middle. I look painfully into Kyle's eyes, and his words make me ache all over. I wonder how many times that angry usher watched me come and go from the movie house and plotted his gruesome revenge for my well-placed foot.

Kyle picks up his story. "I never saw anyone as inflamed as Lester was that night," he goes on. "Jimmy must have caught him in a terrible act for him to be that full of hate, I thought. '*As for you,*' Kanicki said to Billy, '*I'll think of something just as gruesome to take care of you. Maybe punch out your eyes with an ice pick*' I thought Billy was going to throw up. Lester said, '*Now the three of you get off this hill and don't ever come back. I'll be watching you.*' Well, we took his advice and never set foot on Tank Hill after that night."

I am riveted by Kyle's account and completely unhinged over the intense hate Kanicki had spewed at them. Kyle goes silent, and I finally tell him, "I remember asking you one time, Kyle, why we never went back there, even though I was deathly afraid of the sled path. You told me you didn't want to talk about that place, so I never mentioned it again."

"Now you see why, Dave. In all my life, I've never been as petrified as I was on Tank Hill that cold November night."

"But what connection does all this have with your being attacked?"

"Everything, I suspect. You see, two days after Jimmy was found mutilated in the woods, FedEx delivered a small package to my door. Jenny was at the grocery, and I'm glad she was. It was the most horrible experience you can imagine."

He falters and I'm afraid he's about to stop. We're too close now. I can't let him quit.

"What was in that package, Kyle? Get it out now while you still can."

Tears come to Kyle's eyes, and his whole body begins to tremble. "HIS TONGUE, DAVE! HE SENT ME JIMMY'S TONGUE. LESTER"S TOOTH MARKS WERE STILL ON IT." He breaks down and sobs.

I want to heave. It's the most disgusting thing I've ever heard. Many times Kyle had circled his arms around my shoulders and consoled me when I was small. Now I find myself serving as the consoler. He releases the tension that must have brought him to the edge of insanity during the past few days.

We sit for long minutes until he regains control. Then I ask, "You think Jimmy's death ties back to that incident on Tank Hill?"

"I know it does, Dave. There was a note in the box with...you know. It said *'Told you I'd get you all if you talked. Jimmy blabbed and now he's dead'*. It made the night on Tank Hill come back to me like a bad black and white movie. I was living my fright all over again. Lester Kanicki's words in that squeaky voice screamed at me. I saw his clanking teeth and imagined them ripping at my ear. Couldn't shut out his voice no matter what I did.

"What do you think he meant about Jimmy blabbing something?"

"Don't know. And it was too late to find out with Jimmy dead."

"But why are you so convinced the package was from Lester?"

"The note was signed "K". Suddenly, that bad memory came back. I knew it had to be from Kanicki."

"Why haven't you told somebody before now, Kyle? The police need to know about this. If it is Lester, they can find him and put him away."

"And what happens to the rest of us while they're searching? I can't trust Darden and his crew to find Kanicki and put him away before he gets to our families. Who knows where he could be after all these years? What if he comes after Billy or me, turns on you, or even, heaven forbid, goes after Jenny and the boys before they catch him?"

"Police could start looking, anyway," I reply. "And they could provide you some protection."

"Dave, that would only tip off Lester and make him act sooner. Besides, Broadus Darden doesn't have the manpower to furnish full-time babysitters for Billy and me and our families. No, I can't go to the police with accusations I can't prove and expose us all to Lester's wrath."

"But at least Billy should know he's in danger. If what you suspect is really true, it could mean Kanicki thinks either one of you can connect him to some crime, and he's willing to kill to avoid that. What else did Jimmy tell you that night?"

"Only that he saw Lester shoveling dirt and snow on top of something. Then Lester walked back toward a blue car, and Jimmy stepped on some dead branches. Kanicki shined his flashlight toward the trees. He must have seen Jimmy watching him from the woods."

"Where exactly was Lester when Jimmy saw him, or did he tell you?"

"Up over the crest of Tank Hill on the west side. Nothing but an open field and the small cemetery over there as far as I know. Don't know if he was digging or just covering. The ground wasn't frozen hard because we'd already dug a little to build a small campfire to stay warm."

We both sit there silently in the den, oblivious to our surroundings, each of us lost in private thoughts, until at last I ask, "You gonna be all right, Kyle?"

"I am now, little brother. Thanks for making me finally face up to it. Now that somebody's in the fight on my side, I feel much better. In fact, it's like a great weight lifted. My head was ready to explode from the pressure of holding it all in. For the first night since that package arrived, I may even be able to sleep tonight."

"Then let's tell Billy so he can be on guard. We're going after this guy with an organized plan, Kyle. We'll take the responsibility for handing him over to the sheriff. And I swear, if he gives me half a chance, I will personally pound his ass into the ground before we deliver him."

And, I think to myself as I rise to leave, *now the bastard has a name. Lester Kanicki.*

Chapter 21

▼

I return to the Barnwell House thoroughly shaken and confused by the entire weekend. Helen's hot and cold reception, her reluctance to commit, and now Kyle's shocking and disgusting revelation twist and turn in my brain. This may be a peaceful night for Kyle to find some rest, but I have a strong feeling that dawn won't come nearly soon enough for me.

Mrs. Starkey greets me from the parlor with her usual sunny smile, seeming much livelier than she has for days.

"I'm like a new woman, Dave," she tells me. "Can't thank you enough for bringing Meg to me. She's a godsend. Knows what has to be done and goes right to it without prompting. She's even showed me a trick or two in the kitchen. That girl's sure lightened my load."

"Glad she worked out, Mrs. S. Had a feeling she'd fill the bill."

"So how was your trip to Raleigh? Did you get snowed on? You see we have a nice new snowfall her, and there's several more inches forecast tonight."

"I know. It's already spitting out there again. I may sleep in a little late in the morning. Let them clear the roads before I go out."

She points at the silver tea service near at hand and says, "I'm having a cup of tea. Want to join me?"

"Maybe a slight pick up *will* help me climb those stairs tonight. I'm bushed, Mrs. S."

She pours and reseats herself. Her voice tells me she is concerned.

"You look more than just worn down, Dave. You're troubled. Want to tell me?"

"I'll work it out in time. This has been a long weekend, and I'm not sure what it all meant."

"Is your brother all right?"

"Stopped off to see him and his family for dinner on the way back here. Had something important to discuss with him. He's doing fine."

"You're sure there's not something you want to get off your chest, Dave? I'm a good listener any time you need me."

"Thanks for your concern. But all I want to do right now is crawl into that big bed and shut everything out till the sun comes up."

We chit chat a while and finish our tea. Then I say my goodnight and slowly make my way up the stairs. Undress without even unpacking my suitcase. Turn back the covers. Something is lying there with one corner tucked under a pillow. I reach down and slide out the lavender envelope circled with a white silk ribbon tied in a bow.

Sitting on the edge of the bed I untie the ribbon and open the envelope. It's a Valentine's Day card that's come twelve days early. There's some gooey verse that I ignore when I see a handwritten note inside. The note says:

Dearest Dave,

You came to me when I most needed a lift. I don't yet know why, but you are special to me. Please don't go before we know what may lie ahead.

Meg.

Has she misread me? Have I encouraged her too much? That's another of the myriad of things that need to be worked through in the coming days. Beginning tomorrow I must make some progress on several fronts. This will have to be a week of decisions. But for now sleep is all I can think about. I place the card on the night table, shuck my clothes into a heap and roll into bed.

Well into the night I suddenly find myself awake.

A puff of cold air stings my face, and I inhale a musty odor. I open my eyes, try to focus them across the room. At first there is only the darkness tempered by filtered moonlight peeking though the drapes. It creates a liquid gray inside my room that has the feel of a soft, enveloping haze. My eyes sweep toward the far window. A movement catches my attention, a vision somewhere between a filmy apparition and a presence felt rather than seen. It moves slowly, haltingly, across the light from the window and remains an idea without substance, a shimmering image without form.

"Who's there," I ask, fearing the answer that may come from the unlit corner of the room to which the vision has flown.

But there is no answer. I sit up in bed and strain to see what it is that has disturbed my rest. Instinctively, I know if I turn on the lamp, the apparition will disappear in the stark light. Toss back the covers and begin to rise, and the hazy notion gradually becomes a dimly outlined figure. It moves silently, almost floating, ever so slowly toward me. Stops on my side of the bed near one foot post.

The fluttering image gradually takes form, still almost transparent but showing touches of color and depth. I see a youth, a teen turned at an angle to me. The left side of his face is in shadow. The look belies his obvious youth, as if he has lived a lifetime in a few short years. He stands not tall and erect, as his tender years would dictate, but in the slump of someone resigned to an unsatisfying existence, annoyed and searching, tormented and beaten down. As the lines of the vision are defined more clearly, I see he wears a gray cotton tunic open at the collar, and wide leather belts crisscross his chest. His cotton trousers are stuffed into what appear to be riding boots that are brown and shiny as if recently buffed. A hat stands tall on his head, the brim held to the crown with a large pin. There is a small red feather tucked into the hat band.

This has to be the young male ghost Mrs. Starkey told me about in the parlor. The Barnwell House's legendary spirit has chosen to visit my room. Oddly, I feel no fear, only a strange sense of connection with this lonely figure. It's as if I should know the lad, although his manner of dress tells me he's of a time long before I came to be in this world.

My visitor is not pale and ghostly as I would expect. Rather he's tanned and rugged looking and seems to have walked into my dreams straight out of the summer sun. His cheek is burnished a golden brown. His slender fingers reach up and remove the hat to reveal a shock of blonde hair and a forehead burned dark by the sun. Still he stands in front of me nearly in profile, showing me little more than his right side. He turns away to sweep the room with his eyes, looking for something he can not find, then back, never revealing the features of his full face.

When the specter's arm sweeps upward to place the hat back in place, I see something attached to his sleeve. It looks like a rectangle of cloth into which someone has sewn a design. A home-stitched version of the Confederate flag.

The lad slowly turns to face me. Something is oddly amiss in his appearance. His uniform, and I am convinced it is a uniform, seems freshly laundered. But the tunic bears a large red stain where it has been mended by hand at the chest.

He appears to be in the bloom of life, yet I somehow sense that he's met a violent death. The remnants of blood from that tragic event mar his tunic.

His lips begin to move, but I can't make out his words. When he finally faces me squarely, I recoil, not in fear but in shocked discovery. The lad's left cheek bears a crescent shaped mark, a whelp that could have been a deep, ugly wound. Aunt Ethel's words come to me in a rush, and I know, without a doubt, that it's the mark of a horse's hoof branded on his sun-touched cheek. He works his mouth but begins to fade from view. I strain to hear the words he utters, but no sound reaches my ears. I study his lips and shudder as a chill works its way down my arms to my fingertips. Is it only my imagination or can I see them forming the word *Palmer?* No, I must be imagining it.

I reach out to the figure that is growing dimmer and entreat it to stay. "Please don't go! Tell me…are you John Palmer? Let me help you find what you're looking for."

But my intrusion into the soldier's wandering seems to have only hastened his departure. He squares the hat on his golden locks and takes one step backward. The vision shimmers, teetering on the edge of my consciousness, then gradually folds into the haze. The moonlight disappears and there is only emptiness in the silent room.

Chapter 22

▼

After the visit from the shadowy vision, I fall into a deep sleep and awaken to the morning sun. Several hectic days of mind-numbing events are behind me, and I finally feel refreshed and renewed. The whole tenor of the new day seems different, upbeat and promising.

I go down to breakfast and linger over the delicious meal Mrs. Starkey serves. When at last I am the single boarder left in the dining room, she comes around and places one hand on my shoulder. Looks into my eyes in search of something.

"You're a different person from the stressed out, exhausted man who checked in a few days ago. I hope the Barnwell House has been comfortable for you. Helped you gain back your energy. I see a new spark in your eyes."

"It's been wonderful, Mrs. Starkey. I needed a place like this. Had a lot of questions to think my way through. There is something I'd like to ask you about, though."

"Of course, Dave."

"I was visited last night by the young soldier you told me about. He was trying to say something to me, but I couldn't make it out."

"He's never spoken aloud to me or to any of the guests. Maybe you're special to him in some way."

"Oh, there was no sound but he shaped words. I tried so hard to hear him speak. He came to the foot of my bed and told me something. I may never know what it was."

"Then you must have a connection with the spirit. I'm sure of it," she tells me.

Her words ring true. A tingle at the nape of my neck tells me she's confirming a notion that has already occurred to me.

"Tell me, Mrs, S, is he a teenager with blonde hair and a gray cotton uniform?" I ask her.

"That's the way I saw him, Dave. Was the girl with him?"

"No. I saw only one ghost. He was speaking but there was no sound. I caught a glimpse of what appeared to be a bloodstain and hand stitching over his heart. The Stars and Bars were there on his sleeve. My impression was that he could be a young Confederate soldier killed in battle."

I leave it there. My speculation about his exact identity is best kept to myself for the time being.

* * * *

I linger in my room after breakfast, cataloging all that needs to be done during the next few days and delaying my departure from the inn. Have no desire to test my skills again on slippery roads before the road crews have a chance to do some clearing. Atlanta sees much less snowfall and ice. I'm somewhat rusty at skating either my footsteps or a vehicle across slippery surfaces.

I am impatient to get started, though. Have about run out of ways to kill time when there's a soft rap at my door. Meg has stopped by during her cleaning rounds. She's wearing an open collar cotton dress, beige with tiny blue flowers, and a starched, fringed apron provided by Mrs. S. As usual, she's not shy about displaying her attributes—the top of the dress is unbuttoned and spread wide below her neck. Stops just inside the door and takes a prolonged deep breath that accentuates the effect. A sly little smile creeps across her face.

"Well, you are sure enough back," Meg sings out. "How was your weekend?"

"Not nearly long enough. But I had business to get back to here."

"Business?"

"Have to see my brother today. Taking him out for some fresh air and maybe lunch at Snuffy's. It's his first outing since, well, you know."

"Leave some time on your calendar for me. Please." She comes a little too close, and I feel very uncomfortable. Raises her hands as I slide away.

"Like I said, lots of business to attend to."

"And pleasure, too, I hope," she trills. Gives me one of her demure little grins.

"Meg, you and I need to have a talk. I need to make you understand…"

A voice from the bottom of the stairs cuts short my attempt to set Meg straight on our relationship, if it could really be called even that. Mrs. S wants her help downstairs with something, and the opportunity is lost, at least for now.

She wheels and responds, "I'll be right there, ma'am." Then she reaches into the pocket of her maid's apron and hands me an envelope. Waggles her fingers and her bottom in unison and intones, "Toodle-oo, Mr. Dave."

I toss the envelope on the dresser then step to the bathroom with my toothbrush. Standing in front of the mirror, I do a bit of soul searching. *Not really keen on the idea of dropping the cute little blonde, are you, Owens. Want to test your luck, huh? Where's your will power? Cut and run, man!*

I know full well what has to be done. I've been rationalizing that in her current vulnerable state, she doesn't need another disappointment. She's sure she's made a real hit with a new man, and now I'm about to burst her bubble. How heartless can that be?

But I know it boils down to the fact that I'm strongly attracted. Her moves whet my appetite for what might happen next. The face in the mirror reminds me I have a wife and daughter waiting in that big house on Autumn Road. Am I a man of my word or just another horny toad? But I can't seem to decide on my final answer. This other girl is too hot to touch and I'd best make up my mind now.

My coat is halfway on when I glance at the dresser and see the envelope still lying there. I pick it up and see in carefully written block letters *MR DAVE*. Inside is a short note in a hand I now recognize as Meg's The message is:

> Dear Mr. Dave,
>
> My Mommy and I would like for you to come to our house Saturday night for dinner. I like Mommy's fried chicken and you will too. Please come.

It's signed 'Your friend, *T R E V O R*, in carefully drawn letters. Knows how to pluck my heart strings, too, doesn't she? *But, as long as it's Trevor asking…sure, Dave.*

Guess that settles the question. I certainly can't disappoint that charming little guy. Or at least that's my excuse and I'm sticking to it. Saturday night I'll make it clear there's nothing for her to look forward to if she continues to see me. Yeah, sure, I'll get right on that.

* * * *

The snow has stopped. The handyman has cleared the long driveway with a plow and spread salt. It's time to venture out and head for Kyle's house.

I get there with no major trouble. It's still pretty cold, but the roads are mostly clear.

"You think this is a good idea?" Jenny asks me. Is it safe out there? No time to take a chance after all he's been through." She's being a protective wife, and she's very skittish about Kyle's first trip outdoors.

"Trust me, Jen. We're not going far. It really is fine outside. I'll have him back in three hours tops. If it'll make you feel better, I'll call and let you know how we're doing. I'll even feed him so you can take a break from the kitchen." That prompts a brief, nervous smile from her.

Jenny doesn't know our real destination, and I hesitate to tell her. Could raise too many questions in light of recent events. Actually our first stop is less than a mile away to see Kyle's friend Billy Logan. He has to be read in on what's transpired over the past week. I think from our brief encounter earlier that he already suspects someone bent on disposing of him and Kyle may be lurking nearby.

* * * *

We find Billy alone at his house, half dressed and unshaven. A large band aid covers his stitches, but the cheek is almost back to normal size.

"Good to see you're on your feet, Kyle," Billy says. "You still looked pretty rocky when I saw you at the hospital." Billy offers us a soda and pops the top on his. We walk into the living room.

"Said you had somethin' important to talk about so I sent the missus over to see her sister. Me, I was laid off at the plant this last cutback, Dave. Been fartin' around home for two weeks now, so it's good to have somebody come see me."

Kyle strikes a serious tone and begins his message to Logan. "Billy, I know you tried to talk to me about the night Lester Kanicki threatened us up on Tank Hill."

Billy frowns. "Hadn't thought about that for years, Kyle, till I heard about Jimmy. Brought back a lot of good memories and that one bad one. Man, I almost crapped in my pants that night when Lester homed in on me with them wicked eyes. Coulda been him that cut me the other night. That's what I wanted to talk about at the hospital, but you wouldn't."

"I know, Billy. But Dave got me past that hangup. It's time we faced our problem and took some action."

"I'm all for that, pal," Billy says. He touches the bandage decorating his cheek.

Kyle says, "Remember Lester said he'd rip out Jimmy's tongue if he told us what he'd seen? That he'd bite off my ear and neuter Dave unless we forgot about him being on that hill?"

"Yeah, and he said he'd find somethin' gruesome to do to me, too. That's the first thought I had when I found that ice pick. Lester said he may punch out my eyes with an ice pick. Got chills all over. Couldn't wait to see you. But you wouldn't talk about it."

"I didn't want to be the one to have to tell you, Billy. Now I think you're way ahead of me. This has to be Lester making good on his threats."

"Man, the same thought has been tearing up my insides for a whole week. I can't eat, can't sleep."

"He's back, guys," Kyle says. "And it seems Jimmy said something that got back to him about the thing on Tank Hill. Now he's worried enough to come after all of us. You and I just got lucky this time, Billy."

"I've never breathed a word about that night," Billy says.

Kyle answers, "Cost Jimmy his life. Let me tell you about a package that came to the house two days after Jimmy died."

Recalling how I felt when Kyle told me about Jimmy's severed tongue and the note, I am not surprised at Billy's reaction when he hears the same story. First he turns as pale as the walls of his living room, then he charges to the bathroom and loses his soda and probably everything else he's swallowed today. When he's through he returns holding a wet cloth to his mouth.

"What're we gonna do, Kyle? Can we put Darden on his tail?"

"I've already been over that with Dave. Len can't guarantee we'll be safe until he catches Lester. We have to take the initiative and find him first. It's up to us to deliver Lester and stop this horrible rampage he's on."

"Then tell me what to do. Let's nail him before he does any more harm. Won't be able to sleep nights now till he's behind bars," Billy pleads.

"I know the feeling, Billy. That's what I've been going through since the package came," Kyle tells him. "But it was only fair to tell you everything."

"You didn't answer my question. What do I do next?" Billy is sweating profusely now, and he's almost as pale as before he hurled.

I answer him. "If you have a gun, I suggest you keep it handy. And don't take any unnecessary chances or go out alone after dark. You see what that almost did to both of you."

"I got a shotgun that'll blow him to hell and gone, and I ain't afraid to use it, either," Billy announces. But how do we track him down?"

"We're working on that. Just keep your guard up, Billy, till we figure this all out," I answer.

When we're reasonably sure Billy understands everything and is calmed down, we prepare to leave. I ask to use his phone.

"Jenny, it's Dave. We're going to stop off for lunch. I'll have Kyle home before two o'clock. He's just fine. Seems to be enjoying the fresh air, and the roads are almost clear."

"Okay. You fellows behave. I'll be at the grocery store for awhile. Don't eat too much, because I'm cooking a big supper."

* * * *

We drive downtown and turn off Main Street to park behind Snuffy's Restaurant. This place is usually good for an interesting sandwich and maybe a nice bowl of soup on a cold day.

While the three of us are waiting for our food to arrive, Len Darden walks in, greeting people as he moves toward a seat. Must be getting close to election time, I think, the way he's glad-handing everybody. He walks past our booth then spins around and calls out, "Well, kiss my…it's Kyle Owens come back to life!" He reaches for Kyle and bear hugs him, his revolver holster thumping against the booth.

Kyle motions to the open space beside him. "Have a sandwich with us, Len."

"Sure as hell will, old buddy. Hi, Dave. I see you're still in town."

"Told you I was here for the duration, Len," I reply. That draws a frown from the big, ruddy man.

"An' remember I told you to tread careful like. Hope you took that to heart." I nod.

"So how you feeling, Kyle?" He wants to know. "Gettin' back in the groove? Man, I was worried you was hurt bad. Can't tell you how good it is to see you out and about."

Kyle smiles. "Better than a few days ago."

"How's your investigation coming, Sheriff?" I ask.

He looks in all directions before leaning over the table and whispering, "We're checking out leads. Gonna drop a net around that bastard and put him away."

I can't let that go. "Well, it can't be too soon for me. You almost had another death to chase down if that gas station attendant hadn't acted so quickly. I mean

Jimmy and Kyle both. The attacker certainly didn't show Sam any mercy. Went back there the next night and brutalized him. And what about Billy?"

"Hold your voice down, Davey. Got it all neatly tied together, don't you. You're reaching, my man. Who says there's any connection at all between Kyle's mugging and the other incidents."

"Incidents? Sheriff, we're talking about an innocent man carved up, another gutted at work, and Billy almost impaled on an ice pick."

Billy noticeably recoils at my words, and he reaches up to his cheek.

"Your officer found Sam slumped over the counter clutching a fistful of black hair. Billy told me it was a bearded man in black garb that jumped him—same as Kyle's attacker. And did you wonder why he used an ice pick?"

I look at Kyle. He shakes his head, so I stop.

"What's that mean, mister super sleuth?" the sheriff asks in an annoyed voice.

"Just seemed an odd weapon of choice to me. More like an attempt on Billy's life than a robbery."

"Yeah, well, you just let us handle things. Like I say, we're workin' it, Dave." Len obviously wants to move on to other topics. He raises a hand and hails a waitress.

"What you boys havin'? Never mind. Sugar, bring me one o' them big old juicy Snuffy Burgers you got. Don't burn it too long, sort of middlin'. And a choc'lit shake in a paper cup." He waves at someone across the aisle. Then he turns back to speak to Kyle and Bill.

"Man, it looks like the old days out there. Biggest snow we've had in the last ten years. I understand we're in for more, too. Just as soon see gale force winds and white up to our asses. Runs criminals indoors to keep from freezin' their honkers off."

I want to pump the sheriff for more information, but I don't want him on my case again for interfering. Find myself wondering if he has anything of substance on either Jimmy's death or Kyle's mugging. Probably just blowing smoke at us.

We spend twenty minutes listening to Len's tall tales while he gobbles down his burger, grabs what's left of the milkshake, and slides out of the booth. "Got to get out there among 'em, fellas. You take care of yourself, Kyle." He tosses a five and a couple ones on the table. "And Dave, you have a nice *quiet* visit."

Message received, mister lawman.

Only moments after Darden disappears onto Main Street, I glance toward the back of the restaurant and catch a fleeting glimpse of someone staring at us. The instant I see the black beard I bolt from my seat without a word and run toward the back. I burst through the rear door of the eatery and fall down the rear steps. By the time I recover, a brown sedan is pulling out of a parking space, its tires squealing as it pirouettes toward Calhoun Street. The sun blinds me, and I squint to make out the license plate number, but all I can see are the first two digits, a two and a six.

I start to run after the car, but see I'm wasting my energy. The brown car is gone swiftly, screaming down Calhoun toward the center of town. I'm left standing alone panting in the cold.

The best I can do is to shake my fist and vent my anger. "Lester Kanicki—or whoever you are, I'll get you, no matter how long it takes."

Chapter 23

Sheriff Darden isn't going to be much help to us in tracking down Lester Kanicki. Kyle obviously doesn't want to tell him about the Tank Hill incident or even about the package he received. Probably wouldn't believe the tenuous connection we've drawn between Lester and the recent violent events, anyway. Best we leave him and his resources to chase whatever leads he has, if in fact he even has any.

I can't go back to the police station looking for information, and if I show up a second time this soon at the newspaper office, that could raise suspicion, too. Looks like my only avenues are the library and a search of court records. I go to the small library near the middle of town hoping they keep some town historical records that will steer me. To my surprise, a classmate of mine from high school days, Mary Beth Evans, greets me at the front desk.

"Dave Owens, is it really you? Thought you'd left us for the big time. Heard you were some sort of software tycoon now." She has the same cheerful note in her voice, but she looks much the worse for wear after nearly twenty years.

"Nothing quite that spectacular, Mary Beth. Just working down in Atlanta making an honest living." She rolls her eyes. The word is out that old Dave has made it big, regardless of how I bend the truth.

"Heard about your brother. Hope he's okay."

Small town, I reflect. *Everybody knows your business in a place like this.*

"Kyle's fine, Mary. Listen, I need to find some information, general information on events in Springlake over say a two year period beginning twenty six years ago. Think you can point me in the right direction?"

"That's a pretty broad order, Dave. Can we narrow it down?"

I talk through my requirements, being careful not to tie any of my comments to Jimmy Moore, Billy or Kyle. I ask her to include, if possible, any information she may have on the old water tank and its surroundings in the vicinity of Tank Hill. That draws a puzzled look. She starts to jot down notes and studies them, limiting the scope of our search. Mary dispatches me to a nearby table and chair, and she tells me to relax while she does some collecting. I watch her searching the stacks and piling up books and binders on a table by a window. Then she motions for me to sit down at the table.

"That should get you started. Here's a list of other references you may want to check."

I look at the stack of reading she's left me and whistle. "Must have a trailer out back where you keep all this stuff. Lady, you are amazing."

"Been at it a few years. Let me know if there's anything else I can do. I'll be right up front."

"Mary Beth Evans. What a pleasant surprise. Thanks."

"It's James. I'm Mary James now. My husband's a long haul trucker. We have four children—three boys and a girl."

As she walks away, I picture Mary Beth as I first knew her, local beauty queen, a real knockout who put most of the other girls in the shadows with her Miss America maturity. Two decades have added at least thirty pounds and broadened a backside I remembered as classy. She dated mostly college men. I never could muster the nerve to ask her out. No doubt some older, beer belching dude has snagged her, and he probably has her tied down with a house full of runny-nosed kids while he motors down the highways. She probably works at the library to maintain her sanity.

I take a deep breath and bend to my task. Somewhere in these documents there have to be tidbits of information I can follow to something significant. I've bracketed my search to run from September of the year in question through the following April. That still gives me a lot of ground to cover from the looks of the pile in front of me.

A lot of what I read is interesting but not helpful. I scribble down an occasional data bit and note the reference source. Can't tell what may connect back as my reading continues. I linger over items that jog old memories. Have to tell myself to focus and move on. What I'm looking for could get lost in totally unrelated reminiscing.

There is an article written by a local teacher on the history of the water tank that held the town's water supply for so many years. The story relates how funding and construction of a new, much larger and more technically updated water system has progressed. As of three years ago, the old structure on Tank Hill has stood empty awaiting demolition. I carefully read that article and annotate my notes to be sure I can come back to it later. There is a reference in the story to a small cemetery where Confederate heroes are buried and where a Lee-Jackson Day ceremony had honored them in 1930. New markers were placed on their graves. That bears further checking. I'll ask Mary Beth about it.

Then I run across a passing reference to the disappearance of two sisters, Stephanie and Valerie Hurt, during November of the Tank Hill year, as I've now labeled it in my mind. Sounds newsworthy. There must be an article with more details in a back issue of the Springlake Times. I catch Mary's eye and motion for her to come over.

"This story about the Hurt sisters. Think you have an old newspaper account of that?"

She nods and goes to check the archives. I return to my chore, processing the information overload as I continue reading. Can't get the thought out of my head that I've just made a significant find. Must be one of those intuition things Helen talks about. Maybe women aren't the only ones who have the knack.

In a few minutes Mary Beth returns and says, "Found some back issues of the Times when it was still a weekly. One reports the girls' disappearance, and the other tells how the search has been abandoned. Don't know if they ever solved that mystery." I notice she isn't carrying any newspapers, but she gestures for me to follow her to the back.

The articles are on microfilm. She has the first one called up on the machine for viewing. It's dated November 15th.

"Back then the paper hit the street on Wednesday," Mary explains. "This first account tells of the two Hurt girls being reported missing on Monday morning after failing to return home on Sunday night.

I read the article carefully. It relates that an extensive search is underway. Stephanie and Valerie Hunt have both disappeared without a clue. The Times makes a plea for anyone with information to come forward and assist the investigation.

"Now here's the follow up story in the November 22nd edition." She moves the next frame into view on the screen.

That issue reports that Stephanie's body has been identified sixty miles away in the town of Linton after the Times went to press the previous week. She is the apparent victim of a hit-and-run accident on a country road outside the village. There is still no trace of her sister or clues as to her whereabouts. The Hurts have no idea how the older girl could have been that far away from Springlake.

"Do you remember any of this, Mary Beth?"

"Vaguely. My parents told me two girls had been lost. Reminded me that's why they kept such close tabs on me. Said they couldn't take a chance with me such a pretty little girl and all those bad people out there. But you and I would have been only ten or eleven at the time."

"Yeah. Guess it wouldn't have interested us much, would it?"

Then I reread the descriptions of the two girls.

"Says here Stephanie was seventeen and her sister was fifteen. Kyle probably knew at least the younger one, Valerie. I'll ask him."

I read on until my eyes burn with the strain. To my surprise, I find I've waded through most of the documents Mary Beth has gathered for me. Pore over their contents in great detail. Feel like I'm back there in that era. I pocket Mary's list of more reading before opening one more book. Decide that I'll have to return to the library another day to finish.

That final volume is the find of the day. I stop short, my eyes riveted to the table of contents. The book contains a summary of the court proceedings on felony cases for the year following Kyle's fateful November. What has demanded my attention is an entry on a trial with the title 'State of Virginia versus Lester A. Kanicki, March 18.'

My fingers tremble as I fumble with the leaves of the book, hurrying to find the account of the trial. There it is. I rub my eyes, now irritated and beginning to blur, and plunge ahead. Learn that Kyle's old nemesis got on the wrong side of the law that winter by picking a fight with two men in a bar. The fight ended with Lester standing over one of them, broken beer bottle in hand. He had ground the jagged bottle into the man's face then thrust it into his neck, severing the jugular vein. The man bled to death before the rescue squad could respond and stop the bleeding.

The trial summary related that a verdict of guilty of first degree manslaughter had been rendered by a jury of Lester's peers. He had been sentenced to spend twenty five years in prison.

I am sure this has no direct connection with Kyle's confrontation with Lester on Tank Hill, but it confirms the violent nature of someone I fear is at this moment stalking us. The account is like a shot of adrenaline. My system goes into overdrive. I shudder with the sheer excitement of my discovery.

Hurrying to the desk I say, "Mary, there's one more story I need to run down."

She holds up one finger and shushes me. In my excitement I have forgotten where I am. At least three people have stopped what they're doing, and they're giving me a very annoyed look over my outburst.

I lower my voice to a whisper and repeat, "One more story…"

She snickers and says softly, "I heard you, and so did everybody else. Follow me."

There are related stories in several issues of the Times on microfilm. I follow the progress of the trial, which apparently made quite a news splash in this relatively quiet town. Accounts written by someone who must have preceded Randall Bean at the paper tell how Lester's lawyer had paraded his pretty blonde wife and his four-year old daughter, Margaret, before the court at every opportunity to elicit sympathy from the jury. But this ploy had not worked. The crime was particularly violent. Kanicki had plainly sought to inflict maximum damage on his opponent. Even if the sharp glass of the bottle had not pierced the critical vein, the man would have had to live with a horribly disfigured face. Further, the jury was not convinced that Lester harbored the least bit of remorse for his gruesome deed.

I thank Mary Beth for her help, and she replies, "Come around more often. I'd like to meet your family. You are married?"

"Great wife and a beautiful teenage daughter."

"Here with you on your visit?"

"No. Not this time," I admit sheepishly as I turn to leave.

A sudden thought hits me. "Mary Beth, do you think you could find something else for me?"

"Name it, Dave."

"I want to read an account of the battle of Cloyd's Mountain near Dublin in May, 1864."

"Spell that," she says, and writes down my answer. "If we've got anything, I'll find it. Got a number where I can reach you?"

I give her my cell number and say, "Thanks, Mary Beth. You're still my dream girl."

Before I leave the downtown area, I swing by Jordan's Florist. Order a flower arrangement for delivery to the library tomorrow. Mary Beth has been a tremendous help. I want to do something, however small, for her. And I still have a soft spot in my heart for her.

* * * *

The afternoon has slipped away when I return to the Barnwell. Except for a hasty trip to hurry through a burger for lunch, I've been at that library table all day, determined to make a breakthrough somehow. And now I believe that wish has been answered with Mary's help. I am beat, emotionally exhausted, and my eyes beg for the relief of a long, quiet night at the Barnwell.

"Well, it's the missing Mister Owens. Been busy?"

Meg gives me her most intriguing coy grin and sweeps over from the kitchen as I come in from the rear parking lot. Standing on her toes, she whispers in my ear, "Did you read Trevor's invitation?" She manages to brush her breasts across my shoulder.

I hesitate then bring my thoughts back from the library, and her bosom, long enough to answer.

"Uh, yeah."

"So? Are we on for Saturday night?"

She steps in front of me and places one hand against my chest. It leaves an uncomfortably warm print. I'm still reeling from the revelations in those musty old books and the microfilm. But she's pressing me for an answer to something, and I have to collect myself. "Saturday?"

"Yes. The dinner invitation from Trevor. He has his heart set on seeing Mister Dave again. Can you come?"

"Sure. Mind if I bring him something? A gift of some sort? He's such a cute little guy, and sharp, too."

"He'll be delighted, and so will I. Had to take him to the doctor yesterday afternoon with a sore throat, but he's fine now. Thanks, Dave." She finds my hand and squeezes it for an instant. Then she hurries away to finish her kitchen chores.

And then I have a surprise for you, I reflect as she walks away with that rolling sway of hips that leaves a hint of events to come. *It's been fun but it's over, Meg.*

I go up to my room before dinner and dial Kyle's number.

"Have a question for you. The thing you told me about on the hill. Is there any chance you remember the exact date?"

"Let's see. About two weeks before Thanksgiving. It was on the weekend, Sunday, because we were there all day building our sled run. Yes, Thanksgiving was not the next Thursday but the one after that. Jimmy had a lot of work to do helping his grandmother host all the family for the holiday meal. That's as close as I can pinpoint it. Don't have the exact date."

"Close enough. Thanks."

"What's this about, Dave?"

"We'll talk about it tomorrow. I may have some important information for you and Billy."

I hang up and go back to my notes. I had copied down the calendar from the Times issue that held the initial story of the Hurt girls' disappearance. Seemed like overkill at the time, but I was grasping for straws. Now I look down at the page with the hastily drawn boxed calendar and say aloud, "Bingo! Sunday November 12th. A week and a half before Thanksgiving. Those two girls vanished the same night Lester scared the wits out of the boys up on Tank Hill."

But was it just an interesting coincidence or something more? I ponder that question as I walk to the Barnwell dining room and the delectable scents from the kitchen.

Mrs. Starkey has a sparse gathering of guests for dinner this evening. Real shame, too, because the meal is outstanding.

"Can a lonely old lady keep you company for dinner, Dave?" I look up from my appetizer to see my hostess, coiffed and sans apron, standing by my table.

"I'd be delighted," I say, and rise to offer her a chair. "My, you're positively radiant tonight, Mrs. S. Expecting a gentleman caller?"

She blushes and replies, "Just feel so relieved with Meg here to help out. Thought I'd give my hairdresser a visit to see how it feels to look human again. How are you doing with all your running around, Dave?"

"Well, today was a particularly interesting day. Even ran into a friend of mine from high school. Girl I much admired back then."

"Those old flames can be dangerous, son. Remember, you're a married man now." She waves a warning finger at me.

"Nothing like that. Just a dear friend. By the way, Mrs. S, how might I go about finding a town named Linton? Believe it's somewhere in the mountains west of here. Maybe out toward Wytheville."

She gives me the directions for reaching the town from the interstate highway and says, "Not much of a town, more like a wide place in the road. Know somebody out there?"

"No, just want to talk to the sheriff about something that happened near Linton a long time ago."

A coffee pot looms into view and I glance up to see Meg.

"Make you hot?" she asks with a wink. She never lets up.

Polish off a wonderful dinner and enjoy my conversation with Mrs. S. Then I decide to make this an early evening. Have big plans for tomorrow that will keep me on the go until quite late in the day.

Chapter 24

The next morning Kyle and I sneak away to his den as soon as we can. I'm anxious to bounce several things off him before I go charging ahead on my hunches.

"Okay, Dave," he says. "Your turn to 'fess up. What's so important about the date you called me about last night?"

"I've been spending some time at the library, Kyle. Seems there was a double disappearance the exact same night that's never been solved as far as I can tell. Do you remember two sisters named Hurt?"

"Me and everybody else in town. They were a couple of hot items. Val was a sophomore with me and her sister, Steph, was a senior. They just vanished. Stephanie's body was found later. There was never a trace of Valerie."

"What else do you remember about them, Kyle?"

"Like I said, they were well known around town. Had the reputation of being readily available. You know, party girls. Both of them were well endowed and they flaunted it. Where's the connection?"

"Haven't figured it out yet, but it's a strange coincidence. If I could link those girls and Lester in some way, we may have a trail worth pursuing."

"Sounds far fetched to me, but it's on your time." Kyle isn't impressed so far, but I refuse to be discouraged.

We talk on and I relate some of the interesting facts I've run across in my reading. When I reach the story about the Lee-Jackson Day ceremony at the West Ridge Cemetery, he visibly grimaces. "Still hung up on that little cemetery? Why does it have you so fascinated?"

"Two reasons, big brother. First, Jimmy's explanation to you makes me believe Lester's car was parked near that burial plot. Could mean whatever he was doing had some involvement with West Ridge."

"Come on, Davey. Like what? Digging up bodies?"

That sends a shiver through me. It has never jelled in my mind, but a frightening possibility has just jarred me like a bludgeon.

"Or maybe he was burying one."

Kyle looks shocked and turns away for an instant. "You have a weird imagination. That's a creepy thought."

"Damn spooky, I'd say. But we can't discount anything at this point. He was using a spade to do something that seems odd given the time and place he chose. Somewhere out there is a maniac keeping an eye on us, and we have to outwit him before it's too late."

"What's our next move then?" Kyle asks. "I still don't think Len's going to be any good to us. You saw him yesterday, Dave. Now I know what people mean when they describe someone as clueless. Only it's not at all funny in this situation. We're in the crosshairs, and he's fumbling around."

"I uncovered another fact in reading through the articles on the Hurt girls, Kyle. The older one...Stephanie?"

Kyle shakes his head.

"She was found dead near the town of Linton, west of here, the next day. The police said she'd been run over on a back road and left. Called it accidental and never arrested anyone."

"How does that help us?"

"Maybe not at all. But I'm going out there today to ask some questions."

"But what could you possibly learn that will help us track down Lester?"

"Don't know yet, Kyle. But one thing is for sure. We need to close in on Kanicki—or whoever is making life difficult for us—and our time to do that may be limited. I can't just sit here and let him make all the moves."

"Just watch your step, Davey. It may not be safe for us anywhere right now, including wherever you're headed for the day."

"I hear you. Should take me the rest of the day. I'll talk to you tomorrow."

"Do me a favor," Kyle says. "Call me when you get back and let me know you're in town. Promise?"

There is an expression of concern on Kyle's face much like I must have shown those first hours after his severe beating.

"Sure thing. I'll call as soon as I hit town. Should be some time after dark."

I walk to my car and start to pull away. My cell phone rings.

"It's Mary Beth, Dave. Found what you asked for. Have it all right here on the front desk if you want to come by." I check the time and decide it's worth the delay.

"Be there in ten minutes, Mary. Thanks."

*   *   *   *

She is standing there patting a short stack of books as I enter the library.

"Pretty fast service," I quip.

"No, just not much business today," she replies. "Even took the time to read a bit about the battle myself."

I take the books back to a reading table. She's carefully identified each reference to Cloyd's Mountain with a book marker. A brief but ferocious battle was waged in an open valley between two ridges overlooking Back Creek on the east side of what is now known as Cloyd's Mountain. More than 2,500 men died that day in little more than an hour of fierce combat. Although major campaigns were conducted in Virginia for most of the Civil War, this was the largest to take place in the hills of Southwestern Virginia.

Brigadier General George Crook was sent with a force of 6,500 Union troops to take control of the area away from the Confederate Army. He was told to burn the strategic New River Bridge to cripple the Virginia and Tennessee Railroad, the lifeline for moving fresh troops and supplies to the Southern army. The Union forces, much superior in number to their foes, attacked and were repelled by the courageous but outgunned Confederates. Heavy losses mounted as the Union attacked again and again.

The battle of Cloyd's Mountain has faded into history, a minor skirmish when compared to the massive loss of life at epic struggles such as Antietam and Gettysburg. But for the men who died in that high meadow in early May, 1864, even for the ones who somehow survived, the swift slaughter on both sides must have been horrific. And young John Palmer was one of those who lost his life that day.

Three monumental figures played key roles in the battle. John Breckinridge, who had served as Vice President of the United States and was a Presidential candidate in 1860, commanded the Confederate headquarters in nearby Dublin Station. Active Union participants in the actual fight included Colonel Rutherford B. Hayes and Lieutenant William McKinley, both destined to live in the White House.

The more I read, the more absorbing it all grows, and I lose myself in the vivid accounts of the action. The Union troops advance toward the area guarding the strategic bridge below. The Confederate forces, bolstered by local volunteers, muster behind hastily constructed defenses to make their stand. The day is wet and gloomy, and I can almost smell the powder as the muskets hurl lethal shot toward both fronts.

"You are really into that battle, aren't you?" comes a soft whisper. I look up into Mary Beth's twinkling eyes and remember where I am. The wall clock shows I've been reading for more than an hour.

"Got to get a move on, Mary. Have lots to do today." I scramble to my feet, pick up the map I've copied and all my notes, and begin to collect the books to return to her.

"Never mind," she says. "I'll take care of that. And thank you, Dave, for the lovely flowers."

I automatically turn toward the front desk, and see that Jordan's has done a beautiful job on her arrangement. Must have arrived while I was submerged in my reading.

"Least I could do. You've made some important work in here much easier for me."

She's looking at me with a smile lifting her lips, a hint of something going on behind those eyes that only she knows about. I suddenly feel self-conscious, check myself over to be sure I'm all together and properly dressed.

"What?" I'm stumped.

"You never suspected, did you?"

"Suspected what, Mary?"

"That I had a crush on you. Thought you were one of the neatest guys in our class." Now her little grin has blossomed into a radiant beam.

All I can say is, "Wow!" *Never thought I had a chance with the acknowledged beauty queen of our school.*

A few minutes later I motor along the interstate heading west. Looks like a long day given my delayed departure, but it was time well spent. Now I've added a second stop that will require a detour off my route to Linton.

Chapter 25

I'm only a few miles out of town when my cell phone alerts me. I reach down and punch it to life in its cradle, and listen to the speaker.

"Daddy, I couldn't reach you at your hotel. I need your help."

"What's wrong, Melody? Aren't you in school?"

"Teachers' work day. I'm at home alone and Mom's at work."

"What's the problem, honey?"

"Mom and I had an argument last night, Daddy. She's against my dating until I'm sixteen. That's another whole long year. All my friends are already going out and having fun. I think she should trust me and let me date now. I was really upset. Said some mean things to her."

"Whoa. Slow down, sugar."

Helen and I have always had an unwritten rule about the end run Melody may be trying to use on me. We have never let her play off one of us against the other. I know what she wants me to say, but I can't. Wouldn't be fair to Helen.

"I'm just so frustrated, Daddy. She wants me to stay her little girl forever."

"Sweetie, I know it may seem unreasonable to you now. I agree you're level headed and trustworthy. But your Mom is only thinking of your welfare. Please understand that she loves you very much and only wants what's in your best interest. I say *you* should trust *her*. You'll see the wisdom of her decision later on. My folks looked a lot smarter to me the older I got and began to understand their reasons."

"But all my girlfriends…"

"They aren't you, Melody. You're very precious to both of us. We couldn't bear to see you hurt. Just give it time. You have lots of years to do what you want but only a few more years to learn some valuable lessons from the person who loves you more than you can ever imagine."

"I suppose so. But if she has all the answers, why are the two of you still at odds?"

She's stumped me for the moment. And if I'm so smart, what am I doing talking to my only child long distance?

"That's something that has to remain between Mom and me. We're working on it. You should in no way hold her responsible. Mom and you are, and always will be, the most important parts of my life."

"Wish I had both of you here to talk to. When will I see you again, Daddy?"

"Well, if I recall correctly, you have a big day coming up soon. Nothing in the world could make me miss your birthday."

"Oh, I can't wait!"

"Do me a favor. Cut Mom some slack, sweetie. I'll see you soon."

"Okay, I guess…"

"And, Melody, thanks for calling me. You know I'm always thinking about you."

As soon as our connection is broken, I punch in the pre-stored number for Helen at her workplace. She sounds a bit surprised at hearing my voice. "Why the call this time of day, Dave. Is something wrong?"

"I hope not. Melody called me. Said you two had words last night. She was feeling guilty for some things she said to you. But she believes she should be able to date now. Hope I got her set back on the right path. Told her to listen to you about dating, and that she should accept that you know what's good for her."

"Thanks, Dave. I'm just so edgy about the way some of her friends run around. It's too soon for all that. She's so impressionable."

"I understand, and she will, too, once she thinks about it. Give her a kiss for me. Tell her she's precious to both of us."

"Dave, when are you planning to see her again? You know her birthday is coming up on the 22nd. Do you think you could be here?"

"Already made a date to see her turn fifteen. I plan to spend that day with the two most beautiful women in the world. Want to come down and spend the weekend."

"Please don't disappoint her. I know how much she'll look forward to it."

"You can count on me, Helen. I love her. And I love you, sweetheart."

An awkward silence then the line goes dead.

* * * *

I drive out the Interstate and find the exit to Route 100 near Dublin. The site of the battlefield is on private property, but it's available to the public. Feel obligated to stop at the main house and ask for permission to walk around and explore where the battle took place. Tell the owner I have an ancestral tie to the skirmish. Want to see the grounds where my relatives fought. He's most congenial, and points me toward the meadow.

From my reading at the Springlake library, I've laid out this place in my mind. Even have my map from the library copier as a prompter. I study the map again when I pull to a stop along the road, trying to orient it to the actual landscape. I step out and walk onto the ridge, approaching the battle site with the awe of one about to relive history.

I haven't told Kyle this is the other reason for my quick trip. The details of the late night visit from the youthful ghost are strictly a matter between Private John Palmer and me. Okay, I did mention it to Mrs. S, but she's entitled, being the owner of the inn where John has now taken up recurring residence. The image of that young man with his soul in obvious torment won't go away. An idea pounds at me. If only I could understand the spirit's soundless words, they may help unlock a big mystery. And the question still gnaws at me—*How does that small cemetery fit into the Tank Hill puzzle?*

Peering out across the meadow toward Back Creek, I think about that day nearly 140 years ago. A day when the meadow was alive with the noise of battle. I close my eyes and hear the sounds, battle cries of advancing troops, the crack of musket fire and boom of artillery, anguished whimpers of men gravely wounded and dying.

When I reopen my eyes, it's as if I am actually in the midst of that fiery hell; the whole panorama unfolds before me. A cold rain pelts me; an unseasonable gloom hangs over the long ago May landscape. I shiver in the chill wind sweeping across the ridge. Men, horses and artillery bog down in the mud and sink up to their knees in the slimy muck.

I stand behind the Confederate defenders on a rise above their positions. Painfully I watch as time and again they labor to load and fire their muskets. The boys in blue from West Virginia charge forward and are caught up in a withering wave of musket fire. A thick cloud of smoke rises from the weapons to fill the distance between the lines of blue and gray. Gunpowder hangs in the air, the men's faces blackened by its flash. Above my head and on both sides come the whistles of Minie balls whizzing past. I hear the boom of cannon fire. Grape shot sprays the meadow, ripping and tearing at the soldiers exposed by the splintering of their crude barriers. The flooded ground underfoot tugs at me, sucks me down into its mire. Errant metal slugs hurl into the mud with dull thumps, and they send rooster tails of water spraying behind them.

Attackers and defenders alike fall with weapons in hand, their broken bodies strewn and steaming as the cold downpour reaches them. I feel their agony, share their suffering, sense the blinding fear as death reaches out to take their hands. They fall and cry out for loved ones, knowing the end is near. A steady wind buffets me. The cold stings my cheeks. I raise a hand to my face and find tears streaming down. My heart aches at the gruesome and senseless loss of life I know is destined to continue yet for months until a spring day at Appomattox finally ends the insanity of brother against brother, father against son.

Then comes the assault I already know the valiant troops in gray can't drive away. Colonel Rutherford Hayes and his Ohio unit advance in a relentless wave of blue that sweeps over and engulfs the defenders. The outcome is no longer in doubt. Even as a Union victory becomes a certainty, my eyes see only the suffering of the fallen on both sides, young men who proudly wear the blue, the gray, the nondescript garb of new volunteers from surrounding hills. Dirty, hungry men who lie dying in the quagmire below me. They moan and scream their hopeless pleas for help while they writhe deeper into the bloodstained mud that will be their final resting place.

The fierce struggle and the pall of death bring me to uncontrolled weeping. I spread my palms over my eyes and try to make the vision leave. But on that bloody ridge the wet and turbulent May meadow remains.

I wipe away my tears and scan the landscape. In my mind I am still on the battlefield of 1862. The combatants close and hand to hand skirmishes erupt all around me. The pitched battle lasts only minutes as the overwhelming Federal force prevail.

My eyes are drawn toward the road that borders the meadow. A lone Confederate soldier and his Union foe stand facing each other, their rifles raised and aimed for the final moment of truth. A soldier on a gray horse rides between them. The fed raises his barrel and fires, hitting the horseman instead. Faltering in the saddle, the feathered cap falling from his brow, the young reb aims his handgun and fires an errant round at the blue coat. Then the lad falls to the ground.

I move closer to the road as the smoke of battle slowly subsides. Three lonely figures loom before me. A muddy, weary soldier wearing the stripes of a sergeant holds his fallen companion in his arms, rocking slowly to and fro, his bearded face turned upward into the cold drizzle. His voice drifts to me in choruses alternating between a soft crooning and a wail of anguish. The third member of this somber trio is the gray *horse dutifully standing by, nuzzling at the fallen warrior for some sign of movement. His master lies critically wounded by the Minie ball deep in his chest.*

Without even feeling my steps carry me there, I draw nearer to the melancholy figures. Behind his beard and weathered skin, the older soldier appears to be at most in his mid-twenties. The lad he cradles is much younger. The dying combatant's wide brimmed hat lies on the ground and his hair is clogged with streaks of mud, but clearly the hair is long and blonde. On his burnished cheek he bears a large crescent-shaped scar. His free arm dangles, touching the muddy ground. I see something on one uniformed arm.

A small cluster of Federal troops has gathered around the two Confederate soldiers. They seem to share in the sorrow of the moment, not quite knowing what to do next. One blue-coated warrior finally steps forward and levels his rifle at the bearded rebel. His own sergeant steps in front of him and waves him off along with the rest of the group. The Federal sergeant kneels and helps the Confederate lift his dead companion across the horse, says something to him, and the gray clad sergeant leads them away down the dusty road.

As the present slowly reclaims me, my last glimpse confirms what has caught my eye. A colored patch sewn into the young soldier's sleeve—the Stars and Bars.

The intensity of what I have experienced drives me to my knees. For a long while I kneel there on that hallowed ground until I can regain control. Until today I could only wonder about the emotions one felt when he had a true revelation. Now I know. Back there in that lonely meadow I underwent a personal epiphany, not religious but nevertheless life-altering. Never in my thirty six years have I known the focus, the heightening of senses, the sheer intensity that vision brought to my every fiber. Driving down Route 100 to the Interstate I make a silent promise to the blonde youth who in my vision lay there in the arms of a man I believe to be his brother Ira.

"John Palmer, I've heard your plea. I don't know how just yet, but I *will* set your wandering spirit free. Then you can have the rest you so richly deserve."

Chapter 26

▼

He parks the brown car by the side of the road and waits. A chill February wind sweeps down across the ridge and crosses the open field, striking him full in the face as he steps out onto the gathering blanket of new snow.

"Trying my patience, litter brother. Hadn't bargained on standing out in the cold while you went sightseeing. What's so damned important about this place? Thought you'd headed up the road to that hick town where the girl tried to run away from me. You don't know yet the surprise I've arranged for you there."

The dark man laughs aloud, a shrill shriek of a laugh.

Lester reaches for the paper bag lying on the front seat, unscrews the bottle cap, and takes a long swig of the warming liquid. He wipes his mouth and withdraws the rapidly dwindling bottle of bourbon. Exclaims, "Damnation. All's between me and frostbite in this godforsaken place is half a bottle of bug juice. You better hurry and leave. We got an appointment on a narrow road."

The lone figure on the hillside back down the road finally turns toward his car and starts the engine. Lester ducks back into his own vehicle and mumbles, "About time." Lester kicks the car to life and spins away. Wants to be in Linton by the time Owens arrives. This could be an interesting night of fun.

He chuckles to himself, reveling in the pure irony of the moment. Not sure whether he wants to run him down, blow up his car with him in it, or merely scare him out of his wits and save the killing for a more up close and personal time. Well, it's his choice to make, and, after all, that's the real fun of the chase. Keep jabbing and feinting, keep him off guard. Bring him to a state of panic before he finishes him off. Tonight, tomorrow, a week from now—it really doesn't matter. They're all his sooner or later. Make them pay for their taunts and insults, punish them for being where they didn't belong when he was tending to business.

"Damn those boys. Damn those slut sisters. And this little bastard that almost ruined me with his foot and his teeth." He looks at the permanent scar on his arm and seethes with anger.

"I'll send him off with a bang, but first I want him to suffer, to worry about when it'll happen. Makes it more delicious that way."

He guns the brown car and drives back up Route 100. Somewhere soon, Dave Owens is going to get the shock of his life.

Chapter 27

My experience in the meadow on Cloyd's Mountain is so intense I lose track of the time, let the day slip away from me. I see the afternoon is rapidly passing and hurry toward Linton. Have to find the local police station and press my search for clues.

I walk through the front door onto a scene of jumble and disarray. Looks like a twister went through and carelessly tossed everything inside the sheriff's office and jailhouse. A uniformed man somewhere around my age looks up from sorting papers and asks, "Somethin' I can do for you, mister?"

"Need to ask someone some questions, but it appears I've come at a bad time." I peer around the room at the stacked furniture, the open boxes, documents piled everywhere. A pungent smell hangs in the air as if someone is burning paper.

"In the process of moving?"

"Wish it was that simple. Had a fire in here last night. Still tryin' to salvage records and see what the damage is." He straightens up with a pained look and places one hand against his back. "Man, all this liftin' and totin' is about to break me in two."

I take a closer look. See the blackened and crinkled edges on stacks of papers.

The officer grins at me and shakes my hand. Perhaps he's happy for an excuse to take a break from the drudgery. "Deputy Emmit Coleman. How can I help you, sir?"

"Owens. Dave Owens. Drove up from Springlake to ask about something that happened here quite a while ago. Involved a Springlake girl and a hit-and-run."

"How long ago?"

"About twenty five years."

He whistles and shakes his head. "I can't help with that. Only been with the sheriff for five years. Maybe he knows somethin' about it." He goes to the back and returns with an older man. "This is Sheriff Plunkett, Mr. Owens."

Plunkett shakes my hand and says, "Emmit tells me you're asking about that hit and run death we never solved. Don't get many unsolved deaths around here. Hell, I was just a rookie myself when it happened."

"Thought you might have the old reports, particularly if the case has never been closed." He gives me a disdainful smirk. Sweeps one arm in a big arc. Occurs to me I could have answered my own question. If they have any records of the hit and run, how would we find them now?

"You wanta dig into them piles and find the reports, go right ahead, young man. Right now I wouldn't even know where to start." Plunkett rubs his stubble and issues an exhausted sigh.

"Sorry, sheriff. You've got all you can handle without me asking questions." I shrug my shoulders and turn on my heels to leave.

"Wait," he says. "Might save you a wasted trip. You could go see Garth Jenkins. Seems that night was the highlight of his otherwise boring life. If I've heard him tell once how he was first on the scene, I've heard it a hundred times. Claims he saw the car that hit her, too. Couldn't tell us much else."

"How do I find Mr. Jenkins?" I ask with a new glimmer of hope.

"Lives out on County Road 26. That's where the girl was hit. Head down Main Street out here till you see the sign for 26 and turn left. Go 'bout a mile and a half. Look out on your right for a big old red barn near the road and a mailbox with a wooden chicken sittin' on top." He smiles and adds, "Old Garth's the biggest egg producer in the county. He's probably about the biggest talker, too, so I hope you're not in a hurry."

"Got all night. Sorry about the interruption, sheriff. Thanks for the tip."

"Wouldn't wanta lend a friendly hand, would you? Volunteer to help the local law enforcers? We got a real mess here." I shake my head and he grins. "Didn't think so. Oh, well, have a good one, Mr. Owens."

I follow the sheriff's directions. Drive out of town, and turn in at the big chicken sitting on a nest that turns out to be a mailbox. Have to give Jenkins a star for originality, anyway.

The man that answers the door is a strongly built, ruddy-faced man I judge to be in his sixties.

"Yessir?" he says through the screen door.

"Mr. Jenkins? I'm Dave Owens. I'd appreciate a few minutes of your time to ask you a couple of questions about the death of the Hurt girl out there on 26. Sheriff suggested I talk to you."

He looks me over. Seems to be searching his memory banks. Then with a bit of a sardonic grimace he says, "Sure took you long enough to git here, son. That was half a lifetime ago."

"I know. But it may be connected to some more recent trouble I'm looking into. I understand you were an eyewitness to the accident."

"You a lawman?" His tone is one of suspicion.

"No. I just have a large interest in this other matter and it led me to the hit and run."

He holds the door open; motions for me to come in. Shows me the couch where we sit down in front of his roaring fireplace.

Jenkins rubs his hands together and effects a shiver. "Cold as the handle on the shithouse door out there. Whole lot like it was the night that poor girl was run down. Early in the season then, but we'd had a cold snap and a healthy snowstorm. Musta been six inches or more of snow on the ground."

"Mind if I write this down?" I reach for a small note pad and my pencil. He seems all right with that.

"My girls down to the hen house was raisin' a real ruckus along about midnight. Such goins' on can really cut down on their egg output. Figured I had a fox roamin' around. Grabbed my rifle and sloshed out there in the snow."

I glance up from my notes to watch him poke at the fire. A wide smile lights up his face. He is in his zone telling about one of the most memorable nights of his life.

"Got the hens settled down and started back to the house when I heard somethin' on the road. Looked out to see a young woman runnin' hard as she could go screamin' *'Help, help'.*" I jumped and ran towards her. A car come hurtlin' along after her. Swerved acrost the road when the girl ran for the shoulder. Car fishtailed in the snow, bounced off somethin' and broadsided her hard. Threw her musta been ten, fifteen feet clean off the road up against my rail fence. Ugly sight. Terrible."

Garth grimaces and lifts his shoulders in a shudder.

"Did you make out the driver or see what kind of car hit her?"

"All happened too quick. Headlights blinded me when the car spun around. When I saw the car wasn't stoppin', I raised my rifle to shoot out a tire. But it was gone before I could squeeze one off."

"Then there was no clue to finding the driver?"

"Just one thing. Musta hit a big old rock at the side of the road when he slid. Left a streak of blue paint on the rock. Didn't see that till later. My concern was gettin' to the girl and helpin' her. But she was dead by the time I reached her." Garth rises from his chair, walks to the fireplace, stands with one palm against the brick mantle and his head lowered. I wait for him to compose himself.

"Do you remember anything about the police investigation? Any facts that came out afterward? Maybe more about the car or driver?"

"Mostly that they never got a lead and the case ain't been solved. They said she wasn't wearin' a coat so she musta run away from somebody in a big hurry. Found shards of glass buried in the snow. The car's headlight had shattered when it hit her. Police said it was probably from a Dodge or Plymouth. She'd been drinkin' an awful lot, accordin' to one of the deputies, cousin of mine. That's about all I can tell you."

"You've been a great help, Mr. Jenkins."

Garth apparently doesn't get many visitors out here. He spins off into tall tales about the backwoods and tells me all about his egg business. Insists I 'stick around a while and have a couple snorts with him.' He *has* been a big aid in my search for information and the whisky is warming after a cold day. Tastes so good after the beating I've taken from the winds that I temporarily ignore my resolution against all things alcoholic.

"Be honored if you'd take a bite of supper with me, Dave. Got some mighty hearty beef stew simmerin' away over there. Took a batch of fresh biscuits out of the oven when I poured that last pair of drinks."

Once he lifts the lid of the stew pot and I inhale the aroma, I am a willing prisoner for the meal to follow. We eat the hearty stew accompanied by the crackle of flames on the hearth and the faint buzz in my ears from two drinks, which is a couple too many. I savor the fullness the honest country cooking brings to my empty stomach. Realize I've been so absorbed in standing on that mountain and getting to the police station that I haven't eaten since breakfast. Push back my chair. Fold both arms over my newly acquired paunch.

"That's about the best stew I ever tasted, Garth. Guess it's been my lucky day getting steered out here to you. Found out what I wanted to know about the accident, shared some whiskey and interesting conversation with a great host. But that supper tops it all, my friend. You really know how to do a stew."

"Learned that from fixin' hunter's pot for all my buddies. Trompin' the woods gives you a man size appetite. Throw in whatever's handy, spice it up, and cook the dickens out of it." He casts a smug look my way and retrieves the whiskey bottle.

"No more for me, thanks. Got a drive ahead of me." I look across the room and bolt up from my seat so fast I nearly stumble. "Your wall clock shows it's almost ten o'clock. Is it right?" Glancing down at my own timepiece, I confirm the evening is almost gone.

Grab my coat and turn to shake Garth's hand.

"You just drop in agin if I can help with what you're doin', Dave. Enjoyed your company. Stay warm out there."

"Oh, I think you and I have enough antifreeze in our systems to keep us plenty toasty tonight." But I'm thinking to myself *Dave, you klutz, you did it again. Stay off the sauce and keep your head clear.*

*   *   *   *

I leave for Springlake with the cogs meshing in my head. Already I am fitting together the fragments that have been offered up to me. The accident involving a panicked girl happened near midnight some sixty miles away from Springlake. The girl, later identified as Stephanie Hurt, had been drinking heavily, as her blood alcohol test showed. Jimmy Moore had seen Lester near a blue car on Tank Hill earlier that night, and the rock on County Road 26 had a blue smear from a car's impact. The broken headlight and maybe a crumpled fender could have provided a solid lead twenty five years ago, but I couldn't imagine how we'd make that connection after all this time. Stephanie had been crying out for help before she was struck. Sounded more and more like an intentional hit-and-run, not just an accident. Some guy got her drunk, but she fought him off. He ran her down in a rage. If only I could connect Lester more conclusively. He certainly had the violent temper to lose it like that. And the two sisters were reportedly together that night. Where was her sister Valerie while all this was happening?

On the drive down a mountain road toward I-81, I realize how mentally and emotionally exhausted the day has left me. The booze at Garth's didn't help matters, either. I round a bend and swipe across my tired eyes with one palm. Suddenly an oncoming car comes into view. My eyes snap open, and I shake my head to clear the fogginess. The other car is veering onto my side of the road while I sit hard on my horn with no success. When I jerk the wheel to the right, my car careens onto the shoulder. Alarms sound in my head; my brain sends a hundred frantic instructions. I struggle with the steering wheel as the car lurches crazily. Operating on sheer instinct, I somehow manage to slow the car without rolling it. The rear end makes a shuddering move to the right then there is a jarring impact followed by motionless silence.

The sudden need to act and my panicked response have more than cured my overwhelming drowsiness. My whole body sings with the surge of adrenaline. My limbs tremble when I finally relax their tension. I slump forward, sense the wetness of my cheeks against the wheel and slowly release the stranglehold my fingers have on it. I hold my head with both hands. Reality creeps back in.

A quick inspection convinces me the rear bumper took most of the impact against whatever I hit—a rock, a stump, maybe just frozen earth. Won't have any trouble driving the car, but I don't want to push my luck too far.

I mumble aloud, "Davey, you are one lucky dude. Almost bought the big one back there."

Yes, I was far from alert when that brown car rounded the bend and came hurtling in my direction. Brown car? Could be my imagination working overtime.

I stare into the darkness ahead of me. Big floating flakes start to flutter onto the windshield. Within moments they come harder then begin to pelt the car. I turn on the wipers, but the snowfall is going to be too heavy to ward off. My face looks tired and drawn in the mirror.

"Owens, it's time you found a room somewhere and hung it up for the night!"

Chapter 28

▼

I don't wait to reach the Interstate. See a motel sign flickering on and off on the side of the road and pull in. Walk stiffly on nearly immobile legs toward the door of the motel office.

"Whooee! Shut that pneumonia hole. Come in out of the snow." A scrawny little man with gray stubble and a long-ash cigarette dripping from his mouth hugs his shoulders against the cold that follows me inside.

"Got a room for a sleepy traveler?"

If he doesn't, then all his clients are on foot because I see only two cars parked outside.

"B'lieve we might be able to squeeze you in. Sure don't need to be drivin' in that white stuff. Looks like a blizzard comin' on." He wheezes out a chuckle as he spins an old-fashioned register toward me to sign.

I scribble down 'D. Owens, Springlake, VA'.

"Not far from home are you? Bad timin' for this snowstorm, what with you might near home. Long trip, Mr. Owens?"

"Uhmmm," I mumble. No need for further explanation. In miles this has been a short trip, but I feel like I've traveled a century and a half on my weary quest since sunup. I don't think anyone, least of all this geezer, could understand the emotional ride I've been on today.

"That'll be forty two twenty with tax. Cash in advance. Prefer not to deal with credit cards, if it's all the same to you."

Hell, I'll pay him however he wants it if he'll just shut that annoying trap and find me a warm corner to curl up in for a few hours.

"Suits me fine." I offer two twenties and a ten, and he holds up both hands and shrugs. Guess the change can is empty. "Keep it," I say.

"Lemme see, where should I put you?" he toys with me.

"Anywhere you have a comfortable bed and lots of hot water. Maybe the Presidential suite?" I yawn and feel myself reeling. My eyes are more closed than open, and my mind is rapidly slipping into neutral.

With a cackle and a flourish, he says, "Sounds like 101, our finest room with a view."

Produces a key dangling from a hunk of tin with painted letters one-oh-one. Looks like the key to a service station john, but even that would be a welcome refuge the way I feel.

Have no illusions about the quality of my accommodations as I turn the key, but even that mental picture is a cut above what I face in Room 101. I try not to notice the worn fabrics of the chair and rug, the dresser top with cigarette burns and chips, the odor of something, maybe chlorine or disinfectant, hanging in the air. All I demand this night is heat in the room, enough blankets and a hot shower.

I stumble toward the bathroom, shedding my clothes as I go, and turn the hot water tap to full open. As soon as I feel the stream begin to turn reasonably hot, I place the stopper in the bathtub drain. Fight my way out of my clothes and watch the tub fill halfway. Then I pull the plug and turn on the shower. Plop down into the soothing water and put my head under the pelting hot spray. If I had a pillow, I think I could sleep right here. But I'd probably drown before the tub emptied.

Certainly wouldn't expect to find a terry robe in the closet or chocolates on the pillow here in the Taj Mahills. Maybe I can dry off and wrap myself in something to keep from chilling, Already turned the thermostat toward hot, but maybe that's beyond its range.

There's a chore to be done before I can sleep. Kyle wanted me to call him when I returned to town. Better let him know I'm sleeping over and give him an update. Let him know I'm safely tucked in where nobody could possibly find me, not even Lester Kanicki. Towel off and grab a cotton sheet blanket from the bottom dresser drawer. Smells musty, but I'm not choosy tonight. Wrap up tightly before dialing the telephone.

"Hi, Kyle. Decided to get in out of the blizzard. Man, it is slippery as snail snot out there. I'd rather tackle that in sunlight."

"Where are you, Dave?"

"Let's see. The pencil on my nightstand says I'm at the Sunny Morning Motel. It's somewhere on a state road north of Rout 81. Snowstorm got so bad it ran me off the road. Any port, as they say, and this place certainly meets that standard."

"So what did you find out?"

I avoid mentioning the trip to the battlefield. Still not ready to share my feelings about the young wandering ghost. Kyle would likely think me a tad off balance if I described John Palmer's visit to my room and my chilling experience on Cloyd's Mountain.

"Found a man who was an eyewitness to the Hurt girl being hit out on that county road, fellow named Garth Jenkins. He saw a car run her down. Turns out it was blue. Remember Jimmy said Lester was in a blue car that night. The girl was dead before Jenkins got to her."

"What about the local police? Did they have anything on the accident?"

"Police were trying to recover after a fire at the sheriff's office, so they weren't any help. It was the sheriff that told me about Garth. Suggested I go see him."

Kyle's voice changes pitch. He says, "Odd a fire broke out when you were about to check their records. Get the feeling this character that's stalking us is reading your thoughts?"

"Come on, Kyle. That's a stretch."

"Can't help it. This guy sounds insane. Wouldn't rule out anything he might try."

"By the way," I ask, "Have you and Billy talked about our near miss with the stalker at Snuffy's?"

"I told him. He's real torn up over this whole situation. Says he remembered some things we ought to know. Wants to come over to my house in the morning. I told him we'd be here."

"Wonder what that's all about?"

"Don't know, but I'll take anything that helps us close in and put this maniac away," is Kyle's answer.

"Give me time to find the Interstate and get some food in the morning. I should be along about nine o'clock."

"Make it 8:30 and we'll have breakfast here. Billy and I will be waiting. Be careful, Dave."

I pile into the raggedy bed, and hope no other living organisms are sharing it with me. Still feel guilty about my second slip with booze. Made a resolution long ago after my bout with alcohol to swear off for good. Then I broke that promise the night I took Meg to the Auberge. Don't know what got into me. Garth's invitation to share his bottle was also answered much too easily. *Don't backslide now, Dave*, I mumble to myself as sleep finally overtakes me. I feel myself slipping away.

Chapter 29

▼

Must be morning. Bright sunlight pouring through my window. Funny, I don't feel bad at all this morning. Should have an aftertaste like I've been drug through the Dismal Swamp mouth first. Jenkins' booze wasn't exactly the best bottled in bond I've tasted. I need a good ass kicking, too, for letting him talk me into drinking with him. But I guess I lucked out this time. Seven AM by my watch. That means I need to get moving. The hint of cleaning liquid is still in the air, and it's found its way up both my nostrils. I sneeze twice and rise onto my elbows.

Look down at the threadbare rug and the blankets with their tattered edges. Made quite a compromise last night in the face of weather and exhaustion. My only consolation is that it got me off the road. May well have saved my life considering what almost occurred on that winding mountain road.

Then I peer straight ahead at the far wall and come fully awake in shock. The dresser mirror is covered with bright red block letters. Someone has managed to get into this room while I slept and leave without my hearing them. Under the pile of warm blankets a chill reaches me. I realize I could be fortunate to be waking up at all.

I cross to the dresser. With each step forward I'm scanning the room to be sure I'm alone. Facing the mirror, I read the garish red letters written in thick beads of color. The words say 'YOUR TURN SOON.' Reach out to touch the writing and press down, feeling its thick softness. Smear a letter with my fingertip, leaving a red streak on the glass surface and a smudge on my finger. The consistency is one of...rub the red glob between my thumb and forefinger...soft and waxy...crayon, lipstick, candle?

Well, the clerk in the office surely didn't put it there. My stalker is back, and it's clear I'm not safe from him anywhere, not even out here in this desolate spot. I flash back to my fleeting glimpse of that car that nearly ran me off the road down the side of the mountain. More inclined now to believe that my eyes weren't playing tricks on me after all. I'd lay bets the brown sedan has a Virginia license plate that starts with two six. The handgun in my glove compartment has been out of the holster three or four times at most, but beginning today I'm keeping it close at hand.

Then I look back at the bed covers. Something isn't quite right. Walk over and inspect more closely. There on the blanket, inscribed in the same waxy red substance, is a crude 'X'. When I realize it was drawn approximately across my crotch as I lay in bed, I recall Lester's threat and shudder violently. *I already owe your brother…get my knife and neuter him.* Seems Lester wants me to experience the agony in my mind before I feel his blade.

I hurry and leave the Sunny Morning Motel behind me. The early going is a bit slick on the back road. But after I swing out onto I-81 where the road crews have done their work, it's smooth sailing to Springlake. Don't even bother to stop along the way for coffee. Can't help checking in my rear view mirror, though, for brown cars. No bandits so far.

*   *   *   *

I do briefly consider stopping off at the Barnwell for a quick change of clothes. Decide this is no day to begin with a confrontation with Meg. She's becoming an annoyance as well as a threat. For all my outward resistance to her, I am very much afraid she could break through the rather thin, artificial barrier I've thrown up between us. That is one enticing young woman, and she knows how to yank my strings. Despite my determination to fight temptation, my temperature seems to rise every time she walks into the same room. I have to get those pictures out of my head, visions of her lying next to me, supple, hungry, and demanding.

Stop it, Owens! My best defense is to avoid her completely until we can settle the matter of our relationship, or rather the lack of one, on Saturday night.

Kyle has asked Billy to stop by his house for breakfast and our planned discussion. I arrive in time to share Jenny's cooking. We eat quietly, the silence broken only by the normal little jabs to break the tedium. But our faces belie the fact that we have business lurking.

"Jenny, we're going to the basement for awhile," Kyle says, and we troop down the stairs. The wood stove is stoked, and the basement is toasty warm.

They've been known to sleep down here in the dead of winter with the stove roaring away.

"Tell Billy what you found out in Linton yesterday, Dave."

I retrace my steps for Billy's benefit. He perks up when I mention the blue car. "Jeez, Kyle. Remember Jimmy said the car…"

"I know," my brother tells him. "And listen to the rest of it."

When I get to the broken headlight, Billy's mouth drops.

"Yeah," Kyle says. "We were going to trash Lester's sorry old blue Plymouth the next morning after he scared us on Tank Hill. But we backed off. Thought about it and convinced ourselves he'd follow though on his threats if we messed with him. His car had a busted headlight and a banged up front fender. Jimmy noticed it."

"Sounds like that creep Kanicki did the hit and run sometime after he was on Tank Hill." Billy has just stated the painfully obvious.

I ask him, "What was it you wanted to talk to us about, Billy?"

"Well, I was sitting around thinking about this whole mess and it suddenly came to me. You know Kanicki had a reputation for chasing after young girls even though he had his own wife and kid. I watched him try stuff with girls right there in the theater. Saw him take more than one to the balcony, and I could imagine what was happening up there in the dark."

"So?" I ask impatiently.

"So him and Stephanie Hurt was getting it on pretty hot and heavy one night during the movies. He was letting her drink from his flask and her only seventeen. I mean, she didn't have the best reputation in town—but Lester Kanicki? Come on. There were plenty of guys after her. She didn't have to let him. Ugh!" Billy sticks a finger in his mouth and pretends to gag.

"Okay," I tell them. "Let's recap. We can put Lester on Tank Hill at, what, seven o'clock that Sunday night?"

"More like six," Kyle answers. "You know the sun sets early that time of year and it was just about dark."

"All right, six o'clock. Let me wing it and see where it take us. Lester has the two girls in his car. Probably picked them up at the movie that afternoon. Has them drunk by dark. The girls are riding around with him, but something goes terribly wrong. Valerie dies. Maybe Stephanie has passed out. He drives up to the little cemetery to hide Valerie's body in an existing grave. That's when Jimmy sees him."

"Oh, shit," Billy blurts out. "We could show he murdered that girl, or at least give a jury a lot to work with if they found an extra body in one of those graves. No wonder Lester wants all of our hides."

"Unless you've got a more likely story, that's the way it looks to me," I answer.

"Now can we turn this over to Darden and let him chase it down?" Billy leaps to his feet, walks nervous circles around the room.

"I think I agree," Kyle says.

"Wait a minute, guys. Think about it. What if Darden can't find Kanicki before he strikes again? So we hand the evidence to him—what does he do to keep Kanicki from coming after us?" Doesn't have enough people on his force to spare full time wet nurses for all three of us. A few days ago that was *your* position, Kyle."

"I know," he answers. "But I think we need to enlist all the help we can get now. Len has resources and methods we don't."

"Yeah, what do we do," Billy says, "just wait for him to pick us off whenever he wants?" His voice has a distinct note of panic.

"No. We force Lester's hand and pounce on him when he raises his ugly head."

They both look at me with doubt in their eyes, and Kyle says, "You make it sound easy. How do we pull that one off?"

"Not easy at all. Damn risky, but it's the only way to force his hand and get him out into the open. I set myself up as his primary target, and we snatch him when he strikes."

"No way." Kyle punctuates his edict by slamming his fist down on his chair arm. "He's already had shots at Billy and me and failed. He won't miss this chance to do you in, Dave." He gets up and walks away from us. Adds a log to the fire and punches at the coals, repeating, "No way, no stinking way."

"If we don't entice him to make his move," I protest, "there's no telling how long he could keep us running from our shadows. May even go after our families. We don't have a lot of choices, guys."

Kyle stares at me and asks, "How do you propose to pull this off without getting yourself killed or seriously hurt?"

"I have a plan I'm sure will work. Have to talk to somebody about helping us. Give me overnight, and I'll lay it all out for you. Then we can vote on which way to go if you still have doubts." I get two delayed and reluctant head nods.

"Okay, that sounds fair." Kyle still looks skeptical though.

"How about tomorrow morning at the Barnwell? I'll ask Mrs. S to set a couple of extra plates for breakfast. She'll be happy to see that Kyle's recovering, too."

We start to break up, and I turn to Billy. "Be on guard, friend. We're gonna gang up on this crud and put him away, but we all have to stay alive to get it done."

"I'll be there tomorrow. Just hope you know what you're doing, Dave."

Chapter 30

When I call Randy Bean with the promise of an important story, he agrees to see me at the newspaper office. Says he has time for a short visit if I can be there in half an hour. I'm standing in the front room of the Times within ten minutes.

"Mr. Bean…Randy, you were most helpful when I stopped in a few days ago. I have a scoop for you to break if we can agree on how to go about it." That clearly intrigues him.

"I don't know about pre-conditions, Dave. Tell me what you have and we'll see."

"This involves an old news item from years ago, the unsolved death of a young Springlake girl and a possible connection to her sister's death the same night. May even help solve a couple much more recent crimes."

Randy tries to look skeptical, but I know he's salivating to hear what I'm about to toss his way. Could be his big chance for fame. Breaking the story that unravels those two unresolved deaths and solves other crimes at the same time could bring considerable attention to him. He squirms and tries to control his excitement, but his concerted efforts are all too transparent. Got him hooked, I chuckle to myself.

"When did this happen?"

His voice is husky with anticipation. Clears his throat and grabs a pad.

"The girls? More than twenty five years ago. But you'll find there's never been a shred of a clue as to the reason for either loss. One girl was written off as the victim of a random hit and run, and the other has been listed all this time as missing."

"But how do you know all this, Dave? What's your involvement?"

"I've been doing some digging. My brother was the one who was mugged at the service station. Jimmy Moore was his best friend. You remember Jimmy, right?"

"Unfortunately, I remember Jimmy. That's another unsolved murder."

"Why don't we work on finding the answers to all three deaths, Stephanie and Valerie Hurt and Jimmy Moore? And to my brother's near miss. Interested?"

"You make it hard for me to turn you down. What's the risk to me, Dave?" Bean is shedding his reluctance, but he still obviously has doubts.

"There *is* one very large caution I have to issue, Randy. The guy we're setting out to nail could be a real nut case. He could turn on you for helping."

"Seems to me that's part of being a newsman. Lots of folks dislike me for exposing them."

"Not like this maniac, though. It's your call, but you'd be doing a great service to Springlake. Ridding the town of a scourge."

"I can't back away, Dave. This is too important. If you're right, nobody in town is safe until he's locked away."

I can tell that Bean's already hooked and landed. In fact, he's flopping in the boat. I've removed the hook and he still wants in on the action.

"We're going to smoke out the lowlife that committed all four crimes. I'll give you the facts, and you write the article. But it's key that you refer to me as an anonymous source, Randy. Make it sound like you're not even sure of my real identity. Maybe say I sent it in a letter or made a phone call to you. Use your journalist's imagination. I'm hoping the guilty party will figure out who the source is, and he'll come after me. That's when you're going to have an exclusive on the biggest news Springlake has ever seen."

"What about the police? What do I tell the sheriff if he threatens to come down hard on me."

"For what? Premature reporting of facts? You're doing him a favor giving him leads. Getting in his way? They called off the Hurt investigation years ago. Besides, even if they could force you to reveal your source, you've never really met me face to face. Right?"

The tradeoff should be too good to resist. This could make Randall Bean a name well known around the state, maybe even the nation. The risk is one he *has* to take.

"Just be sure you stay alert in case the loony decides to add you to his list of targets, Randy. And don't hesitate to call on the sheriff if you sense he's getting near."

"Okay, Mister Anonymous, let's get on with it," he says.

* * * *

That went even better than I expected, I reflect as I walk down Main Street. My conversation with Bean put him on the fast track to a new headline story for the Times. Gave him the information he needed to write the article. I've asked him to hold off printing it until Monday morning. Have to be sure we're as prepared as possible for the reaction I hope it will prompt. I look forward to zeroing in on that article, and my intended target will certainly be equally interested. We carefully worded the story, and I gave him just enough facts to whet Lester's appetite, wherever he is out there. Even dropped some clues about my identity in case Lester has any doubts. At this point no one can link Kanicki with what Bean is writing, so he'll have a strong incentive to silence me before I tell more. From now on, I'll keep my handgun on me and stay very alert.

Drop by Snuffy's for some lunch. Len Darden and one of his deputies are already laughing it up with the customers and gobbling their burgers on the fly. When I walk past Len, he drops a big, hairy arm in my path like a toll gate.

"Hope you're enjoying your stay, Dave."

"Turning out to be most interesting, Sheriff."

He thinks about that for a moment then asks, "How's my buddy Kyle?"

"Coming along fine, Len. I'll tell him you asked."

"Do that. And, Davey, I hope you're taking my advice and being a quiet visitor to our town."

"Just like a little mouse."

He holds up one thumb in approval. I smile to myself and walk past him to my booth.

After lunch I set out to do some window shopping. Not much left on Main Street except specialty shops. Most of the stores have moved to the malls in the nearby city. But there are a couple of interesting stores, and I need some time to clear my head. Events are moving too fast for me. I want to kick back, feel the cold air in my face and enjoy the sunny day while I mull over what it all means.

As I leave Barlow's Men's Shop with two new shirts in a bag, I sense someone on my heels. I whirl around quickly, and spot that same dark man in the long overcoat as he darts into the hardware half a block behind me. Take off at a dead run to catch up to him. The sidewalk is icy. Have to steady myself with one hand against the store entrance and skid to a halt.

A quick scan of the store tells me my quarry is nowhere in sight. I turn to the clerk and bark, "Man in a long dark coat. Came in seconds ago."

The counterman points a finger past me. "Went right through and out the back door."

I wheel in the direction he's pointing; charge past the counters of nuts and bolts, hammers and saws. On instinct I drop my bag and grab one of the ax handles standing in a wooden barrel. Wave it in front of me.

When I emerge from the hardware into the back parking lot, I hear a car engine come to life. Sprint in the direction of the sound. Brandish the ax handle like a club and hurtle toward a brown sedan, the same one I've seen once before. Twice if I can count the near miss on that mountain road. Without warning the scenery around me comes unglued. I stab at the ground with the handle to break what is about to be a nasty fall on the slick pavement. Hit the ground hard. In this case I'm more than happy to land ass first. The car speeds away, and I catch only the last digit on the license plate, a seven.

The clerk from the hardware store helps me to my feet. I hold up the axe handle. "Maybe you should label these things as life preservers," I tell him. "That might bring a higher price."

"Looked like a serious fall you took. Want a doctor?" he asks.

"No, I'm fine. But if I hadn't been holding this thing, both my head and your parking lot might have needed some major repaving. Did you see the car?"

"Sorry to say I didn't." He can't help laughing now that it appears I'm uninjured. "Too busy watching you. Thought for a second you'd do a somersault for sure." He loses it and doubles over with laughter.

"Damn. Black Beard slipped me again," I say and rub my butt.

Chapter 31

▼

Mrs. S has told me all along that I'm a special guest because of her affection for my mother. I invoke this privileged status, and ask if I can invite two guests out for breakfast. She doesn't disappoint me. In fact, she's excited at the news that not only is Kyle on the mend, he's coming to the Barnwell so she can see that for herself.

"Haven't seen that boy in ages. I know Ruby, bless her soul, would be proud of both of you."

"Well, he's a solid citizen. Can't say much for his little brother, though." I wink. She admonishes my flip attitude with a tsk tsk.

I manage to time our get together so we will be at the laggard end of the morning meal brigade. Don't want any extra ears within range. Kyle, Billy and I linger over our coffee and the room finally clears. All through our meal Meg hangs nearby, trying hard to listen in on our conversation. We stay as bland as possible until we are virtually alone in the room.

"Can I give anybody a warmup," she asks. We were just about to get down to the real reason for our gathering. I try to cover my annoyance at her interruption, and calmly make a request.

"Meg, can you bring us a pot of coffee? We want to move to the back corner and hold a very private conversation."

"Oh, that's quite all right. You just give me a shout. I'll come running with more."

"No, Meg. The pot and some quiet time. Okay?"

She turns on her heel and stalks away, a hurt expression setting her jaw and turning her mouth down. Has to be one of the most persistent, single-minded women I've ever met. She and I still need to have that long talk, though I now suspect it won't be a pleasant scene. Her looks are silken, but her claws are set, and I'm the quarry.

When I'm sure we're safely out of earshot, I open the serious part of our discussion.

"There are a couple of things I need to tell both of you. Haven't been totally above board with you. The situation we're in dictates that you know as much as possible." They home in on me, their eyes boring holes through me, probably wondering what choice bits I've withheld that may have placed them in even graver danger.

"First, let me tell you that the plan I proposed is in motion. It involves getting Kanicki's attention with the message that I can connect an unnamed person to three murders. Talked Randy Bean into planting a story in Monday's edition of the Times. We'll see how quickly it draws out Lester, or whoever has been stalking us."

Kyle reacts. "Don't like you playing decoy for that monster, Dave."

"It's all right. I know to stay on my toes, and I have a handgun at the ready. Billy has his weapon, and I suggest you protect yourself, too, Kyle. Don't you still have that pistol you used to shoot targets with?"

"Haven't fired that thing in ages, Dave."

"Well, now is a good time to dust it off and keep it handy. Get yourself some cartridges." His expression tells me I have finally gotten through that the showdown is coming. It's time we ganged up on our stalker. Kyle comes to grips with the need for defensive measures, and he gives me an affirmative head nod.

"Now, there are three other items I need to tell you about. I was on a mountain road in Pulaski County when a brown sedan ran me off onto the shoulder. Nearly flipped the car. I could have rolled down that mountain side. That's when I decided to get off the road. Spent the night at a cheesy motel and called Kyle."

"You think there's some connection to the rest of this mess?" Billy asks, and he rubs his head nervously.

"I'm coming to that. But first you need to know that when I woke up Thursday morning, someone had scrawled a message on the dresser mirror."

"Not sure I want your answer to this question," Kyle stammers. "What did it say?"

"Said 'Your Turn Soon'. That tells me I'm not the only target. We have to assume it's Lester Kanicki who's after all of us. The scary thing is he's playing games. He obviously could have killed me in my sleep. He also left a red X on the bed right where my family jewels would have been while I was sleeping on my back. Remember what he said about cutting me, Kyle?"

Kyle shifts uneasily in his seat, and the blood drains from Billy's face.

"One more tidbit. Remember, I chased that guy out the back door of Snuffy's the other day?"

"Yes, I told Billy about that. Didn't make him any too happy, either."

"Got that right," Billy chimes in. "Sounds like this son of a bitch is everywhere."

"When I left the newspaper office yesterday, I took a stroll on Main Street," I continue.

"Somebody followed me. Only caught a quick gander but it appeared to be the same guy. Had a beard and dark cap and wore a big black coat. Ran after him through the hardware. But I fell on the way. He got away in a brown car."

Billy comes unglued. "That's enough for me. Man, I'm through wettin' my pants every time a door slams," he squeaks. "Let's hang this on the sheriff and back out." I look at Kyle and he's pleading with his eyes. I'm outnumbered.

"Okay, guys. I give in. Time to pay a visit to good old Broadus Darden."

Chapter 32

When we all three walk into the police station with our determined looks, Len Darden is leaning over a deputy's desk, busy reviewing something with him. Our expressions must be revealing. When the sheriff looks up at us, it's with an air of disdain as if he already anticipates an argument. Even his greeting is combative.

"Well, what have you amateur sleuths been up to now? Got some more advice for ol' Len?"

I let that pass. "We'd like a few minutes with you, sheriff. I think it will be worth your time."

He wags his big old gourd of a head slowly from side to side. Len turns his back on us, and motions for us to follow him to his office.

Once the door is closed, he makes it clear we're not the most welcome visitors.

"I'm gonna hear you out, but this amateur detective bull shit's gotta stop. Don't need smart asses, local grown *or* imported, tellin' me how to run my business." He retreats behind his desk, points to chairs for us to pull up, and throws both booted feet onto his desktop. "Okay, spend your wad, fellers. You got five minutes."

I can't bear his pigheadedness any longer. At the expense of furthering alienating him, although that doesn't seem possible at the moment, I return fire.

"Damnit, Broadus, if you'd go into receive mode for a few heartbeats, you may learn something."

Wrong approach. He bristles when I use that old nickname. Probably thought it had been buried long ago. This is going to be like pushing a tractor uphill, but I had to get that out of my system. Conceited ass has gone too far with me.

Darden splutters and his big jowls flush pink. He fishes an unfinished stogie from his ashtray. Chomps on it and fidgets while his temper cools. "Clock's runnin'. Now you got less time than before."

"Sheriff," I continue, "We have a stalker out after all three of us. He's very likely the same one that mauled Jimmy Moore, killed Sam and cut Billy. He's breathing down our necks, Len. We need to know for a certainty what you're doing to stop him."

"What kind of cockamamy story is this? Man, Davey, you got too damn much imagination for your own good. We got leads on both killings and we're workin' 'em. Don't you get in the way or I'll run right over you. Leave boot tracks all over you."

"When you're through flapping your gums and threatening us, I have some information that may help you, sheriff."

I'm as riled up as Darden is now, not taking any more of his bullying. He hasn't changed in twenty five years. Still a big blowhard.

My outburst catches him off guard. He rises halfway out of his seat then plops back down. Extends one big arm toward me palm out. "Okay, you got the floor, but this better be good."

"Sorry about the attitude, Len. Just seems you aren't listening to what I'm trying to tell you. We truly believe all three of us are in immediate danger, and we don't see anything happening to corral this crazy that's after us. I think you'll understand after I tell you all the things that have happened the past few days."

The sheriff seems to calm down a bit. He reaches into a desk drawer and finds a fresh cigar, makes it ready and lights up. Not that I would have accepted one, but in his typical fashion he doesn't even offer smokes to any of us. He fills his cheeks with smoke, and rares back in his chair. I slowly, carefully relate our suspicions about Lester Kanicki. Tell Len I'm convinced Lester is the one behind the deaths of Jimmy Moore and Sanjay Samderiya, Kyle's beating and the attack on Billy. When I repeat the tale about that night on Tank Hill he scans back and forth between Kyle and Billy. Silently questions them for agreement, and they nod to back up what I'm saying. I'm beginning to think I finally have a willing listener in this big blonde bag of wind.

When I reach the part where I start to connect Lester to the hit and run in Linton and repeat Garth Jenkins' words, the sheriff tips his chair forward and hunches across the desktop to stare at me. My two sightings of the mystery man perk up his interest, particularly since he had barely missed the incident himself at Snuffy's.

"Wish I'da had a crack at him. We'da run his ass down and *solved* this little problem for good."

"Wouldn't call it a *little* problem, sheriff. It could cost any of the three of us our lives."

I go on with my accounts of the car running me off the mountain road and the threatening messages on the motel mirror and bed. Len is listening, concentrating now, and I sense a breakthrough. He stands up and walks to the window, looks out onto Main Street and goes silent.

When he turns to face us, Darden answers with noticeable hesitation. "I can see how you could make a case, but there's no hard evidence. Can't tell you any more, but we have leads to suspects in both the Moore killing and Kyle's mugging. Can't say we've had a breakthrough on the station attendant's killing, but we will. Damnit, Owens, I can't go charging around in all directions on supposition and a bunch of maybes."

"If you don't believe me after I tell you the most horrible part of all, I don't know what else I can say, Len. A package was delivered to Kyle days before that bastard attacked him at the service station."

"So?"

"Remember you slipped and told me Jimmy had been butchered? In the package was Jimmy's severed tongue. Had tooth marks where it had been ripped out. This guy is a lunatic."

Darden visibly reels, and I'm sure I see his knees buckle for an instant. There is no way I could have known about Jimmy's tongue being bitten off. I can see it seeping into his skull at long last. Maybe I'm telling him the truth after all. He stumbles back to his big swivel chair and sits; rests both elbows on the desk and mumbles, more to himself than to us.

"Shit and two makes three. I'm sorry, Dave. Is there more?"

"The package had a note inside." I repeat to him the language in the threatening message. "It was signed 'K'. Lester's our man, Len, I'm sure of it."

"Well, now, *that's* a problem. We got no clue where Lester Kanicki could be. We know he served 18 years of his 25-year sentence for manslaughter. From what I read about the case, how he maimed and killed that guy in the bar, Kanicki shoulda rotted in jail for the rest of his life. Weak-livered jury let him off too light then some softhearted parole board turned him out. Wasn't on the street more than three or four years before he was sent back for drug dealing."

"Real winner, huh?" I toss at him. "Then why can't you track him down?"

"Because, smartass, they freed him again last year. Parole officer's been looking for him ever since. Lester just completely vanished."

"Don't you see, Len?" I pound his desk and stare him down. "Kanicki is a two-time loser. With convictions for manslaughter and drug dealing, he's run out of free passes. This time he'd go back for life as a three-time felon. Could be facing the death penalty for any one of four murders, the Hurt sisters, Jimmy, and Sam. Lester's out of options. He's willing to kill as many times as it takes to avoid facing another jury."

Darden leans across his desk and sneers at me. "Can't lock him up if nobody's able to find him. Hell, he could be dead by now. Maybe got into another bar brawl and some other nut made ground meat out of *him* with a broken beer bottle. That'd be poetic justice, wouldn't it?"

"You don't believe that. He's right here in your town, and he's outsmarted us all," I tell him. "While we sit around wringing our hands, he's deciding when and where to strike next. How many people does he have to kill before you stop him?"

The big man trains his sad eyes in turn on each of us and says, "Guys, I barely got enough men to go around now. Can't spare anybody for protective details. Maybe one rover to check on all of you periodically."

I stare across at Billy with my 'told you so' look, and he's obviously reached his limit.

He explodes. "So unless you catch him in the act of killin' one of us, you don't have a clue how to arrest him. Not good enough, Darden. You supposed to look after folks, and I don't see it happenin'."

"Told you we have other leads, and we'll act on what Dave's given me today. Takes time to pin these things down."

Kyle calmly adds his voice to the din. "We don't have any time left, Broadus. You either nail him or he takes three more people down."

Len is so engrossed he doesn't even react to Kyle's using the derogatory nickname. I'm sure for Kyle it was merely an innocent flashback to their friendship as youths.

"Listen," Darden begins. He jabs a finger in my direction. "I'm not gonna say this again. We'll do what needs doin' the right way. My deputy will take down everything you tell him, and we'll get on it. You're only gonna screw up whatever we do with your muckin' around. Cool it or get the hell out of my town. I'll dump your scraggly ass in one of those cells back there for the duration of your stay in Springlake if you don't butt out of my business."

"On what charge, sheriff? Aiding and abetting the sheriff's department? Shoring up the weak arm of local law enforcement?" I start to get to my feet, but Kyle reaches over and places a hand on my arm to rein me in.

"I'll think of somethin'," Darden returns. He stabs the air with his cigar. "Yeah, you *better* talk some sense into him, Kyle. He's walkin' a thin line."

Len turns me over to a deputy, and he closes his office door to make it plain he's through talking to the three of us. Kyle and Billy sit glumly by while I help the deputy document the facts I've given to the sheriff. When I spell out the details of the package delivered to Kyle, the policeman stops and squints up from his keyboard.

"We see some pretty bad stuff. Thought when I looked into Moore's bloody mouth and saw that jagged stub of a tongue, I'd come full circle. What sick mind would taunt your brother with a thing like that?"

"The worst mind you could ever imagine. And he's out there somewhere just biding his time."

When we leave the police station, not one of us says a word on the way to the parked car. In fact, we're nearly to Billy's house before Kyle breaks the heavy silence.

"Not very reassuring, huh?

"I'm not surprised," I flip back. "Guess we had to see for ourselves how little we can depend on the sheriff. It's up to us now if we're going to outwit Kanicki."

Billy sits in the back in constant motion, fidgeting all over, stuffing gum into his mouth until he's chewing on a huge wad. "Can't take this any more, guys. I'm so edgy I'll probably shoot the first person steps through my front door just to be sure. Hell, I'm gonna be dangerous to my neighbors, maybe even my own family. Feel like I wanta go somewhere and hide."

"Keep it together, Billy. You panic now," I tell him, "you're only making it easier for Lester to get at you."

Kyle sits quietly, staring out the windshield at the light mist starting to fall from gray skies. "Not the best day I've had," he says softly.

Chapter 33

Saturday morning. I greet the day with new energy but a feeling of impending disaster. Everything around me is in fast forward. The facts are piling up. We're heading for a showdown with our stalker. Darden has agreed to get moving on the case. I have high hopes that my future with Helen is looking better. Kyle is definitely on the mend but not yet back to normal. Long time till golfing weather. I'll know he's okay when we take a turn around the links together.

But the dark man has appeared twice in four days. He's definitely getting bolder. Does he actually *want* to be seen? Is he flaunting the fact that he can get near me any time he chooses? No doubt now he's the one that forced me off the road. Lester's the one that left the bone-chilling message on the motel mirror and made the ceremonial X on my bed that pained almost as much as a real blade. If he wants to jangle my nerves, he's doing a good job. Have to force him out into the open on my terms as soon as possible.

The story Randy Bean and I planted in the Monday Times will call Lester's bluff. That is, if it really is Lester stalking us. If not, I don't know where to turn next. What I want now is to force him to actively pursue me, try to get to me. Randy's article will leave the impression that his "anonymous source" is about to tell all, a disaster Lester can't allow. I haven't mentioned that plan to the sheriff. That would only speed up my confrontation with him that's bound to happen soon. And he has the badge to back him up.

I greet Mrs. Starkey when she scurries in from the kitchen with my morning coffee.

"My, you're looking chipper this morning, Mrs. S. Have a lightness to your gait and a million dollar smile. Makes me feel brighter just watching you."

"Have you looked out the window, Dave? It's a glorious day. Temperature's still below normal and the snow is like white powder. Have a new dusting of flakes from last night. Looks like a picture postcard."

"I know it was a wonderful night for sleeping," I respond. "Went out like a light and slept straight through."

"No visitors?" she poses and lifts an eyebrow.

"Oh, you mean...no, just peaceful rest."

John Palmer has been in my thoughts. I'm still reeling from my experience on that rainy battlefield. The images were so stark and real. But the young soldier hasn't returned to my room.

The scene outside the dining room is stunning, I note and sip my coffee. Reminds me of winters past in Springlake when we scampered in the snow, crouched behind fortresses of stacks of firewood to pelt each other with snowballs. Crisp days when we huffed and puffed our way to the top of Tank Hill, and I faced that awesome, terrifying downhill run.

When I remember the hill, my nemesis, I suddenly find the scene framed in my window not so exhilarating after all. I tear my eyes from the snow-covered lawn and hover over my cup. A chill works its way down my back.

"Good morning, stranger. Been avoiding me?"

Meg is standing near my shoulder, coffee pot at the ready, quizzing me with her dewy brown eyes. She's waiting on tables wearing one of Mrs. Starkey's bright aprons with its starched lace fringe over a simple cotton dress. But she does things for that apron and dress that render them almost obscene.

"We seem to miss each other in our comings and goings," I offer. "How's the Barnwell treating you, Meg?"

"Just what I needed. And I have the best boss in the world. She's a darling lady. Want me to warm you up, Dave?"

Funny how her words reach my ears in a whole different context than she means. Or do they? I confess I am fascinated by the way the sunlight pours in the window and casts golden flecks in those beautiful eyes.

"Oh, coffee. Yes, I could use a refill."

I look at the upward curve of her lips. She knows full well how her question threw me off balance. She leans forward and pours. More than her apron presses into my shoulder. I want to be annoyed at her boldness, but my hormones won't allow it.

She sweeps closer to my ear and says softly, "Don't forget we have a dinner date tonight."

Meg doesn't wait for my reply, just whirls and moves away to fill the cups at the next table. In the rush of events, I'd totally forgotten about tonight. My visit to her and Trevor will be my chance to set matters right. Have to be firm and decisive this time. She believes we have some sort of budding romance. She's working hard to fan the flames. Well, it may not be a showdown to rival my baiting of Lester, but it's a hurdle I have to clear. We'll have a nice evening together. Trevor will get his wish. Then Dave, old boy, you've got to suck it up and put an end to her false hopes. Helen and Melody own you. It's time you made that clear—to Meg and to yourself.

When I get up to leave the dining room, Meg is hovering in a corner. She looks at me, and her reminder about tonight still hangs in the air. I give her a head nod that brings a smile to her face.

*   *   *   *

Stop at the mall to buy a gift for Trevor. Nothing extravagant, just a token to show I genuinely like the little guy. Have them gift wrap it. Half the excitement for a child in receiving a present is the thrill of opening it. If things go as planned this evening I may not be seeing Trevor again. No way to predict how Meg will react when I hit the off switch on something already gone too far.

The small house on Juniper Street is lit up, and the porch light glows a welcome. Meg's battered white van sits in the driveway, its windows frosted and patches of ice still clinging. I pick my way along the brick walk to the front door. A couple of near misses on parking lot pavement have me leery of my footing.

I ring the doorbell. A charming young man in a suit and bright red tie answers. Trevor peers up at me with his most grownup face. "Howdja do, Mister Dave. Please come in."

Meg is standing across the room beaming at her little man. Trevor grasps my hand and leads me to her. "My friend Mister Dave is here, Mommy."

"Quite a guy, this Trevor," I tell her. "Think I may have something for him." I hand him the package I've been holding behind my back. His eyes sparkle, and he sits down to open it.

Meg giggles. "He's planned the whole evening, Dave. Decided he wanted to wear his suit then told me what I should wear."

I approve of his choices for both of them. She looks like a fancy wrapped present in a low-cut red dress and red pumps. Wonder if she arranged the small red bow at her shoulder to be the secret to opening my own delicious package.

But I strain to push back such thoughts. Remind myself why I'm here—to bow out of her plans permanently.

Meg has a pitcher of martinis and snacks set out. She pours our first round. I take my glass but leave the drink untouched. Trevor finishes opening his box. Finds the shiny truck I've brought him. He runs over to give me a big hug. "Thank you, Mister Dave. How'd you know I like trucks?" he asks.

"Little bird flew by and said 'Trevor looks like a truck man.'"

He grabs a handful of munchies and returns his attention to playtime.

"He's really special, isn't he, Meg?"

Her tone is sincere, almost dramatically serious when she answers, "He's all I could ever want in a son." Her eyes mist over.

"You never told me about his father."

"Takes after his daddy in so many ways. The hair, the eyes, even the way he moves. But he's even better looking."

"And where is his dad now?"

She thinks about that for a long moment then answers in a near whisper, "Drowned in the river. Trevor was only a year old."

"Sorry." I can tell she doesn't want to pursue this subject. "Do you have family nearby? Other than Marcy, I mean." Meg composes herself.

"Just her folks. My aunt and uncle and Marcy's little sister."

Trevor chimes in, "Fambly? How 'bout…?"

Meg cuts him short. "You'd better hold off on those snacks if you want to leave room for my fried chicken." He drops a handful of crackers and returns to his truck.

"You didn't answer, Meg. About your family."

"Lost track of my mother years ago. She walked out on my father. I do see him now and then, but he lives too far away to come more often."

She steps to the kitchen. Brings back the pitcher to refill our drinks. "You've hardly touched your martini. Something wrong with it?"

"No, Meg, it's fine. Remembered a New Year's resolution I've already broken twice. Time to start keeping it. Swore off alcohol."

"Didn't stop you on our first date," she chides.

"That was the first of my two slips. No more for me, please."

She frowns then tries to cover her surprise, maybe her disappointment. "I admire people with will power. Then I'll have just one more." She pours then sets down the pitcher, and snuggles closer to me on the couch.

"Now it's your turn. Tell me about the mysterious Mister Dave. I know you live in Atlanta and have one child. But you're not living with your wife. So?" She pumps her hand to prompt me for the next installment of my life story.

Trapped, I grumble to myself. "She and my daughter live in Raleigh. I got too busy making my fortune, and we sort of drifted apart."

"And you told me you grew up somewhere around here."

"Born and raised right here in Springlake. Even lived here for awhile after I married."

I'm ready to meet our problem head on and get all the words out. Search for my opening line, but Trevor comes over and tugs at Meg's arm. He pulls her down to his level and whispers something to her.

She sighs. "Bookmark it right there, Dave. I want to know everything about you. But Trevor says he's hungry, so I guess it's dinner time."

I came so close. Maybe I should just say, *Thanks but no thanks, Meg. There's no way this is working out, now or ever. So long!* But that wouldn't be fair to the boy. Surely there will be quiet time after he's down for the night. Then we can get this whole thing settled. I want to help this lovely young woman and her son any way I can. But she has to understand I'll be her friend, nothing more.

The chatter over dinner is directed at Trevor, but there's a decided undertow. I get the strong impression we're using him as a conduit to reach each other.

"Tell our guest about your school, Trev." He looks at his mom, and she encourages him.

"Well, I'm in kingergarden. Teacher says I'm a good reader, and I like my numbers. Let's see, what else?"

His question is directed across the table, and Meg quickly takes his prompt. "Tell him about how you love to draw."

He hops down from the table. Meg shakes her head. "Get back here and finish eating, young man." But he scoots away.

Trevor reappears holding up a drawing. He's carefully drawn and colored with crayon the picture of three people, a little boy and two larger figures. He hands it to me proudly and waits for my reaction.

"I see somebody that has to be you right here standing with a pretty lady. And a man up in the top corner looking down at both of you. Tell me about it, Trevor."

He crawls up on my lap. Points his finger at the woman with yellow hair holding his hand in the picture. Meg clears her throat nervously and watches.

"That's my Mom. She likes my drawing."

"And the man? The one up here?"

He touches the other figure with his palm almost like he's caressing it. "This is my daddy. He's in heaven."

"He has black hair and dark eyes like you." Trevor nods yes.

"I like your drawing, too, Trev. Wish I could draw like that."

"Now get back up here and finish that chicken," Meg tells him. "Or there'll be no dessert for you, mister."

She's said the magic word—dessert. He busies himself with cleaning his plate.

"Does everybody in this family have black hair except you?" I ask Meg. She shakes her head.

"My mom was a blonde. Guess I've always been partial to dark haired men. At least up until now."

I let her words hang and fade.

*   *   *   *

Much later Trevor's evening comes to a close. He's played himself out and his suit, pitifully rumpled by now, has been replaced by pajamas. Meg says something to him, and he comes over to shake my hand. "Glad you came to see us," he intones in his adult voice. A healthy yawn escapes.

I can't help myself. He's so adorable. I kiss his cheek. "Good night, pal. You're a great host." He waddles over, takes Meg's hand and goes off to bed.

When she returns, Meg wastes no time resuming our earlier conversation. "You were going to tell me more about yourself—and your family."

"My brother, his wife and two sons still live here. Came to town to see them."

"No. I mean the family in Raleigh. You're separated?"

It's launch time, Dave. Get on with it.

"Meg, I've been trying to say this for days and kept backing away. Yes, I'm separated from my wife, but I hope that's coming to an end now. Those two girls are the most important people in my life. I'm about to right things with them."

A concerned frown creeps across her face, and she visibly stiffens. I think she knows what's coming even before the words are out. She obviously doesn't like the feeling.

"Meg, you're a lovely, desirable woman. Witty and charming. Someone to be prized and cherished by the right man."

Her frown transforms into a look of pain. She places her hand over my mouth.

"I don't think I want to hear the rest. You don't know what I feel for you, but I can show you in so many ways." She slips even nearer. Her warmth sweeps over me.

"No. Damn it!" I jump to my feet. "You have to listen to me. God knows, it's been hard keeping my hands off you. At any other time you'd have to fight me off. But I'm about to put my life back together. One more backslide and those chances are gone. You and I have no future other than as friends."

She's coiled on the sofa ready to pounce. Meg launches her attack, but it's strictly verbal.

"Then why did you encourage me? Why lead me to believe you had feelings for me?"

"If I gave that impression, I'm sorry. Sure, I wanted you but not in the way you think. It was purely physical. There were moments when I wanted you so much I'd have taken you in the middle of Main Street if you'd offered. But I made one mistake, and I'm not about to repeat it. Please understand."

Now she loses control, and her assault turns physical. Leaping to her feet, Meg pounds my chest with both her clenched fists. No weakling, this woman. I find myself retreating, my chest stinging with the force of her blows.

"Damn you, damn you," she repeats over and over. "I wanted to give you everything. I hate you, Dave Owens."

She looks up at me with tears streaming down her face. Without warning, her eyes soften. She presses her lips to my mouth and kisses me deeply. Then I feel a warmth on my chin, and I wipe the back of my hand across it. She's bitten my lower lip.

I rip her away from me, and she lands heavily on the sofa.

"No more, Meg. I could have been your friend, but it's all or nothing with you." I find my coat and start for the door.

"Wait, Dave. Please. Give me a minute to collect myself. You affect me like no man ever has before." She gulps down the remainder of her martini then takes a deep, calming breath.

I blurt out, "Sorry I pushed you so hard. You startled me. My lip hurts like hell."

She starts up from the sofa then holds out both palms in a gesture that tells me she will keep her distance.

"As much as I want it to be different, Dave, I know your mind is made up. We're natural together. If it can't be more, I'll accept for now that we're only friends. Just remember that if things don't work out with your wife, you have another option. That's all I ask."

I gaze deep into those big browns. Try to find sincerity, but there's no clue there. Her turnaround is entirely too abrupt to buy on face value. I want to think about this. But, for the moment, it gives me a way to exit without having to run for my life.

"I know you're going through some rough times, Meg. I'll help you and Trevor any way I can. Money isn't a hurdle. And you deserve a hand."

She follows me to the door, carefully keeping a safe distance between us. I'm at least hopeful one worrisome crisis has passed.

* * * *

I drive through the freezing night back to the Barnwell House, mount the hill and park. My watch shows nearly ten o'clock. This has been another bummer of a day. I seem to be running harder and losing faster with everything I try to do.

I reach for my cell phone.

"Hello." The voice is drowsy and edgy.

"Helen, it's me. Didn't wake you, did I?"

"Sitting here reading. You know I'm a night owl. Why the late call?" I can hear that she's annoyed.

"Just wanted to talk to you. Sometimes a guy needs to hear a special voice to right his world."

"Something's wrong, isn't it, Dave. I can hear it in your voice."

"No, honey. Suddenly I have this overwhelming feeling that absolutely everything's going to be great." We both go silent.

"So, is that it?"

"No, honey. I want to talk. Hear you talk. Sit here and think about better times."

Where are you, Dave?"

"Sitting in my car, Helen. Outside the Barnwell House. It's a frosty night. Lots to ponder, but your voice is so soothing. Talk to me, baby, really talk to me."

"You're scaring me, sweetie. Are you sure you're okay?"

I do a double take. She hasn't called me that for months. Is it a slip born of genuine concern or something more? I'll choose to believe she used the term on purpose. Right now I desperately need to believe that.

"Helen, honey, I'm as right as I can be with you there and me here. I want us together again. Us and our sweet Melody. It can't be soon enough for me."

"Dave, promise me you'll be careful. I have a queasy feeling you're not telling me what's really going on up there. Promise you'll take care?"

"For you, Helen, anything. I can't wait to see you again. I love you, lady."

She replies but her words are clipped. I want to believe she answered in kind, but there's no way of knowing for sure. Now the line is dead.

Chapter 34

▼

No choice. I have to face another problem head on. My dilemma with Meg Kane's playfulness is only a temporary matter. This other challenge is something that's plagued me for more than twenty five years. It's Dave versus the monster hill. Best I face it in the bright sunlight of a midwinter day. I could never do this in the dark. My gloves and wool stocking cap are in place, my oversized galoshes flop on my feet. It's now or not at all, Dave.

One last chance to back down. I take full advantage of the opportunity. Tank Hill is only a short walk across the fields in back of the Barnwell House, but I'm still hedging. Leave by the front door, walk down the long drive and onto the sidewalk on Main Street. My first test of will power is at the bottom of the drive. Have to force my feet to turn left in the direction of my dreaded destination. My footsteps fall ever slower. I'm consciously delaying the time when I have to turn and face that hill.

I hunker down inside the collar of my down jacket and blow out my quickening breath. It's only a block to walk, but my legs seem heavier with every step. I know my fear is unreasoned. Some would say it's downright silly. A grown man faced down by an inanimate object. But my long held fright doesn't need reason or explanation. It's there inside me, and it's as real as ever.

Now I have a fresh reason to loathe that hill. It holds the answer to why my brother and his friends have been under a long-term death threat. A threat that may soon be carried out by a crazy man. I think Kyle is as frightened by Tank Hill as I have been for most of my life.

At the small brick church I turn and walk the curbing. There was a gravel road when I last stopped by this side of the hill. Now a paved street leads to a cluster of homes. I know the dreaded rise is looming on my left, but refuse to look up and acknowledge it. Finally, I stop and lower my head. Can't avoid the showdown any longer. I turn slowly and peer upward, my palms wet, my mouth as dry as overdone toast, trembling. It's not the cold that chills me, it's the thought of the climb I have to face and finish. My head spins as my eyes move slowly up, up to the crest of Tank Hill.

"Well, Kyle," I whisper into the wind, "I always had you to protect me before. This time I'm on my own. It's just that mini-mountain and me. Wish me luck."

My first shaky step onto the snow-covered slope pierces the white crust. I sink halfway to my knee into the cold wetness. Nearly break and run. But to where? No more turning back.

Cast a last tentative squint into the glare of the morning sun and trudge forward.

"Only takes a step at a time, old boy." Now I'm working overtime, giving myself pep talks.

Each halting step is followed by a long pause and a quick glance ahead of me. The monster hill seems to rise up and defy me. It swells and grows steeper. Years of pent up frustration and cold fear wrack my body. The small voice of a child pleads over and over, *'go back, Davey, please go back.'* I clamp my jaw and cover my ears to drown out the voice of that youngster. He's trembled for too long at the thought of this behemoth. Now a grown man, he stands shivering in the cold, afraid to look up, humming under his breath to drive away the gathering demons of doubt.

Tromp, stumble, plop. My progress is slow, but I look back and see my footprints multiplying. I fall and pick myself up, fall again and struggle through the drift. My worst mistake is when I have scaled more than halfway to the top. I twist around to look back toward the bottom of the hill. All of the old paralyzing fear of that long drop closes in around me. Spin and struggle upward, leaning forward to free my boots from the deep snow's pull, falling face first in the snow and biting into its iciness. Panic stricken, I flail and attempt to stand upright, only to find that I'm sliding, rolling backward toward my starting point. When I come to rest lying in my own chilling wallow, I take in short, fast gulps of air that sear my lungs.

My first impulse is to dig down into the white blanket of snow, pile it over me and let it hide my embarrassment. I lie face down for long minutes. The snow burns my cheeks, turns bitter in my mouth. Force myself to roll over, lie on my back and squint up into the sunlight. Even with the bright red sun blazing overhead, the cold soaks through every corner of my body. I make a conscious effort to move my limbs, but the fear and the cold halt even the slightest movement. A sudden fright sends emergency signals to my brain. If I lie here long enough, someone will find me frozen to death right here in the middle of town!

I'm on the verge of failing in my simple attempt to mount the snow-laden hill that has taunted me for so long. Grit my teeth and mount a final offensive. Anger-white hot, fire breathing, damn the torpedoes anger-courses through my veins. I somehow scrabble my feet underneath me and rise to face the climb. A burst of renewed courage and my utter contempt for that hill propel me forward.

"Damn you, Tank Hill. Somewhere up there you're holding the key to this whole dirty mess. I won't let you buffalo me again. I'm gonna force you to yield to me."

I plod resolutely to the top, shaking off each misstep and flop as mere annoyances. This is my victory lap, and I won't be denied. I'm cold, wet, exhausted and shaking all over. But my goal is clearly in sight.

When I get my feet under me and stand at the hill's summit, I am Rocky atop the stairs, Jeanne-Claude Killy the master of the slope, Sir Edmund Hillary planting the flag on Mount Everest. I've shed my albatross—the fear of returning to the top of that run. The final triumph I'll share with Kyle on a shiny new sled, zipping to the bottom of the hill before I leave Springlake. That's a promise.

For a long while I traipse all around the area where the old water tank stood. Try to picture in my mind's eye what those three boys must have experienced that long ago night. Then I walk beyond the crest and slowly make my way down toward the small cemetery.

I go to a line where I remember three Confederate graves lie with their bronze headstones. A solid blanket of drifting snow covers the entire fenced area, but the relentless wind has exposed a corner of one of the markers. Kneel and set about scooping the snow to clear all three bronzes. Apologizing to the dead heroes, I thrust my hand through the snow's crust over the first plot to a depth halfway up my bicep. Gauge that to be eighteen inches from my fingertip. A test at the third plot makes my arm disappear to about the same depth. Then I move to the grave in the middle, the resting place of Private John Palmer, and shove my hand tentatively below the surface. My middle finger jams painfully against solid ground. My forearm is only half submerged in the snowy cover.

"Wasn't my imagination after all," I say to no one in particular. The wind answers with a low moan. I scrape armloads of snow from all three plots and compare them. There is no doubt now that Palmer's burial plot is not nearly as sunken as the other two.

My discovery is interrupted by a rustling in the distance. I look up quickly in the direction of the sound, and see the fronds of an evergreen moving, the snow falling from them in clumps. There is a sound of crunching, and I picture dry branches being crushed underfoot. But I've reacted too late to see the cause of the movements and sounds.

I take the short return route. Stop at the Barnwell's back door to knock the snow from my boots. Mrs. Starkey hears the commotion. She peeks out at me through a frosted pane.

"Get in here, Dave. You'll catch your death out there in that cold. Look like you've been burrowing in the snow." I kick off the boots now caked with ice and leave them behind. Hurry inside, and stand, frozen and trembling, in the hallway. But this time it's strictly the cold that makes me quake. I've defeated my fear of Tank Hill.

"Burrowing? Guess you could call it that, Mrs. S. Took some tumbles going up the hill the long way around. Had to shake a monkey off my back." My hostess obviously hasn't the slightest idea what I'm talking about.

"Whatever. Go in by the fireplace and warm yourself. I'll bring you some hot tea."

I shiver by the glow of the gas logs in the old fireplace. Certainly beats hauling in firewood as they must have long ago, I muse as I ponder the blue and orange flames. Realize how cold I've gotten and how soaked I am. The circulation is slowly returning when Mrs. Starkey shows up with a steaming cup for me.

The big, hot mug feels good to my stinging hands. I sip the bracing tea. I'm about to return to semi-normal after my terrifying, puzzling adventure. Mrs. S looks me over and asks, "What on earth were you doing out there cavorting in the snow drifts?"

"Didn't feel like cavorting to me. More like exploring," I reply.

"Exploring for what, pray tell?"

"Answers to some hard questions, dear lady. Important answers." I concentrate on the flames, and my feet scuffle up as near the fire as I dare.

"Well, did you find any?" I hear her question as if it comes from far away.

"Find what? Oh, answers. Yes, maybe I did."

"Now don't you budge, Dave Owens, till you're warm. Haven't lost a guest yet, and I don't intend for you to be my first casualty. I'd swear your lips were blue when you came in from outdoors. I'll bring you more tea."

"I'll stay put. Can't imagine I could find a place more comfortable than this," I say.

"Soon as you warm up a little you need to get out of those wet things and take a hot shower," she tosses back as she walks away.

I stand gazing into the fireplace. Ponder what my discovery at the cemetery means. Can it help place Lester Kanicki at the cemetery that tragic night? How? And how do I convince Len Darden that the Private's grave should be opened? That would amount to desecration of the burial site of a war hero. We could both be driven out of town for that.

Altogether, though, I'm satisfied that it's been an encouraging start. I've mounted the hill, fought my nemesis to a standstill. And another clue has been added to a growing list of possible breakthroughs. Now if I can only last out the week. Randy Bean will dangle our bait, and Lester will come looking for me with homicide on his mind. Helen, honey, root for me. It's crunch time in Springlake.

Chapter 35

▼

Today we set the hook. Find out if my stalker is who I think he is. We'll see whether Lester is close by and if he's paying attention. I can't wait to pick up a copy of the Springlake Times and read Bean's story. If Kanicki does the same, I'll have to be on guard every minute. He'll be itching to silence the kid with the flailing feet. That could be the only way for him to avoid a final kick in the groin that will put him away for life.

My morning starts routinely enough. There won't be any return engagements rolling in snow banks this day. I take my time getting ready to go downstairs for breakfast, and turn on the radio for some music to accompany me as I shave. An altogether refreshing wakeup for a change. I hum along with some old tunes.

Then the news break on the hour brings an announcement that upends my day.

"We're getting an alert that there has been an unexplained death of a Springlake resident. This is the second time in less than a month that a tragic event has shaken our normally peaceful community. A man identified as William Logan of the Oak Heights area was found in a parked car near Lexington early this morning. Police have given no further details except that this was a brutal murder. In mid-January police found lifelong resident Jimmy Moore dead on Wildflower Road. Stories persist that Moore had been mutilated by his killer, and to date there have been no promising leads. Now a second mysterious killing has occurred."

I flop down in a chair and put my head in my hands. Why didn't I cook up my scheme with the newspaper article sooner? Maybe Billy would still be alive, and Lester would have been concentrating on me instead. I can only imagine the condition Billy was in when they found him. What was it Kyle said Kanicki would do—'*something gruesome, maybe poke out his eyes.*'

A breath of fresh air is what I need after this shock. And I'll check in with Kyle. If he hasn't heard the news, he needs to know and be on guard.

"Going out so early?" Mrs. S asks as I whisk through the foyer.

"Be back in five minutes for breakfast. Just want to see what it's like outdoors." I step out onto the front porch and look south toward the mountains with the sun on their white slopes. Then I reach for my cell phone and punch in Kyle's number.

"Mornin', Jenny. Is he up?"

"He's in the den as usual, Dave. Something about a Monday morning show on the sports channel. Has to get all the basketball and hockey scores from yesterday. That's his winter fix when football season is over and he can't play golf yet."

"Can I talk to him?"

"Hold on."

I hear the television going full blast when she carries the phone to him. He mutes the sound and quips, "Out and about kind of early, Flywheel." *Damn*, I think, *he hasn't heard.*

"Hope you've had your wakeup coffee, Kyle. I'm about to shake up your day."

Silence. Then a long sigh from my brother.

"Bad news?' he asks.

"It's Billy, Kyle."

"No. Please, no, Dave." I feel like he wants me to go away and say no more. Maybe if I don't actually say the words…but I don't have a choice.

"He's been killed. Billy was found up the valley this morning. Kyle. It had to be Kanicki's work."

Again there is a long pause. The news must be suffocating him. He's lost his two closest childhood chums, both victims of violence. I can imagine the sense of loneliness and sheer fright that thought brings him.

"Why are you so sure, Dave?"

"His eyes. Just like Lester threatened."

Kyle's voice trembles. "Where? Was his family harmed?"

"According to the radio, police pulled him from his parked car near Lexington in the wee hours. That's all I know, but my next stop is the police station and Len Darden. I'll tell you more when I know. Please be careful, Kyle."

"You, too." His voice is small and quivering. Think I've just let all the air out of his cheery morning. He's more than shaken. My words have rendered him disoriented, fearful and withdrawn.

* * * *

I try to put up a good front and cover the thoughts racing through my brain. Mrs. S looks at me in a way that tells me I'm not succeeding.

"What is it, Dave? Need to talk?"

"Not just yet, thanks. Have a lot to think through first. Nothing I can't work out."

Yeah, sure, Owens. Three people dead, your brother narrowly escapes. Now you've deliberately arranged for this madman to come after you so you can trap him. I can hear what Billy Logan would have said about that: "You and what army?"

One thing is for damned certain. It's time Len Darden and I stopped going at cross purposes. Need to help each other find this maniac. Got to stop the bloodshed and havoc. I have information that can help. He has to come down off his soap box and listen.

I'm concentrating so completely on what to do next that I'm in my own little cocoon in that dining room. Then I see fingers waving before my eyes and emerge from my self-hypnosis.

"Hello, there. I said do you need a refill?" Meg is across the table facing me with a bright smile. She's bending over the table, apparently to be sure her eyes aren't all I see. Persistent, this one. Thought we had all that settled.

"Sure. Fill it up. I was in another world for a minute there." I grin and she sees my embarrassment.

"Just trying to be helpful," is her reply. "Want an ear to bend?"

"You'll have to stand in line. I must look like a charity case this morning."

From the reactions I'm drawing, it's clear by now that Kyle isn't the only one distressed, even mortified by the day's news.

I finish my meal and hurry through preparations to face the cold weather outside. Grab my coat and gloves, and turn toward the door when Meg appears. Now what?

"Dave, I want you to know I took to heart what we discussed Saturday night."

"Good," My manner is intentionally curt and abrupt. I really don't want to encourage this conversation right now. But she isn't ready to leave.

"Hear me out, please," she coos and takes two steps toward me. "It's no secret I'm attracted to you, Dave. More than you can possibly know. And my son doesn't remember a lot about his father, but he thinks you're the coolest man he's ever seen."

"Cool…and married, Meg."

"I know. Let's be friends for now. Just want you to know that if things don't, you know, work out for you elsewhere, I'm here. Don't mind waiting my turn."

Her words sound entirely too smooth and patient to me. I've seen how touchy Meg can be. Saw her smoking passion when she flung herself at me, and her intense anger sparked on Saturday night when she attacked me like a wildcat. My chest still aches from the pummeling she gave me. Hard for me to buy this suddenly docile front.

* * * *

Back to the police station I go. Len Darden won't be happy to see me this morning, particularly with a new murder to solve. But I've been trying to nudge him into action. Now it's time I applied a hefty shove.

Sure, I'm pressing my luck. But it's my carcass that's on the griddle, and Lester's turned up the heat. Billy tried to run, and Kanicki issued a strong, bloody warning that wouldn't work. When he reads that article in today's paper, I could be down to a matter of hours left in my present state—breathing, that is. And as screwed up as my life has been, I can finally see a hint of daylight with Helen. Nobody's going to deny me that chance.

Walk into the squad room and ask, "Sheriff in?"

I can feel the tension in the air when the two uniformed officers do a double take and stare at each other. Must remind them at this point of the naïve man with his hand in the pit bull's cage calling out, *'here, nice pooch.'*

The man behind the station desk can't resist. He looks at me as if I'm the biggest moron in town and asks, "You sure you wanta see the sheriff today of all days? Anybody tell you what happened to Logan last night?"

"That's why I'm here. Damn right, I want to see him."

The officer shakes his head, and he turns to his coworker. "Fred, I guess there's no saving him from his temper. Tell Sheriff Darden Dave Owens is here." He looks back at me, grins and shakes his head before finishing his instructions. "Then get ready to hit the wall real fast."

He looks quickly at me and goes to Darden's closed office door, knocks and opens it slightly. He says something too softly for me to hear. But I clearly hear the chair scraping across the floor and the heavy footsteps as the deputy clears the way. Broadus Darden comes storming toward me. His face is red, his fists are clenched, and I'd swear he's snorting steam from his nostrils.

"Dammitall, Owens, I told you…"

I hold up a hand and cut him off with, "Stabbed out his eyes, didn't he?"

Darden seems to suspend his charge in mid-step. He unclenches his fists, and the blood instantly drains from his face, leaving him pale and stunned. "How?...get in here," he orders. Waves me toward his office with one big, meaty arm.

He closes the door behind us.

"How are Billy's wife and daughter, Len? Did Lester go after them, too?"

Darden looks frustrated that I've grabbed the initiative. He stands there puffing then says, with a wave of his hand, "They're okay. Got somebody watching out for them."

"Did she tell you how Billy ended up in Lexington last night?"

"Said Billy wigged out, grabbed up her and the kid and they took off. Took along his shotgun. Swore he'd use it if Kanicki showed up."

"Didn't do him a lot of good, did it, sheriff?"

"That's for damn sure, Dave. His killer musta caught him by surprise. His wife said Billy went out for cigarettes and soda pop and never came back."

Darden stops for a moment then his face takes on a pained, almost sickened expression.

"Dave, the son of a bitch not only gouged out his eyes, he blasted Logan with his own shotgun. Lexington police said it was a gruesome scene."

There's nothing I can add. The sheriff has said it all. I sit in shock and feel the raw anger surge in me. Billy Logan, the big lovable brute of a man, was savagely killed.

Darden points his finger at me and almost shouts, "Now answer my question. How the hell did you know Billy's eyes were gouged out? I'm one step away from throwing you into a cell and holding you as a material witness in a murder. Hell, maybe you're doing the killings yourself."

"Maybe now you'll believe what I've been trying to get through that thick head of yours, Len. That night on Tank Hill the boys were each threatened in their own way. Kanicki has a warped imagination and a good memory. He told Jimmy he'd rip out his tongue if he ever repeated what he'd seen. Went that one better and tore it out with own his teeth. Threatened to bite off Kyle's ear for listening to Jimmy. Damn near gnawed that off the other night. Said he would poke out Billy's eyes. Made good on that the second time around. Had a special treat planned for me."

"And what might that be?" Darden asks, turning toward his chair. "Sewing that sassy mouth shut?"

Guess I earned that remark with my earlier outbursts directed at the sheriff. I wet my finger and hold it up in the air. "Touche. That's one for you, Len. Remember when I kicked Lester in the groin?"

"Balls," Len corrects.

"Whatever. He swore to get even with me, according to Kyle's account. Said maybe he'd just get his knife and neuter me. I don't plan to let that happen."

"So tell me what you want me to do with all your circumstantial evidence. Even if I could lay my hands on Kanicki, that is."

"Jimmy, Kyle and Billy were all punished exactly in the ways Kanicki swore he'd get to them. Sam's death was a bonus for this homicidal monster. What else do you need?"

"Doesn't prove he did either the killings or the mugging." Darden won't budge.

"Swear to me that you have other credible leads, and I'll leave you alone, Len." I wait and he squirms in his seat.

"Okay, let's say Lester Kanicki *is* our man," he sneers. "What's our next step according to mister master detective?"

"I've already set it in motion, sheriff. You need to read the article that was printed in today's issue of the Times. It clearly implicates an unnamed party, whose identity is known by an anonymous source, a party who's responsible for at least three murders. Kanicki will know I'm the source, and I can pin the murders of both of the Hurt sisters and Jimmy Moore on him—or at least I want him to believe I can."

I'm winging it now because I haven't even read the paper yet. That's my next action as soon as I tear myself away from here.

"Yeah, Carl showed me the paper already," the sheriff says. "Had a strong notion the fool that baited that hook could be you. Damn stupid of you, Dave. Now you're a sitting duck if your theory is right."

"Had no alternative. I didn't see anything happening on your end, and time was getting shorter. Have you even seriously tried to find out where Kanicki may be?"

"Told you we'd look for him and we did. All dead ends. Told you everything I know. He's faded into the woodwork."

"His wife and daughter, too?"

"Wife got a divorce. Moved up north. Almost fifteen years ago. Just dropped out of sight. Poof! She was gone. Police up there have no clue where either Lester or their child may be. Can't keep tabs on him if we don't even know where to start. He just seems to have dropped off the face of the earth."

"Well, he'll come after me, Sheriff. You can bet on that. And I'm warning you, I'll do whatever is necessary to protect myself."

"Look, Dave," Darden continues, peering across his desk with a guilty look, "I'll admit our search could have been more thorough. I'll pull out all the stops beginning now. If I tell you I'll bring Lester in, come hell or high water, will you promise to leave this whole thing to me? It's that or I'll have to put you in jail for your own good. At the very least, you'll be obstructing justice by getting in the way of a police investigation."

"I'll agree to stop searching for clues, Len. Suspect I've found out everything that's important already. But I'm watching over my shoulder, and I *will* take him out if he comes after me."

"Davey, I'm gonna put Carl on you morning to night for the next few days. That's the best I can do with us short handed right now. Have to depend on you to let Carl know if you need to be out after dark so he can call in relief. If this guy does try to get at you, we'll have somebody there. You don't have to play vigilante."

"I'd rather you protected Kyle and Jenny."

"You heard what I said. Carl's gonna be your shadow. At least, you're one suspect I won't have to worry about.

"Suspect? Are you out of your head, Len? What does it take to convince you who's behind all this. And what if Kanicki sees Carl tailing me and it scares him away? Maybe even makes him go after Kyle's family? Len, please. I know your resources are limited. Use them to protect Kyle, Jenny and the boys."

"Not your call, Dave. You go nowhere from now on without Carl. Understood?"

"Sure."

My answer doesn't sound convincing even to me.

Chapter 36

"Bet that curled their hair," Lester laughs as he watches the morning news. "Dummy Logan thought he could get away from me by running. Don't know why he took along his shotgun. Couldn't slip me twice. He didn't stand a chance when I came up behind him and buried that ice pick in his ribs."

He calmly sips his coffee and gnaws on a piece of overcooked bacon. Swirls his toast in egg yolk and licks at it as if it makes the taste of revenge even sweeter. Then he picks up the Monday morning Times to reread the article by somebody named Randy Bean. His black eyes flash, and his anger rapidly reaches the boiling point once again.

"Anonymous, huh? Well, Mister Bean, you and I are about to have a talk about this twit Anonymous. Don't think you'll hold out on me for long with what I have in mind."

He crumples up the newspaper and walks to the front of the trailer. Looks out at the bright morning sun. A fine day for a little fun. Sunday was a banner day, but today is going to top it. Lester picks up a small pouch from the side table and extracts a stainless steel scalpel. He admires its keen, gleaming edge; carries it to the kitchen and tests it on a raw chicken leg. Ahh, just like cutting through butter.

"Logan was foolish to think leaving town was the answer. Maybe he thought he'd lure me away from his family and the others. What a special feeling it was, knowing the last thing his eyes saw was his own blood on the pick as I scooped his eyeballs out of their sockets. I thought blasting him with his own shotgun was a nice finishing touch, too."

The fresh memory of his latest conquest is more than he can bear. He reaches again for the scalpel, draws it across his thumb, and savors the taste of his own bright blood. Then Lester Kanicki tilts his head back and emits a sound that begins as a low squeal and grows into a shriek of hysterical laughter. The sound fills the confines of his small trailer.

Chapter 37

▼

I walk to a newsstand and pick up a copy of the Monday morning Springlake Times. Carl lingers close behind me in his patrol car. Randy Bean has done a great job of putting together our bait for Lester Kanicki. There are enough details to let him know the 'anonymous source' is ready to pin the deaths of both Hurt sisters on an unnamed assassin. The circumstances of their untimely ends are provided in small spoonfuls, teasers that imply the source has solid evidence. But those words stop short of laying out the specifics. Only I know that's because I don't have any hard facts, only strong suspicions that I believe are accurate.

Finish the story and lean back in my seat in the small Main Street coffee shop. Reward myself and Randy Bean with a broad smile. I'll drop by his office shortly and deliver my thanks to him in person.

The waitress says, "You look like the fox that got away. Something funny you want to share?" I grin back at her.

"More like I'm about to snare the fox. Think I'll have another cup of coffee and one of those big sweet rolls."

The feeling of elation is short lived, however. I have the odd sensation that someone is watching me. Jerk my head toward the street window. Nobody there but a little old lady hurrying by with an armload of packages. This is going to be an intense day for me. The tingle I feel isn't all excitement. *Dave Owens, you phony, you're scared numb, afraid Lester will get the drop on you before you can react.* I know Carl is out there in his patrol car keeping watch. Nevertheless, the handgun comes out of the glove compartment and stays with me until this is over. Won't trust anyone else to protect me now, certainly not one of Len Darden's Keystone Cops.

Rising from my seat, I grab the paper and turn toward the front door of the café. My cell phone comes alive, and I reach into my shirt pocket to retrieve it. Before I can speak, a voice in sheer panic shrills at me.

"Dave, help me. Melody's missing!" She breaks into sobs and struggles to continue.

"Hold on, Helen. Take a deep breath."

A few moments of silence, then she speaks again, still on the verge of tears.

"Oh, Dave, she didn't come home last night. None of her girlfriends have any idea where she could have gone. I'm going crazy. So many bad people out there and her so young and vulnerable."

"Honey, I'm on my way. Hold on. I'll be there as soon as I can."

"Please hurry, Dave. Help me find her."

"I'm heading south. I'll stay in touch with you by phone. Call somebody, Beth or Marge, to stay with you till I get there."

Suddenly the only thing in the world that matters is getting to Raleigh to stand by Helen and find our daughter. If Lester wants a shot at me, he'll have to wait. By the time I emerge onto Main Street, I'm running headlong toward my car.

Carl must think Kanicki is already after me. He flies out of the police car, weapon drawn and sweeping in front of him. "What is it, Owens?" He covers the distance between us in a flash. People on the sidewalk scatter in all directions.

Gasping for air, my heart thundering in my chest, I manage to blurt out, "It's okay, Carl. Put your gun away."

The bright sunshine of the frosty morning sends my head spinning. I feel dizzy, confused, nauseous all at the same time. I lean on my car, supporting myself while the moment passes so I can get myself together. Carl holsters his weapon and jams a helping hand under my arm.

"Thought the demons of hell were after you," Carl says. "What on earth happened in there?"

"Deputy, my daughter is missing. My wife just called. I have to go to Raleigh immediately. Looks like you get the day off babysitting me. Can't waste a minute."

He considers my words and makes a hasty decision. "You follow me. I'll take you the shortest route out of town toward Raleigh. I can call the sheriff on the way to tell him what we're doing. Then I'll see you safely out of the county and make sure nobody's following you. Give me your number. I'll relay whatever the sheriff tells me."

"Give me five minutes to go by the Barnwell and throw some clothes in a suitcase," I ask.

Mrs. Starkey sees the stunned expression on my face when I charge into her home and bound up the stairs. I literally toss together enough necessities to get me through a few days in Raleigh. Hurry back down the stairs to find Mrs. S waiting in the front hall.

"Can I help you with something, Dave? You look white as Aunt Fanny's laundry."

"Have to be gone a few days, Mrs. S. Family crisis. I'll be back. Hold my room, please." I speed out the back door and hoist my bag into the back seat, signal all ready to Carl and kick the car to life.

We leave town, Carl with his lights flashing, me in hot pursuit. He clears the road to the county line and calls me on the cell. "Boss says be careful and keep an eye out. He expects to hear from you regularly till you get back to town, then you're to come see him first thing."

"Thanks, Carl."

"No problem. And, Dave, I hope it all turns out for the best. Just don't kill yourself or get arrested for speeding."

Carl pulls over, turns off his blinking lights and waves me on as I speed by.

* * * *

By the time I reach the house on Autumn Drive, Helen and I have already had several conversations. Each time I sense she is calming down a bit now that she knows we can face this crisis together. I've reassured her over and over that Melody can take care of herself. We have to think positive thoughts. All the while, though, my gut is grinding. I repeatedly push back the terrible scenes that erupt in my mind. What if my precious Melody is lying somewhere, bleeding at this very moment, calling out for a father that is too far away to help her? What if some evil man, or one of her own friends, has taken advantage of her innocence and made her a woman before she's ready?

Then the most horrific thought of all strikes me so forcefully it sends a sharp pain rocketing through my chest. What if, God forbid, Lester Kanicki is behind her disappearance because I've forced him to up the ante in our vicious game of cat and mouse? Did I foolishly bring her into this without thinking?

Reach Raleigh in record time, miraculously without landing in jail. Can't wait to hold Helen close to me and dry her tears, tell her that everything will be all right. The car has scarcely stopped rolling when I turn the key and leap out.

Helen runs to me and throws herself into my arms. We hold onto each other. I hear sounds like soft whimpers of pain, feel a warm dampness where our cheeks meet, and realize that we are both bawling like babies. No words come and none are necessary.

"Let's get you in out of the cold where you can fill me in, sweetheart." I steer her toward the porch and press her close to my side. She leans against my shoulder trying to make her convulsive sobbing subside.

Once we are in the warm living room and she's thanked her friend Beth and sent her home, Helen pours out the whole story to me. She and Melody made up after their argument. Melody told her she was sorry for being so unreasonable about Helen's dating rules. Everything was fine.

"I agreed to let her spend the night with her friend Judy next weekend, Helen said. "But she was to be home last night with school work. Melody told me she had finished her homework before dinner. Then, after the meal, she asked if she could go over to Judy's for a short visit. I said okay and cautioned her to walk home before dark. If she ran late, she was to call home and let me pick her up. Didn't want her walking alone after dark, even in this quiet neighborhood."

When the sun set, Helen had begun to wonder and worry. She called Judy and learned that Melody had never arrived there. Now she started to panic. She contacted Melody's other close friends. They hadn't seen her, either. Helen made each of them promise to call if they learned where she may have gone. She fretted and walked the floors for the next couple of hours then called the police. They assured her they would be on the lookout for Melody, but she had not yet been gone long enough to be considered missing.

"Don't think I slept at all last night, Dave. I called the police again when Melody wasn't home by dawn. They told me to come by to fill out a missing person report. Then I called you as soon as I left the station."

"Must have been pure hell for you getting through the night alone, baby," I tell her. "But I'm here now, and the police are working to find her."

We go over the events of the past few days, but find no clue to what could have prompted Melody's disappearance. That leaves only circumstances beyond her control keeping her from returning home on time. Points to the possibility that someone snatched her off the street within the short distance between here and her girlfriend's house. Had someone been lurking outside waiting for her to appear? All I can see in my mind's eye is a dark man with a very black beard and a maniacal smile, and he's mocking me.

Chapter 38

By early Wednesday we've spent two long days and two agonizing nights worrying about Melody. The police press their search. Both of us try to help, but there is little more we can tell the investigators. Melody is a stable, level-headed girl. We can think of no reason she hasn't come home unless someone has prevented it. She and her mother had a misunderstanding, but it had been worked out.

I can see it in the police detective's eyes. He's trying to shield us from what he fears at this point. Young girl gone from home two consecutive nights, no trace of her after she left her house, doesn't look good at all. I can tell he's thinking kidnap, rape, other possibilities I refuse to face.

Helen and I sit alone in the house. Without Melody, the house feels as cold inside as the February day is outdoors. Helen has been talking non-stop, reliving all the wonderful times of her daughter's childhood. I guess that's to keep her from dwelling on the cold, hard fact that she may have loved her in that beautiful past and lost her in the harsh present. Although she smiles at the memories, pain is etched in her face. The truth of our dilemma threatens to overwhelm her. I can only wonder what part of the blame she assigns to me and to my absence at the time Melody most needed me.

"Maybe we should try to get out for awhile, Helen. Breathe the fresh air and get a meal or something. We can give the police our cell numbers in case there's news."

"I'm not moving from this house, Dave, until they find my baby."

She looks away and withdraws into her own thoughts. I share her distress, but she needs to be busy, not sitting here dwelling on all the bad things that could have happened. At this point I'm worried about losing both of my ladies. Oh

God, did I say lose? Melody has to be safe somewhere. I couldn't bear it otherwise.

Something has to pry Helen out of her self-destructive despair. I hazard an opening.

"Let me be here for both of you, Helen. Melody's coming home then I don't ever want to leave either of you again. You're the two people who define my whole life."

"I can't think about that now, Dave. We have to get our daughter back then we can talk about our future."

"No. Don't you see, her disappearance has brought us together, and I don't want that to ever end. Melody will be back soon. I know it in my heart and so do you. This house will be the home it once was and more." I cross to where Helen is sitting and cup her cheek in my hand. She looks up at me with a hint of that familiar sparkle in her eyes.

"I love you, Dave. I've never stopped loving you." She pulls me down to her. This time her kiss is no peck, no mild affection for show. This is the real thing.

"You're all I ever wanted to make my life right, Helen. I'm sorry for what I've put you through, but we can put all that behind us. Time for me to come back where I belong."

We are so engrossed in each other and the prospect of a new start that we almost miss an all important sound. The telephone is ringing, and we both dash for it. I grab it first, hand it to Helen and hold her hand.

"Yes? Yes, this is she. Thank God! When? Yes!" Her face is aglow.

"Tell me, baby."

"Melody is safe. They found her in a fleabag motel down the road, exhausted but unharmed. The police have questioned her briefly, and they're bringing her home. They should be here in a few minutes. We're a family again." She breaks down and sobs.

Helen's relief is immediate. My heart soars. I grab her and lift her off the floor, swing her around and repeat over and over, "I love you, I love you."

*   *   *   *

We face our daughter, each of us holding one of her hands, and feel blessed that she has been delivered to us with no apparent ill effects from her ordeal. The police haven't told us what their questioning revealed, so we wait to hear the story from Melody's lips.

"We were both worried sick about you, sweetheart," Helen tells her. "Please tell us what happened—that is, if you're up to it."

Melody starts hesitantly, her words barely audible. "I'm so sorry. Made a terrible mistake, and it all turned out wrong." She lowers her head and mumbles, "I'm ashamed."

Just hold on, I tell myself. *Let her do this her way.*

"The whole thing started out as a way to coax you two back together. I planned to run away so you'd call Daddy and get him down here. Then I could plead with you to bring our family back together. It's tearing me apart seeing you separated when I know how much you really love each other."

"Then nobody took you away? You did this on your own?" Helen's voice shows a spark of anger, but she continues to stroke Melody's hand and bask in her being home again.

"Not exactly. That's the way it started, but it got out of hand."

"What do you mean?" I demand. "How did you get to that motel?"

"That's the most embarrassing part of all, Daddy. I had arranged for Eddie Morgan to drive me out of town. He said he knew a motel owner, and he would arrange a room for me. I only planned to stay overnight, just long enough for you to come to Raleigh and let me talk some sense into both of you."

"But you nearly drove me insane with worry, little girl." Helen's tears are streaming, but she bores a hole through her daughter with those brown eyes.

"I know, Mom. It was a foolish thing to do. More foolish than I even imagined at first. Eddie used the situation, and he tried to take advantage of me."

"If he harmed you, I'll dismember him and every male member of his family." I stand and pace about the room, anxious to get my hands on anybody that would do such a thing to my daughter. But the word "tried" finally soaks in.

"My stupidity taught me something, Mom. I know you've only been trying to protect me by being so strict. I turned Eddie down flatly. Told him I never want to see him again. But I couldn't face you after what I'd almost gotten myself into. It's a nightmare I don't ever want to repeat. Just sat in that room and dreaded coming home to take my punishment."

"Honey, you've punished yourself enough. We're so relieved to have you back. I just want to forget the whole episode. Right, Daddy?"

"You bet. Some lessons we learn the hard way. The only important thing is that we both love you very much and want what's best for you." Melody finally begins to smile.

"Now, young lady," Helen says, "I'll bet you're famished. What can I cook for you?"

"Anything but hamburgers. That's all I could get at the fast food next to the motel."

"You just sit there with your Daddy and I'll put a meal together for you."

The next two days are the happiest I could imagine given the clouds still hanging over my life. The three of us share with each other like we always did before my own stupid period, taking great pleasure in hearing what is going on in each other's individual little worlds. The only topic I dodge is my suspicions regarding the murderous rampage in Springlake. And I carefully avoid mentioning my fear that Lester Kanicki would have sought revenge on me through Melody. I report Uncle Kyle's health as much improved, almost normal after his scary beating. But I deflect any further attempts by either of them to find out why the attack had taken place or what was being done to catch his assailant. That whole subject is out of bounds.

At the last moment before arriving in Raleigh, I remembered the holstered gun that has become my full time companion. It now rests securely locked in the car's glove compartment once again. The presence of that little item on my person would have been enough to raise too many questions I was not prepared to answer. Since we had never been accustomed to having a gun in the house, it would have frightened both Helen and Melody to know something in my present life made me feel I had to carry a weapon.

Helen and I made a breakthrough on that first frightening day of Melody's adventure. We both spoke our love and held onto each other. But it hasn't gone beyond that crucial point. There is no answer from Helen to my plea to return home and stay. I decide to let that ride for now and see what develops by the time I leave. As much as I want to stay here, the business in Springlake must be finished or we'll always be under a threat.

Valentine's Day rolls around and I have two dozen roses delivered, a dozen red for Helen and a dozen pink for Melody. I present both of them with elaborate greeting cards that invite them out to dinner. We spend a lovely evening, and Helen tops it off by baking my favorite dessert. But still she doesn't offer a permanent truce, and I impatiently wait and hold back.

On Saturday morning I resign myself to the drive back north to face whatever fate unfolds in Springlake. I've stayed in contact with Kyle this week, and he's indicated there is nothing new to report. Len Darden has not yet pinned down Lester Kanicki's whereabouts, and there has been no further news about Billy's death. If I have calculated correctly, Kanicki has by now concluded that I present the greatest danger to him, and he's probably frantically searching for me. I check my handgun once again to verify that it's ready, fully loaded and on safety.

At breakfast there is an air of cheery lightness. The real question between Helen and me, however, remains a mystery hanging over us.

"This has been wonderful," I begin. "Wish it would never end, but I have one more trip to make to Springlake."

I look at Melody and catch her peering at Helen as if to say, '*Okay, Mom, it's your move.*' But Helen stands and walks toward the coffee pot.

I call after her. "My calendar says there's an important date coming up on the 22nd. Can I get a date with you two beautiful women to celebrate a fifteenth birthday?"

Melody beams and says, "I refuse to have this birthday without you. And I really don't want to be fourteen for another year. It was too difficult the first time." She looks at Helen and awaits her reply.

Helen asks, "Can you come down on Friday and stay the weekend? That will give us more time to do something special. What would you like to do on your birthday, honey?"

"Mostly, I want to enjoy being with my family," Melody tells us. "Beyond that, how about an elegant dinner out somewhere we have to dress up?" My daughter is excited at the prospects, her eyes all sparkly. She has been suddenly thrust into a grownup world by her trying experience this week. It's time I acknowledge that she's about to bud into a young woman.

"I'll be here Friday night," I confirm. "Helen, you always did know more about Raleigh than I do. Pick out the swankiest place you can find. Book it for us, please. I'll give both of you a birthday to remember."

We dawdle over breakfast. I get the feeling none of us want this visit to come to an end. But I can't delay my departure any longer. I wander off to the guest room to finish my packing. When I return, Melody is dressed for outside. She comes over and gives me a hug.

"Have to cut out to the library. Judy and I have a school project that's due Monday. Her dad is driving us. See you Friday, Daddy. Love you." She kisses me and leaves.

"Looks like she's back to normal," I remark. Helen nods and gives an approving smile.

"Thank goodness for that. I see you're about ready to brave the cold, too."

"Places to go and people to see, but none as important as the ones I'll see on Friday. By the way, I want Melody decked out right for her birthday celebration. Get her a special dress from us." I press a wad of large bills into her hand.

"And, Helen, wear the blue dress for me." She knows the one I mean. It's the last dress I bought for her before we parted, and she's never looked better.

Then she catches me flat footed. "I know you're waiting for a commitment from me, Dave. I've been thinking a lot about us. Give me until next weekend then let's seriously talk about our future."

"I'm ready for that now," I quickly answer.

"Just a few more days. Please?" She kisses me warmly. I turn and force myself to leave.

Chapter 39

A dreary day on the road from Raleigh. Lots of time to think. Started this trip in a state of all out panic but it ended on a high note. Melody's childish attempt to force Helen and me together by running away almost turned to tragedy for all of us.

But with that episode behind us, we had spent a couple of beautiful days together. The atmosphere between Helen and me is worlds better. I see signs that we could be together soon. She's still holding back a bit, hasn't welcomed me fully back into her life. Don't quite know what to make of that. She promises we'll talk about a decision next weekend.

On the other front back in Springlake, I have no idea how close my pending showdown may be. Has Lester set his plan for closing in on me? Kyle called to check on us but said nothing about our stalker. Lester's had time to read and react to the newspaper article. My handgun is nestled close to my side. I'm putting my head in swivel mode to guard against a sneak attack.

* * * *

Mrs. Starkey greets me with a concerned frown when I enter the Barnwell House foyer.

"Should I ask, Dave? About the family, I mean?"

"Oh, yes. Guess I *was* pretty cryptic when I left. Everything's fine in Atlanta. I'm back for probably another couple of weeks at most."

"I was worried. All you said was 'hold my room for me, I may be out of town several days. Family crisis.'"

"All worked out, Mrs. S. My two girls are fine. I'll be going back for Melody's fifteenth birthday next weekend."

"You know I can start and stop your room rent anytime you want. No use paying for nights you don't use," she says.

"No. I'm a business man, too. I committed to a room. Want it here for me until I leave town. Gives me a place that feels like home." That draws a warm smile.

"I never did ask you what you do for a living, Dave. If you don't consider it prying, I'd like to know what Ruby's boy has been up to since you left Springlake."

"Don't mind at all, Mrs. S. Some would say I've prospered, at least for the past eight years. Started a software company in Atlanta with a partner and we've done quite well. In fact, I really don't have to work any more. Just don't like the idea of being a thirty-six year old retiree."

"Ruby would have been proud, son."

She leads me into the parlor to sit with her.

"I hope so. My personal life hasn't been the best for a few months, but I think that's getting set right now."

Something in her eyes tells me she's already guessed as much. She seems to want to say something more but is holding back.

"What is it, Mrs. Starkey?"

"May not be my place to say this, but I hope you'll watch your step around Meg. I suspect you're trying to patch up your marriage, and she's a threat to you."

"You're pretty perceptive. I wonder if others have noticed?"

"The way she's taunting and teasing you? Not very subtle about it, is she? Dave, she has her cap set for you. I hate to see you caught in a trap."

"Thanks for the warning, Mrs. S. Finally hit me on this trip home how permanently committed I am to my wife. Helen and I are about to shed some history and get back to being a happy family with Melody. Won't let anyone, Meg included, jeopardize that. But thanks for your concern."

I take Mrs. Starkey by surprise by bussing her cheek.

I've taken my time crawling back up the road. Compared to my mad dash to Raleigh, the return trip was a cakewalk. Most of the day has slipped away by the time I unpack, call Kyle to say I've returned, close the shades and flop on my bed fully clothed. All the tension of the past few days seems to drain from me. I fall into a deep sleep.

* * * *

Someone seems to be talking to me from a distance, but I can't make the words form in my mind. I stir in bed and raise one eyelid to glimpse a murky image. Feel its presence only inches from my face. Instinctively, I reach for my holster, roll away from the figure, and fall to the floor. But the holster is empty!

"Looking for this?" a feminine voice asks.

I stare into the dark to see Meg Kane standing on the far side of the bed. She's holding my pistol with both hands, pointing it directly at my nose. I don't know whether to throw my arms into the air, shout for help, or merely melt into the carpet. Talk about a woman scorned! Figure I have seconds to make my peace and quietly die.

But the muzzle flash doesn't come. There's no sound or explosion. Meg speaks softly.

"Why would you be carrying a gun? Seems to be some things you haven't told me." She lays the handgun flat in her palm and offers it to me.

"Hells' bells, Meg. You nearly scared me to death. Ever wake up looking down the barrel of a gun?" I reach over and take the pistol from her, return it to its holster with a great sigh of relief.

She sits on the side of my bed, and looks at me with a childishly playful grin. There's something disturbing about how casually she's treating my being scared out of my wits. I take a seat opposite her. Lean heavily on the headboard mopping my damp brow. Must have aged a couple years in that tense moment when I was dead certain she was about to put a round squarely between my eyes.

"You were sound asleep. I was just curious about this thing. What has you so scared you're carrying a gun?"

"It's too much to explain. Anyway, I'm still pretty dazed. Thought I was dead there for a second. Just let me say I have good reason to protect myself, and let's leave it at that."

"Fine with me, Dave. I know all about harassment. Watching over my shoulder everywhere I go. Lying awake nights expecting someone to come out of the dark and grab me. Wondering what will happen to my son if I'm not there for him. Sometimes I wish I could take a big, nasty knife and hack away at my tormenter."

She raises one arm and clenches her fist, brings it down on the bed cover time and again in forceful strokes as if stabbing some invisible target. I stay her arm and hold her hand until she calms.

"Tell me about it, Meg. Let me help."

She shakes her head and refuses to speak.

We sit for a long time staring at each other. I try hard to delve the depths of those stunning eyes. Wish I could understand the anguish, the intense anger she has bottled up inside her. She stares at me, and waits for my answer to her question about the gun. I'm not about to give her any more of an explanation. And she's obviously not ready to say more about her tormentor.

She slowly composes herself. "I see you're back from your trip. Mrs. Starkey wouldn't say where you'd gone, just that you went away for a few days. Visited your family, didn't you?"

I nod. "Spent awhile at home."

"Well, you missed the special valentine I had planned for you," she trills and strokes my arm. "Had a sweet surprise all ready for you."

Do we have to plow this ground again? She never gives up.

"Meg, listen…"

"It's never too late, you know. I can still package your surprise anytime you decide you're ready. It'll be the nicest ribbon you ever untied." By now her hand is caressing my cheek and she's leaning closer.

I jump to my feet. "Meg, damnit, I thought we had an agreement. There's nothing more in this for you other than friendship. My family is in North Carolina, and we're about to make a new start. Back off!"

She falls face first onto the comforter when I pull away. Then she raises herself with both hands and purrs, "Please, Dave. I lost my head. Friends…I'm okay with that."

"You say that now. Seems you have a short memory. I mean it. I'm committed, Meg."

"Whatever you want. Just don't shut me out completely. I…we need you to lean on you for awhile. Then, if you insist, I'll leave you alone."

Her pleading is more than urgent, it borders on hysteria. And she said there was something *I* hadn't told *her*. She appears ready to break down. Now she's reached out to me as her remaining thread of stability. How can I take that away? But the games have to end now.

"Meg, you have a lot going for you, and I'm very fond of Trevor. I'll do whatever I can to help both of you, but that doesn't include jumping into bed with you. Understood? I'm married, and I intend to stay that way. Now tell me about whoever it is that's tormenting you."

"Not here. Not now."

"If you won't tell me about your problem, how can I help you?"

"I have work to do, Dave. Not comfortable talking about it here. Let me choose the time and place, and I'll tell you everything. Feel better already now that I can count on you."

"Remember, Meg. Friends, right?"

"Okay, Dave. I'll control myself. I have so much to tell you. I know you can help us. Just don't turn away from me."

"You know the rules. No more slips."

Meg rises from the bed, straightens the covers and turns up the corners of her mouth in a sly response. She turns and slinks away, rolling her hips in that tantalizing fashion of hers. Mumbles something that sounds like, "We'll see about that."

Chapter 40

▼

Feel like I'm moving through a sea of molasses. Everything is slogging by in slow motion. This is nerve wracking. A few days ago I just wanted a breather from the fast paced events cuffing me from all sides. Now I crave action but have no way to control what happens next. My life in Raleigh is on hold until I show up in person and try to coax my way back into Helen's good graces. The situation in Springlake is disturbingly quiet.

If Lester Kanicki has swallowed the bait, he certainly hasn't tipped his hand yet. He has to have seen the Times. It's been more than two days since the story appeared. I've heard the buzz on the streets, in the Barnwell dining room, at the post office, at Snuffy's. Everybody in town seems to be speculating about who the anonymous source can be. They're wondering what shocking new information he…I…will drop next time. It's like waiting for the next installment of the serial at the old Colonial Theater. Where are you, Lester? Let's get it on. Finish this business now.

Deafening silence.

I'm sitting at breakfast trying to puzzle my way through how to kick start the action before I go buggy when there's a nudge at my arm. I look up to see Meg Kane. She's wearing her most alluring smile this morning.

"Boy, your mind was on another planet. Thought I was going to have to do something naughty to get your attention."

I choose not to deal with that, fearing what she may have in mind. She's already done everything short of…enough of that. "Did you ask me something?"

"No, I brought you this. Mrs. Starkey told me to hand you this note, but you were far away outside that window daydreaming."

"Thanks, Meg. Little more coffee, too, please?" She pours and moves on.

I watch her go. Her behavior is about the only encouraging part of these past two days. Except for that little tease just now—and I'm beginning to believe that's just a part of her normal makeup—she's left me alone. No sudden popping up in my room. No come hither glances from afar. Maybe I've finally gotten through to her that she's wasting her time vamping me.

Let's see what this note is all about. A message from the sheriff. Says he wants me to come by the station for a talk. Must be something new. I followed his instructions and checked in when I returned to Springlake. All he had to say then was, "Keep behaving yourself, Davey. We're working all fronts."

Maybe he'll put some zip in my day. Better hurry down to the station.

Mrs. Starkey comes through with empty plates, and she stops off at my table. "See Meg brought that note to you. Sheriff called shortly before you came downstairs. Said not to wake you or anything, but he was sure you'd want to hear what he had to tell you."

"I'm almost through, and that's where I'm headed next. By the way, did I tell you I'll be in Raleigh this weekend?"

"For a special little lady's birthday you said. And other important matters, too, I surmise." She gives me that expression Mom always used to let me know she was a lot more savvy to what was going on than I might think.

The wind is particularly cutting this morning. I park and open the car door. The handgun is snugly stored in the glove box again. Don't want to have to explain that to the police force.

I dash into the jailhouse. Hope the cold has chased Darden indoors. I expect some significant news from him. Can't imagine why else he would call the Barnwell so early.

"Grab a mug of grounds and come on back, Dave," Len Darden says. He stirs a freshly drawn cup, and starts to turn toward his office.

I decline, saying, "All coffeed out, sheriff. And stuffed. You ever had one of Mrs. Starkey's morning meals?" He grins and continues walking away. I follow.

"Have a seat, friend. Got some information for you, but I want to be sure you still understand the ground rules. Remember I agreed to run down all I could find on Lester Kanicki and his family, and you said you'd stop interfering. Still got a deal?"

"That's what I said, sheriff. What have you found out?"

"Already told you about his troubles with the law and his two prison stays. Last time he was sprung was about fifteen months ago. Left a facility down near Lynchburg with instructions to check in regular with his parole officer."

"Okay. What's new?"

"Tracked down his wife, or at least found out what happened to her." He reached for one of those obnoxious big stogies and lit up.

"So where is she?" I'm getting the impression he's stringing this out.

"In the cold, cold ground, pal. Seems Carrie Kanicki gave up on Lester. Tried to start over, but she was never quite right after he was put away."

"Not right? What do you mean?" I want to put him on fast forward, but he's plodding along.

"Well, she turned up back in Virginia. Living with a new guy somewhere up the Shenandoah Valley. Seemed to be doing okay according to those that knew her. Then nearly fifteen years ago her live-in boyfriend found her in their trailer with an empty bottle and a razor blade, blood everywhere. Went out of her gourd, slashed her wrists and bled to death."

"Are they certain it was suicide?"

"Hey, Lester may be the nutcase of the century, but he can't kill somebody from inside prison walls. It was four years later before he got out the first time."

"What about the daughter—Margaret, was it?"

"Story is she kept going back to see her daddy in prison. Must have been the only one that thought he was worth saving. Anyway, she must have been tainted by the two crazies she had for parents. Ended up in a looney bin herself."

"How long ago was that, Len?"

"Lessee, she was sixteen, so it woulda been..." He hesitates. "Jumpin' up Judas, she went to that facility the very same year her mother killed herself! Girl spent three years out in Marion. Convinced them she was cured, so they turned her loose. After a couple more years there's no record of a Margaret Kanicki anywhere."

"So we're left with a lot of loose ends and a madman on the loose. Any progress on finding Lester, Len?"

"Working on it, Dave. Working on it. I tend to believe the case you've built, so we don't intend to let down. Remember our bargain. I'm doing my part. You do yours."

He walks slowly toward his office door. Guess my visit is over.

"Gave my word, Len. Anything I do now will be strictly in my own defense if I'm attacked."

"See you remember that." He whirls around to face me and points a finger. "And, by the way, I did some checking on you. Seems you have a gun registered in Atlanta. A handgun."

"Yes."

"May have a license to carry that thing back in Georgia, but you discharge it in my county and you're gonna be in lots of trouble with me."

"I hear you, sheriff."

Can't start another pissing contest with Broadass Darden over that. But if Lester Kanicki gets within range, I'll blow him away and gladly serve the time.

Chapter 41

▼

Don't know why I feel so compelled to visit that place again. I know what has to be done to confirm my suspicions. But there's not much chance anyone will go along with digging into a Confederate grave. Maybe I just want to collect my thoughts, feel good about something like the fact that I've shed my fear of Tank Hill.

I pull on my coat and cap and start the climb to the West Ridge Cemetery. The sun hasn't made its appearance yet, so I pick my way carefully through the dark with a flashlight beam. Maybe a matter of minutes before the new day arrives. Most of the last big snow has melted away after a couple of sunny days, so the trek up the hill is not nearly as difficult as before.

Take my time and walk around West Ridge, shining my light on each bronze marker in turn. No doubt John Palmer's grave is curiously rounded on top as I had detected even when the whole cemetery was blanketed. I wonder how the signs of digging had escaped detection twenty-odd years ago until a new carpet of grass covered John's plot. Maybe it wasn't as well attended back then as it is now.

I stand in the cemetery as the first glint of sunlight peeks over the tall pines. Kneel down and touch the brass marker, trace the word Palmer slowly with my fingertips. I remember vividly those moments in the high meadow when I witnessed John's death—or at least my idea of how he died. Silently thank him once again for saving his brother from a Yankee bullet so Ira could live and become my forebear. And my mind goes to Aunt Ethel whose rich stories of our ancestors opened the way for me to find my connection back to two brave soldiers.

I raise my eyes toward the tree line beyond. Imagine how Jimmy must have watched from their cover. How he'd peered this way as Lester finished his grisly chore of hiding Valerie Hurt's body in this unlikely place. The feeling is so real I scan at my feet for signs of tire tracks from a blue Plymouth. Find myself straining to hear the rustle of motion and the snap of fallen branches underfoot in the stand of pines.

As convinced as I am of what happened on this spot, it's of little consequence, because the sheriff isn't about to close in on the maniac Lester. Unless we can find him first and get the drop on him, Kanicki's going to come after us one at a time, and I don't know what chance we stand of fending him off.

Decide it's worth a trip to the crest of the hill to scan out across the valley and watch the winter sun rise. Some of these daybreaks over snow laden hills can be spectacular. I need a lift, if it's only from a colorful landscape. The wind is blowing hard, but it's not a bad morning, considering that I'm standing in a Virginia winter in mid-February.

Take a stance at the summit and look down, laughing now at how I could have harbored such an unreasoned fear of Tank Hill for so many years. Well, that's behind me now. And with a little luck, this whole episode of murder and mayhem in my old home town will soon be in the past. I for one don't intend for Lester Kanicki to survive long enough to be put away. I want no chance that he will ever surface again to devil Kyle, me, or anyone else in this town. Jimmy and Billy, you paid a dear price. It's up to me to see that Lester's vendetta stops here and now. The code of the old West we used to watch every Saturday at the Colonial no longer applies. I'm shooting first and asking questions later.

As I turn to retrace my steps toward the Barnwell, there is a hint of something in the corner of my eye, something oddly amiss. A change in the order of things atop the hill that I can't quite put my finger on. I walk slowly and carefully toward the old town water tank now rusting away behind a stand of pines and underbrush.

When I find my way through the vines and emerge into the open, I stand in frozen shock at the horror facing me. What had attracted my attention was a metal sound and a hint of movement. My eyes are riveted to the reason for both.

Suspended before me is a body spread-eagled on the lower x-frame of the tower's metal support bars. The hands and feet have been securely bound with lengths of chain and heavy ropes, and its weight shifts in the wind. The poor soul's head droops, chin against chest, so that I can not clearly see a face, only a crown of slightly graying hair. His shirt has been ripped open and a large K pattern has been cut into his hairy chest, the blood now congealed into a dark red monogram. Below that point on the disemboweled corpse is an unspeakable gore of inhumanity that could only be the work of a twisted mind.

As much as I dread my next move, I have to know. Walk to the hanging figure and gently lift his chin until the approaching daylight reveals the truth of what my mind fears.

I step back and stare, wishing myself away from this place that has found a way to impose itself anew into my brain with a fresh, horrible fright. Want to forget I ever became entangled in the disgusting events of the past four weeks.

I fall to my knees and pound the frozen ground with both fists. Raise my eyes to the reflection of the sun's shifting rays on the most hideous sight of my life and scream into the morning air.

"Damn you, Tank Hill. Damn you, Lester Kanicki."

Above me, the gentle breeze rustles the chains at his wrists, and he silently looms over my anguish. Beyond help, still and frozen.

Randy Bean!

Chapter 42

The coroner says Bean died after enduring savage torture. Only an evil beyond my comprehension could have inflicted the wounds he describes: slow, agonizing abuse, cuts from a keen blade, dozens of painful slashes applied over a long period of time, possibly hours.

Len Darden, as I might have expected, is all over me with accusations and blame.

"Now you see what meddling in my business can come to. Can't lay this one on Lester alone. You brought it on, Owens."

"Oh, sheriff, for God's sake, shut up. You think I don't already feel bad enough. Randy understood the danger from the outset, but he signed on, anyway. Breaking this story would have been the biggest thing he'd ever done as a newsman. Still, I know I goaded him into it."

"Well, maybe you'll cool it now, and let me do my job, smartass. Think you've done enough damage?"

At that instant I come about as close as I've ever been to spending the night in jail. My fingers flex, and I form a tight fist. Debate the most vulnerable spot I can level a blow on this mound of blubber. But that would ruin any chance I have of going after Lester and settling things once and for all. I force my fist to relax, and turn my back on the sheriff. Start to walk away.

"You're not out of the woods yet, Dave," he hurls at me. "Better walk the straight and narrow. Always seem to turn up at the wrong places. You ain't off my list of suspects yet."

* * * *

On the way back to the Barnwell, my nerves severely shaken, my spirit on the verge of breaking, I think about the irony of this gruesome death. For days now I've been moping around wanting action. I'm beginning to see shadows and things that aren't there. People's expressions disturb me, sudden sounds spook me. Lester's game of nerves is going in his favor. Think I'd rather have him jump out of the bushes and give it a go. At least I'd have a chance to defend myself. The grinding suspense is wearing me down.

Now he's struck in the most chilling way possible, savaging perhaps the most innocent person in the mix, somebody that only sought to do a public service.

Len Darden had told me just yesterday that his blood hounds weren't having much success. They'd followed up on a couple of possible Kanicki sightings somewhere in the mountains west of here. But nothing developed from that. Kyle and I have been gnawing our nails down to the quick waiting for Lester to pounce. Now poor Randy has been caught in the crossfire.

Two more days and I'll be in Raleigh with my girls. Have to concentrate on that and what it could mean to me. I'm so beat today. Just can't wait to crawl in that bed. Put all my worries behind me. Snuggle down and think about Helen…and Melody…and home.

* * * *

After an hour of twisting in anguish, picturing the vacant eyes of the ravaged body crucified on the water tank, of the red K carved into his flesh to taunt us all, I finally drift off to sleep. The big house on Autumn Lane shimmers into view. It looks warm and inviting. Feel like I could glide up onto that porch without my feet ever touching the ground. My heart says the long wait is over and I'm back for good. No more guarded answers, questions that hang in the air, invitations offered and somehow withheld. No more guest room and living out of a suitcase, feeling like a visitor in my own home.

Helen and Melody stand in the entryway. My daughter is in her new gown. Helen is wearing that special blue dress. Looks so delicious I want to sweep her up in my arms and…*whoa, Dave. One step at a time.*

"You're beautiful, princess." I bow to Melody and she rushes into my arms.

"Daddy, you're the best birthday present of all," she whispers.

Helen beams and coos her approval. I turn to her, take her in my arms. Cradle her and savor the feel of her warmth next to me. Taste her lips and the past falls away. Just dim memories locked up and forgotten.

"Daddy, we have a wonderful weekend planned," Melody tells me. She takes my hand and steers me into the living room.

When I look back at Helen she's standing in the soft light of the foyer, a vision in blue, her long brown hair sparkling and her eyes sending silent signals. Her lips are still pursed as if our kiss never ended. I know I'll never again forget that here in this house are the only two people that matter. Nothing will ever come between us—not work, not alcohol, certainly not a casual fling—not even Lester and his threats. I really am back.

But the scene begins to fade. No matter how hard I try to stay in that house, I'm slipping away. Melody's hand slides from mine and I reach out, but she drifts farther away. Helen has vanished. I stand alone in an open field.

The setting is familiar. It's the rise behind the Barnwell and the West Ridge Cemetery. I can hear only the sound of a horse pawing and whinnying off to my left. Spin around and see, through the rolling mist, a gray steed with a blonde youth in its saddle. The youngster peers down at me, a question in his eyes, his lips moving, but no sound reaching me.

"John, I saw that terrible day on the mountain. I know the pain you feel and the sorrow it brought to your brother. But Ira took you home. You rest in hallowed ground."

The soldier nods and tries again to speak. I work hard to hear what he's saying but without success.

Movement, footsteps. A girl appears clad in a skirt and saddle shoes. She is clearly not a teen of John's time and certainly not of today. Oddly, she wears no top garment, only her bra, and she shivers in the cold air. With great difficulty she hoists herself onto the gray horse behind John Palmer, pulling and tugging at his uncooperative arm and the saddle to lift herself up.

The girl speaks to John and places her arm around his waist. He stiffens, shrugs her off with his free arm, disdainfully urging her away until she slips unceremoniously to the ground. She pleads, but he sits high in his saddle and looks away. She stands and turns toward me. Hugs herself with both arms, shudders and speaks. I instantly recognize the girl from the old news photo in the Times. She's the younger sister, Kyle's classmate, Valerie Hurt. Her words are not clear to me, but she's pointing at something behind me. I turn around and see the alley leading up to the cemetery, a small wooden building and the rear of the Barnwell House.

The girl apparently realizes I can't hear her, and she throws both arms into the air in frustration. She walks away toward the cemetery and disappears into the mist.

The young man's sad eyes plead with me. His message needs no words. If the heavens had opened and sent a bolt to me, it could not have been clearer.

"I understand, John. Your spirit still wanders looking for the peace you can't find. Your burial place has been violated. You're not alone there, are you? The girl is in that grave with you."

A new light shines in the lad's cornflower blue eyes. He exhales perceptibly as if a great moment of relief has finally come to him. His broad smile is all the reward I ask.

"Private John Palmer, you are a hero. You saved the life of your beloved brother Ira. He lived a long life and sired a large family. My own mother was one of his many descendants. I thank you, John. I'll make it right so you can be at peace in your resting place. I swear it, John."

Palmer draws himself up to his full stature and snaps his arm up sharply to his brow. He offers a salute then spins and urges his mount forward over the crest of the snowy slope. I stand alone on Tank Hill. John has returned to his grave with my assurance of a respite in his torment. Somewhere in the distance a lonely figure suspended from a crumbling tower silently pleads for this ordeal to be over.

*   *   *   *

When I regain my senses and snap awake, the dark room is hot and stifling. I kick away the covers and lie there in the stillness, my pulse tattooing at my temple. Sleep is impossible now. The gamut of emotions those too-real scenes thrust upon me have me reeling and racing ahead to wonder what is coming. I hold my head under the tap to let the cold water jar me awake.

My watch tells me this is no time to be wandering about befuddled while the world sleeps. But I need to think and the room is sweltering. Maybe I'll turn the heat down, take a walk and wait for my bedroom to cool. Better bundle up against the chill night air. I dress and slip away down the hall, along the winding staircase and out the front door, leaving it unlocked for my return.

The cold air announces itself as soon as I emerge onto the porch. After the first frigid gulp sears my lungs I relax. The air wakes me, gives my systems a wakeup, sets my brain whirring. I turn toward the driveway and carefully step onto its paved surface. No new snowfall for the past several days, but I remember too well my recent adventures with slipping, sliding and bumping my way through falls. I reach Main Street without incident and turn west.

Set out in the direction of Lake Spring, and roll over in my mind the warm moments my dream forecast at the house in Raleigh. Will my homecoming be as I pictured it or are there still hurdles in my way? Why is Helen so reluctant to shed the past and get on with our new life together? The more focused I become the faster I walk. Find myself approaching the spring and quickening my gait to a trot.

What of the encounter with Private John Palmer? Has my mind tricked me or did that deep sleep actually reveal the answer to connecting the night on Tank Hill and Lester Kanicki's guilt in the Hurt sisters' deaths? Could Valerie be wandering around the Barnwell looking for something she's somehow lost? Something to shield her from the cold?

I want Lester put away where he can never again harm my brother or any other innocent soul. And that's really the last major hurdle to my going back to my ladies with a clear and bright future ahead of me. When I go home it has to be with no sword of Damocles hanging over us, no bearded man lurking just out of view.

My own steps echo thunderously in my ears. I breathe heavily, my heart pounds and both legs tighten. I seem to float along almost as if I'm detached from my own body. Glance down and see that my feet are moving furiously in an all out gallop. I force my brain to slow down. Bring the pumping legs to a halt. Stand bent forward, hands on thighs, sucking in the cold air and gasping for oxygen. I resume at a more reasonable pace.

Streetlights and store signs dimly light my path as I pass one side street and approach a second one. A car lumbers by on an almost deserted Main Street. Its headlights flash across the street sign—Juniper Street. Without knowing why, I start down Juniper and scan ahead for Meg's small house. All reason tells me this is the last place I should be, given my resolve to put her out of mind and concentrate on returning to Helen. But logic is somehow overshadowed by an urge, more a need, to talk to someone, to pour out my thoughts and confusion and relieve myself of a weighty burden. Meg is near so I home toward her bungalow.

Almost one AM. A light glowing near the rear of Meg's house. I feel a sudden lift, a desire to find Meg and unload to an understanding ear.

Turn around now, Dave, and work this out on your own. Of all times to get her involved—Don't do it! I stop and stand on the sidewalk, debating my next move. A strong man would get out of here while he still can. He'd forget about knocking on that door. But I plod on toward her front walk, ready to turn in and find her.

The front door opens and two figures are dimly outlined in the soft glow from inside. A man and a woman. I know the woman is Meg, but who is that with her? He bends down, and her arms encircle his neck. They kiss as he steps back onto the stoop.

I watch from behind a shrub. Stand motionless while the man turns toward the street. He is a hulk of a man, tall and broad, clad in jeans and a fur-collared parka. He peers in both directions before leaving the porch then proceeds down the sidewalk away from me. But his face is outlined long enough for me to identify him.

It's Len Darden!

Don't know how long I stand rooted to that spot. My shoes are riveted to the ground as surely as if someone has nailed me down. I do have the presence to crouch behind the shrub away from the street when Darden swings his car around down the block and heads back in my direction. My second view of him confirms beyond a doubt that Meg's late night visitor is Len Broadus Darden, local sheriff and two-faced slug.

No wonder he's been so hostile to me. Don't doubt for a minute that he's plugged into everything that's happening in this town. That certainly would include keeping close tabs on his personal squeeze and all her movements. He knows I took her to the Auberge, went to her house for dinner, must see her almost daily at the Barnwell. Not only does he think I'm pushing him too hard with his investigation; he believes we're competing for Meg's attention. Well, on that last count he's dead wrong. He's welcome to the deceiving little wench.

I spin on my heel and skulk away down Juniper Street, conflicting thoughts battling in my head. A part of me feels betrayed, angry that the likes of Broadus Darden has been sharing with Meg what I thought she wanted with me. But more importantly, I'm relieved that any lingering thoughts of being with her are gone for good. As alluring as she may be, I wouldn't touch her now.

Chapter 43

The things I saw in my dream and outside Meg's house should keep me frustrated and awake for the rest of the night. Strangely, they have exactly the opposite effect. Out there in the cold air on Juniper Street I made some decisions about where to go from this point. The shock of learning that Len and Meg are involved clears an important stumbling block for me. Sleep like a winter bear for the last half of the long evening.

I go down to breakfast, and Mrs. Starkey brightens my day as always.

"Morning, Dave. Restful night?" She sets my grapefruit juice in front of me and whispers, "Found the homemade scrapple you mentioned. Don't tell the others. Picked up some just for you and me. Scrambled eggs with it?"

"You're too much, Mrs. S. Scrambled will be fine." I turn to the newspaper, check the weather and the sports section. Get absorbed in the paper and my morning coffee.

"Well, don't you look fit this morning?" Meg has arrived with my plate, standing there with that maddening smile, looking like the definition of the word 'perky'.

"Thanks. Must have been a great night for you, too," I reply. "Bright and sunny as all outdoors." I return to my paper. She can't possibly know the hidden meaning in my comment. Doesn't know what I saw on Juniper Street.

I read on and nibble at breakfast. More than once I glance up to see Meg staring across the room from the entry to the kitchen. All this week she's been cool to me. Had almost nothing to say on the occasions when we passed each other or I sat here for meals. There's something very different this morning. It's like she has more to say, but she doesn't know how to begin. When I laid down the rules and told her to back off, she was obviously shaken. Her silence has made for a much less encumbered stay at the Barnwell this week. I'm enjoying not having to joust with her. Sure, I have mixed emotions after finding out she has a thing going with that Pillsbury doughboy of a sheriff. But that's okay, she's his worry, not mine.

As soon as breakfast is over, I'll give Kyle a shout and get over to see him. This is my last chance before I head for Raleigh this weekend. He's endured two shocks already since Monday with the horrific deaths of Billy and Randy. Want to be sure everything's right with him before I leave him here alone to face the whims of Lester Kanicki. By now we're overdue to hear from Lester again.

What I want even more, though, is to confide in him what my trip to Raliegh is all about. He will surely have some words of advice to offer, and he'll do it without sounding like he's prompting me. I wouldn't make this important trip without first hearing what he has to say about my upcoming reunion with Helen.

I haven't been back in my room long when I hear a soft rap at the door. Finish buttoning my shirt and call out, "Come in." Meg Kane steps into the room still looking fresh as spring flowers.

"Dave, I need to talk to you."

Yeah, I think, *and I needed to talk to you last night, too, but you were too busy entertaining that big dumb ox.* But I'll listen and try to be civil.

"There isn't time now to tell you everything, but I'm in serious trouble, Dave. I need help desperately, and the only one I can turn to is you." Her voice reaches a panic pitch. When she says 'you' it comes out more a squeak than a word.

"What is it, Meg? Money troubles? Something wrong with Trevor?"

"Those are things I could deal with. What's so frightening is that I can't do anything about this. It's totally beyond my control."

"This is about whoever is harassing you, isn't it? You ready to talk about that now?"

I watch the color leave her cheeks, the bouncy lightness turn to a cold fear. She's trembling and wavering, and looks near to collapsing. I reach out and drag the desk chair to her, urging her to sit before she falls. She drops heavily to the seat. I resist the urge to put my arms around her. Caution is still the byword around this unpredictable charmer. I'm taking no chances.

"Slowly, Meg. Tell me, how can I help?"

She recovers enough to go on.

"I'm being stalked, Dave. Trevor and I aren't safe here. I need your advice on what to do."

"Then give me the whole story."

"No, someone could overhear. Meet me somewhere. You know the gazebo at the lake?"

"Sure."

"Meet me there at six o'clock. Just the two of us. No one else to listen in."

"I'll be there, Meg. And try to calm down. We'll make things right."

* * * *

I make my way toward Kyle's house. What Meg has told me bounces around in my head all the way there. She's a complex and puzzling woman. This could be another one of her schemes to bait a trap for me. But no one could fake the terror I saw in her face. She's tied in knots, concerned for her safety, for Trevor, scared out of her wits. For some reason she's chosen to turn to me, not to the logical choice, to rid her of her stalker. Len Darden certainly has the know-how and the resources to solve her dilemma. Why me?

"All quiet, Kyle?" He's sitting in the den reading, feet propped up and a soda standing by. Looks calm and relaxed.

Kyle says, "Not a peep out of you know who. Maybe you put too much heat on him and he's left town."

"Wouldn't stake my life on it, brother, particularly after the three horrific killings he's pulled off. Len and his boys say they're hot on his trail, but how much of that can we really believe? I do almost miss Carl tagging along everywhere I go, though."

"Yeah, got to know him myself when you left so suddenly for Raleigh, Dave. But he explained they needed to pull him back. Said he'd be on call if I needed him. Things have seemed pretty normal since then."

"Don't let your guard down, Kyle. Lester could be counting on us to do just that."

He thinks about that, and I change the subject.

"Tell me something about Len Darden, Kyle. He has a family, right?"

"Couple of grown kids and a wife that Jenny and I knew back in high school. Nice girl. Not at all crude like Len. Why do you ask?"

"Met a girl when I first came to town. She works at the Barnwell House now. Found out last night Darden is seeing her. Well after dark, I might add."

"Doesn't surprise me. He's always had a reputation for a wandering eye."

"And remember he admitted he wasn't playing it straight about checking on Kanicki. Did a sloppy job the first time then came up with more information than he was willing to tell us. What's going on with your old chum, Kyle?"

"Same old Broadus. He'd lie to your face if it was to his advantage. Guess he never outgrew it. But folks seem to think he's a good lawman. They keep electing him."

"Well, there are a lot of questions I'd like to hang on the sheriff. But how can I trust his answers? Now there's little miss perky, his nighttime squeeze. Could be a little awkward to confront him now that I know about his relationship with her."

Kyle's reaction is predictable.

"Sounds like you may have more invested in this than merely a dislike for Darden, Dave. Want to tell me about it?"

Caught. Nailed. Never could fool him.

"Okay, I briefly had this thing about the girl he's seeing. Nothing happened, but I was toying with thoughts I shouldn't have been having."

He frowns and asks, "So?"

"It was a non-starter, big brother. I know where my future lies, and there's no room for a dangerous flirtation."

"Good."

We drop that subject. Kyle and I have a nice long visit. Talk like old times. I slide into a discussion of my upcoming trip over the long President's Day weekend. He brightens. No need for pretense with Kyle, he knows from my tone the high hopes I have for patching things up with Helen.

"Put all this mess up here behind you, Dave. Concentrate on what matters. We'll do just fine. Tend to your girls in Raleigh."

"Exactly what I plan. Take care of them. As soon as we remove the threat from Kanicki."

Kyle nods. He knows as well as I do that neither of us will have a normal life until we deal with Lester.

"See you as soon as I get back, pal. Stay warm and safe."

"Don't worry, Dave. You'll be okay. Helen loves you."

That's all I need to buoy me on my way to Raleigh tomorrow. But first I have an appointment to keep at Lake Spring.

* * * *

Six o'clock. I'm standing in the Lake Spring gazebo. Weather's improved. Not as windy or cold. Still, I hope Meg and I don't have to be out here long with a cold night coming.

Meg arrives looking like she's in a hurry, her movements skittish, her head jerking about to check our surroundings.

"Settle down, Meg. We're safer here than any place I can think of. It's totally public but out of earshot. Calm down and tell me what's going on."

"I'm terrified, Dave. Can't sleep, can't eat. The pressure is unbearable."

"You said this was about a stalker. Who, Meg?"

"Can we leave that unsaid for now?"

"It's your story. Tell it like you want."

"Everywhere I go I can feel him close by. Probably watching us now, but thank goodness he can't hear what we're saying. Trevor and I are alone. He could walk in any time and hurt us."

"But why? What reason does he have for hovering over you?"

"It's somebody from my past. Somebody who's extremely jealous and possessive. What matters is I need for him to go away." Her fright gets the best of her again. She lights a smoke, and paces back and forth in the small enclosure.

"Dave, he called me at the Barnwell this morning to remind me he can get to Trevor and me anytime he wants."

"So you're talking to him, too."

She doesn't answer. Breathes hard and looks away from me.

"That's why your mood changed so abruptly after breakfast. Why don't you call in the police and let them handle him?"

She continues pacing. Shakes her head vigorously at my suggestion. "Can't do that, Dave. Don't ask why."

"Okay, but let me tell you something you don't think I know. About you and Len Darden."

That stops her dead in her tracks. She freezes and looks up at me with a helpless expression. "Darden? The sheriff?" A feeble attempt at a defense.

"Yeah, the guy that was at your house after one o'clock this morning. *That* Len Darden."

All the air goes out of her. She flips her cigarette butt into the water, turns to me and resigns herself to the fact that I've found her out.

"I won't deny it. He's good to me and to Trevor. Big brute can be rough, but he's got a good heart."

"So how long has this been going on? Certainly longer than you've known me, I take it."

"He's been courting me for several months. Always comes around after dark. Doesn't want any rumors flying. He and his wife are not on the best of terms. If it wasn't for his support, we'd be out in the cold by now."

Courting. That's a new term for what's been going on out on Juniper Street.

"I think he's well paid for his help. Looked mighty satisfied when he left your house last night."

"Are you snooping on me, Dave? Thought you didn't have feelings for me. Maybe you're not being as honest as I thought." She slides a little closer.

I back off and say, "No. I meant what I said. Friends only. But I needed someone's ear last night and you were near by. Unfortunately for me, you were otherwise occupied."

"You don't understand. I need Len until I get on my feet again. I have genuine feelings for you, Dave, but you'd made it clear you weren't interested. What do you expect me to do?"

"Oh, you bet I was interested, but you came along way too late. I have my commitment. Now let's get back to the stalker."

"There are certain things the sheriff would find out if he dug deep enough. Matters I want left alone. Tell me you'll help me."

"Is there somewhere you can go, Meg? A friend you can stay with? Maybe if you leave your place, the stalker will show up there one time too many, and I can bag him for you. Best I can offer."

All the while I'm telling her this I'm wondering why I would take on a new burden, but it's done now.

"I have a girl friend out in the country that I'm sure would take us in for awhile. I can't stand this constant pressure."

"Then let's take Trevor and go to her place. Where is Trev now?"

"At my aunt's house. I'll get him and we'll pack."

"I'll pick you up in an hour. Pack two suitcases, no more. Call your friend now, and ask her to meet us at the grocery down at Lakeside. I'll lead the stalker on a merry chase he won't be able to untangle until we have you safely in her car."

She looks relieved that she may have a way to elude her stalker, even if it's only temporary. Her eyes, however, continue to dart about. Still expects to see someone watching us.

"Thank you, Dave. Oh, thank you!" She steps toward me and I wave her off. "Friends. Remember?"

I mentally kick myself as I walk back to the Barnwell. Could be the biggest rube in town. Is she using me? Can't take the chance. If she's being truthful about the stalker, I know exactly how she feels. *Don't I, Lester?* Besides, Trevor's had some bad breaks, and he deserves a hand.

Chapter 44

Meg and Trevor are waiting when I reach her house. We hastily put their possessions in my car and speed away. I'm scanning in all directions looking for signs of being followed. No suspicious cars in pursuit, but I wouldn't expect the stalker to be obvious about it. I make a series of unorthodox moves, turns and cutbacks to be certain. We arrive at our rendezvous location, and she points out her friend's car.

"Dave. Dorothy," she says. I carry two suitcases and a large box to Dorothy's car. The tall brunette smiles and opens the trunk.

I press an envelope into Meg's hand. "Here. My cell number. Call if you need me." She will discover later that the envelope also contains three hundred dollars in cash to tide her over.

"Thank you, Dave." This time she's a bit too fast for me, and I find she has me in a fierce lip lock. Feels too good to regard her as only a friend. "Here are the directions to Dorothy's place in case you need them," she says, "and her telephone number."

I look down at Trevor who obviously doesn't understand what all this activity means. To him it's merely a late night adventure.

"See you sport. Look after Mommy." He offers his small hand.

* * * *

I return to the Barnwell and park beside the small shed in back. Walk toward the back door when a thought strikes me suddenly and stops me short. When the Tank Hill incident took place, this would have been the Starkeys' home, not yet the Barnwell House. West Ridge was probably closer to this house than any other. And a tool shed stands behind the big house. What if Lester stopped in the quiet alley behind the Starkeys' with Valerie, or maybe both girls, in his car? Garth Jenkins had told me that the hit and run in Linton occurred after dark, and the boys saw Lester on Tank Hill at around six PM the same night. Maybe things had already started to go wrong for Lester before sundown.

The shed looks to be quite old even though repainting has kept it from being an eyesore. Mrs. S has someone who keeps the grounds for her. I'm reasonably sure the gardening tools and lawn mower are kept in this building. Her helper has dutifully placed a lock on the door hasp, but behind the plate, the wood is rotting away. I have little trouble prying the lock and hasp off using a forgotten rusty rake for leverage. I'll apologize to Mrs. S later.

A musty smell greets me from the inside of the small shed. There is no electrical wiring, so I bump around in the dark until I decide that's a lost cause. Go back to my car and retrieve my flashlight from beneath the front seat.

I poke around and search every corner, not knowing exactly what I expect to find, but the potential reward is too great to pass up. The wood plank floor, badly in need of repair, yields and creaks underfoot, and my searching raises long-dormant dirt and dust that fill the air. I choke and sneeze my way around. Garden tools hang on string loops around wall nails. A weather-beaten straw hat sits on a shelf. I find several old cardboard boxes and a wooden orange crate stored on leaning metal shelves. Play the flashlight beam inside the crate and feel around, extracting two small bottles, an old tobacco tin, a few other discarded items. Then my efforts are more than rewarded. My fingers grasp what seems to be wool cloth and I lift. Bring out a bulky yellow sweater. Turn it over and discover a large dark spot at the neckline. Bingo!

My mind races. I can picture the scene that November night. While the older sister, Stephanie, lies passed out or otherwise immobilized in Lester's car, he takes Valerie into the shed for fun and games with a child of fifteen. She tries to fight him off, and he hits her with his hand or something else. She bleeds and he panics, probably decides to finish her off then and there. Then he hits on the idea of taking one of the handy shovels and digging a shallow grave somewhere nearby. He'll worry about Stephanie later.

After stuffing the blood-soaked sweater down into the crate, he grabs a shovel and drags Valerie up the hill to the cemetery conveniently waiting for her. Minutes later, Jimmy Moore sees Lester performing the end of that heinous deed.

These days there is a new weapon for connecting evidence to cold cases. DNA! Now I have the link that can convince Len.

Chapter 45

Early the next morning I leave the Barnwell without waiting for breakfast. Mrs. S seems puzzled by my haste, and she insists I take time for toast, juice and coffee. Then I hurry out the door, professing that I'm on my way directly to Raleigh.

I swing east and stop at the police station. I've carefully placed the yellow sweater in a plastic shopping bag. Tried to treat it as gently as possible for fear of disturbing any genetic evidence it may still contain.

"Morning, Carl," I greet my new acquaintance and erstwhile babysitter.

"Out kind of early, aren't you, Dave?"

When I place the bag on his counter, he looks quizzically at me and asks, "What's this?"

"Precious cargo, Carl. Handle it gingerly." He's stumped.

"What the hell are you pulling now, Owens?"

"That's evidence, Carl, a bloody sweater from a long time ago that could link Lester Kanicki with the death of Valerie Hurt. Maybe this will convince the sheriff we need to dig her bones out of John Palmer's grave."

Carl reaches for the phone.

"Who are you calling," I ask.

"The sheriff, of course. He needs to hear this right away."

"It'll keep till he shows up for duty. Tell Len I'm on my way to Raleigh. He knows how to reach me there." I walk away and close the door behind me.

Before leaving town I swing by Meg's house and take a quick check. Quiet and peaceful just like last evening when I drove over and sat watch in my car until the heater made me unbearably drowsy. The stalker is either well hidden or we've eluded him for the time being. If I do encounter him, my first call is to the sheriff's office, but Meg doesn't know that. Not my job to arrest him, just to make sure they do. I have urgent business in Raleigh.

Meg had called me last night just before I hit the bed. She reported they were safely installed at Dorothy's house. Said she'd opened the envelope and owed me. I had visions of the return of misreads we'd already been through and gotten beyond. Told her she owed me nothing other than staying safe and keeping Trevor away from harm.

* * * *

The sky is clear and the day is bright when I arrive in Raleigh. I step into the foyer and call out, "Anybody here to greet a tired traveler?"

Both Helen and Melody appear, Helen coming from the direction of the kitchen and Melody bouncing down the stairs. I walk over to my wife, and she accepts my embrace and kiss willingly. She even returns a kiss of her own. Melody forgets she's about to turn a mature fifteen and squeals with delight. Not exactly the greetings I pictured in my sleep the other night, but it's a very encouraging start.

"How was your drive down, Daddy?" Melody wants to know.

"Too long. Couldn't wait to get here. Brought lots of clothes so I could dress up for my two favorite dates." I set my bags down in the hallway.

"I put some manly soap in your bathroom this time," Helen says. "Got rid of that 'froo froo' scented muck as you called it."

Guess that takes care of one big answer. It's back to the guest room for my bags and me. Well, can't expect her to cave in and *really* invite me home. But there's a long weekend ahead.

Turns out to be a lovely evening. Helen has obviously told Melody she's to take the lead as our birthday girl and decide what we'll do. Her choices are simple but they take me back to the times we spent by the fireplace laughing and teasing each other, loving every minute of our time together.

Helen works her usual magic with dinner and I stuff myself. She knows how I love key lime pie, and produces huge slices of the home baked version with coffee as Melody and I sit by the fire. We end up on the rug, a big bowl of popcorn between us, playing games by the light of the fireplace.

"The room feels so much warmer with the lamps low," Melody says, and she turns them down.

Helen shrugs, sticks out her hands as if feeling her way through the dark, and joins us at the game board. I realize Melody has made it easy to dispense with our game playing. We can hardly see the board with the lights so dim. Father and birthday girl find a better sport—throwing popcorn at each other and all over mother's clean carpet.

Helen picks up a handful of kernels and tosses them in my direction. "When you two kids are finished, the vacuum cleaner is in the hall closet."

Melody takes a shot at Helen with some fluffy missiles then attacks me and bowls me over. Our enthusiasm catches Helen up in the playfulness, and she begins to tickle her daughter. Before any of us quite realize it, we're tangled and rolling, with popcorn and playing pieces scattered in all directions, the three of us roaring hysterically.

"I have an idea," our not-so-little-anymore girl announces. "Since tomorrow is my birthday, I'd like to see those tapes we have of past birthdays. You guess my age in each one."

She fishes the tapes out of a cabinet, and slips one into the player. A younger version of our cutie cavorts for the camera in the back yard of this very house. Then she tries her best to mimic a proper young lady until someone who looks a lot like her mischievous father rubs cake icing on her nose.

"Age?" she quizzes.

I answer without a moment's hesitation. "Your tenth. You were so proud of that party dress."

"Haven't decided what I'll wear tomorrow. Mom said she made a reservation at the Crown Room. Has to be the swankiest place in town."

I cast an inquisitive look in Helen's direction, and she returns a knowing grin. As the tape ends and Melody searches for another, Helen slips quietly out of the room. She returns with a large, ribbon-tied box under her arm.

Melody pops in the tape, and turns around as Helen holds the box out to her. "Daddy wanted you to shine on this birthday, honey. This is for our celebration tomorrow night."

Her movie game is temporarily forgotten. She holds up the shimmering silver dress and hugs it to her cheek. Helen offers her the matching silver pumps.

"I couldn't have wished for a more beautiful dress. It's perfect. Thank you, Daddy. Thank you, Mom. I'll treasure it always."

She sits and strokes the fabric of the dazzling garment. Helen and I take our places on the big leather couch.

"Mom, do me a favor," Melody says. "My most favorite birthday before now was my fifth, the last year we were in Springlake. Put the tape in, please. I just want to sit here and hold my new dress."

Helen starts the tape and returns to my side on the couch. A cute little preschooler dances across the screen, comes closer to the camera, showing off the gap where two front teeth have recently disappeared. Helen nestles closer to me. She lets me take her hand.

We didn't have a lot of material things in those days, but no three people could have been happier than we were. Upstairs apartment with two tiny bedrooms and enough love to fill a mansion. Five-year old Melody continues her frolicking and Helen squeezes my hand. I look at my wife. See something I haven't seen in months. The spark is definitely back, and the pain and frustration have dissipated. There is no longer any question that we're ready to rekindle our life together.

"The girls will be looking for me," Melody says. "They don't know I've already figured out our sleepover is actually a pajama party for me and all my closest friends. But I'll be home as soon after breakfast as I possibly can. I want a full day with the dearest parents a girl could have."

She gathers up her new clothes and heads off to her room. Helen and I sit there with the log light softly glowing in the darkened room. I realize I'm still holding her hand in mine. Raise her warm hand and press it to my cheek. She's looking at me with anticipation. I kiss her. She responds.

"Tell me this is how it's supposed to be, sweetheart."

"Yes, Dave, this is day one of a whole new us."

Melody flutters into the room. There should be little doubt what's happened in her absence. We both must be flushed. She bends down to give each of us a peck. "Love you both."

She turns to go, but I trap her arm. "Not so fast, young lady. It's dark out. I'm driving you."

"Oh, Daddy, it's only three blocks," she protests.

"No matter. Tonight you get chauffeured," I tell her, and retrieve my keys.

"Don't go away, Helen. Hold that thought. I'll be right back." Melody looks at us, but she doesn't ask. Just smiles.

To say the evening was just beginning would be a gross understatement. Once the floodgates open, we both find our voices. End the terrible hiatus in our lifetime of sharing.

"I've been so lonely without you near," Helen tells me.

"Baby," I answer, "I know I was the one that ripped us apart with my thoughtless actions. That made my loneliness all the worse."

She presses a finger to my lips then replaces it with her own sweet lips.

"Helen, honey, nothing can ever come between us again."

"Come home to stay, Dave. I love you."

Feel like I'm back in her parents' parlor courting her all over again, but this time it's definitely for keeps.

We meld together until we can stand the wait no longer. Without a word, she rises from the sofa and takes my hand. I follow, but my impatience takes hold. Soon I'm leading the way. As we pass the guest room, I say a silent farewell to beds with one warm side and an empty pillow, to a burning ache that will soon be quenched. We spend a sleepless night. Savor every moment of our celebration—our own pajamaless party.

Chapter 46

"You can run, but you can't hide from old Lester, Owens. Show time is getting nearer."

Kanicki opens another beer and wolfs down a long draught, letting the foam trickle down his beard. It's been a memorable time, these past three weeks. Surges of seething anger at all the people lined up against him, then the immense relief of cutting three of them down, silencing them forever. He reflects that it's an acquired taste, a need that grows more intense each time he kills. A new goal to reach that exceeds his previous successes.

"Logan, it's over for you, but it's just beginning for the Owens brothers. Damn your eyes, I've got those baby blues in my cooler to prove it doesn't pay to cross me. That stupid Indian got in the way and caused his own death. And you, Bean, you gullible man. Let little brother talk you into getting in over your head. You're my first signed work; I left my mark for everybody to see, for all the good it'll do them in catching me."

He stumbles to the sink and lathers his beard. Takes the straight razor and makes the first long sweep, rinses the blade and watches the black whiskers disappear down the drain. Hesitates for a moment then nods his commitment to continue. The coarse black hair collects in the stopped sink until he dumps it in the trash.

He views his new look from all angles and approves heartily of his decision. This will mark the next phase of his long struggle to cleanse himself of all the people who wish him harm. They can't be allowed to live. Only he and Margaret will be left standing when it's finished.

"My, my. You've still got it. Is it any wonder the women have always given in. Oh, a few of them needed convincing like that Hurt girl. She didn't know what a favor I was doing her making her first time an experience with a real man."

Yes, this may be his smartest move yet.

"They're chasing a beard and black clothes. I'm about to become the cleanest-cheeked best dresser in town. Better make your peace, Owens boys. Before the week is over, you'll be fitted for your coffins."

Chapter 47

The rest of the weekend in Raleigh with my girls is beyond fantastic. Almost too perfect to believe. Helen and I save the best news to be delivered as our proudest birthday gift to Melody. She is overjoyed that our family will be restored.

My daughter is a knockout in her gleaming silver dress, though I confess I feel a note of sadness. My little girl is about to grow up. Helen is positively stunning in that blue sheath. I proudly waltz each of them around the Crown Room. Melody has carefully planned the entire weekend as her birthday present to us. She fills our days with activities. Helen and I have no difficulty finding our own entertainment at night. We cling to each other like newlyweds.

Monday dawns. It's nearly time for me to tear away and return to Springlake. There really is no alternative. Until the business is settled in my old hometown, we won't be safe and secure anywhere. Helen wants me back, and I can't wait to get the loose ends cleared up. One way or another, I'll force Lester Kanicki into the open and dispense with him.

I prop up on one elbow to watch Helen sleep. She stirs and opens her eyes.

"What?" A smile creeps across her face as she reaches out to touch my cheek.

"Just watching you and wondering."

"Wondering what, Dave?"

"How you want to make our new start."

"Seems we've already launched." She draws me down to meet her lips. I almost forget to ask the important question I have for her.

"Ummm. But where? Is Raleigh home or should I carry you away to some exotic spot? Live on the beach in Tahiti. Hire a tutor for Melody."

She gives me a serious look and asks, "What about your business? You'd leave Atlanta?"

"In a heartbeat. Wherever you choose. Already made that decision. Talked to Bill yesterday. He's agreed to buy me out. My only job now is to make you and Melody happy."

"But you thrive on being busy. What will you do?"

"Honey, I don't have to work another day in my life if I choose. There'll be other opportunities. Something low-key, less demanding. Maybe you and I should find a business we can run together."

"Have you ever considered going back to Springlake, Dave?" Her tone hints this is not the first time that option has occurred to her. And it's exactly the answer I wanted but couldn't press for. Had to be her decision.

"I've thought about it. More times than you can imagine. Lot of happy memories up there. How do you think Melody would feel about going home?"

"Dave, we've never been happier than we were in that town. Let me bounce it off her and see how she reacts. I'd want her to finish the school year down here, but we could relocate during the summer break."

Now I have *to make Springlake safe for us.*

*   *   *   *

Mrs. Starkey is in the kitchen when I reach the Barnwell late Monday afternoon. I set my bags in the back hallway, and slip into the kitchen while she scurries about finishing the evening meal. I take one look, discard my coat and roll up my sleeves. She is so absorbed in her work she hasn't even noticed me.

"Need a hand, Mrs. S?" She turns with a start. Nearly backs over a table full of carefully prepared salads.

"Glory be, Dave. Scared me out of a year's growth."

"Perfect opening for one of my short people jokes, but I don't want to upset you while you're holding a skillet."

She smirks, swipes a hand across her forehead, and returns to her task. "You could serve those salads. I counted ten people in the dining room."

I move from table to table greeting the guests and placing their salads. Get a bit of a puzzled look from some of them so I explain. "Mrs. S is short on help tonight. Same great meals, less appealing wait staff. Think I should wear an apron?" A couple of the patrons even manage a half hearted chuckle.

When the hurried pace of dinner service is finally past, Mrs. S and I sit in the kitchen taking a well deserved breather. She surveys the kitchen and sighs.

"Glad you showed up. I was about to fizzle out. It's been an exhausting weekend. Meg hasn't been here since Friday."

She starts to clean and stack dishes and I pitch in.

"I know. Meg has a serious problem." She frowns and takes two dishes from me. Insists on using good china in the dining room and hand washing everything.

"Oh, is there anything I can do? Wish she'd called me instead of just not showing up."

"She's hiding out, Mrs. S." That brings a shocked expression. She stops to listen.

"Meg is being harassed by a stalker. She's afraid for herself and her son. I can reach her, but I don't think she'll be back to work—at least not for awhile. Didn't have a choice."

"Poor thing. Wish I could help her." She washes another plate and places it lovingly on the drying rack. "Found temporary help for a couple of days but the girl wasn't reliable. Couldn't follow instructions, and I won't compromise on our guests' comfort. I've been running my legs off today."

"Wish I could tell you more, but that's all I know, Mrs. S. She can't come out until the stalker is gone, and she doesn't want the police involved. I'd say you'd better look for a full time replacement."

"Oh, heavens. I'm so fond of that girl. We make a great team."

I look at her tired eyes. Wonder how long she can keep going at this stride.

"Go relax in the parlor, lady, and I'll make us some tea." I try to shoo her out of the kitchen. She waves her hand then turns back to wiping and storing the china.

"I mean it, Mrs. S. Scoot on in there. I'll serve."

She gives me a long stare that gradually melts to a resigned, "Do need to sit down. You're a dear. Bring our tea and tell me all about your trip."

Give her awhile to unwind while I put the china and silverware back where they belong. Put on one of her frilly aprons then carry the teapot into the parlor. She's on the verge of dropping off to sleep. I wheel around to exit. She needs sleep more than refreshment. But she calls out to me.

"Don't you dare. That won't keep me awake tonight. Besides, you're so cute in that apron I wouldn't miss this for the world."

I set down the tea service and do a pirouette and curtsy. She laughs until her cheeks are wet.

"Now I want to hear aall about what happened in Raleigh."

I'm sure my lips must be curled up in a grin that she quickly decodes because she amends her words.

"Well, most everything, anyway."

"Shows in my attitude, huh? Couldn't have asked for better results. The three of us will soon be back together permanently."

"Hallelujah! I know you're ecstatic about that, Dave. So, will you be living in Raleigh?"

"Don't know yet. Wherever they want to live is fine with me. Maybe I'll coax them back to Springlake and take a job as a handyman at the Barnwell."

"How about as kitchen help? You're pretty handy at that," she tells me.

We talk on and sip our tea by the hearth. I see her day is about to fade into an early bedtime. She dozes then comes around with a sudden jerk. "Believe I'm about ready to finish that kitchen work and toddle off to bed."

"Kitchen's all tidied up. You have a pleasant night. I'll watch over the parlor for awhile and lock up."

She stoops to kiss my cheek and says, "Thank you, Dave. I'm so glad for you."

* * * *

I sit alone in the quiet of the parlor enjoying the soft music. All the guests have returned from their evening outings so it's almost time to secure the Barnwell for the night. The warmth of the events of the past few days overwhelms me, fills the room, and makes the fireplace an unnecessary ornament. I'll never be cold again.

Maybe I'll turn the TV on low and channel surf. Should be worn out, but I'm not quite ready to call an end to this beautiful day. History Channel, huh? Let's see why it's one of Kyle's favorites. Documentary about the British royal family. May be interesting.

The narrator is relating how England's citizens revere the royals despite the family's shortcomings. He tells of the young king who abdicated his succession to the throne to marry his American love. There's a lengthy review of the inauguration of Elizabeth II and the coming of age of the bonnie prince Charles.

The voiceover dwells on the special affection all Brits felt for their beloved Queen Mother who never failed to add grace and dignity to the royal family. Vignettes show Princess Margaret, Elizabeth II's sister who died in the same year her revered mother passed away. Few ever referred to the princess by her given name. She was never Margaret to the English, merely Meg.

Meg! The word strikes with such sudden force I leap from my seat and blurt out, "Of course. Margaret, Meg. Kanicki, Kane. Where has my head been? That could explain everything." I plop back down and stare at the wall. A possessive person from her past is after her, she said. Her father? Could that connection be what she didn't want the police to find out about? Sure, I could be diving head first off a steep assumption, but why not?

If Meg Kane is, in fact, Margaret Kanicki, it would also explain why Lester's daughter had seemed to vanish. If Lester is back and harassing her, it means he's lurking in the vicinity of Springlake. He could sooner or later make the mistake of showing up when I can catch him off guard. She could be the key to the whole problem and the way to solve it.

Where is that slip of paper with the directions to Dorothy's cabin? I find it folded up and tucked into my wallet.

I turn the door latches and hurry up to my room. Priority one now is to confront Meg and sort this all out. I'm bushed, but there's an early morning drive to the country that is definitely on my schedule.

Open the door to my room, stand back and gasp at the state of disarray.

Everything in the room seems to be out of place, turned over or spilled. The bed covers are piled in the center of the big four poster. The dresser drawers have been dumped and left on the floor. The closet door stands open, and my clothes are off their hangers, heaped in a jumbled pile. Looks like everything in the room has been searched thoroughly then tossed.

Then my eyes are drawn to the mirror attached to the bathroom door. Something is scrawled in garish scarlet across its shiny surface. Looks like it could be paint or nail polish. The way it's run down the mirror it's almost like a message written in blood. *KYLE THEN YOU* the words shout at me. A chill rushes through me. I reach for the phone. Have to call Kyle now!

One, two, three rings. Where is he at this late hour? Four, five rings followed by a recorded message. I impatiently wait for the tone and say, "Kyle. Get help from the police. Lester's about to make his play. I'll be at your house as soon as possible."

I don't take the time to right the room. Mrs. S will be in shock, but I have no time to spare. Reach for the wallet in my pocket and tuck the folded sheet of paper back into its hiding place. Well, that's a relief! At least I kept the directions for finding Meg on me if that's what he was looking for. Or maybe he just wanted to terrorize me again for the pure enjoyment of it all. I grab my coat and flee toward my car.

On the way to Kyle's house, I punch in the number at Dorothy's and wait. A sleepy, somewhat annoyed voice finally answers.

"Sorry, Dorothy. It's Dave Owens. Urgent I speak with Meg."

"I'll get her," she says. The phone drops then I hear indistinct background noises.

Almost a minute passes before Meg says, "Dave?"

"Don't talk, Meg. Just listen. He's been here. Left a warning and trashed my room. Don't think he knows where you are, but we can't take any chances. Get out of there and take Trevor and Dorothy with you. Go to the police station in Springlake. I'm on my way now to check on my brother."

There is a long silence from her end. I wonder if my words have sunk in. She's likely still trying to shake herself awake. At last she speaks.

"Who, Dave? Who did this?"

"Your father, Meg."

Again, she goes quiet.

Finally, she says very softly, "It's my stalker. He's taunting you. Part of the vicious games he loves to play to mess with your mind. That's how he's kept me stressed out all this time. Must have a plan in mind or he would have waited for you and attacked you right there in your room. He wants you to suffer till he's ready to do you in."

"Don't let down your guard, Meg. He could be after all of us. I'll track him down after I check on Kyle. You go to the police station now."

"We'll be all right, Dave. I'm as safe here as anywhere. Dorothy has guns and we both know how to use them."

"Meg, listen. I think it's your father. Am I right?"

No answer.

"Lester Kanicki, Meg. Your father. He's the one that's stalking you, isn't he?"

Silence.

"Talk to me, Meg!

The telephone goes dead in my hand.

Chapter 48

I try again to reach Kyle. No answer. How could all four of them be gone this time of night? He and Jenny never stay out late, and both boys must have school tomorrow. I take all the shortcuts. Skid to a halt by the hedge-lined yard. Hurtle from the car and take the handgun; leave the holster on the front seat. No telling what I may encounter inside the house.

No lights on. But then I wouldn't expect anyone to be up this late. I take out my key and fumble with the lock in the dark, hoping the noise doesn't alert the wrong person. Enter the foyer and carefully check the main level. Nothing out of the ordinary. Hesitantly, fearing what I may find, I cautiously climb the stairs.

Both of the boys' beds are undisturbed. I work my way down the hall expecting to be attacked at any moment. But I sense no movement, hear nothing at all except the steady tick, tick of a wall clock. I inch toward Kyle and Jenny's bedroom, and snake my arm through the doorway, feel for the light switch. Click it on. Crouch in the doorway almost in the same motion. Scan the room. Bed made. All appears to be in order.

Then I remember. Sometimes in the middle of winter, Kyle and Jenny retreat to the basement to sleep by the wood stove. I work my way back, through the kitchen and down the long basement stairs. This time I decide to leave the room dark, and carefully make my way down the steep stairs. Wait at the bottom and strain to listen for any sound at all that will tell me I'm not alone. Finally I fumble for a switch and light the room. No sign of them.

I sit down on the steps and take stock. Stumped. Bewildered. Where now?

Hear footsteps above me. Reach for my gun. I'm so spooked it falls from my fingers and clatters to the floor.

"Got you." A voice roars down from the kitchen.

My first thought is, *It's all over, Dave. You blew it.*

"Police. Hands up." Never thought those words would sound so comforting. For a second I was sure Lester had nailed me.

I turn and peer up toward the figure framed in the doorway. My friend Carl does a double take then holsters his weapon. "Sorry, Dave. Could have been anybody."

"Kyle and all his family are missing, Carl. Wait a minute. Why are *you* here?"

"Hold on, man. Kyle and the boys are fine. They're down at the station talking to the deputy on duty."

"Wait," I answer cautiously. "You said Kyle and the boys. You didn't mention Jenny."

"Come up here, and I'll tell you everything I know," Carl says.

I don't like the tone he's using. Something is terribly wrong. The gun is lying at the bottom of the stairs, but I leave it there. Saves a possible argument about why I'm packing a weapon.

We stand in the kitchen, and I ask, "What aren't you telling me, Carl?"

He starts slowly and carefully. "Kyle made a call for help and I came out here. Said Jenny was missing, kidnapped. We took him and the boys down to the station to give us statements."

"Kidnapped?"

"Seems she walked down the road to the church for some sort of meeting, and it ran longer than expected. She called Kyle and told him, but the church is close by so he wasn't worried. Said she'd have one of the girls drop her off when the meeting was over."

"And she didn't show up?"

"Not quite that simple. Man snatched her right out of the parking lot before her friend could react. He knocked the other woman to the ground then grabbed Jenny and took off with her."

"Did she give you a description? Of the attacker or his car?"

"Said it was a man in a long black coat. He shoved Jenny into a dark colored car, maybe brown."

I feel like my guts have been ripped out. Hold my stomach and try to keep from heaving.

"He's got her. Damn, Carl, he's got her."

"Who, Dave? Who's got her?"

"The one that's been stalking Kyle and me. Lester Kanicki. The bastard your boss can't find is about to add another victim to his list."

Carl looks right through me, trying to absorb the impact of what I'm saying. Then he points toward the front door. "Come uptown with me, Owens, and we'll sort this out."

* * * *

By the time we get to the sheriff's office, Len Darden has arrived. Don and Tom are sitting out front talking to a deputy. I'm told the sheriff is closeted with my brother.

I put my arms around the boys' shoulders and tell them, "We'll get her back safe and sound. Hang in and keep your dad's spirits up." I spin around and head toward Len's closed door.

"Wait. I'll let him know you're here," the officer on the desk says.

"Screw that. I'll announce myself," I say and shove the door wide.

"Broadus, you damn well better have some answers."

The sheriff scowls across his desk at me and, right away, I know it's face off time between us.

"Sit down and don't hand me any crap, Owens."

Kyle is clearly in a state of shock. I cross to where he's sitting.

Darden continues in his most officious tone. "Looks like your suspicions about Lester Kanicki could be right. But that don't give you any call to bust in here spoutin' off. Got a place for you to cool down if you can't manage it on your own."

"So you finally believe what I've been trying to get into that thick skull of yours?"

"Watch your mouth, Dave. You're right on the edge"

I'm on the attack now, not about to back off. "What was the outcome of the tests on the yellow sweater I brought in? That should give you the link to the Hurt girls' deaths."

"Tests aren't back yet. We asked the parents for blood samples, too."

"He's killed at least seven times, sheriff, and four of them were on your watch: Jimmy, Sam and Billy, and Randy."

"You don't know that yet. Lester could be a dangerous man, but we're hot on his trail now."

"On his trail? You're as lost as ever. He's got my sister-in-law, for God's sake. No telling where he's gone while you fill out reports and get organized. When are you gonna get up off that fat ass and do something useful?"

He kicks up out of his chair and shakes his big, meaty fist at me. "No more passes for you, Dave. Bad time for you to piss me off. Think I'll just toss you in back for a while." His face is beet red. Kyle nods toward a chair and I sit, still fuming.

"Okay, what's your plan, sheriff?" I make a serious attempt to settle my temper. The big windbag doesn't scare me, but he's the one with the badge.

Now it's Len's turn to foam at the mouth, and he struggles to keep control. But he strains hard to play the efficient lawman.

"Got men out searching. Looking for a brown car. Not many people out and about this time of night. We're calling all the motels to be on the lookout. Alerting the state police. The service stations that are open this time of day know to report any brown cars that show up."

"Tell your men we're looking for a Virginia license plate that starts with two six and ends with a seven. Caught that much when my stalker showed himself twice before." He writes that down and calls Carl, hands him the pad with the numbers. Carl nods his understanding.

"Now I suggest you all go back to Kyle's place and wait for a call from the kidnapper. We believe he's only after Kyle. This is his way of getting to him. We'll send Carl with you, and I'll keep him read in on our progress."

We prepare to leave, but I want another minute alone with Darden. Guess it comes under the heading of being a glutton for punishment with him already on a rampage. I shut the door and face him.

"What now, Owens? Better quit while you're ahead." He stares menacingly at me past his big, stinking cigar.

"I know about Meg." I stop at that. Let it hang for effect.

"What does that mean?" he replies defensively. But he's no longer puffing the stogie. He's twitching nervously. I've struck a nerve.

"It means I'm fully aware you have a girl friend on the side. I know about your late night visits to Juniper Street. You know I've been seeing her, too, don't you? Got you in a jealous rage. Well, on that count you have nothing to worry about. She's only a friend."

He smirks. Obviously doesn't believe that friend part.

"Better forget about that, Dave. None of your damned business who I see or when. Forget anything you think you saw. Leave it alone for your own good."

"Don't you see, Len? She's involved in this up to her pretty ears."

Now he's completely flustered. "What are you doing, Dave, grasping at straws? Her involved? You gotta be shittin' me. Not Meg."

"Think about it. You know she hasn't been home since Friday. Want to know where she went? Tough. I'm not telling."

"Run right through you, smartass, if you don't spill what you know."

"No you won't, sheriff. Last thing you want with election time coming around is a scandal. I can ruin you in this town."

Darden picks up his cigar. Puffs so hard I expect to see smoke rings come out his ears. Not a thing he can do to me. Got him by the short ones this time. Worst part for Broadus is he's ruined either way. I expect to return to this town. Can't do that under a cloud like an irate sheriff looking for ways to get revenge. Politically he's dead meat. I can sink the hook in him whenever I choose.

As I drive toward Kyle's house, I try Dorothy's number again. Ring it a second time as I pull into Kyle's driveway. Still no answer. Meg was supposed to leave the cabin. I can only hope they got away before Lester showed up. Her final words over the phone worry me, though. She sounded about ready to snap. Guess I didn't realize the intense mental pressure her stalker had caused for her.

Nothing I can do for her now. She knows how to get in touch with me, and I have no idea where she's gone. Obviously didn't take my advice or she would have been at the police station.

One more try. No luck.

The pitiful moan Meg issued just before she left the phone was gut wrenching. Where could she be wandering now? And what about Trevor?

Chapter 49

The all night vigil begins at Kyle's house. A couple of bleary eyed Owens brothers are about to go out of their skulls with worry. We send Don and Tom off to bed, and Kyle promises to wake them if anything important happens. Then Kyle and I put the coffee pot on. Settle in for the duration. We hold our collective breath and listen for the phone to bring news.

I look at Kyle, sense his overwhelming concern for Jenny's safety, and find it hard to make conversation. He's tearing himself up inside wondering what he can do to bring her home. I think about the subhuman monster that brought this down on him, and wish I could personally teach Lester the last lesson he will learn on this earth.

Kyle rescues me from my awkward silence.

"Didn't ask you about your visit at home, Dave. Anything you want to tell me?" My brother nervously fidgets while he stares out the window at the inky night.

"You don't want to hear about that. We have more important things to think about right now." Somehow it doesn't seem fair that my life is finally falling nicely into order while his world may be shattering. But he persists.

"Humor me," he says. "Maybe it'll help calm me. You can see I'm a basket case."

"Helen and I are back together, Kyle. The war has ended, and things are as good as ever between us. As soon as we collar old Lester I'm on my way back to those two sweet girls."

Kyle thrusts out his hand and pumps mine vigorously. "Best news I've heard in a long time, little brother. Man, am I happy for you. But why wait? They need you down there in Raleigh now, not in Springlake."

"Can't go till he's locked away, Kyle."

"Don't stay on my account. We'll get through this somehow. Lester will make a mistake, and Darden will collar him."

"No, it's for all of us. See, I plan to bring Helen and Melody back here to live."

"What about your business? Not going back to Atlanta?"

"Had more success than I can handle. Need peace and quiet and people I love near by. It won't be safe here for any of us till we conclude this Kanicki affair, though. First we get Jenny back safe and sound, then we put Lester away permanently."

For two hours we sit and talk, reminisce about things both of us barely remember but talk about like they happened yesterday. Even break the tedium with a few laughs over ancient escapades of the brothers Owens. But always there's that emptiness in his face that belies his near panic over Jenny's absence. For the first time I realize Kyle and I are alike in another important way. He's only half a person without his mate. So am I.

Seems the clock is in slow motion; the hands are stuck on daylight minus too long. We both need to sleep, but it wouldn't work. No need to lie down. We're too tired to sleep and too drowsy to make sense. Mostly we continue to drone at each other, our words humming like distant music and dying in midair.

Rinngg! Both of us are wide awake and out of our seats.

I caution Kyle, "Careful. Slow and easy." He punches the button to go to speakerphone.

"That you, Owens?" comes a squeaky voice through the speaker. You know who this is."

"Yes."

"Let's make this quick. I have your wife and a lot of ideas about fun things to do to her. So listen up."

"Lester, I swear I'll pull your guts out through your mouth if you hurt her," Kyle tells him. I didn't know my brother had it in him to get this enraged.

"Wanta hear her scream?" A muffled cry for help sounds near the phone. What is that sleaze doing to Jenny?

"I can make her death very painful. Now shut up and listen," Lester orders.

"You there, little brother?"

"Damn right I am, you sorry piece of shit. Meet me and let's settle this man to man." I want at him so badly my knuckles itch.

"Temper, temper, chaps. You're wasting valuable time. Dave, you know where a certain girl is that I want to find. I won't share her with you or that dunce of a sheriff. That punk Johnny she married found out, too. Drowned him, watched him choke for air and die a slow death. Last face he saw was mine."

Lester's shrill giggle makes me shudder. I wonder how many people this madman has killed along the way.

"Now, Dave. Write down the directions to where she is, and put them in the mailbox down at the next corner. Mailbox says 2135. Do it now. Leave immediately. If you stop for more than 10 seconds at that box, she's dead."

"Got it," I say.

"Good. Noon tomorrow, Kyle, you drive up to Shaws Corner. Turn on Hilltop Road at the grocery. Watch for a signal. You'll know it when you see it. If you're not alone your woman's a goner. Follow my lead and you'll find us. Then we'll talk about trading her for you." His shrill laugh is enough to send chills all over me, one only an insane mind could produce.

"No tricks. I'll come alone, and I want you to let her go," Kyle pleads.

"We'll see. Have a nice night, boys."

Click.

I drive to the corner mailbox to leave the note, peer around quickly for signs of a person or vehicle. Nothing in sight. I want to get my hands on Lester's throat and squeeze the life out of his sorry body. But I can't put Jenny in jeopardy. Wheel about and drive back to Kyle's.

Chapter 50

▼

"It's done, Kyle. He has the directions and a head start. He's on his way to find Meg. I have to call her now." I nervously endure the wait while Dorothy's telephone rings.

After six or seven rings, Meg answers. Oddly, she sounds calm.

"Where have you been, Meg?"

"What is it, Dave? More bad news?" Her voice quivers but there is no panic.

"No time to explain. He knows how to locate you. Had to tell him to save Kyle's wife."

"Don't tell me…"

"Lester has her, Meg. Threatened to kill her if I didn't tell him where you're hiding. Then he arranged to meet Kyle in Shaws Corner tomorrow morning. I know Lester plans to kill him."

"Oh, Hilltop," she says. Her answer stumps me.

"I've been calling for you, but got no answer. Get out of there. Head for town and go to the police station, Meg. All three of you."

"Don't worry, Dave. We'll leave now."

"Wait. One more thing. He boasted about killing your husband. Lester killed Johnny. Please, Meg, take Trevor and run."

Her labored breathing stops abruptly. A low, pitiful moan escapes, and Meg finally answers through tears. "No more, no more. I can't bear it."

She emits a shriek as if in excruciating pain. The crash of the phone dropping punishes my ear. I wait for more but hear nothing.

"Meg. Speak to me. Meg!" I activate the speaker, and we both listen for identifying sounds. There are only muffled voices and the click of the receiver. The connection is broken.

"I have to go to her, Kyle. Maybe I can stop Lester and bring him in. More likely I'll just shoot the sonofabitch and be done with him."

Remember my gun lying on the stairs and hurry to the basement to retrieve it. When Kyle sees me holding it in my hand, my eyes belying my murderous intent, he sounds a warning.

"Careful, Dave. Jenny's life hangs in the balance. I'm going with you." He leaves no room for argument.

"Bring your pistol, too, Kyle. Let's get going." He jumps to his feet. Goes to talk to the boys. Returns with his gun and says, "Let's get him, Dave."

As we speed away, I turn to Kyle and ask, "How much do the boys know?"

He stares ahead into the misty blackness with the first signs of sleet tapping on the windshield.

"Couldn't bear to tell them a maniac has their mother. They only know we have a break and have to respond now. Told them I'd call them as soon as we had good news."

I turn on the wipers. The icy pellets begin to build. My brain is in overdrive. Try to process all the possibilities, most of them bad. *Yes, Kyle*, I think, *let's hope it's good news.*

* * * *

The pavement turns more treacherous as we leave town and proceed on secondary roads. Kyle has the directions in front of him under the car's map light so he keeps me on course. Twice I feel the tires slip on a surface now rapidly turning to ice.

Kyle signals to me. "I think the road to the cabin is just ahead. Careful."

But something has already caught my eye. A brown car sits on the shoulder of the road. I try to apply the brakes, but we're going too fast. The car lurches and the rear wheels start to come around to meet us. I steer out of the slide just before we hit the shoulder. A spray of gravels thumps the car's underside. Bring the vehicle to a stuttering stop. Look back at the brown car, driver's side door open and dome light glowing.

"What are you doing, Dave?" Kyle queries.

"Could be Lester's car. Have to check it out before we go on. Cover me." I hold my gun ahead of me, cautiously approaching the darkened vehicle. Kyle is close behind. The Virginia license plate on the brown Dodge bears the numbers 264-8137. The driver's side door is ajar, and the keys dangle from the ignition, as if the driver has momentarily stepped away expecting to return.

Then I see a figure on the back seat. I raise my gun and jerk the rear door open. The prone figure squirms and cries out, muted words and bleats.

I do a double take at the form, the upper torso draped in some sort of blanket crudely wrapped with circles of rope. My heart is in my throat as I nearly choke on my words.

"Kyle, I've found Jenny!"

My brother charges past me into the car. "Hold on, sweetheart. It's Kyle. I have you now." He claws at the ropes to free her.

I step back and keep a constant watch for the missing kidnapper. Can't let our exuberance cloud our judgment. Madman could be setting a trap using Jenny as the bait. I reach behind me, still scanning all directions for signs of movement, and give Kyle my pocket knife. "Use this."

He rips at the rope, flings the blanket away. Jenny reaches to throw her arms around him. I step away while they share their private moment of reunion.

Back in the warmth of my car with Kyle and Jenny huddled in the back seat, we pause to catch up. "She's fine, Dave. He didn't harm her, other than a couple of knicks with a sharp blade for effect."

I vow Lester will pay many times over for that.

"Can you tell us what happened back there?" I ask Jenny.

"Confusing as it was, I'm not really sure," she says. "I've been blindfolded with my hands tied and mouth gagged so long. Had no idea where we were. Then he walked me to his car and threw something over me. Tied me up so tightly I could hardly breathe."

She's on the verge of breaking down reliving the horrors of her experience. Kyle holds her and says, "You don't have to say any more."

Jenny sits up to look directly at me. "No, I want to get it all out. Anything to stop this lunatic from whatever it is he's planning. We drove for awhile. Then I heard a loud sound like a tire blowing out. We seemed to slide around and finally stop. I heard the car door open then noises in the trunk and outside. After some time there was something like a choking sound followed by dead silence. Must have been lying back there alone for ten or fifteen minutes before you came."

"Give me a minute," I say and walk back to the brown Dodge, flashlight in hand, to check inside and out. Play the beam all around the interior, but find nothing that might help. Step to the passenger side. Find a jack on the ground and a tire lying on the road shoulder. Somebody had finished changing a rear flat.

I step back from the car. The grass rustles behind me. Fumble for my gun, draw and fire without waiting to see what is there.

A small animal scoots past my feet, under the car and beyond. Better put this thing away. I'm going to hurt somebody, maybe myself, as jumpy as I am.

When I look down, another object catches my attention. I kneel to inspect closer. Nausea fills my throat and nostrils. A human ear is lying on the icy road surface, cleanly severed and still pink but now flecked with glistening dots of sleet. I carefully retrieve it with my handkerchief and jam it into my coat pocket.

Chapter 51

▼

We find the winding gravel road just ahead. Make our upward climb toward a log cabin sitting on the brow of the hill. Lights burning even now after midnight. Either Meg has not left as she should have or Lester is inside. I turn off the car lights and roll slowly toward the cabin.

"Wait here for me, both of you."

"You may need help," Kyle replies. "I'd better go along."

"Stay here with Jenny. She doesn't leave our sight again." He readily agrees to that. I crouch and plod toward the side of the house. Already the heavy snow is drifting, and my progress is slow. Inch along the rough hewn surface of the structure, round the corner, climb over the side railing onto the front porch to avoid the windows. Cautiously, I sneak a quick glimpse through the corner of one window. Meg is sitting calmly in front of a wood fireplace with Trevor huddled in her arms. Too quiet and peaceful. Puzzling.

I wait for more activity inside the room, but it all seems so serene. How can this be when she knows Lester is on his way? If he's here, there is no sign of him. Haven't seen Dorothy, either. Have to take a chance. Keep my gun ready for a surprise.

Meg answers my knock, and she registers shock when she sees my pistol pointed at her.

"What...Dave? I don't understand."

"The warning I gave you. What are you doing still here. And where is Dorothy?"

"Oh, she had a trip to take. Wanted to get an early start."

I am so flustered by the confusing scene of tranquility that it doesn't occur to me how illogical that is. Heading out in a sleet storm? Trip couldn't be that important. I also don't realize Meg is closing the gap between us, her face raised to mine, her mouth open and hungry. She drapes her body against me from shoulder to kneecap. Pulls me forward with both hands around my neck. I feel like her tongue is performing a tonsillectomy on me.

"My warning," I gasp when I eventually break away. "You promised to leave. You're in danger and so is Trevor." At the sound of his name, the boy stirs awake, gets to his feet and stumbles over to us.

"Mister Dave!" His eyes twinkle. I see no fear or apprehension. He is clearly unaware of what could be about to take place if the stalker is out there.

"Hi, Trev. Give me a few minutes to talk to your mom then we'll visit."

He returns to the floor. Starts to toast a marshmallow in the fireplace. My head is spinning. Am I the only one in this room who expects Lester Kanicki to come crashing through the door at any instant? Maybe I've finally gone over the edge. Maybe everyone else is sane and I'm the one that's flipped out.

I steer Meg into the small kitchen. "We need to talk. Why didn't you take off for the police station like I asked when I called?"

"Called? When was that?"

For the first time since entering the cabin I take a really close look at Meg. Her mouth is turned up in a little smirk, and her deep brown eyes are fixed on me. But I find only emptiness in those eyes, a blankness in the way she looks back at me, as though her mind is far away, not here with me at all. I find this jarring, downright frightening.

"Tell me, Meg. Do you remember my asking you if your father Lester Kanicki is after you? After his daughter Margaret?"

A spark of recognition crosses her face, and she mumbles, "Margaret. Dear little Margaret. So innocent and trusting. But he betrayed her."

"Who, Meg? Who betrayed Margaret?"

"Her daddy." The words come out in a childlike whisper. "She believed in him. Hated the people who wanted to harm him. Even the boys he told her about on the hill. Margaret understood he had to stop them from telling their lies."

"But he went to prison, didn't he?" If this was the only way to draw her out, I would go along.

"Yes. Bad people took him away from her. Margaret never gave up on getting him back. Ran away from home when she was thirteen. Saw him every chance at that cold, ugly place."

"And he told her about how everyone was out to get him?"

"Couldn't let them hurt him. Margaret had to take care of her daddy. Then the bad people sent Margaret away, too. Locked her up for soooo long." He voice is becoming a child's singsong.

"And later Lester came looking for Margaret, didn't he?"

"Oh, yes. And she was so happy. He told her she was the only one he had ever really loved. She wanted to believe him."

I prompt her. "Then she found her own love, Trevor's father Johnny. But he drowned."

"Drowned, yes. Margaret loved Johnny."

"You know deep down, don't you, that it wasn't an accident. Margaret knows it was Lester who killed Johnny."

She looks at me with those blank eyes, and something registers in them. Meg tilts her head to one side, peers at me like she is only now fully aware of my presence, projects a look of anguish. The face gradually hardens, and I see anger, hate, pure frenzy.

Meg is on her feet. The innocent, trusting Margaret has given way; her brain has been seized by an enraged Meg.

"Kill him!" she shouts and runs to the counter. Snatches up a large carving knife, drawing it across her fingers until they bleed, then tastes her own blood. Another piercing scream and she charges toward the kitchen table. I'm dead, I think, and cross my arms in front of me in defense. But Meg stops short and swings the big knife down at the tabletop.

"Kill Lester. Horrible, lying Lester." She strikes blow after blow until her anger is spent. Then she slumps into a chair and pounds her head on the table, wailing and mumbling, "Daddy. Daddy."

I stop her violent self-punishment, pry her fingers from the knife and try to comfort her. There is no longer anyone behind those brown eyes, only a vacant wandering, a complete detachment from all reality. I stroke her hand gently.

Sizzling in hell is too good for Lester Kanicki. His venom and lies have ruined the life of the daughter who adored him. I hope it was his ear I found. Maybe someone has scattered the rest of him across the countryside. God, I think, it's even rubbing off on me.

Meg looks up into my eyes with the sudden naked terror of a doe trapped in bright headlights. She breaks away and runs out the rear door, sprinting and stumbling through the snow that is now coming down furiously. Disappears into the trees. I slip and slide after her; search for as long as I feel there is a chance of finding her. But in her present state she's a danger to both of us. If I wander too far into the dark woods, she could turn on me. This is now a matter for the police to handle.

On my way back to the cabin, I make a most disturbing discovery. Someone lying in the snow a few feet away from the path of my outbound footsteps. I reach down to the still form and turn it slowly over. Dorothy stares fixedly at me, but she's beyond seeing. No pulse. Still warm. I can't leave her out here like this. Mark the spot with a large rock then lift her into my arms to carry her inside.

I plod back to the cabin to find Trevor. His whole family has collapsed around him, all gone mad or suicides. The one person who might have helped salvage his life, the father who could steer his son and love him, never had a fair chance to nurture the boy. Lester's insane, possessive jealousy drowned Trevor's best hope.

Kyle meets me at the kitchen door, and I gently lower Dorothy to the floor. Jenny and Trevor are by the fireside, already well on their way to becoming friends.

"Trev doesn't need to hear this. We have to call the police and get them out here," I say. Kyle signals to Jenny and closes the door leading to the living room. I reach the police.

"Murder off County Road 130. This is Dave Owens."

The policeman launches into a series of questions. I stop him.

"No, just listen. I have the dead girl here."

He wants to know if we need an ambulance.

"Too late for that. Please just send someone. Killer could be out here in the woods somewhere. First road to the right after the bridge over Ridge Creek. Cabin on top of the hill.

"No, damnit. Would I be standing here talking to you if the killer was still here? I'll tell your people everything when they get here. Hurry."

I hang up before the officer can quiz me further.

Pause then turn back to Kyle. "Wanted to ask too many questions. We'll cover the details when they arrive. Got some dangerous people on the loose who could return."

* * * *

Two uniformed policemen burst in while we're warming by the fire. Len Darden, dressed in his civvies with a sidearm strapped under his coat, follows them in.

"What the pluperfect hell you got yourself into this time, Owens?' Then he sees Jenny and his tone softens. "You found her."

"Come in the kitchen, Len. Let's make this as private as possible." I nod toward the boy.

When we're alone I take Len to the body lying next to the back door. He checks her over and declares, "Looks like one blow with an axe or meat cleaver. Cracked her skull and punctured her brain. She musta died right away."

Now it was my turn to take another dose of Darden's wrath. "Thought you was done with stickin' your nose in where it didn't belong, Dave. You got a death wish or somethin'?"

"Lester came here looking for Meg Kane," I snarl at him. "Called us at Kyle's and demanded the directions or he would kill Jenny. Meg is Lester's daughter."

That nails his attention. He homes in on me as if he wants to pin me to the wall with a glare.

"Daughter! I'll be damned. How'd I miss that?"

"Probably because she had you charmed like she did me. It's true. She's Margaret Kanicki. Admitted as much to me though she likely doesn't realize what she said. Lester has mentally abused her until she's lost touch with reality. She's a mental case, Len, gone totally insane. And she's out there in the woods right now wandering around."

He gulps hard. Wonder if he's thinking what I am. She could have caught him with his pants down, literally. Could have gone bonkers and killed him during one of his late night visits.

"We'll track her down. Can't get far without wheels," Len declares.

"Speaking of wheels, sheriff, did you see the car down on the county road, the brown sedan?"

"Wasn't there just now. Why?"

I swallow hard. "Oh, great! That's where we found Jenny. It was the car I saw twice when the bearded man was spying on me. The car your people have been searching for tonight. And I found this lying next to the car after we pulled Jenny out of the back seat."

I reach into my pocket and hand him the handkerchief. He unfolds it, stares at the ear wrapped inside and goes pale.

"And Lester ordered Kyle to meet him in the morning at Shaws Corner. Somewhere along Hilltop Road. When I called to warn Meg, she mentioned Hilltop before I could get it out. Guess she knows where Lester's been hiding."

With no hesitation Darden speaks into his two-way. Orders two uniformed cops to be sent for an immediate sweep of the Shaws Corner area.

"Now if you don't need us, we're going home," I announce. "This has been one of the worst days of my life. I'm out on my feet."

"I'll send Carl with you. Don't you stir from the Barnwell House until he tells you to. I consider you a material witness in protective custody. May find you're more than that."

"Suits me, Len. Too bushed to argue. I'll ride with Carl. Jenny and Kyle can take the boy home with them. They'll get in touch with his aunt."

Considering the fate I could have suffered at the hands of a lurking Lester Kanicki—or a Meg/Margaret gone berserk—riding back to the Barnwell with Carl as my watchdog doesn't seem so bad.

Chapter 52

The wind swirls the snow. I get the sensation we're driving down a long, dark void with a line of white flakes revolving around it. Don't know how Carl can see to drive. Hope Kyle can make it home in my car. I'm so tired. It didn't hit me till we found Jenny in that brown sedan. All the tension dropped away when I saw she was safe. Wanted to curl up somewhere so I could forget about the scary things that had happened today.

Meg ruined that plan. When she raised that butcher knife…it was the second time I thought I was dead at her hand. Haven't quite gotten over her pointing my own gun at me.

Damn, the brown car *is* gone. Forgot to pull the keys. Too excited about finding Jenny. Then I found that bloody ear. Damn.

"Bad time to distract you, Carl, but I just thought of something."

The deputy keeps his eyes glued to the road and asks, "Important?"

"Could be. The license number of the car that was sitting back there when we went to the cabin. The Dodge where Jenny was held."

He listens to the number and calls it in then focuses all his attention to maneuvering on the slippery road.

"Now take a snooze, Owens, and let me be. That's some bad stuff out there, mix of snow and sleet. Don't need any distractions."

I burrow down into my seat and close my eyes. No snoozing for me, though. Meg could be on the loose with a car to elude the police. Or Lester could still be running around, minus an ear, his evil mind in a rage. What new horrors is he dreaming up, determined to have both Owens boys as his victims?

* * * *

Carl beats the odds and gets us safely back to the Barnwell. The steep driveway is a challenge, but he spins and slips up to the parking lot. Suggest to him that the back alley may be his best bet when we leave. He gives me a 'where were you with your advice when I needed it' stare.

As much as I hate to disturb her, I have to wake Mrs. S to let us in. She looks at Carl and asks, "Dave? Why the police? What's going on?"

"It's okay. He's staying the night. We'll make do in my room." She looks unsure.

He goes upstairs with me to my bedroom. Pulls up a chair across the room, loosens his tie, and settles in to sit watch over me.

"Grab some sleep, Dave. You look terrible."

"Thanks, Carl. I really needed that. You're not so beautiful yourself."

"Got no time to listen to you trying to be cute, friend. Just cool it. And don't try to sneak out on me. I like you, Dave, but I'd shoot you like any other suspect if you try to escape."

"Suspect? What do I have to do to get you guys off my back?"

"We still have only your word for why all these weird things have happened this past month. What if you're lying to us and it's you that did it all?"

"Come on, Carl. You don't believe that."

"I'd rather not, Dave. But being careful is what's kept me breathing through a lot of tight squeezes. The sheriff isn't exactly your biggest fan, you know. Can't take any chances. Just rest. I'll sit right here and watch you."

Maybe I just have a guilty look about me, I tell myself, as I stuff my face into the pillow and try to sleep.

* * * *

I toss and turn, roll and moan in bed. One thing is for sure. Neither Carl nor I will get much rest in this room tonight. When I do finally feel myself slipping away, it's to endure a fitful thrash with the bedcovers for a few hours. Can't get it all out of my mind.

The police are out there searching for Lester. Some of them are scouring around the cabin for clues to Dorothy's death. Did Lester kill her to try to get to Meg? Poor little Trevor is in a warm place for now where people will take care of him, but what will all this mayhem and family tragedy do to him?

Sometime around dawn I crawl wearily off the bed, my clothes soaked with cold sweat, and turn on the shower. Hear Carl moving around. He taps on the door.

"You gonna make it, Dave? Thought you were about to take off and fly around the room a couple times last night."

The best I can manage for a reply is a sound akin to 'blurrbbb'. He laughs and says, "Guess that means you're alive."

I feel like my turning in at all was a bad decision. If there's anything worse than no sleep, this has to be it. I swear I could pack three days' clothes in the bags under my eyes, and my pupils fight me mightily before they open to the morning light. Tempted to give the whole day a pass, but it's not an option. Too many balls in the air to drop my hands, even if they do feel like wooden blocks. Shape up, Owens.

Put on my best face, and stumble out of the bathroom.

"You hungry?" I ask my chaperone.

"I could eat the ass end out of a walrus, pal. Reckon Mrs. Starkey would set an extra plate?"

"Carl, my man, you're in for a treat. Better let that belt out a couple notches. I'm about to introduce you to the tastiest breakfast you ever wrapped your mouth around."

Mrs. S intercepts us in the front hall.

"What's he doing here, Dave?" She nods toward Carl.

"This is my old buddy Carl. He's my nursemaid the sheriff posted so I wouldn't run away."

She looks completely confused.

"Long story, Mrs. S. No problem, really. Carl wants to sample your dee-licious food." I take another look at her. "You seem troubled. What is it?"

"Wish I knew, Dave. First there were sirens out on Main Street. Heard later on the radio there's been a death out near Shaws Corner. What are we coming to with a new horror every time I turn around?"

Carl walks into the parlor, keeping an eye on me, and activates his two-way radio. Must have the volume way down. I hear mumbled words but he's careful to speak directly into the mike. Watches us for any reaction to the conversation.

Mrs. S turns to me and says, "Dave, I just couldn't wait any longer for Meg to return. Hired a new helper. Nice girl but not as efficient."

"That was your only option with her gone for so long. Pained me to see you wearing yourself down. Besides, I don't think Meg will ever return. She's gone from here—physically and mentally."

She's trying to dissect my strange statement when Carl returns from the parlor and says, "Let's eat, Dave."

Mrs. Starkey guides us toward the dining room. "You two find a place to sit and I'll fix you right up." She leads us to the dining room where her guests stare and whisper when they see a lawman with me.

"Not going to tell me, are you?" I pose as soon as we take our seats.

"Police business. You'll hear soon enough."

"Carl, don't shut down on me. Shaws Corner is where Lester told Kyle to meet him. This has something to do with Lester, and I want to know."

He makes a show of ignoring me. The new helper brings us coffee. Carl hides his face behind his cup. Goes quiet, but it's a thoughtful silence punctuated with fleeting glances across the table. At last he comes to grips with my request, and he offers some jarring information.

"Okay," he says barely above a whisper. "I know you've been through forty kinds of hell since you came back to Springlake. Guess you're entitled to know. Found a body in Shaws Corner. In a trailer off Hilltop Road. Could be Kanicki."

I sit in stunned disbelief, scanning his face for something more, but he's said all he will for now. Could our frustration and fright be over? Is Lester really gone? I want to shout for joy, but this raises disturbing new questions.

How...who? My head spins with the implications. If in fact Lester has been killed, does that mean we're home free? Or is there someone else still running wild killing people?

I slide my chair away and loom over my breakfast companion. "Deputy, I'm going to find the sheriff. This is critical for me and for my family. I'd rather not wait for the headlines."

A buzz starts around the dining room. Carl glares at me.

"Sit down or I'll have to restrain you," he says harshly.

"Do what you have to, Carl. The sheriff owes me some answers—right now."

I stride out of the dining room with the lawman in pursuit.

He catches up to me in the hallway. Shoves me roughly toward the kitchen. "Dave, let's not have a scene here. Cool down so we can work it out. I don't want to have to put you in cuffs. If you'll promise to stay where you are, I'll get in contact with Sheriff Darden."

I nod and he steps out onto the back porch with his radio. He watches me through the window pane in the back door, being sure he never breaks eye contact with me.

Soon Carl is back with me in the kitchen.

"Sheriff said for me to bring you to the coroner's office. May even help in case you have something else you haven't told him yet. You're the only one's had a look at Kanicki recently—alive, I mean."

"That's more like it. Thanks, Carl."

"Now can I finish my breakfast?" he asks. We return to the dining room full of gawking boarders.

Fortified against the cold, windy morning, we head out across town through snow flurries. Len Darden is at the coroner's office when we arrive. Looks frustrated and mad as hell.

"My peaceful town turned to shit 'bout time you showed up, Owens."

"You mean when Lester showed up, don't you, Len? Already had a death and a mugging before I ever got here."

"Yeah, well, it ain't gettin' any better, that's for damn sure. This is Doc Jamison. Dave Owens."

We follow the white coated coroner into an antiseptically austere room. A table stands in its center. A white sheet is draped over something, a form I'd just as soon leave covered if they'd let me leave now.

"Doc, let him take a peek at that body. May be able to identify it." I feel beads of sweat break out on my brow.

"Brace yourself, Mister Owens. This is ugly."

Doctor Jamison pulls the sheet back to reveal a face white with death. I gag so hard I puke, and the sheriff jumps away to avoid being sprayed.

"Jeez, Owens, I asked for an ID, not a bath."

Lester Kanicki was, without a doubt, a raving homicidal maniac. But whoever he encountered during his last hours on earth must be every bit as cruel. This cold corpse does resemble the bearded man I saw twice before for an instant. But he has no beard, and his face is smeared with dried blood. He's no longer dressed in black, either, but in a tan suede shirt heavily stained with his own blood and dark brown slacks. His mouth is open wide. I see only the stub of a tongue. There is no way to judge whether he had the same black orbs that had peered at me. His eyes simply are no longer there. And one ear is missing as if it has been cleanly sheared away.

"We matched the ear you found," the doc says. "It was his all right. Sliced with a blade sharp as a scalpel. Having it checked for fingerprints."

"Yeah," Len interrupts. "Now we have almost a whole body to work with. Whoever did this probably did the community a huge favor, but they'll pay for it as sure as Lester paid." The sheriff reaches for a cigar and the coroner barks, "Not in here, sheriff. How many times do I have to tell you?"

"That's all I can take," I say to the doctor. "Cover him up. No way I can identify him as Lester or anybody else in that condition."

Darden sneers at my queasiness. He says, "You ain't seen nothin' yet, kid. Show him the other end, doc." With a frown of disapproval, the coroner turns back the sheet to reveal a nude body that has been disfigured in ways I never imagined possible.

"Lost some other parts here, too." The sheriff chuckles as I turn away in disgust.

Doctor Jamison speaks in a very clinical tone while I try to get my breath. "Most wounds I've ever seen on one body. My opinion is he was tortured slowly and could have been conscious for most of the time. No single mortal wound. Appears death was due to accumulated loss of blood."

I steady myself on the table edge with one shaky hand. Doc holds a wet cloth to my face. Len is amused, but I'm out of it. Not the kind of scene I want to view even once in a lifetime.

The sheriff takes the opportunity to hammer away at me as we leave the autopsy room. "If I didn't know Carl was with you every minute since you left the cabin, I'd suspect it was you gettin' revenge for your friends. Some of them wounds looked mighty familiar. Sort of a package deal. Revenge for Jimmy, Kyle and Billy in one fell swoop. Wonder, though, what the butcher job on his crotch was all about?"

Lester's words about what he'd do to Kyle's little brother come back to me. I have the answer to Len's question but it's too personal and painful to think about.

"Where exactly did they find him, Sheriff?"

"Trailer up a dirt road past Shaws Corner. My man said it was so full of blood somebody coulda been slaughterin' hogs in there."

Only one living person other than my brother and I could know the exact series of threats Lester uttered on Tank Hill twenty five years ago. His daughter. That last bit has special significance for me. I know if Lester had ever gotten his hands on me, I was going to be carved up that way—neutered as Lester had termed it. Suddenly I wish my stomach wasn't empty because the dry heaves that follow are even worse.

"Okay, Sherlock," Len challenges. "Your suspect is dead, and we have a new killer on our hands. Any *more* bright ideas?

"Only one, sheriff. But you should have figured that out by now. Your girl friend. She's loony as a bedbug, and she had a score to settle with him. Seemed to know where he was hiding—mentioned Hilltop Road to me."

His jaw drops so far the unlit cigar falls from his mouth.

Chapter 53

I need a note of sanity after the raw scrubbing my nerves have taken in the past twenty four hours. Only one place to get my thoughts back on an even keel. Kyle is waiting for me in the warmth of the wood stove downstairs. Trevor is snuggled up by his side in an overstuffed chair eating potato chips and watching TV cartoons. The little fellow sees me and charges across the room to hug my knees. I sweep him into my arms.

"How's my buddy today?"

He hugs my neck and whispers in my ear. "Is he really your big brother, Mister Dave?"

"Sure is, pal. Taught me most of what I know. Big brothers are special people."

"I like *him*, too." He pauses. His mouth turns down. "Where's my mom, Mister Dave?"

"She can't be here right now, sport. Marcy and your aunt are coming for you to stay there till Mom gets home." That satisfies him for the moment.

"Can I take Mister Kyle for a few minutes while you watch cartoons? We'll be right back."

Kyle puts him in the big chair, and he munches away, spellbound by the action on the television set.

"Kyle," I begin. "Don't think I can handle this but once so let me spill it all. You know Meg Kane is Lester's daughter. She's also gone insane and homicidal to boot. Lester abused her for years and poisoned her mind. Drove her over the edge. Now her mind is so confused, Meg doesn't know who she is. Seems to switch identities and spin off without warning."

My brother stares, eyes welling up. Tries to absorb what I'm saying. He doubles over and holds his stomach.

"I think she intercepted Lester before he made it to the cabin. Shot out a tire and waited till he changed it, then attacked him. That's the activity and the choking sound Jenny heard. Sometime during their struggle Meg cut off his ear then dragged him away. I think she left him outside and retrieved him, still alive, after she ran into the woods. Probably took him back to the car and drove to Shaws Corner to the trailer. Doctor says he died over a long period of time from loss of blood. God only knows what took place in that trailer."

"So you're sure it was Lester's body you saw?"

"As certain as I can be given the shape he was in," I tell him. "Trouble is, we knew what Lester was up to. Can't predict what Meg may do now that she's out of her skull. At least I think Darden understands the danger, and he'll put all his resources on finding her."

"Where does that leave us?" Kyle asks, glancing back to see if Trevor is still occupied.

"The one and only thing that *is* predictable is that Meg will never leave Trevor behind. He's her whole world. Sooner or later she'll come for him, and the police will be ready for her."

"But his aunt is coming to pick him up."

"Makes it even simpler. She'll do anything to get him back. They'll blanket that place and trap her. The sooner we get him to Marcy and Meg's aunt, the sooner this can all play out. Meg would never hurt Trevor. Now I'm going to the Barnwell for some sleep."

* * * *

I hang out the Do Not Disturb sign and pile under the covers for a much needed visit to slumber world. Beg off giving any of the gory details to Mrs. S, but promise myself I'll fill her in as soon as I feel human again.

This time my efforts meet with success. I lose all touch with the conscious world, don't even dream, just go into a state of suspended animation. Absolutely nothing disturbs me until a distant alarm sounds in my brain. The telephone! I drape one arm over the night table and pick up the receiver.

"Um—hmm?" is about all I can get out. But the urgent voice that answers my mumble brings me wide awake.

"Dave, please tell me. Is Trevor all right?"

I'm sitting up awake instantly. "He's fine, Meg. Where are you?" She ignores my question.

"I know he's at Marcy's but I can't get to him. Police all over."

"Yes, but he's safe and well. Meg, you have to let me help you. Where are you?"

"Sneaked into my house. Need some things to take with Trevor and me. Can't stay."

I stand up and look for my clothes. "Wait. Give me ten minutes, Meg. I want to help you. Don't leave."

"Ten minutes. Yes. Hurry. He could come here for me."

I check the time. Nine PM. Where are those shoes? Don't let her get away.

* * * *

The house on Juniper Street is dark, but I'm not surprised. She's smart enough to know that any activity here could bring the police force down on her. I douse my car lights and drive past then race through the back yards to her kitchen door. Can't be sure where the cops may be positioned. Try to knock as noiselessly as possible, but I hear no response. Rap again.

Seconds pass then I try the doorknob and it turns. I step inside and feel my way through the room. Whisper, "Meg? Are you here?" and wait for the answer that doesn't come. Have a strange sensation I've made a terrible mistake coming here, and I turn to retrace my footsteps.

A hand reaches out of the darkness from behind and covers my mouth. A voice whispers, "Had to be sure it was you."

I feel relieved but only for a second. A sharp point has been thrust through my coat and painfully into my ribcage.

"Meg, easy, it's Dave."

"Meg? Lester has you, stupid. You're a dead man."

The point digs deeper as I struggle to break his hold. Lester? Who was that on the coroner's slab? Does he have a twin?

I take one step backward and stomp down as hard as I can with the other foot. My assailant screams in pain. I turn and swing wildly in the pitch black, guessing where he stands, flailing furiously with both hands. A blade grazes the back of my fist, and I wince at the sting of its slashing blow. I lunge for the door. Try to put distance between that razor edge and me. But hands clutch and claw at me and I fall to the floor short of the doorway. With a surge of energy fueled by fright, I roll over, bend both legs at the knee and thrust them forward. Somewhere above me the attacker expels a lungful of air and hurtles backward, falling over a chair and clattering to the floor.

I'm no hero. This is a fight I don't need to win. Just want to survive. I find the knob and practically tear the door from its hinges in my haste to exit.

I scamper down the block, jumping hedges, tumbling over unseen obstacles, watching porch lights come on. People emerge to see what the ruckus is in their back yards. I reach my car at the end of the block; search for my handgun. As I lunge from the car, a dark figure comes from between two houses and crosses the street behind me—a figure with a beard. No chance for me to get off a shot.

Chapter 54

▼

The shock of my near miss has me doing mental gymnastics. My methodical engineer's brain is trying to add up the confusing inputs, but it keeps coming up with too many disconnects. Thought I had everything figured out. The encounter in that cottage defies all the logic my mind has neatly lined up.

By now the cops have Trevor under surveillance so he should be safe. If Meg was telling me the truth on the phone, she was at her house only minutes ago. Did she see Lester coming and run from him? Where could she have gone? The cabin? The trailer?

I doubt she would return to the scene where that pitiful corpse was savaged. If it was Meg that killed that man, she'd want to give the trailer a wide berth. If not, she certainly wasn't looking to run into Lester on his own turf. But she may not know Dorothy is dead. She may believe the cabin is still a safe haven. I turn toward the county road.

A warning sounds from somewhere in my subconscious. I punch in Kyle's number.

"Kyle, I'm on my way back to the cabin. Have a strong notion Meg is there, and she could be hard to handle. Call the police and send them."

"Don't go, Dave. Let Darden handle this," he pleads.

"Too late. It's my problem. Got to stop her. And Lester, too, if he's still alive. Call Darden, Kyle." I break the connection.

The highway crews are out and the main roads are much improved. Minutes later I turn onto 130. I find it piled with several inches of drifted snow, enough to hold my wheels in the road. Turn onto the snow-covered gravel road and up the hill toward the cabin. Stop before reaching the top, draw my gun and flip off the safety. Sitting to one side of the cabin at the end of a set of long skid marks is the brown Dodge. As much as I dread the answer, I must know who brought it back here. Lester? Meg? Another demon I didn't even know was involved?

Concealing my approach isn't easy given the lack of cover between the road and the house. I crouch and dart from clump to bush to tree. Come alongside the car. No sign of life inside the cabin yet. What's this in the car? A large box piled high. I ease the back door open and slip inside, reach into the box to explore its contents. Looks like clothes for a woman and a child. And there's the dress Meg wore when she wowed them at the Auberge.

I slide away from the box to back out the car door. But as I stand, a blinding pain shoots through me from the skull down. I'm sliding down a long mountain of black.

* * * *

Floating. Gliding along in a murky shadow world. Weightless. My head throbs.

A rapid jumble of scene fragments flashing past. I stand in a mud-covered meadow while muskets roar around me. The pain of suffering and death overwhelms me, and I sink to my knees. Now I am kneeling at the babbling brook, filling my water skin to its brim. The snow gathers around my feet. I stand and peer upward from the base of that monster hill. A bearded man slogs down the slope toward me, a sword raised high above his head. I rise to challenge him. He comes closer, sneers with contempt and spits insults at me.

"Little shit, you kicked me and left me in pain. You hurt me once but I have you now. I'll cut off your legs and gouge out your middle for good measure." His bearded face and cold eyes fade into a bloody visage, a mask of horror; the eyes become sightless black holes. My head threatens to explode with pain.

My eyes open and I blink at the blinding overhead light. A sharp, searing agony in my head is like a spike driven deep into my skull. I can't focus. Then a shape looms between me and that glaring light above, a shape that takes human form. I blink until my vision slowly clears.

"Back with me, are you? Thought I'd hit you too hard and spoiled all my fun."

Lester Kanicki is standing over me. I can't move my arms or legs. He giggles and says, "Got you tied down for the carving, little brother."

I feel the room spinning. Start down that dizzying tunnel again. Cold water splashes in my face and revives me.

"Don't you black out on me again. I want you to feel every knick, every little slice." My captor leans in closer, and he tests the tip of his knife by pricking the sensitive skin of my nipple.

I wince and a chill washes over my body. Realize I'm naked and vulnerable to the whims of this raving madman. I strain mightily, but he has me securely strapped to the table, unable to fight back. A feeling of utter helplessness sweeps through me. Totally at the mercy of a maniac bent on making me suffer the most horrible of deaths.

I close my eyes and think about the last time I looked into the face of the person I thought was Lester Kanicki. Think about how that face had been ravished beyond belief. Somehow the crud who's stalked us has survived, and now I'm about to die. My mouth is dusty dry, my throat threatens to close. I try to concentrate on visions of Helen and Melody and prepare to say my silent goodbyes.

My own voice echoes in my ear. But it seems far away. "Wait. At least tell me why you're doing this. I only defended my brother. Surely I shouldn't have to die for that."

"You made my Margaret love you, set out to take her from me. Then you threatened to turn me in for what happened on that stinking hill. No more time for you, Dave Owens."

I feel cold steel piercing the skin of my stomach, a blade so keen it hurts only after the blood begins and the burning starts.

"Too easy for you," the bearded man shrills. "How does *this* feel?"

He draws the knife's point across my chest and rips it away. I shudder with the pain. He bends and flicks his tongue to taste my blood.

The coal black hair slips to one side, and I see gold beneath. When he draws away, blood on his lips, I focus on his eyes. Brown! Deep brown.

"Meg. I know it's you. Listen to me. He's in control, but you can break out. Please listen. It's Dave. I care for you. Don't do this."

The head turns to one side. Now I'm certain my eyes aren't deceiving me. The beard isn't real, the wig is askew on her head. Meg is about to slice me up.

"Meg, please. You don't hate me. You love me. And you love Trevor. Don't do this. I can save both of you from Lester."

A flicker in her eyes. Is it a note of recognition? She drops her arms and stands as if uncertain what to do next.

"Dorothy tried to help Margaret." The words are spoken in a coarse, male-sounding voice. "Told Margaret to get mental help. But I planted an ax in her. Nobody wanted to accept Margaret for who she was. Only I really loved her."

"No, Meg. Fight him. Let me take you and Trevor away from here."

I'll promise her anything to break this spell Lester's spirit wields over her. And to stop her from peeling me like an onion.

"That's it, Meg. Untie me and let me rescue you from Lester. Tell me what you want."

She looks directly at me, and I'm certain I've gotten through to her. She looks at the blade in her hand and lowers it slightly.

Then the fire returns to her eyes and she raises the knife high above her head, grasping it with both hands.

A splintering sound and voices erupt behind her.

"Police. Drop it now." *Sheriff, you have a voice like an angel.*

Meg turns toward Darden. She strips away her fake beard and wig. Holds out both arms as she rushes forward to embrace him. For a split second he hesitates.

That indecision is his undoing.

She thrusts the knife hard and it disappears into his gut. The sheriff's startled face melts into a mask of shock and pain. Meg rips the blade upward in one continuous stroke. Darden falls heavily as shots ring out.

Meg twitches violently when the bullets tear through her. She crumples atop the sheriff.

Carl lowers his handgun and kneels to check the sheriff for a pulse. Frowns and shakes his head.

"What did she do to you, Dave?" The most welcome voice I could hear in my wounded, frightened state. Kyle is bending over me, his face contorted as he surveys my bleeding body.

"I'll be okay. At last it's over, big brother. You pulled my fat out of the fire, just like you always have. Thanks for bringing the cavalry."

He beams with relief, steps back and covers my middle with his jacket. "Never could teach you any modesty," he throws out at me.

"Kyle, you are one beautiful sight."

He leans over and whispers in my ear. "I was scared to death I was going to lose you."

Chapter 55

▼

When I was growing up in Springlake, I always thought of March as a cold, windy, generally dreary month. Locals delighted in saying that March 'came in like a lion'. My Dad liked to add that the lion usually had 'big, cold teeth that gnaw at your ass.' This year will be no exception.

I step out onto the front porch of the Barnwell House and drink in the chill air. It fills my chest with the sting of a winter not yet ready to die. A solid mantle of white lies over the ground. Each time a sunny afternoon melts the snow's top layer, the night winds refreeze its surface into a crust that crunches underfoot. Neighborhood kids have their snowmen built, their sled paths iced and fast. The child in me delights in memories of windswept frolics in the frigid outdoors, cheeks and fingers soaked and reddened then warmed before the big kitchen stove.

A shiver courses through my veins. It's born not of the morning frost but of recent memories too painful to accept yet too real to purge from my mind. February has been a watershed month in the life of Dave Owens, one that has taught me some hard lessons, but days I would prefer never to have to relive. When I first reappeared in this town, my personal life was in a shambles and my brother lay gravely injured, brutally set upon for no apparent reason. Now all that is behind me. I finally see a bright future ahead. Still, without considerable luck, and perhaps the hand of providence, the outcome could have been vastly different.

The morning is a personal challenge to be met. I step from the porch onto the glistening carpet of snow. Feel it crumble beneath my footsteps.

"Hey, little brother. You're gonna freeze your tookus off out there."

I look around to see Kyle staring down at me.

"That's Flywheel to you." I punch a hole in the snow's slick crown and make a ball from the snow beneath. Send it hurtling toward my brother. Bullseye!

He accepts my challenge. Steps down and arms himself. We begin pelting each other. He charges me and knocks me down. We wallow in the snow and wrestle until I catch my breath enough to call it off.

"Truce! Snow balls and wrestling always were two of your strong suits."

Mrs. Starkey appears on the porch and calls out, "When you kids are through playing around, I have a warm fire and cocoa in the parlor."

We dust ourselves off and make a beeline for the parlor before the chill sets in. In front of the roaring gas logs I realize this is the first time I've relaxed—really let myself go—in the past month. Feels like a whole new me.

"Kyle, it's mind boggling to think where we were when I got back here. You banged up and holding on, me with my life going to pieces on all fronts. It's hard to believe how much has changed since four weeks ago."

"We still make a pretty good combination, Davey. Had no doubt we'd come through given time." He slaps my hand to salute our victory.

"I've always known you had an iron will," I tell him. "It was like a glimpse into the past, my big brother taking on the world and whipping the bad guys. I shudder to think what would have happened to me if you hadn't brought the police to the cabin. Rescued me from that madman…madwoman?"

"Puzzles me, Davey, what happened and why. Guess that poor girl Meg's mind was so full of poison from Lester's lies she was no longer herself, only a confused reflection of Margaret Kanicki."

"Yes, she had careened through my life, teasing and scheming, inviting and ranting at me. Her intense hatred for her father finally took over completely. Many times I've heard that imitation is the highest form of flattery. I wonder if hate doesn't rival love in its depth and intensity. At the end it seems that Meg so despised her father for his mental abuse she made him suffer a thousand cuts of death."

"But why did she turn on you?" Kyle asks.

"Her insane mind must have turned down the only twisted avenue left to it after she killed Lester. She became Lester herself with all his hatred and vengeance. That was the worst part of all."

"Do you think she could have been changing identities before that, Dave? Jumping back and forth between personalities?"

"Exactly what I was thinking in those last moments when she was ready to carve me up. Was she the dark man who had stalked me, the driver who forced me off that mountain road, left me warnings in the motel and in my own room? How many times was I at the mercy of Meg turning her Lester identity off and on? She held a gun on me, rushed me in Dorothy's kitchen with a butcher knife, had me at her mercy when she offered herself to me."

"Well, that's all behind us now, Dave. I talked to Helen last night. She called and asked me to tell her what's really been going on up here. I knew you'd find it difficult to tell her how hard things had been for you in Springlake."

"I know, Kyle. She called me after midnight. Told me she and Melody will be in Springlake by week's end to stay. Melody can finish the school year here. The only thing that matters now, in Helen's words, is that our family be together as soon as possible."

We sit in silence for a long while sipping our cocoa and thinking our private thoughts. Then Kyle speaks up.

"Carl is the interim sheriff, I hear. He's going to see that the grave in West Ridge is opened as soon as the ground thaws."

"I know. He told me the DNA on the yellow sweater is a close match to samples from the Hurt girls' parents. Finally your classmate Valerie can be laid to rest beside her sister."

"So that wraps it up, Davey," Kyle says, stretches then sinks back into his overstuffed chair. "Feel like I could take a snooze right here."

"Not just yet," I tell him. "There's something special I have to do, and it won't be complete unless you're with me." I stand and pick up my coat drying by the fire.

A puzzled expression crosses his face, but he gets to his feet, grabs his coat and says, "Lead the way."

We go out the back door of the Barnwell and start the climb up the hill. Press on past the cemetery, and make our mark in the drifted snow up the back side of Tank Hill. Kyle stays a few steps back, and I tug on the rope trailing behind me. Finally we stand at the top of Tank Hill, and I look down that steep slope. Stare at the shiny run packed hard and slick by the youngsters, no longer fearing it; feel the anticipation surge through me.

"Wish me luck," I say. I yank the rope to sweep the shiny new Flexible Flyer up into my arms. Take a full running start and fling myself headlong onto the sled. Speed over the crusted snow down, down, curving and dipping, steering over bumps and swales. When my mount at last thuds to a stop, I lie there and relish the moment. Then I roll over and over in the snow, glorying in its cold wetness.

Feel a hand reaching down to help me to my feet. I rise and turn to share my joy with my brother, and get a shock. It's not Kyle standing next to me but a young blonde soldier with sunburned skin and a crescent scar on one cheek. He shakes my hand, salutes and swings aboard his gray horse to climb Tank Hill. I stand motionless, unable to react. Look down at my hand and remember the split second when I felt Private John Palmer's warm flesh.

Then I stand like a six-foot snowman with right arm upraised in victory. Kyle is in full flight down to meet me.

"What was that all about, Davey? Looked like you saw a ghost."

"Just saying goodbye to an old friend."

Kyle puts his arm around me, and we start our climb up. After thirty years the monster has yielded and I own Tank Hill!

I think, *Whoever it was that said 'you can never go back home'—stuff it, pal.*
DAVE OWENS *IS* HOME!!

0-595-33688-4

Printed in the United States
24028LVS00003B/211-237